K. J. DAWSON

Cover art by Deranged Doctor Designs

Published by Oliver-Heber Books

0 9 8 7 6 5 4 3 2 1

Nylann'or
Trinth
Northern Channel
Unaria
Carrus
Neidrei
Beggarton
Blackmore
Easthill
To Aggord
Shoals End
Ironport
Heikton
The Haunted Sea
Yllalen'al

CHARACTER LIST

Ivala "Ivy" Balrel: House of Seeds, daughter of Councilor Balrel
Orion Arya: Captain of the Unarian Night Guard
Breccia "Brecc" Feldspar: House of Minerals
Kolvar Phiro: House of Tides, son of Councilor Phiro
Nym Phiro: House of Tides, daughter of Councilor Phiro
Lial Darcassan: House of Tides, son of Omasys Darcassan
Magdud "Maggie": orc warrior residing in Carrus
Zelbim "Zel": gnome residing in Neidrei
Wirenth Olaxisys: House of Seeds ambassador
Omasys Darcassan: the right hand of the Tides Councilors
Adviser Daecyne Obsin: House of Tides treasury advisor
Adviser Bellas Sylceran: House of Tides law advisor
Ash: a Lenonius Draco

The Elven Council:

Ialant Balrel: House of Seeds Councilor
Emmyth Phiro: House of Tides Councilor
Mormaris Roble: House of Tides Councilor
Lonsdaleite Meorise: House of Minerals Councilor
Lazuli Carfina: House of Minerals Councilor

Fae Realm Royals:

King Eldrin Cor'arya: Winter Court
Princess Selleth Zrin'arya: Winter Court
Prince Rime Zrin'arya: Winter Court
Prince Devain Seral'Rey: Summer Court

Alysatraee, the Mother of Magic: deity creator of both realms and all creatures

PROLOGUE
LORE OF ALYSATRAEE

Alysatraee, the Mother of Magic, longed to create. So she touched the ground, and there a tree grew. One root was the sylph, another the mermaid, and many other fair creatures who took to the sea. Branches reached forth. One was the centaur, another the fae, and many more which were all the creatures of the land and air. Many children did she create, all with magic gifts imbued. She molded a realm for them, which was vast, ethereal, and as diverse as her mind could conjure, which was great.

As the eons passed, Alysatraee's creative spirit yearned for more. Once again, she reached out and touched the ground, and a new, cousin tree sprang forth. This tree was smaller but no less beautiful. Its roots and branches were all called humankind. The Mother fashioned another realm, a softer, fertile land, punctuated by a majestic range of mountains that cut to its heart.

Alysatraee cherished both her creations and desired cooperation and peace between the cousin realms. She charged the fair ones to assist their younger cousins.

And the elves she entrusted with a unique responsibility: to be the keepers of peace and live apart from their own kind. But the elves were sad to reside apart from their fae siblings. Alysatraee recognized their sacrifice, and she gifted them a reward; in exchange for watching over the humans and representing their needs to the fair ones, the Mother bestowed special gifts upon the elves—seeds.

The elves now gather at sacred trees, in special events set aside for the purpose of collecting the magical seeds. For they live a hundred years in the fae realm, but with the seeds, a thousand in the human realm. Elven longevity enables them to stabilize both realms through generational relationships and hard-won wisdom.

But as Alysatraee does, if her rules are corrupted, so too are her rewards.

I

SEEKERS

The vial of seeds warmed Ivy's trembling hand. She couldn't afford to take one. Not unless her situation was dire. And it wouldn't come to that. Not if she timed her escape sufficiently.

She flinched at her internal lie. No, she had to time it *perfectly*.

The double moons' light reflected off the snow as Ivy crouched in the alley, behind a pile of refuse and stacked crates. She exhaled, and a white cloud formed at her lips as she waited, her muscles tense.

She tucked her enchanted-glass pendant inside her coat, hiding the seeds it held, and scowled at the steel-faced door across the alley. It'd been over a hundred years since the War of Realms ended, and she highly doubted the human landlords even knew the origin of the steel-door tradition. By looking at the shoddy craftsmanship, they definitely didn't. The door might keep out their fellow humans. It might cause a fae to hesitate. But it certainly wouldn't stop her.

Angry voices rumbled down the alley. A woman shouted jumbled words, punctuating the night. Ivy pushed her sight to the other end of the alley until several Seekers stumbled across the opening ... turning inexplicably in her direction. She'd evaded more in the past; still, she rasped a breath as her attention caught on one in particular.

He almost looked healthy, like it hadn't been long since he'd eaten regular meals. His fine-spun merchant clothing was intact. Even more noticeable, he wasn't barefoot—he wore shiny boots. Even the weakest Seekers were fearsome. She didn't want to even *think* about fighting this recently corrupted, full-belly-fancy-boots directly. The Seekers lumbered closer. Too close.

Ivy's heart thumped, and she bolted toward the door. Her shoulder slammed into the metal, ripping the hinges from the jam, and the door crashed onto the floor. A twinge of pain shot from her shoulder up her neck.

Blasted Iron. It didn't stop her, but it stung.

Yells erupted down the alley, but Ivy didn't look back. She raced through the housing complex hallway and up two flights of stairs, her stomach twisting in dread. Once she reached the last apartment on this floor, she'd have easy access to the lower roof. She counted the rooms as she passed, 32, 33, 34 ...

A woman stood outside number 35, fumbling with the latch. Ivy swallowed. A stone felt like it slid down her throat, thudding into her stomach.

"Oops," the woman giggled, her words slurring. "That's not the right door."

The Seekers were headed this way. In the woman's state, she might do something foolish. Like fight back.

"Here we are ..." Then the woman dropped her key.

A scraping sound swept up the stairs. The Seekers were mere steps away. Instead of running past the woman like any sane elf would do, Ivy improvised. She jumped forward and kicked in door 35, breaking the latch.

The woman yelled, justifiably so, but Ivy yanked her inside, doing her best to stay calm. This was *not* the plan.

"Seekers are coming. Hide!" Ivy tugged the woman to her bedchambers. "Stay out of their way, and you'll be fine. They're after me, not you."

Ivy's heart thrummed a warning: *run, run, run.*

But she kept her composure and repeated a popular children's rhyme:

Merciless, tainted, none can abide.

Against fae magic, run or hide.

Technically, the human rhyme didn't get it all right, as usual. Still, the general advice was accurate.

"Stay hidden," Ivy warned.

Shouts from the hall grew louder, and the woman gave a halting nod. Ivy slammed the woman's bedchamber door shut and then sprinted for the window overlooking the front of the building. With a quick thrust, it opened; the cold breeze was a breath of hope against the sweat on her brow.

Ivy scrambled onto the window ledge, assessing, already wishing for her easier, original exit point. But she'd made her decision and reversing course would only compound the risk. Ivy climbed out slowly, careful not to knock icicles onto the unsuspecting revelers below. She pulled herself up higher onto an angled portion of the roof. The upper four stories, a later addition, sat unevenly with the rest. Digging her fingers into the stones, Ivy climbed the wall, safeguarding her seeds and the scent they carried. No, she hadn't planned to reach the roof this way, but she'd learned long ago to map out multiple escape routes.

Her stomach tightened at the thought of the Seekers storming through Room 35. But she reminded herself that they ignored all creatures unless they riled the Seekers ... or got in their way.

The glass vial burned next to Ivy's skin, taunting her. She cursed under her breath; four months was too long to survive with only two seeds. Fate was cruel.

Clouds raked across the night sky, but more than enough light remained for an elf to find one particular balcony on the sixth floor. The apartment owner was a lower noble who spent his winters elsewhere. A perfect escape route.

Ivy had identified buildings throughout the city, including this one, with the highest chance of distancing herself from her pursuers. Meticulous planning had kept her alive, safe from the Seekers; the corrupted humans who maimed, plundered, or murdered any who kept them from the elven seeds they sought.

Though she was confident the apartment's owner was gone, Ivy held her breath as she pressed her hand to the painted, wooden door. The eccentric owner had locked his "inaccessible" balcony with an exquisitely carved wooden board across the inside. More importantly, the too-narrow board was set at a slight angle. A dwarf would be horrified at the imprecise craftsmanship.

Ivy was grateful for it.

She rocked the door back and forth until the board clattered to the floor inside. Ivy shoved the door open and dashed through the rooms filled with velvet draperies and handsome furnishings. Though she hadn't left any tracks in the snow, it wouldn't confuse the Seekers for long.

Seekers shouldn't be able to sense Ivy's seeds—not when inside enchanted glass. Yet they did. They could follow Ivy like a wolf tracked a rabbit.

What had changed, Ivy didn't know. She had never been in one place long enough to figure it out. As a lone elf living among humans, her options were limited.

Ivy unbolted the front door and sprinted down the building's communal, wide hallway. The railing on her left blurred by, which faced a soaring, four-story-high window centering on the majestic Blue Mountain. On her right, she counted the doors to the residences.

She slid to a stop, spun, and dashed up the stairs, her view of the mountain shifting with every step until she was on the highest floor. The access point to the roof wasn't far now. From the top, she could leap to the eastern building. She'd already tested it, just like she'd done in other, targeted structures around the city.

Seed Seekers were terrible jumpers. Ivy leveraged every advantage. If she didn't stay a step ahead, they'd overpower her. She wouldn't be the first elf they'd killed, let alone the last.

A muffled crash sounded from below. But thankfully, no screams. Most humans in their apartments wouldn't notice the disturbance, but Ivy did. The Seekers had likely tracked Ivy beyond the lower building, out onto the lower roof's ledge. Anxiety threatened, but she gulped a breath and pushed away her mounting fears.

Room 777 caught her eye. An elven lucky number. She skidded to a stop. If it followed the pattern of the other numbers, it should've been '77,' but the owner had added a '7.'

And the door was cracked open.

Through the slit, the room boasted a riot of color and texture, unlike any she'd ever seen. From the ornate, gilded frames around the many oil paintings to the plush rugs and the green, silk-covered sofa, the apartment was the definition of luxury. Ivy frowned, emotion churning so fast and hard inside her that it threatened to boil. Her self-preservation instinct urged her to ignore the insult and run, but the exhausted, bitter part of her crumbled.

How dare this human take an elven lucky number? Why should they claim luck and fortune when I have lost everything? My kind cut-off. My House scattered.

What wouldn't Ivy give for a peaceful life at the base of Blue Mountain? No hiding. No fear.

Her family surrounding her.

Without thinking, Ivy sent a swift side-kick at the door. As her foot connected, she noticed the iron lining the length of the doorframe. She tucked that information away to examine later.

The door swung wide, slamming into the wall, revealing a massive sculpture that dominated the main room ... and a petite man faced it. For half a moment—a singular beat of a hummingbird's wings—Ivy's world stilled.

Her breath caught, her whispered word never leaving her lips.

Father?

The petite frame, grey hair pulled back in a queue, and the way he held himself ... could it be?

Even before he turned, she knew it wasn't. The ornate decor, and the silk tunic, and most glaringly, no long, pointed ears—it wasn't him. He faced Ivy, his skin and clothing sprinkled in a fine coat of white dust, which had settled into the wrinkles around his eyes. He held a small hammer in one hand and a chisel in the other. His hand was raised, moving to attack, when he stopped mid-swing.

"Well, well. An elf," he said, seemingly more amused than angry.

Then you'll know a tiny little hammer won't bother me much.

In a heartbeat, Ivy analyzed his work: a sculpture of a woman, the folds of her gown as delicate as actual fabric. Her ears were gently pointed—a half-elf? The masterful spectacle almost distracted Ivy from her goal. Almost.

Something slammed into the wall down the hall. Hard. Ivy closed her eyes, chastising herself for the delay. Seekers were decidedly *not* athletic creatures, but they still moved nearly as fast as any other human.

"Danger is headed this way," Ivy warned. "I'm sorry. Stay in your apartment." Ivy retreated, cursing her foolish pride as she grabbed the doorknob.

The man shouted from behind her, "Wait! Get back here!"

Ivy spun around. "Seekers! They are moments away. Stay inside!"

His eyes widened and he didn't budge as Ivy slammed his door shut. Sprinting to the edge of the hall, Ivy closed the distance to the roof access. She had checked this exit routinely, and it was always left unlocked. Warfare favored the prepared.

She yanked the door open, and hope sprang within her; she had reached the last, long flight of stairs to the top of the building. She glanced back as stomping feet echoed up the stairs to the seventh floor. But elves could easily outpace Seekers. If she could cross the roof without coming into contact with one, she would escape unscathed.

Her heart thrummed, but she held her ground. After stepping into room 777, she needed to draw the Seekers directly to her. Yes, they should follow her scent, but she could afford to wait and ensure the man's safety.

Ivy slammed the lower access door, making a ruckus. Growls echoed and the sound of thudding feet stormed up the stairwell balcony. Ivy shouted for extra measure, "Looking for me, you heartless, half-dead ...?"

Without finishing her insult, Ivy dashed up the steps. Three at a time. The lower access door thudded shut behind her. And Ivy grinned.

Clamoring sounded below, thuds from bodies colliding with walls.

Wait, that wasn't normal. Ivy slowed as a realization surfaced: luck-stealing-777 was fighting the Seekers. Why did he leave his apartment? Seekers didn't wander into rooms without seeds to steal. Plus, his door was actually well-crafted.

His door was actually well-crafted.

A warning shot through Ivy. This human knew the fair folk traditions, but he didn't truly understand the danger. Ivy groaned. Foolish humans with straw for brains. He'd attacked *them*.

Ivy shook her head at his grievous error as she grabbed the handle on the final, upper door leading to the roof. The latch was ice cold. Winter—and freedom—awaited on the other side. Yet guilt twisted her stomach. Unlucky-777 was in over his dimwitted, tiny-hammer-wielding head to think he could fight off a pack of Seekers.

Ivy turned and hurried back down the steps. But before she reached the bottom, the hallway access door creaked open. Ivy's heart jumped into her throat. A gaunt woman with pale lips and feral eyes blocked the doorway. Her stained dress and satin cloak hung limply on her frame.

Out of time, Ivy scrambled back, unable to take her eyes off the Seeker. The woman lunged. Ivy spun and leapt for the handle to the roof access, blood pounding in her ears. Plunging into the cold, Unarian night air, she rushed toward the eastern edge. The roof was slick with slushy snow, but Ivy didn't hesitate. With all her practice, her body moved without conscious thought. She tugged her hat tight over the length of her ears as she took a deep breath.

At the edge, she pushed off and jumped, sailing over the wide alley. For a moment, the world silenced. Only stars and moons and exhilaration as she slipped through the greedy hands of death.

Her feet slammed into the snow-covered surface of the neighboring rooftop. She tucked, rolled, and was back on her feet, sprinting forward. Getting down the little-used emergency ladder took mere heartbeats. She dropped the last two stories to the ground through the air, landing in a graceful crouch. Not her fastest performance, but not her slowest, either.

Glancing around to be sure she was alone, Ivy strolled out of the alley, blending into the boisterous evening. Locals laughed and bragged about their day on the mountain.

"Hello there, darlin'," a man who'd obviously imbibed more than a few drinks called to Ivy. "You're too beautiful to spend the night alone, lass."

Ivy tucked her chin and lost herself in the crowded street. Guilt curdled her stomach and her mind raced.

Why did you fight, 777?

Not that his reasons mattered; in the end, his demise was Ivy's fault. The Seekers would've passed right by his door, him none the wiser, if she hadn't let her pride and frustration dictate her decision. The timing of her evasion routes was critical, and she'd let an offense distract her. It could have cost her a seed, but it surely cost 777 more than that. She gripped the vial hanging from her neck, trying to tap into the feeling of security it usually brought.

It didn't work.

The ache to take a seed almost drowned out the vibrating pains her body was just beginning to register from her chaotic night. A seed would heal her, even give her a moment's respite from the mental anguish threatening to claw its way out. Each seed was a gift; each one could bring her back from the brink of death, revitalizing her elven body, flesh and bone.

Distracted, she bumped into someone. In an instant, she recognized the official uniform: a guard. Glancing at his face, she noticed his green eyes, and her heart squeezed. Before he looked down, she dropped her attention to his hand. A ring with the duke's crest glinted on his middle finger. She sucked in a breath, knowing who she'd run into—Orion, the Captain of the Night Guard.

Of all the nights!

But of course, he'd be investigating the destruction. She tilted her head, keeping her identity a secret, or hoping to. She felt his attention on her, as if he was peering into her soul, calculating her guilt. Her body thrummed, but she forced herself not to sprint away. Instead, she mumbled an apology and hurried on.

The entire interaction happened in a blink, but even so, Ivy's mind spun. He had an unsparing reputation, one that extended beyond Unaria, and she knew what that would mean if he ever discovered her. Ivy had worked to avoid his notice.

She picked up her pace and shoved the seeds out of sight, a hand pressed to her chest, putting aside the temptation to take one. Instead, she slipped a leather pouch from her pocket. The spherical stones inside were not nearly as powerful as the seeds, but they held more magic than most humans would ever experience. She selected the smooth one with a familiar dip in one spot and held it tight. The healing stone was slow but safe for humans and fair folk alike.

Ivy turned her focus to her next move. Beyond the Seekers, the human captain would soon be looking for her. She calculated she had less than a day to escape over the mountain or die trying.

2
CAPTAIN OF THE GUARD

The crowds skittered out of Captain Orion's way as he and two of his guards marched through the street. Most of the citizens were oblivious to their presence as the roads were packed with revelers. At first glance, the night appeared to be like most others, but Orion had been given an alarming report—one he had to investigate himself.

Next to Orion, the young recruit's brow scrunched. He'd been the one to relay the news of attacks in the city center. "We're not far from the trouble in the main square." The recruit kept his voice too low for others to distinguish. "Why aren't people panicked?"

"Because your report is inflated nonsense, li'l one," shot back the older, bearded lieutenant.

"People must have noticed the bizarre visitors?" the recruit spoke quickly, ticking off his reasoning. "They're not dressed for the weather. They hardly speak, but they're destructive. We tried to stop them, but they were strong. Really strong. And—"

"Hush it," the older guard snarled. "You already said the attackers had no horns, tusks, pointed ears, or any other real ...

strangeness." The guard avoided the dreaded words, "fair folk." "Sounds to me like a few people got piss-drunk. That's all."

The lieutenant sounded more irritated than worried. But Orion knew fear bubbled under the deflection. No human wanted to believe that the fae nor their ilk might return to this realm. Over a hundred years ago, humans had triumphed in the Fae Wars, but the stories lived on. Brave mortals were wary of magic. The wise trembled before it.

Perhaps the woman he'd bumped into not a quarter-hour ago had witnessed something she wished she hadn't. He had glanced down just long enough to see distress behind her dark eyes. She held her arm tight against her body, and he nearly asked if she was injured, but she darted away. By the blue color and tailored cut of her coat, he guessed it had the silver stitching of the Blue Mountain Climbing Guild on the right front pocket; she was likely one of those misguided elitists. Perhaps she'd injured herself in a hiking expedition. He had shrugged off the encounter and continued forward, his investigation far more important than a random guild injury.

"People see what they want and ignore the rest," Orion explained to the young guard, turning the situation into a training opportunity. "People come to the Blue Mountain for a holiday. For fun. Plus, who will they gossip with? Many people out tonight are visitors, just here to enjoy the mountain."

"But a woman thrashed three civilians and pulled two trained guards off their horses," the recruit insisted. "I was there. I saw her. She looked frail, but ... she wasn't. I still don't know how she escaped."

The crowd shifted, revealing a group of people staring in shock and others animatedly talking to each other. They stood at the edge of an outside dining area, yet unlike all the others, no one was eating.

Orion held up a hand, and his guards immediately

responded to his change in course. Drawing closer, Orion noted the people gawking around the edge of the chaos. The restaurant owner was picking up pieces of broken chairs next to a table crushed to splinters. Rivulets of ale ran through the cracks between the stones, shattered mugs littering the ground. Near an overturned table and shattered glass, Orion picked up a short length of rope from the ground.

"The restraints, or what's left of them," the restaurant owner said, approaching Orion. "An elderly man barreled through this dining area, knocking into diners, spilling drinks with his erratic movements. He ignored the customers cursing at him. The old man seemed half-dazed ... until two guards caught up with him. They tackled and secured him. But, somehow, the man broke free. You just missed him, but your two guards are after him."

The recruit gave Orion a side glance. There were not one, but two unusually strong and violent individuals in the city.

"I'm sorry for the disturbance and the damage. A guard will return and question you further, after the culprit is apprehended," Orion said, dismissing him. He turned his attention to the rope. "The fibers on the ends of this rope are shattered." Orion paused, lowering his voice. "The Seeker ripped this apart with brute strength."

"Seeker?" the young recruit's voice cracked, his expression reflecting similar horror as the other guard. "They're bedtime stories parents tell their children, so they'll behave."

"I assure you they're as real as elves," Orion said. "Elves are just better at hiding."

"How can you ... n-no, that can't be—"

Cries jerked their attention to an adjacent street. The guards followed their captain and ran toward the screams. They didn't make it far before getting swallowed by a wall of people fleeing in the opposite direction. The guards pressed forward and the crowd finally thinned, revealing a dark alley. Not far inside, a man raged, ramming his fists into a stone wall. The man's once-tailored clothing now hung in stained tatters, and bloody cuts covered his bare feet. His blond hair was dark with oil and dirt, limp and unkempt.

Several people cowered, trapped on the other side of the Seeker. Seekers were unpredictable; with one foot in death already, they were dangerous.

A young man attempted to charge the Seeker. The Seeker's attention turned toward the movement. The young man slammed into the Seeker, perhaps trying to clear a path for the others. But, even with the full momentum of the boy, the Seeker hardly budged. With one deliberate stroke, the Seeker back-handed the young man, sending him tumbling. Before the boy could recover, the Seeker had grabbed his arms. He screamed as the Seeker pulled.

Not wanting to watch the boy lose his limbs, Orion drew his sword as well as the Seeker's attention. The Seeker snorted and released the boy, who curled into a ball against the wall. Dropping into a crouch, the corrupted pressed his hands against the wet cobblestones. Orion took a single step closer.

The Seeker leapt, snarling as he attacked. In that moment, Orion registered the rock in the Seeker's hand hurtling toward his skull. With a thrust, Orion drove his blade between the Seeker's ribs.

As the Seeker crumpled, the recruit muttered a prayer and touched his heart and chin. Steps away, the young man's whimpering turned into sobs.

"Thank you. Thank you, Captain," a woman said, hugging herself as she stumbled toward the fallen young man.

"People won't be able to ignore this any longer," the recruit whispered. Orion looked over at his lieutenant, who stared at the scene in shock. Orion didn't blame him—no one wanted to believe that Seekers had inexplicably descended on Unaria.

Orion shook his head as he cleaned his sword; the seeds had destroyed far too many lives. Thanks to the seed's poison, the Seeker had been on a path to death long before Orion met him, but he never enjoyed taking a life. Any guilt and anger he felt were eclipsed by more cries echoing around the city.

The young recruit strained to see the roofs surrounding them. "That's not good. How many Seekers are there?"

"We must hurry while the tracks are fresh," Orion said, glancing at the dead Seeker and the injured boy.

"Go," the woman said to the guards. "I'll fetch a healer."

Orion nodded his approval, then directed his lieutenant to clear away the Seeker. "The body may still be tainted with poison. Be cautious."

Captain Orion took the recruit and they followed the Seeker's bloody footprints in the snow. The tracks joined with others, at least a dozen more. He'd never seen this many Seekers in one location. Seekers were volatile; a single one could endanger many lives. But they were lone hunters, which made it possible to overtake them. So, the idea of Seekers working together chilled him.

The tracks converged at a seven-story building overlooking Blue Mountain. This was usually a quiet area of the city, preferred by the leaders of the Mountain Guild and lower nobles. Not tonight.

The large window was now a pile of glass shards, glittering like bits of snow in the moonlight. Shocked residents congregated together, shivering in their night clothes. Several spoke in loud, rapid tones, attempting to explain what'd happened to the guards.

Seeing Orion, an officer marched to his side to report.

"We're checking the rooms, one by one," she said. "We're currently working through the third floor."

Orion explained that Seekers had infiltrated the city. To his guard's credit, her shoulders stiffened only slightly as she took in the news. Orion dismissed her back to her work, and he and the recruit investigated around the building, finding a breach in the alley entrance, with the door dented near shoulder-height.

On the third floor, things got interesting. Inside a thrashed apartment, a guard was questioning a woman. The soldier gave Orion a deferential nod before continuing.

"So, they didn't hurt you?"

The woman wrapped a blanket tighter around her shoulders. "It happened so fast ... I watched their movement through the crack under my bedchamber door. I was horrified. I still can't believe it. How is this happening?"

Orion studied the room, noticing the damaged, open window. He prepared to follow the destructive path but turned to his recruit before continuing. "Get this cleaned up and cover the window until it can be repaired. Then meet me upstairs."

"If it weren't for that stranger," the woman shuddered, "I would've been caught unaware. I might have been ..." Her voice trailed off as she blinked away some unseen worry.

Orion paused. "What stranger?"

The woman wrung her hands as she explained how a stranger had saved her life.

"Could you describe her?" Orion asked.

"She had brown hair. Or black? Dark. I think. Her coat was teal. Maybe green?"

"A dark shade? Or pastel?" the recruit piped up as he swept the floor.

She shrugged, unsure.

Orion turned away from the window. "I can help you remember if you'd like."

The woman nodded.

"Close your eyes and think about what you were doing before you saw her." Orion turned his back on the others, hiding his face.

Then he let a layer of his glamour drop away.

When Orion's glamour faded, the woman relaxed, smiled, and reached for his outstretched hand. His face didn't look much different to strangers, but his guards would notice. Without his full glamour, his appearance calmed her, and his magic trickled forward, clarifying her memory.

Orion preferred not to use magic. No matter how careful he was, he risked being discovered. But, with Seekers in the city, he needed answers.

"What do you remember?" he asked.

"Brown hair under her blue hat. Her skin was tanned, and her nose was a little red across the bridge. A smattering of freckles. Looked like she was in her early second decade. And she wore a blue jacket with silver stitching." Her grip tightened. "Mountain Guild. I see it so clearly now."

"We appreciate your cooperation." Orion wrenched his hand away, but the woman reached for him again. He pulled his glamour back into place and moved to the window. The woman paused, cocking her head.

"Get some rest," Orion said. "We will secure your room."

Orion climbed through the window and perched on the ledge. The woman started to follow, but the guard caught her arm. He shot Orion a quizzical look before guiding her to a cup of tea. The captain ignored them both, pulled himself onto the lower roof, and followed the Seekers' tracks to the open balcony. Inside, almost everything was in place, but a bitter chill cut through to the hallway beyond.

In the communal hallway, the wind whistled past bits of stained glass still clinging to the lead design, which framed the moonlit mountain beyond. On the right, fist-sized holes marred the wall. Something had excited them when they reached this point. Ahead, one door was open and askew on one hinge, with ripped pillows and feather-stuffing around the entrance. Orion slowed, alert, a sense of foreboding trickling down his spine.

What other dark thing would be required of him tonight? The captain stepped into the apartment. Three bodies lay on the floor. Beyond them sat a slender male with his head in his hands and a small hammer dropped by his feet. No fae features, noting that his hair covered his ears but was pulled back, making it impossible to hide pointed tips. And Orion didn't sense the slightest tickle of glamour; he was dealing with a human.

The captain cleared his throat. The man gazed up, his expression vacant. Orion tensed, preparing to fight another Seeker. But the man's eyes focused as he rubbed his chalky-coated hands on his trousers.

"I'm Captain Orion Arya. What's your name?"

"Brecc."

"Are you injured, Brecc?" Orion checked for pulses from the emaciated forms of the Seekers on the floor, still keeping an eye on Brecc. The Seekers' feet were blistered, bloody, and probably half-frozen, judging by the blackened toes. One wore a wedding band on her finger.

They had all been human, once.

Technically, they still were, but only in body. Not in mind. Orion wondered if this woman had known what she was getting into when she first swallowed a seed. Was she after eternal youth, like the tantalizing tales promised? Or had her family scraped together the funds to secure one seed, hoping to save her from an illness, at least hoping to postpone its effects? Or had it been given maliciously by an enemy?

"I was attacked," Brecc said, staring ahead.

"By Seekers." Orion studied the man's reaction. Nothing. Either Brecc already believed in Seekers, or he was in shock. Time to rattle his cage. "By the looks of your door, you've been expecting trouble."

Brecc grimaced in a mixture of superiority and disgust. "Excuse me?"

"Let's not play games. Seekers are roaming my city, and innocent people are getting hurt. We don't have time for nonsense. The interior of your door is lined with thick metal. You might play it off as expensive, eccentric art to visitors, but I know the truth. No one does that unless they're worried about security. Either you're afraid of elves, who aren't usually aggressive. Or you're afraid of Seekers, who are quite rare. So which is it?"

Brecc's gaze slid to his door and then back to Orion, his lips pressed shut.

You're nervous about both?

"Why did you fight them?" Orion pressed. "If you know enough to line your door properly, you know Seekers won't fight unless you keep them from what they want."

"I was distracting them."

"From the young woman in the blue jacket?"

Brecc's cheek twitched. "Yes."

A lie.

Only the high fae couldn't lie, but Orion found them to be the most deceitful of all creatures. By comparison, Brecc's lies were easier to follow than any map. Orion glanced around the room, noticing the blue coat on the hook, charcoal sketches on parchment of the city from a distant perspective, and what appeared to be an art studio beyond the half-closed door.

"You work for the Blue Mountain Climbing Guild?" Orion moved to the coat and pointed to the guild seal, a mountain, stitched on the front.

Brecc didn't answer.

"So, how well did you know the young woman who came through the door?" Orion pressed. "What kind of illicit business are you running together? She came to you for help, but you sent her away?"

Brecc shot to his feet. "What? No!"

The recruit burst into the room. "Captain Orion, if I may."

Orion hid his irritation. "Yes?"

The young guard paused, catching his breath. "The guards are speaking to the emissary of the Mountain Climbing Guild downstairs. She came as soon as she heard about the attack, specifically to check on this man, Brecc. The emissary claims that Brecc has worked on the mountain for ten years and is the best guide they've ever had."

Brecc folded his arms, looking ready to gloat.

"That doesn't mean you're not involved in a crime," Orion said. "Tell me about the woman from tonight."

"I'd never met the intruder before," Brecc said, his voice steady. "Seen her from afar, yes. But nothing more. Furthermore, I would never draw Seekers to the city, let alone to my home. Only someone with a death wish that entailed endangering dozens of innocent people would do such a thing. I have more respect for life than that."

Finally, some truth.

Yet, Orion didn't trust Brecc; he was hiding something. Perhaps several *somethings*. Judging by the room, Brecc was spending more coin than a Mountain Guild member could afford, even if he *was* the best guide they'd ever had.

The officer he'd spoken to outside arrived, and Orion signaled for her to finish the questioning and oversee the removal of the bodies. Orion didn't demand Brecc remain in the city; the man seemed the type to panic and run if he felt cornered. Not expecting to learn anything more, Orion followed the destruction to the slush-covered roof.

The Seekers had gone to the edge of the building but hadn't crossed. Instead, they'd scattered throughout the city.

How had the woman escaped? Orion scanned the far roof, only five stories high. If the roof had been snowy, he might not have noticed where the runner had landed; slush was easier to disturb. Orion had never met a human who could leap that distance, leave so slight a mark, and vanish without leaving footprints. The scattered clues he'd found started to come together.

He was hunting an elven culprit. Or so he hoped, for her sake. Though he had little respect for elves, she'd pay a steep price if she was a human playing with seed magic.

"We lost her." The recruit frowned.

She'll return to the mountain, Orion told himself. Once he found the elf, he'd crack open her life like a walnut shell and discover how and why she'd drawn more than a dozen Seekers into one place.

Another cry punctuated the air.

"Captain?" the recruit straightened.

"Let's go," Orion said. "Our work tonight has just begun."

3
DEATH ON THE MOUNTAIN

The overcast morning sky blotted out the snow-laden tops of the Stormbringer Mountains. Ivy dug her boots into the snow, a habit she'd formed to leave prints.

"You're strong for such a slight thing," the man said, gesturing to her heavy pack. Ivy couldn't remember his or his son's name. Did they start with an 'M?' All the clients seemed to blend, including the twenty she was assisting over the mountain. "Are you sure you can carry that pack?"

Embarrassed that a "slight thing" must carry most of your son's gear and half of yours? Ivy reminded herself that her safety lay over the jagged mountain. Between this snobbish, belittling man and a relentless Seeker, she'd take the former.

"The mountain air makes our guild lean and strong," the guild leader boasted, shooting Ivy a warning look.

Ivy swallowed a chuckle as the client's gaze shifted to a burly guild member on their excursion crew who looked like he had lifted more sweets than weighted bags. Ivy worked for a guild that assisted wealthy travelers over Blue Mountain. Seekers were strong, but they couldn't follow her for two reasons. Firstly, they lost the scent in the open. Secondly, few were aware enough to survive the elements for long. By the time Ivy returned, the Seekers would be scattered or captured. She'd get her earnings and get out of the city. She'd escaped far worse before.

She'd considered leaving Unaria without her coin, but she'd done that at her last residence. She was long overdue for a new identity, but the tedious, risky process would cost her. She hadn't been able to afford a new "life" in over a decade, and it was bound to catch up with her.

A woman called out in an overly cheerful voice from behind the staging area. Behind the painted fence dividing paid travelers from everyone else, a woman blew a kiss to the man and his son, two people Ivy was guiding. Next to the woman was a little girl who held up a carved, cube-shaped blue stone. Ivy casually turned her back to the box, hiding her face.

The two men enthusiastically waved at the girl and her box, their images recorded for their future entertainment. Perhaps the box would be trotted out at a dinner party, their projected images on display, and the 'M'-clients would brag about their adventure.

The boxes combined fae magic and dwarven craftsmanship. Not that humans remembered. Humans used them to record fun adventures, and honestly, elves did, too. But lately, elves needed the blue boxes for more tragic, utilitarian reasons.

"What happened to your nails?" A fellow guild member nudged Ivy's arm as they started up the mountain. He was a pleasant fellow with bushy eyebrows and frequent jokes. "If the master finds out you ignored the guild requirement, he'll dock your pay. Again."

Ivy feigned a smile. The guild couldn't have blue "remembrance boxes" on display around the kingdom with shabby-looking guild workers in the background, now could they? "I did some gardening last night."

"Of course. *Very early* spring gardening." He gave her an exaggerated wink.

The day before the Seekers had discovered her, Ivy had already been anxious. She'd been in Unaria for three months, and she rarely stayed in any city for much longer. So, Ivy had begun her preparations to move. She hitched a ride in a farmer's wagon out of the city, then doubled back to a dilapidated farm nearer the gates. At dusk, Ivy crept into the barn and dug up a drawing of her family and her stones where she'd hidden them when she'd arrived.

Gratitude washed over her, relieved that she'd not had to leave the items behind. She'd been fortunate because she'd fetched them just in time—before the Seekers caught up to her. Now she was headed in the opposite direction, over the mountains.

She couldn't imagine fleeing without the only thing left of her family—a drawing of the six of them together. It was too precious and too dangerous to carry around, normally. With it, Ivy's elven identity could get discovered. Without it, she feared she'd forget what her family looked like.

Ivy's tension uncoiled a little more with every step up the mountain, away from the populated city. Bushy-brows rambled, trying to start up a conversation. A futile endeavor. Even if humans didn't live such short lives, Ivy was never in a place long enough to make friends. She'd stopped trying long ago.

"Rumors say this mountain was a once-sacred elven refuge," he said. Of course, those words grabbed Ivy's attention. Her hands shot to her hat, making sure it covered her ears. Feeling the comforting material, she took a breath and half-listened the conversation.

In the human realm, few souls had Ivy's knowledge: a dwarven cave carved into the far side of the Blue Mountain had an entrance shaped like an open maw, with jade eyes that glowed when any elf drew near. In fact, the light was a warning to her kind, not built by them.

"Or so the scholars believe." Bushy-brows puffed out his chest, ready for a compliment.

Even if someone stumbled upon the entrance under the vines, an internal rockslide blocked the city deeper within. Ivy had investigated the cavern, of course. Though never her home, she contemplated the thousands of dwarves who had once trod that path. She mourned the families who'd fled. The dwarven stronghold had fallen long before she was born. The thought still caused a lump to rise in her throat.

"Their sacred books say, 'Where the sky tucks into the land, the Blue Mountain blesses,'" bushy-brows droned.

Ivy's hand drifted to the image of her family in her pocket. If dwarves and elves had joined forces all those years ago, perhaps things would be different today.

"Conveniently, the fair folk's lore makes this human guild rich," Ivy said, her voice edged in bitterness.

He frowned and nearly smacked right into the young client, who had stopped in his tracks.

"Who's that?" the boy asked.

He pointed at figures higher on the mountain. They wore the mountain guild's fitted blue jackets, but the last expedition had left yesterday. As the people crested a mound, Ivy spotted a sled pulled behind them.

The boy's eyes widened as they neared. Ivy looked back at the lodge. Sure enough, in the main brazier, a blaze burned, signaling danger. Thankfully, none of the clients seemed to notice the unnaturally orange flames. According to rumor, it had only been lit once since last spring, after an avalanche.

Near the brazier, a guild member directed visitors away from the painted fence to make room for an approaching healer's wagon. Ivy swallowed, spotting several guards. It was one thing to invite a healer. It was quite another to call in city guards.

Ivy tugged her cap down further, her body growing heavy with dread. Her climbing group watched the morbid procession with the sled, the prone body completely covered, including the face.

The group whispered to each other, panic rippling. A guild member rushed up the mountainside past them all, her arms pumping with the effort. She stopped at the head to speak with their expedition leader. The newcomer lifted a gloveless hand to the elder man's ear, relaying a hushed short message.

"I've been informed that the injured individual was not with our guild," their leader addressed them loudly. "It was an unsanctioned attempt at crossing the mountain. We are perfectly safe."

The group moved forward, the initial scare making the hikers even more excited to conquer the mountain. But before Ivy could follow, the gloveless messenger grabbed her arm.

"You're to report back to the Mountain Guild Emissary," she instructed. "She asked for you, specifically. I'm to take your place on the expedition."

"What? Why?" Ivy's heart raced. She avoided all official representatives of the guilds. They were well-connected and knew too many people.

"You were here early, right?" She tugged the bulky pack from Ivy's back.

Ivy had slept in the guild dressing rooms, but she wasn't about to admit it. With Seekers hunting her, she hadn't dared go to her shared housing unit. The guild lodge was empty at night, separate from the other buildings; it was safe. Wasn't it?

Ivy's gaze was drawn back to the form on the sled. Though it was at the base of the mountain, near the wagon, she could see every detail of the guild members and the body between them.

"They want to question anyone who might have seen the victim this morning." She hoisted Ivy's pack onto her back. "His death is 'suspicious.'"

"They?" Ivy said, still watching the sled below.

"Our emissary and the Captain of the Night Guard." She gave a wistful sigh as she slid on her gloves. "I wish he'd investigate me."

Ivy ignored her as guards helped lift the sled into the wagon. The wind caught the material, lifting it from the body. Ivy sucked in a breath. The man wore merchant clothing and shoes—shiny boots.

No sane person would attempt the mountain in such ill-suited clothing. A Seeker would. He was likely the same Seeker she'd seen last night.

But how did he track her up the mountain? It was one thing to catch the seed scent in an enclosed space and follow at a close distance through a narrow alley. It was another to track seeds through a wide-open expanse ... one she hadn't crossed in five days.

Her mind whirled. Ivy had already gotten unlucky-777 killed. She could be leading other dangerous Seekers to the lodge.

"Hurry up." The guild member nudged Ivy down the hill. "They're waiting to question you."

"But I didn't see anything worthy of report."

The woman shrugged and hurried to catch up with the group.

If the captain interrogated Ivy, he'd likely figure out she was the "wrong" species. If he discovered her two seeds, he'd confiscate them, and she'd likely end up in some dungeon for future questioning. The Mother of Magic, Alysatraee, had created seeds for elves to consume when ill or injured. When elves suffered from neither, they could still take one a year and survive in the human realm for a thousand years ... or so Ivy had been taught. But Ivy never seemed to have enough, and she had no one to rely on but herself.

Mother. Father. Where are you? Why have you abandoned me and Iris? Her hands curled into fists.

Her parents wouldn't want her to languish in some underground human prison. Ivy pushed down her threatening emotions. Forget her coin. Forget the new identity.

Despite the Seekers still hunting her, she had to take her chances in the city. She braced for a desperate sprint to the gates. Ivy gripped the glass vial at her neck and ran.

4
ELVEN ESCAPE

In the heart of the duke's castle, Orion stilled at the messenger's words: a Seeker had died of exposure on the mountain.

Orion tapped the pommel of his sword at the unexpected news. No Seeker would trudge through knee-deep snow unless the scent of the seeds drove them. Had the Seeker been chasing the same culprit Orion was hunting? Had she climbed the mountain under cover of darkness? Orion needed to get to the mountain before the weather elements erased the evidence.

Orion dismissed his guards from their meeting. The next visit was for him alone.

The captain hurried into his room and peeled off his clothing, still marred with dirt, mud, and blood. A member of the local Mountain Guild was the culprit behind the Seekers' attack, the same woman he'd bumped into the night before. Or was she an elf? Either way, he needed their emissary's cooperation in finding her.

Once he questioned the mysterious female at the center of the Seeker activity, Orion could make an official report; one he knew the king would study. Seekers weren't born; they were made—with magic. The king would demand to know who was behind this debacle. So, the information Orion gathered and the content of his report would impact the kingdom far beyond Unaria's walls.

Orion threw open his door and marched toward the guild's headquarters at the base of Blue Mountain. The cool morning air tugged at the edge of his long, quilted, formal coat. As he stormed up the streets, he processed the events of the night before.

Dozens of Seekers in one location were unheard of, and Orion's responsibilities included gathering all fair folk-related activity. If he failed, he could lose his position after a lifetime of work, or worse. He swallowed, attempting to release the tightness in his throat.

He would succeed. There could be no other outcome.

Before the lodge was in sight, the warning flame announced trouble. Orion cursed under his breath. Why alert the crowd? There was nothing to be done for the dead. If the culprit Orion hunted hadn't already gone over the mountain, the guild's incompetent flame had warned her away.

A healer's wagon trundled down the hill toward him. Orion held up a hand, and the wagon stopped. A quick investigation of the body confirmed that it was, indeed, a Seeker. Seeing Orion, a guard jogged to the captain's side.

"Captain, the Mountain Guild Emissary is gathering all those present this morning for questioning," she said. "The emissary awaits your arrival."

Orion gave a curt nod and followed the guard, but he scanned the crowd for lurking Seekers. Instead, he spotted Brecc. What was he doing here? Why was he gawking from outside the guild's property when he was one of the few who could enter?

Orion glanced from the orange flames to the guard leading him. "Go ahead without me. I'll be with the emissary shortly."

The soldier nodded without question and continued to the lodge. Most of the crowd was riveted on the departing wagon, still visible on the road below, but Brecc's focus was unwaveringly on the mountainside. Several women crowded unnecessarily close to Brecc, but he didn't seem to notice their proximity.

Clues Orion had observed earlier started falling into place. Brecc's slender stature, his skill on the mountain, the metal door, and the way humans were unknowingly drawn to him ... it all made sense. Orion would've laughed at the irony if he wasn't so annoyed.

Brecc was an elf. Or at least part elf, by the lack of pointed ears.

Yet, Brecc hadn't tried to help the female elf; Brecc had been protecting himself. So, why would an elf fight off three Seekers?

Seeds.

A flare of anger sparked in Orion's chest. Brecc probably had a reserve of seeds in his home. Had they been properly secured? Were the Seekers actually after Brecc? The elder elf turned, as if sensing Orion's gaze, but the captain ducked down, hiding in the crowd.

Orion considered the situation anew. Brecc was upset last night but not utterly devastated. So he probably wasn't robbed of his seeds. Then why did Brecc show up here? Morbid curiosity?

The letter that Orion had received months ago came to mind. The anonymous sender had asked to meet and discuss the elves. Orion had nearly ignored the message; he'd heard countless nonsensical theories about fair folk, but the sender had enclosed a distinctive purple leaf.

Orion later met the elf outside the city. The elven male didn't say much—but he was obviously worried. Paranoid. The elf visitor asked questions about Orion and his work. Orion got the distinct impression he was being tested. He already distrusted elves and their seeds. He liked random tests even less so.

The elf had declined an invitation to the duke's castle, instead requesting another meeting before the summer equinox. But in Neidrei, which was nearly two weeks' travel by horse. Orion had initially hesitated—elven politics were not worth his time—but thankfully, he'd agreed. After last night, Orion was keen to speak with the mysterious elf again.

For now, Orion resolved to task his best spy with tracking Brecc and, with any luck, locate the elf's seeds. At the very least, he wanted to rule out Brecc's involvement with the Seekers. Orion's instinct was that the mysterious female was the true culprit. He'd track her, himself.

It wasn't surprising that both elves worked on the mountain. Elves had the stamina needed for the arduous work, and elves longed for nature, especially when residing in a city. Only dryads were more connected to the trees than elves.

The captain pivoted, searching the same area that Brecc had been looking toward. An expedition group climbed the mountain, but Orion had no idea if the elf he hunted was with them. He'd barely glanced at her face, and the individuals were too far away to distinguish.

But, Brecc had likely seen her. And elves could see great distances. Orion straightened and looked for Brecc in the crowd, but the elf was gone.

"That's the guard," a voice sounded behind Orion.

Orion turned and saw the young man he'd saved the night before. Fresh, purple bruises and cuts marred his face. He was in a group with several others about his age, all staring at Orion.

"Come off it," a tall, skinny young man jabbed his bruised friend in the ribs.

Orion ignored them, continuing to look for Brecc, but their animated voices enabled everyone to hear the conversation.

The injured boy continued. "I'm telling you, he moved so fast, he was a blur."

"Another drunken tale," the skinny one spat.

"Leave him be." A young woman cut in, defending the injured young man.

A little girl squealed and pointed at the two young men who began pushing each other. Then an undisciplined, wide punch flew. Recklessly, the young woman stepped in, trying to stop them.

A father hastily yanked his child back, but the crowd had already swelled forward in a tight circle, fascinated by the brawl. The bruised boy grabbed his lanky friend's jacket in his fists and swung him—straight into the young woman.

She thudded to the ground, and the crowd shifted, swallowing her. Orion pushed through the onlookers, prepared to calm the situation before anyone got seriously injured.

"You're pathetic." The skinny boy was breathing hard already.

"At least I don't punch like a pixie."

"By order of the Duke, stand down," Orion announced, keeping an eye on the father who'd picked up his little girl, a protective hand at her head.

Both boys blanched. The lanky one dropped his gaze to Orion's sword and stilled. The young woman got to her feet, glaring at her two companions.

Before they could offer an excuse, someone else cried out in the distance. A commotion stirred near the fence that divided the paying "elite" hikers from the masses.

"Ivy!" a man in a blue coat called to a woman as she darted

past the fence and into the crowd. "Stop her!" the guild member shouted as he chased her. "She's needed for questioning!"

"Go home." Orion waved off the young men and moved to intercept the fleeing woman. But as he did, bodies collided into him as onlookers darted out of the way of an oncoming horse. Someone galloped past them all: Brecc.

Brecc pulled to a stop next to the woman. She stepped back, seeming to recoil.

"Ivy!" the guild member shouted again, coming after her.

Orion pushed through the crowd, sensing she was the culprit he was pursuing.

The woman, Ivy, turned in time to see guards closing in. As she did, Orion got a good look at her face. Was she the same woman he'd bumped into last night? She spun back to the horse, reaching up to Brecc. In a quick motion, he yanked Ivy up behind him onto the horse.

She was mere steps away. Yet, with the jostling crowd, Orion couldn't reach her in time. He needed to distract her long enough for the nearest guard to stop them.

"Ivy!" he called her name.

She twisted around, and their eyes met. The intensity of her expression caught Orion by surprise, jolting him from head to toe. Her scowl softened to ... curiosity? He couldn't be sure. She wore her cap low to her brow. Her hair, the color of earth after the rain, curved over her shoulder in a long braid. Her lips parted, and her grip on Brecc relaxed. For a heartbeat, Orion half expected her to jump down and run to his side.

"Halt!" the nearest guard yelled, reaching for the horse's bridle.

Brecc urged the horse forward, and for one sickening moment, Orion feared Ivy would be thrown. But, adjusting her weight, Ivy stayed seated as the horse lurched forward and galloped down the hill toward the city gates. Orion grabbed the collar of the guard who had scared her off.

"Fetch my horse!"

Orion was almost certain Ivy was an elf—the same one he'd hunted last night. The combination of her ability to jump across the buildings the previous night, her classic, petite elven frame, and her easy way with horses all indicated elven blood. He wouldn't know for sure until he observed her more, but preferably, he wanted to speak with her.

Orion didn't trust Brecc; the elf lied.

And Ivy had just joined him.

The situation was spiraling. Orion's official report would be woefully incomplete without confirming that Ivy had drawn the Seekers, as he suspected. But at the same time, dozens of Seekers wouldn't go unnoticed.

Over the last decade, there had been very few conflicts with fair folk, which made this attack all the more shocking. If Orion didn't report before rumors reached the wrong ears, his reputation would suffer. Haughty members of the court who were waiting for an opportunity to discredit him would latch onto this blunder.

With Orion's skill, he *would* catch the elves. And he'd do it quickly. Vultures filled the courts, but Orion refused to be the carcass.

5
THE ROAD TO RUIN

Ivy didn't mind riding in a saddle, but it was terribly uncomfortable to ride *behind* one, especially at a gallop. Still, she was grateful she'd escaped the city of Unaria with her last two seeds. Perhaps it was even more fortunate that she'd escaped Captain Orion, who'd come to question her. His glaring intensity had indicated he wouldn't let her go easily. Though she could out pace any guard across the kingdom of Trinth, they were not to be trifled with—fair folk were their ancestors' sworn enemies.

After they passed several branching paths off the main road and the sun was near its zenith, Brecc finally slowed his horse, Sunshine. It didn't take Ivy long to figure out that Brecc was an elf. Instead of the revelation bringing comfort, it only added to her growing anxiety. Seekers would find them much quicker with two elves traveling together.

Ivy spent the next two hours looking over her shoulder, despite their growing distance from the Seekers in Unaria. With few options and fewer seeds, she'd have to lay low until the spring Gathering. Away from civilization, she could survive. Of all her options, it was the least terrible.

"I appreciate you taking me this far," Ivy began. "There is a fallow field near here with a decent barn. I can walk there."

"You know, once Seekers need seed," Brecc said, "they lose their minds until they get it."

Do you think I don't know that?

Brecc continued, "It would be better if we stick together."

"Traveling with me is like aligning with a lightning bolt in a field of dry grasses. Incineration."

"Are all Protectors so dramatic?"

Ivy bristled that he'd guessed she was from the House of Seeds, casually using the nickname, "Protectors." As if it meant he knew her. He didn't. It wasn't much of a stretch to guess correctly, as only three elven houses existed. Even a blind squirrel occasionally found a nut.

She dismounted from the still-walking horse, landing softly on the ground. "I'm sorry, again, for turning your life upside down. If I could go back and do things differently, I would."

Brecc pulled Sunshine to a halt, looming over her, pausing as if picking his words carefully. "If we're being honest, I assumed you were a thief. A strong, fair folk thief who gave a ridiculous excuse for her intrusion. I didn't believe you when you warned of Seekers. I went to follow you, and ... things went badly. I'm only complaining because I'll miss a few things about my apartment, that's all."

Ivy knew Brecc missed "the most comfortable chair he'd ever owned" because he'd whined about it for the last hour.

"And I haven't been completely honest with you, Ivy," Brecc tightened his grip on his satchel's strap. "I remember when you first arrived on the mountain. I knew almost immediately *what* you were. Your presence brought back memories I wanted to forget."

Ivy's gaze flicked to his ears. His surgically cut ears. If nothing else, it indicated he'd forsaken his elven life. It wasn't her place to question what he'd done or why. It *was* her choice to leave him behind.

Movement in his satchel caught her attention. An object, the shape of an apple, turned. Slithered? No, Brecc must've shifted. Ivy ignored her over-active imagination. "Perhaps our paths will cross again."

Ivy stepped into the forest, and Brecc called after her. "Elves keeping secrets from each other is foolish, Ivy. It's not Alysatraee's way."

She spun to face him, irritated at his naïve reprimand. He knew nothing of her life.

"Do you know what's not right? You, working on the same mountain, yet ignoring me. Why didn't you say anything?"

What if I needed help? I did *need help.*

"I knew you were trouble. And I was right, just not in the way I expected. I'd lived in Unaria undetected until you arrived. I had just gotten into a rhythm—I'm usually in a city for twenty years before I need to move again."

His words were a slap. He had lived in luxury and security; she moved every few months.

"H-how have you lived in one place without Seekers finding you?" she asked.

Brecc stared past her into the trees, his age-marked hand resting protectively against his satchel. "I've witnessed a lot. Learned. I likely trained more years in my elven House than you've been alive. I fought in the war, said goodbye to friends who fled to the fae lands, watched humans build a civilization on our ashes, and I've seen the destruction the seeds bring to human lives, up close and personal." Brecc blinked, swallowing back the tightness in his voice. "Perhaps Alysatraee put us on a collision course because I can help you."

Something moved in Brecc's satchel; it definitely wasn't her imagination. A scaled paw reached over the edge, shiny little claws digging into the cloth. An adorable dragon peeked over the side, staring at her with slitted, vertical pupils. The creature was deep blue, the color of early evening when the double gibbous moons peeked over Stormbringer Mountains.

Ivy opened her mouth and then snapped it shut. She'd heard the stories as a child but had never seen a dragon. The noble creatures had retreated to the fae realm at the end of the war, or that's what she'd been told.

"Ivy, meet Ash." Brecc put his hand down, and the dragon scuttled up to Brecc's shoulder like a lizard. A lizard with wings. "She's a Lenonius Draco."

"How ... where ...?" Of all dragon species, Lenoniuses were the smallest.

"Strictly speaking, it's not completely legal for me to keep a dragon in a human city. I thought perhaps you'd come for Ash. Either for yourself or for a reward. It wouldn't be the first time an elf reported on their kind to garner favor with the high fae."

Ash settled on Brecc's shoulder, and the elf grinned. "After that Unarian guard questioned me, I climbed the mountain under cover of darkness to retrieve my seeds—it's the safest place in Unaria. I hurried to get back to Ashie to prepare to leave the city this morning. Then, by the Mother's providence, I saved you, too."

Ivy's mind still latched onto the fact that he had stayed in a single city for years. Decades. The concept seemed ludicrous, but somehow, Brecc had done it. With a dragon in tow. "If I stay with you, will you teach me how to hide?"

"I'll spill all my survival secrets."

The sun peeked out from behind the clouds and reflected off patches of snow. If Brecc would take the risk to teach her, shouldn't she be willing to try?

Brecc dismounted and took Sunshine's reins loosely in his hand. Ivy sucked in a breath and stepped next to him. As

Sunshine silently accompanied them down the road, Ivy dared allow a pinprick of hope to pierce her heart.

"Why is her name 'Ash?'" Ivy finally asked, staring at the dragon on Brecc's shoulder. "It seems an odd name for a blue creature."

"Pick her up and find out."

Ivy raised a brow but plucked the dragon off Brecc's shoulder. Her scales puffed out in the most delightful way. She pulled back her lips, flaunting a row of sharp baby teeth, and opened her mouth, almost in a yawn.

And a cloud of black dust blasted Ivy in the face.

She coughed, shoving the dragon as far away from her as she could. The taste of burned ash coated her tongue, and Ivy gagged and spit, still holding the little earth-core-spawn in her grip.

Pick her up and find out, my arse.

Brecc laughed. *Really laughed.* Ivy wanted to smack him, but she couldn't risk dropping the dragon, either. Though Ash acted too lazy to fly out of her hand, Ivy didn't want to offend the horrid little creature. With her eyes still squeezed shut, Ivy spat again and cursed, stepping to where she *hoped* the air was cleaner. Finally, the earth-core-spawn's weight lifted from her hands. Using the back of her tunic to wipe her face, she squinted at Brecc, whom she now wanted to pummel.

"I'm sorry. I couldn't help it. Ashie is harmless, but she hates pretty much everyone and everything." He chortled. "She barely tolerates even me."

Ivy glared in his direction, barely seeing him through the smudges across her lashes. He sobered, seeing her expression. Sort of. He still wore a grin, which deepened the wrinkles in his eyes and cheeks.

"I'll make it up to you." Brecc offered Ivy his water, though the bladder was mostly empty.

Typical.

After getting herself semi-clean, Ivy pulled her cap back on, daring to ask a serious question. "Did they get any seeds from you? The Seekers?"

"You mean, did I spare the corrupted humans their misery? Help them return to the life they knew?" Brecc frowned. "No."

"You regret *not* giving them seeds?" Ivy asked, confused.

He sighed. "The Seeker who died on the mountain, he was following my trail. Yet another mistake from last night. I retrieved my seeds, but in my haste, I didn't seal them." Ivy tensed, and he quickly added. "They're secured *now*. Completely."

Brecc seemed haunted by the Seekers, a memory perhaps. So, Ivy didn't press further. For the rest of the afternoon, Brecc chattered about his work on the Blue Mountain and other cities where he'd lived. But, he spoke nothing of his family or life before the war.

Sunset ignited the jagged slopes of Stormbringer's snow-covered mountains, setting them ablaze. Seekers didn't sleep much, but they couldn't travel quickly, even if they did manage a lucky guess and follow the same road. The elves ignored the few riders and wagons traveling to Unaria, but they hid from the handful of riders who came up fast behind them. Their sensitive hearing forewarned them in plenty of time.

A small, walled city came into view. Once past, they could select nearly any animal track and rest without worrying about getting discovered. But instead of skirting the city, Brecc continued to the gates.

"Here? We're not stopping *here!*" Ivy's heart thumped at the thought of entering another populated area. Besides, Ivy had salvaged her seeds but no coin. She couldn't afford to eat or sleep at an inn.

"Live a little. I'll take care of your supper and your room.

Consider it my apology for tricking you." Brecc slid Ash back into his satchel. Even with his face angled down, Ivy could still see the smirk on his face. "Besides, Sunshine needs pampering. She's a bit spoiled."

Why am I not surprised?

Brecc continued. "There's an excellent inn here. Even their feather beds are tolerable."

Ivy resisted rolling her eyes, but just barely. "I'll order the most expensive food available as payback."

"Worth it."

"And I'm calling that dragon, Ash-face," she muttered.

"Um, check a mirror."

Ivy silently groaned, remembering the mixture of tears and ash smeared across her face.

At the gate, Brecc spoke with the guard, who, surprisingly, didn't require a bribe. The city inside was well maintained, from the buildings to the streets, almost like a storybook—about wealthy people. Brecc handed Sunshine's reins to a hostler.

"I want my horse's coat to shine," Brecc said, finishing his lengthy instructions. Ivy cocked her head to the side, evaluating Sunshine's pearly coat, wondering if the horse had a bit of unicorn blood.

Brecc led Ivy along a cobblestone road that was so shiny it reflected the last light of the sunset. Two women, parading in fine dresses and long cloaks lined with rabbit fur, walked into the nearby inn.

"I don't think I'll be welcome here." Ivy ran her hand down her messy braid.

"Nonsense." Brecc pulled her through the entrance and left her standing alone while he spoke with a barmaid.

Within moments, the barmaid whisked Ivy and Brecc to a table with a velvet curtain edged in gold satin. The curtain was probably to hide Ivy, who looked like she'd fallen into a hearth, but Ivy repositioned her chair to watch the inn's entrance. The barmaid recited the menu, her attention firmly on Brecc the whole time. The prices were so high Ivy wouldn't have purchased a single mug of ale here, even if she *did* have the money. Brecc and the barmaid flirted for what seemed like ages, which her growling stomach found incredibly annoying.

"I can't let you buy such an expensive meal for me," Ivy whispered before standing to leave. Everything about this place itched under her skin, and she could gather edible roots from the forest.

"Please, sit." Brecc then ordered mushroom soup along with spiced wine for them both. As he spoke to the barmaid, his sleeve slipped up past his wrist, and Ivy realized why his sleeves were tailored long—they covered the scars on the back of his hands. She'd thought they were age spots, but they were the remains of minerals. Ivy averted her gaze, trying not to stare. When the barmaid finally left, Brecc explained. "The proprietor of this place is paying the coin. It's less than nothing to him. He's happy to do it. Trust me."

Ivy raised a brow.

"I saved his son's life."

"You gave a human boy a seed?" she hissed.

"What? No!" He winced. "I would never choose that fate for a helpless, human child. I used a stone, of course. It was slow, but effective."

Ivy blinked several times before his words sunk in. Brecc had relationships. With humans. Friends. What would that be like? Ivy pulled out the sketch from her pocket. Her heartbeat slowed as she ran her finger over her mother's face, and her body unclenched. For humans, their treasures were gold; for her, it was this drawing of her family. If she was honest, she knew her family was dead. It'd been fifteen years. Fifteen opportunities to meet her at a Gathering since they'd parted ways.

"Is that your family?" Brecc asked.

She ran a thumb across the edge of the drawing. "Back in happier times."

"May I?" Brecc held his hand out.

Ivy pinched the image in her fingers before sliding it across the table.

A sad, tight smile flickered on his face as he admired the drawing. Brecc turned it over, and his smile vanished. He held the image up to the candlelight and tilted it back and forth, his face stern. He inspected the message of well-wishes on the back. Nothing special. He smelled the parchment, and his brows furrowed, deepening the wrinkles on his forehead.

He shot his hand out, like a bird of prey, and grabbed Ivy's wrist. "Who wrote this note on the back?"

Ivy tensed at his sudden change. What did she really know about Brecc? Only that he'd abandoned elven ways. And that he'd killed Seekers.

Brecc squeezed her wrist. "Who?"

"The ... the midwife. She w-was nice to us."

"Let me guess," Brecc hissed. "You bury this with your stones, but when you retrieve it, suddenly Seed Seekers find you?"

She started to argue but paused. That was exactly what happened.

"Ivy, after you dug up this illustration, how much time did you have until a Seeker found you?"

She bit her lip, thinking. "Hours?"

"This writing on the back." Brecc pointed to the back of the photo. "Rock, pulverized into dust, is mixed in the ink. The House of Minerals keeps the secrets of—"

"I-I'm not supposed to know these things," Ivy cut him off.

"Hoarding information will be the downfall of our kind," Brecc snapped.

Ivy pulled out of Brecc's grip and cupped her palms over her ears. "You shouldn't be ..."

This is how he's survived.

If she wanted to know the source of her family's demise, this was her chance. She pressed her hands to the table. "Tell me."

"This ink is combined with bits of azurite. See the grainy texture?"

She grabbed the photo and inspected it. "I think so. Does that matter?"

Brecc opened his satchel, and Ash poked her head out. Brecc dug around and pulled out a leather pouch. From the pouch, he dumped five cylindrical stones on the table.

"Brecc," Ivy hissed. The stones were sacred, not to be shared around humans.

"Azurite is a stone we use to find each other," Brecc explained, ignoring her warning. "When held, it broadcasts your location to other elves. Like an ancient beacon. This signal isn't a gentle caress, Ivy. It's like suddenly getting dunked in the icy northern channel. It'd wake you up from a dead sleep. I haven't carried azurite since the war."

Ivy stared at the writing as horror dawned. She covered her mouth, pleading with and cursing the Mother simultaneously. All these years, she'd believed she'd made a mistake with her seeds or that Seekers had gotten smarter. In reality, she panicked and called the Seekers to her side every time she unburied the image.

"*All* elves should be taught *all* the elven ways. True power comes from collaboration, not compartmentalization. However, " Brecc thrummed his fingers on the table, "azurite doesn't explain everything. I doubt those Seekers in Unaria could keep track of anything, let alone a stone. I'm missing something." Brecc lowered his voice, his nostrils flaring. "I shared knowledge of the minerals and earth which helped you. You should share knowledge of the seeds and trees. You can grant access to the Seekers."

"What are you saying?" Ivy feared she knew exactly what Brecc meant. "You think elves should give *more* seeds when they are poison to humans? The Mother tasked elves to bring peace to both worlds, not to condemn one."

"Someone I knew was corrupted by a seed," Brecc said. A piece of his grey hair slipped from its band, but he didn't smooth it back. "Watching her devolve ... I can't describe the pity and horror I felt. After she died, I spoke at a Gathering on the Seeker's behalf. No one listened. That's when I realized that elves didn't care about humans. Not anymore. I didn't turn my back on elves. They turned their backs on me."

The two companions fell silent as the barmaid delivered their food, but Ivy's appetite had vanished.

"The Seekers will eventually be extinct." Ivy's hands shook as she clutched her goblet. "That's what the Council says. The Council tracks every seed now—they're more careful."

"You think your House *protects* the seeds. Your House controls, monitors, and hordes the seeds for elven benefit alone." Brecc sighed and sipped his soup, seeming to drop the topic. Ivy was glad to let it go.

A movement behind him caught Ivy's attention. A woman in a nightdress with a silken robe shuffled across the room. Her jerking movements were subtle, yet they set Ivy's heart racing.

"Grab Ash-face and follow me," Ivy snapped. "A Seeker found us."

6

THE DESPERATE MIDWIFE

Appalled, Brecc watched Ivy shove two swinish bites of the finest truffle soup into her mouth before she darted away from the table. Her little act was dramatic enough to fit right in with the high fae's Spring Court, which was saying something.

He moved to stop her when a muffled yell sounded from outside the inn. Was a fight breaking out? Then he noticed a woman, mere steps away, in a silken nightdress with exquisite stitching lumbering past the tables. Her disheveled hair and waxy skin signaled her corrupted nature.

Ivy darted to the kitchen, but Brecc stood frozen in awe. The strength of the azurite was stunning. Yet, this fast response indicated that the signal was more than just the bits of stone. Something else was going on—some unknown magical combination bent on destruction.

Brecc tucked Ashie against his chest and chased after Ivy. The dragon snorted, her muscles tensing under her scales. "Don't even think about it. I won't be able to see if you spout." Above the din, Ivy warned the cooks. "Seekers are here! Stay calm!"

A door in the back was propped open with an oven-baked brick. Outside, tobacco smoke assaulted Brecc's senses, and a ribbon of the gibbous moons' light revealed the narrow alley.

"Where are we going?" he asked.

"Away from here," Ivy shot back. With a gloved hand, she tested an iron ladder attached to the back of the adjacent building, which was several stories high. "Evasion and speed are essential. Direct confrontation won't end well. You don't have your toy hammer, and I don't know this place ... we're in trouble."

Brecc placed Ash on his shoulder, and Ivy shoved napkins at him. "Wrap your hands to protect them from the iron."

His jaw dropped. When had Ivy grabbed napkins from the table? Iron wasn't deadly, but it weakened.

She scrambled up the emergency ladder. "What are you waiting for?"

Plates crashed in the kitchen. Brecc furiously wrapped his hands, his heart racing. He jumped onto the iron ladder and climbed, Ash's pointed claws digging into his collar.

"We can't risk going higher," she said, stopping at a darkened window. "We'll need to jump, and three stories is the most my body can take without needing a seed."

"But—"

"Stones aren't fast enough," she interrupted his argument.

"So, punch out the glass, and we'll climb inside."

She placed a single hand on the pane, smirking at him. With a gentle push, it smoothly opened. "You'd burn through all your seeds in a month with that attitude."

Shouts sounded in the alley below as Ivy slid into the dark room.

"I know it's cold, Ashie, but follow from the skies." Brecc wriggled his shoulder, and Ash flew higher, skimming up the wall, her small frame blending with the shadows.

Brecc squeezed through the window and sidestepped bulky furniture in the dark. “Where to, now?”

“Out of Carrus and into the forest.”

“This Seeker activity isn’t normal, Ivy. I’ve lived in Unaria for over a decade and visited Carrus many times, and I’ve only seen one Seeker before you arrived. Heard rumors of them, yes, but nothing like *this.*”

Brecc generally avoided attachment to humans. They were fragile and short-lived. But, against his better judgment, he’d grown attached to the Carrus boy he’d saved. He and his family lived above the inn. If the boy’s family were to get in a Seeker’s way ... Brecc’s stomach clenched.

They ran down the hallway, passing several doors to residences. Brecc knocked on the door at the end of the hall.

“Just pound the door down,” Ivy growled. “An iron ladder isn’t going to slow a Seeker.”

Brecc nodded and leaned back, ready to ram the door, but it swung open. The woman’s scowl melted away at the sight of Brecc.

“How can I help you?” she fluttered her lashes.

Ivy muttered under her breath and pushed past them into the room, darting to the window.

“I apologize, but Seekers are coming,” Brecc said. “Do you have a safe place to stay for a few hours?”

“Brecc!” Ivy shouted as she opened the window.

Brecc led the woman into the hall. “Take the stairs to the next floor, just to be safe.”

Glass shattered down the hall. The woman’s eyes widened, and she hurried to the stairs. Brecc spun into the woman’s apartment, slamming the door behind him. Ivy was gone.

He ran to the window. Ivy was already on the ground, frantically waving for him to jump.

"Most generous of you to wait for me," he muttered sarcastically.

The door flew open behind him, and the nightdress-wearing Seeker ambled into the room, her eyes alight.

Brecc grabbed both sides of the window frame and launched himself into the crisp night air. He didn't have time to think, but his years of military service paid off. He hit the ground and rolled, unhurt. The Seeker screamed in frustration, her hands gripping the window frame.

Ivy sprinted north. Brecc wiped a bead of sweat from his brow and followed. They turned down an alley, dodging crates and refuse. Ivy slowed to a jog, scanning the streets from left to right.

"How often do you do this?" he asked, trying to catch sight of Ash. She wouldn't be far.

Footfalls pounded the stones not far behind, shaking Brecc to his core.

"You know this city better than I do," Ivy said. "Which is the best way to get back to your horse and the gate without retracing our steps?"

"Right. We need a way back untainted from your image's scent. This way." Brecc ignored Ivy's pained expression at his accusation and raced to a low fence. Vaulting over it, they landed in a communal garden next to a row of tall, narrow homes. Frozen blades of grass crunched under their feet as they ran. Brecc turned back to see if they were followed. No movement, yet.

Suddenly, he went down, tangled in a mess of wires—forgotten supports for a long-gone vegetable garden. Pain blossomed from his shins. Momentarily dazed, he felt Ivy gripping his arm, pulling him to his feet.

By some miracle, she'd come back for him. He tried to run, but pain reverberated up his leg, and his ankle screamed. He limped forward, warmth trickling down his shin. One of the thinner wires must have sliced into his leg. Was his ankle sprained? Of all the ways to hurt himself ... foolish, foolish.

"When we tell the story of our glorious escape," Brecc joked, despite his rising panic, "let's leave that part out."

Ivy snorted. "If you get us out of here, I'll spin the story however you wish."

Voices echoed on the other side of the fence. Terror rose higher in his chest. How many were there?

How could this happen? He'd been drinking tea and sculpting marble just yesterday while enjoying his neighbor's harp practice.

Ivy pulled his arm across her shoulder and tried to run, but Brecc couldn't keep up. He grabbed for the vial of seeds at his neck, but his hands shook too hard to loosen the cap.

Ash dove from overhead at the figures near the fence. With a squeaking roar, a dark cloud surrounded the two Seekers. Blinded and coughing, they still pushed forward, their other senses guiding them. The dragon circled higher, sounding a warning cry.

Ivy yanked up the leather strap at her neck, revealing her seeds. She hesitated, and Brecc could see why. She only had two seeds. Mother of Magic, he hoped she had more hidden somewhere. She tilted the vial, rolling one into her hand.

He was torn between pity and harsh judgment as she shoved the seed into his mouth. Brecc choked it down. He would repay Ivy by showing her the truth.

Another shadow dropped into the garden. The elves were out of time. Ivy supported Brecc for three steps, then strength flooded into his limbs. He sprinted into the lead with the familiar surge of energy. Past the homes and into the street, Brecc's mind quickened, fully alert. The road widened, the double moons' light revealing a Seeker crouched and waiting.

"Ivy."

"I see him."

They'd be overtaken before reaching the eastern gate. So, he veered down another alley as he formed a new plan, still alert for any signs of movement. He was strong enough to forcibly take the drawing of Ivy's family and destroy it. It would save Ivy, but she'd never forgive him. She'd never listen to him.

He reeled back, noticing a Seeker on a rooftop. These back alleys weren't working. As possible plans formed in his mind, he analyzed them and cast them aside until a single path remained. Ivy wouldn't like it.

His new path required a route back through the crowded, vibrant part of the city. Though the outcome wasn't guaranteed, it was his best chance to save Ivy and get justice for the love he'd lost.

He led Ivy and the Seekers to a populated park that circled the untamed, off-limits forest inside the city. Nothing else like this forest existed in all of Trinth.

The wealthy strolled the periphery to see and be seen as they traversed the city in their jewels and furs. Brecc sprinted for several blocks, taking a few sharp turns, until they reached the edge of the busiest portion of town, abutting the park's entrance.

Brecc and Ivy crossed the manicured park, past the dormant flower beds and under barren trees. Motes of light floated daintily in the naked branches, a magical luxury few cities could afford. Young couples walked back and forth on their way to elegant dinner parties or intimate, influential gatherings. Brecc and Ivy slowed their pace, blending in like any other father and daughter. Brecc whispered as they walked. He had too little time to explain things only an embittered elf of the House of Minerals would know.

"This is my best guess: humans strategically placed

midwives in communities where protector elves might settle. Who knows how long your sister's midwife waited to birth an elven baby and entrap the family? To be fair, who knows what lies the midwife was fed."

Ivy turned her face away, refusing to look at him. "Perhaps the midwife was simply greedy, lusting after the rumored chance at immortality."

"The reason doesn't matter, Ivy. The midwife's tainted ink leads them straight to you." Brecc grabbed her arm, desperate for her to understand. "Even when I give you a seed, you'll only have two. You'll never survive until the next Gathering. You must destroy the picture."

Brecc tugged at the leather around his neck. Two vials. Twenty seeds. Gifts he'd believed Alysatraee had granted him. But the night's events cast his assumptions into doubt. Perhaps the Mother intended his seeds for another purpose.

"Seeker," he warned, moving faster. "Behind me, on my left."

"There's more than one."

He glanced over again. Two Seekers moved straight toward them through the crowd, blindly knocking over a bystander while never taking their focus off Ivy. He and Ivy would have to be quick to slip past their pursuers. Brecc ducked around a raised garden bed and sprinted down a tree-lined path toward the sound of the rushing river.

"How can there be this many Seekers in such a small town?" Ivy said, panic rising in her voice.

"This is beyond any mathematical probability. The writing on your drawing is not only calling to Seekers but also speeding or amplifying their corrup—"

Something smashed against Brecc's head; his temple exploded with pain. His world tilted, and he found himself staring up at the blurry night sky. His mind struggled to grasp why he was on the ground and what was happening. A Seeker kicked him in the side. Brecc curled up, using his arm to protect his body. He couldn't scream; no air to give. Blows thundered against his side, again and again. Rolling to his stomach, Brecc strained to crawl away, suffocating, desperate. Ivy crashed into Brecc's attacker, and the beating mercifully ended.

Brecc collapsed, his ribs screaming with every labored breath. A step away from him, Ivy caught a punch. In a blur, she used the Seeker's arm as a lever, throwing him into another attacker, and both Seekers went down in a tangle.

Already a third, desperate Seeker sprinted toward Brecc, hands outstretched for the seed vials at his neck. The scents were contained, but the Seeker must have spotted them.

Ash flew down behind the Seeker and dragged her claws across the back of the attacker's neck. The distraction was enough—Brecc kicked up, hitting the Seeker in the stomach with all his strength, which wasn't much. Half-blind with pain, Brecc gripped Ivy's outstretched hand, her necklace swinging forward like a pendulum. The Seeker lunged, one hand clutching his stomach, the other catching the lace of Ivy's necklace with a hooked finger.

Ivy pulled back, and the vial snapped. She stumbled as the vial flew through the air, end over end. It clattered to the ground, the ping like a siren's call. In a heartbeat, two Seekers pounced, smashing the glass. Ivy gasped and dove for the seed. Elbows flew, and her head snapped back, blood flowing from her nose.

Brecc pushed himself to his feet and grabbed Ivy, pulling her back from the fight. "Leave the seed. More Seekers are coming!"

Dragging Ivy away, he watched in growing horror as the Seeker he'd fought also converged on the single spilled seed in a mad frenzy. Three Seekers. One seed mixed with glass in the cracks of the cobblestones.

"Brecc," Ivy wiped the blood from her face, smearing it across her cheek, "this is bad. Right after the Seekers get seed—"

"I know." Brecc led her to the forest. Once the Seekers devoured a seed, for a short period of time, they became *much* more deadly.

Each breath brought a sharp, stabbing pain in Brecc's side. He slogged across the small river, but Ivy quickly jumped it. Did she realize, yet, that they were trapped? Without seeds, she'd never survive a direct fight. There were too many Seekers.

And they were closing in.

Brecc wanted to blame Ivy for their desperate situation, but she had warned him. He'd thought he could save and teach *her*, but it was becoming clear that she would save *him*.

Save him by finishing the work he had lost the heart to do. His new plan was a risky gamble, at best. However, to give Ivy a chance, there would be no escape for him.

He pressed a cold, wet hand to the seeds under his tunic. "I'm coming home, my darling."

7
ELVEN SECRETS

Ivy grabbed Brecc's hand, pulling him out of the river as Seekers entered the other side. Ivy's body screamed to run, but she steadied her companion instead.

"Which way to the gates?" she pressed.

"East."

Brecc stumbled through a cluster of pines, cedars, and birches. The sounds of humans enjoying their evening were lost, replaced with a prickly warning down Ivy's spine. Could they hide? Brecc wouldn't make it far in his condition.

"I'll help you get a seed," she grabbed for one of the vials at his neck.

He knocked her hand away and limped a bit faster.

"I loved someone once," he said. "Sariah, a half-elf. She relished gardening and her flowers. She loathed deer. But in a remote village, deer reigned. She purchased a repelling elixir from a traveling "wizard" for the perimeter of her garden. But the mixture killed everything it touched and didn't stop the deer from eating what was left." Brecc started to chuckle but winced. "Between her growing up around humans and me keeping our elven secrets, as I was taught, Sariah knew little of fair folk. She'd heard rumors of seeds enabling elves to extend their lives. When she found mine ... she just wanted us to grow old together." His voice grew tight. "She was my whole heart, my forever companion, and my dearest friend. The seeds I received at the Gatherings couldn't keep up. Eventually, I ran out."

Horror and sadness snaked through Ivy as she imagined Brecc doling out seeds to bring Sariah's mind back for a day. An hour. A moment.

The trees thinned, and Brecc led her to a mature pine. Brecc stumbled to the tree and leaned against it, struggling to catch his breath. A faint rustling announced Ash just before she dropped onto Brecc's shoulder.

"We're not going to the gates, are we?" Ivy asked. She recognized a last stand when she saw one. This wasn't the way she wanted to die.

"Of the two of us, I know Seekers best. I need you to trust me. Climb." Brecc pointed to the branches overhead.

A twig snapped, and Ivy spun to see the woman in the nightdress enter the clearing. Another Seeker with a bloodied temple followed. It was the Seeker they'd fought already. Another one with a fur cap entered the clearing, much closer to Ivy's location.

A curse caught in Ivy's throat.

"Ivy!" Brecc gasped. "Climb!"

She backed up and took a running jump at the tree, wrapping her arms around the trunk and climbing. She grabbed a branch, hooked her knees, and quickly reached for Brecc.

"Take my hand!"

He wrapped his arm around his ribs. He looked up, his face oddly serene. "I figured it out. The ink. The midwife must have added ground seed to it. The azurite acts as an amplifier, signaling your location to every Seeker within your proximity. That's how the Seekers track you. Elegant, in a way."

Brecc turned to the oncoming Seekers and lifted his vials. If he took one, he could climb the tree without her help. Even so, Ivy reached out her hand, ready.

"I made a mistake, Ivy." Brecc's voice was soft.

"Take the seed!" Panic flooded Ivy's senses.

"I should've kept fighting for the Seekers. After Sariah, I let my anger boil and turn to resentment."

"Take my hand!" Ivy shouted, stretching her arm further as the nearest Seeker closed in.

"But they'll listen to you," he said. "A seed protector."

The scene below seemed to slow as Brecc opened his vial. He tipped it upside down, and every seed spilled to the ground.

Brecc spoke quietly to his dragon, ignoring Ivy as the Seekers rushed forward. The nightgown-Seeker dove to the ground as Ash shot into the sky. The dragon's silent, graceful ascent was discordant with the Seekers, screeching and clawing at the dirt near Brecc's feet. He stood stoic as more Seekers emerged from the trees.

Blood pumped through Ivy's veins, throbbing in her ears. She could barely count them all, but there were at least a dozen.

Brecc opened his second vial and removed a single seed. Then he tossed the remaining contents in an arc. The horde rent the air with their cries, rushing forward before their crumbs of liberation even hit the ground.

"Brecc!" She stretched her fingers, willing him to take the last seed pinched between his fingers.

The human cries made her skin crawl. Seekers fought each other, kicking, punching, biting. Instead of eating the last seed, he placed it back into his glass pendant with a shaking hand. Then he threw it into the air. Ash darted from the sky and grasped the vial in her talons before soaring out of reach.

A Seeker slammed into Brecc's knees, and he collapsed to the ground. Ivy screamed. The Seekers paused, looking up at her.

"Don't let this be in vain, Ivy," Brecc called up with a thin voice. "Speak for the humans who our seeds have poisoned."

She bit off her scream, though the horde already knew her location. She fumbled for a corner of the drawing of her family; her salvation, and her ruin. They wouldn't want her to let Brecc sacrifice himself for an asinine cause. Below, Brecc had curled up in a ball next to the tree. Ivy pulled herself up and prepared to drop next to him. With the Seekers distracted, she had a sliver of a chance to grab Brecc and run.

She swung her leg down, but Ash darted from the sky before she could jump, flapping her wings and screeching a warning. Ivy paused, and Ash retreated. She swung her leg down again, and Ash dug her talons into Ivy's braid, pulling her back. Ivy desperately flung her arms, vainly shooing the dragon; if Ash breathed her smoke, she'd blind Ivy, making it impossible for her to help anyone.

One Seeker emerged from the mass directly below Ivy's dangling leg, triumphantly propelling bodies back. He crouched and stared at Ivy, the moons' light cutting through the branches and across his face.

Ivy froze, her breath coming in rasps.

He skulked toward the trunk, his movement smooth. Quick. Ivy's insides shriveled.

Ash cried out, breaking through Ivy's fear-stupor, and she snapped her leg up. More victorious Seekers followed the newfound leader. They howled and snarled like a pack of rabid beasts.

Then they attacked. Wrapping their arms around the trunk, they pushed and pulled with newfound strength, causing the tree to sway to a violent beat. Shortly after Seekers ingested a seed, their strength multiplied and their emotions heightened, making them nearly impossible to defeat.

Brecc's body was still, even as one Seeker trampled him underfoot. Ivy whimpered, grabbing the branch with both arms, clinging with her waning strength. The trunk moaned and cracked. Behind them, more Seekers fought each other for the remaining seeds while others lay lifeless on the ground.

With a sickening snap, the tree shuddered and tipped. Ivy's stomach lurched as the tree fell, gravity shifting.

Ivy nearly closed her eyes, trying to shut out her dire situation. But Brecc's last words rang in her ears. She took a breath and adjusted her body weight. She jumped just before the tree slammed against the ground. Clearing the branches with the force of her leap, she tucked and rolled. She slid her hand into her pocket, finding her healing stone as she blindly ran deeper into the forest.

After only a few steps, a Seeker wrestled her to the ground. She tried to kick free. The Seeker's grip tightened. The burst of energy Ivy had conjured to escape the falling tree was quickly spent. Was this how her family died? Knowing their end was near? Helpless? Trapped?

Ivy twisted enough to see her attacker's unseeing, wild eyes start to roll back into his head. His grip loosened, and he collapsed on top of her. Ivy dug her fingers into the dirt, desperately trying to pull herself from under his weight before another Seeker arrived.

Once free, she got into a defensive crouch as she scanned the forest for the path of least resistance. But the only Seekers in view were collapsing, one by one.

Phase two was mercifully beginning.

Ivy staggered back to the tree through the carnage, but Brecc wasn't at the base. She picked through the bodies. Some, like dormant trees in winter, were internally regenerating. In a few hours, the surviving Seekers would awaken—the Seeker's final phase.

The final phase was a special kind of torture for humans. A recently corrupted Seeker might have hours of lucid thought. Perhaps weeks. They were often tormented by what they'd become, especially knowing they would quickly devolve again.

Ash shrieked, and Ivy followed the sound to the river's edge. She discovered Brecc face down, his hair splayed, with Ash on the ground next to him. Ivy rolled him over and held his head in her lap.

"Brecc?" She wiped the dirt away from his face. His hair was slick with blood, but he had a slow, faint pulse.

"Go fetch the last seed Brecc gave you," Ivy commanded the dragon.

Ash lifted her wings, and her back arched as if ready to attack Ivy. But instead, the dragon hissed and flew away.

Gently, Ivy ran a finger across the puckering where Brecc's ears had been cut. Ash perched on a nearby tree, her scales criss-crossed with angular shadows, giving her a menacing, hard look.

Ivy tamped down her anger and tried begging the dragon, "Please, *please*, the seed."

Brecc opened his eyes and coughed, grabbing her attention.

"Tell Ash to bring your seed," Ivy pleaded. "I don't know where she put it."

He gave a pained smirk. "The seed is not meant for me. You'll need it."

"I'll throw it away."

Brecc swallowed, his attention drifting.

"Why?" She searched his face, looking for answers he couldn't or wouldn't give.

His breath grew labored. Ivy's heart ached, knowing it

would be easier to get a seed at the next Gathering, hundreds of miles away, than to steal the one Ash hid.

"Sariah loved tulips. She tried everything to cultivate them, a fool's errand at the forest's edge. But she would have figured out a way. Probably ten different ways." He tilted his head to look at Ivy. "Sariah wasn't your enemy. The Council hopes Seekers will simply die. But humankind is richer than we give them credit. Speak for the Seekers at the next Gathering. The fair folk have vast knowledge. We can help them if we try. I know we can. I saved who I could. Now it's your turn."

A lump grew in Ivy's throat, too big for her to swallow. Tears burned as she clutched his hand. Council members spoke at the Gatherings, but she never had. Standing up in front of a thousand elves wasn't something she'd ever planned to do.

Brecc grinned, his eyes closed. "And ... get rid ... of that wretched ... drawing."

Ivy laugh-cried, tears spilling down her cheeks. Ivy pressed her healing stone into his hand, clutching it between them. As the night darkened, Brecc slipped away.

Ash let out a screech and lit into the sky, and Ivy knew Brecc had returned to Alysatraee. Ivy hunched over his body, clutching his still-warm hand in hers. She let herself cry, ugly and hard, for the first time in a long time.

She cried for Brecc, her father, her mother, her niece, her sister's husband, and her sister. Ivy curled inward, alone. Logically, she knew her family was dead. So she'd refused to allow the thought to surface. And she'd not allowed herself to dwell on her loneliness. Her deepest heartache and gut-wrenching turmoil had been caused by Seekers. How could she ever genuinely speak for them? Her feelings about Seekers warred inside her, vitriolic anger and the most profound pity. Seekers had driven not just her family apart but her entire House. Yet, were they victims, too?

She would honor Brecc's last wish and speak for the Seekers. But she wasn't ready to forgive them.

Ash returned, landing several steps from Ivy, Brecc's glass pendant with a single seed in one claw. The little dragon didn't hop closer. She didn't perch on Ivy's shoulder. The dragon didn't close the mournful distance between them. Still, Ash was there. For the moment, Ivy wasn't completely alone.

A branch snapped in the forest. Ivy sucked in a breath, and Ash crouched lower to the ground, her wings spread. Ivy kissed Brecc's forehead goodbye and wiped away her tears.

Her night wasn't over.

Ivy yanked out her drawing and took one last look at her family. Then she ripped the parchment in half. Her heart cracked with each subsequent tear and shattered when she dropped the pieces onto the river bank. The river would wash the remnants away, but before it did, the ink would call any remaining Seekers here, giving her a chance to escape.

Ivy gritted her teeth, attuned to the forest around her. She was vulnerable without a seed, so this was the last place she could stay. Even so, thoughts blared in her mind. Someone had given the midwife azurite dust and ground seed. Now that Ivy considered the ink, it was unlikely that the woman was even aware of the seed in the ink. Otherwise, she would've consumed it or given it to whomever she was attempting to protect.

Seekers were the weapons, but someone else had manipulated them. Why? And were the culprits fair folk or human? Were they after Ivy's family or just Ivy?

She didn't know, but she was determined to find out.

"Ash, time to go," she whispered, clutching her healing stone in her fist. "We have a Gathering to attend."

8

THE FAE PORTAL

The last stars faded as Captain Orion arrived in neighboring Carrus. With a flash of Orion's ring, a gate guard quickly escorted him to the scene of destruction.

Despite the predawn hour, the meticulously maintained periphery of the forest was a whirl of activity. Guards restricted access, but it didn't stop the onlookers from trying to peer between the trunks and needled branches. Half the city milled about; everyone from well-dressed residents to personal guards to servants. A few cheeks glistened with worried tears, but most were likely braving the frosty morning in hopes of local gossip.

Orion dismounted and pushed through onlookers, approaching Carrus' inner forest. One of the city guards apprised him of the recent horrors.

"I'll help you find the lieutenant," she said, leading him into the forest beyond.

Carrus was unusual because it boasted a section of forest inside the walls. But then again, the citizens of Carrus were unusually wealthy.

"I've never seen so many Seekers," she continued explaining

what little she knew as she marched through the forest. "They were chasing a male and female who had been dining at a local tavern."

Her ensuing description sounded eerily like Brecc and Ivy. He berated himself for not arriving sooner, but tracking elves was no easy feat.

The temperature dropped, and crystalline frost rimmed the brittle leaves on the ground. Before they even reached the river, they encountered a guard standing near a body wrapped in white cloth.

Orion released the reins of his horse and checked the body. Sometimes regenerating Seekers were mistaken for dead, their pulse barely perceptible. But no such luck for this one. The guard touched her heart and chin, a whispered prayer on her lips.

"What happened here?" Orion asked.

"I haven't been informed." The guard didn't make eye contact nor venture a guess. Smart woman. "There are only three healers in the city today," the guard continued. "They're attending, um, survivors ... as quickly as they can."

Orion and the Carrus guard continued across the shallow river. As they moved closer to the heart of the forest, the back of Orion's neck pricked, a sense of foreboding seeping under his skin. Though birds were usually noisy at dawn, their songs were silent.

In the small clearing, two guards stood near several blanket-covered bodies on the ground.

"In Carrus, healers use a red blanket when the patient needs immediate care," the guard quietly explained.

Orion counted five red and many more white coverings. He surmised that those with white covers were beyond the healer's reach. He continued forward and spoke to the guards, one of whom wore a lieutenant insignia on her fitted coat.

"What happened here?" Orion asked.

"It appears that the fight between the Seekers and the man and woman culminated there." The lieutenant pointed to a pine tree that had snapped in half, then to a nearby form covered in white. "The man is dead, and we don't know what happened to the woman."

Orion internally reeled at the news. Was Brecc among the dead? Was Ivy?

"We found a handful of Seekers alive," the second, more grizzled guard said. "Though I'm not sure why the magistrate called for the healers. We should kill the Seekers while we have the chance."

Any of these Seekers could have family nearby; perhaps they'd get some closure before the seeds retook the corrupteds' minds and were locked away. But Orion was in no mood to attempt to explain.

Instead, he turned his focus to the morbid scene. Orion still hoped to find Ivy alive; he needed answers before he made a report. Gossip would spread about these salacious, deadly events, especially in Carrus. Those who resided here were especially well connected. His account needed to reach the king before the gossip.

The lieutenant sent Orion's guide back to her post, then led Orion to the fractured tree. Though blood wasn't visible, the copper scent hung in the air. Orion studied the gouges, calculating the number of hands that had dug frantically into the soil.

"Careful of the glass," the lieutenant warned.

Orion picked up a piece and put pressure on the edges. As he'd suspected, it was enchanted. Difficult to break, but a Seeker could shatter it. How many seeds had been inside? How many Seekers had wandered away before falling unconscious? And where was Ivy?

Orion moved around the area, and his gaze fell on debris near the river. Parchment. He wanted to know precisely what it revealed before he shared it with anyone, just like he always did when investigating fair folk.

He'd kept his suspicion that Brecc and Ivy were elves to himself. Any rumor of fair folk always resulted in some level of undue panic. So, he needed to investigate without prying eyes.

"Lieutenant, I don't know what the protocol is in Carrus, but in Unaria, when a captain arrives to investigate a crime, usually another captain greets him."

The lieutenant leaned back, "Our captain has been a bit busy today, Captain."

"Yet I've been through the forest and haven't seen him," Orion said, knowing the captain was looking forward to retirement and was probably questioning people in the comfort of his guard station.

"I'll send a guard to fetch him," the lieutenant said with tight lips before she spun on her heel and marched away. He didn't have much time to search without her watching his every move.

Orion hurried to the prone form covered in white, dread filling his bowels. This body was set apart from the others, away from the seeds. Orion took a breath, then pulled back the sheet. The recognition and sense of loss struck him all at once. Though he'd not cared for Brecc, he'd never wanted this end for him.

"I wish you'd told me what was going on," Orion whispered. "I would've tried to help."

Brecc's ear was visible, revealing puckered scarring, another confirmation of his elven blood. Orion covered Brecc's body, the tension in his limbs mounting as he wondered if Ivy was alive or dead.

Orion pushed forward with his investigation and moved to

the riverbank. Bits of ripped parchment lay in the mud. Orion crouched closer, strategically placing himself so an evergreen partially blocked the guards' views. Still, Orion sensed a watchful presence, likely the lieutenant returning or one of the many forest inhabitants upset by the night's events.

At a glance, Orion realized the ripped-up parchment was once a drawing. He flipped over the pieces, trying to fit them together. A family? Several portions were missing, likely floated away in the water, but recently, judging by the cleanliness of the remains.

He flipped over a piece and a familiar face greeted him. His heart nearly stopped, and the parchment slipped from his fingers back into the mud.

A screech sounded from deeper in the forest, light and high-pitched. Unfamiliar. Orion's hand went to his hilt as he listened for movement.

From the forest's shadows, a bright teal-colored creature emerged. It scuttled quickly forward and then froze in place, seeming to evaluate its next meal. Although about the size of a barn cat and hissing like one, too, it was distinctly reptilian, despite the vibrant yellow feathers on top of its head. In the dim light, Orion didn't notice its red eyes until too late. His limbs stiffened.

The creature charged, but Orion couldn't move a muscle. Foam bubbled up from its lips. The creature's mouth snapped open, revealing a hundred tiny, pointed teeth.

"Princess, stop!" a deep, female voice commanded. Orion knew the accent well—the magistrate of the city.

The reptilian creature slowed but still stepped closer to Orion, its body low to the ground. The captain struggled to move, magic pinning him in place.

"Princess!" The magistrate reprimanded the creature like humans did to impetuous toddlers.

Orion strained to close his eyes, breaking the bond. He stumbled back, the tip of his blade slicing through the air. Even without looking directly, he purposefully kept his blade from hitting his attacker—a young cockatrice.

"Orion Arya," the magistrate's voice rumbled. "Don't even *think* about it. I will not hesitate to chop off your blade-wielding hand if you harm her." The magistrate's voice then changed to a soft coo as she scooped up the cockatrice. "Don't you worry, my little, sweet princess."

Orion sheathed his sword. "You'll chop off my hand? You know I can't grow back appendages, Maggie."

"Unfortunate." The magistrate gave him a flat stare. She was tall for a human female. But then again, she wasn't human. "What have you found?" she asked, noticing the bits of parchment in the mud.

"You first," Orion said, narrowing his eyes at the reptilian creature in her arms. Behind her, both the guards had vacated their station.

"Shall we?" She glanced over her shoulder and walked deeper into the forest.

Orion grabbed the piece of parchment he'd dropped and slipped it into his pocket before following the magistrate. Once they were alone, far beyond the broken pine tree in the clearing, the magistrate ran her thumb slowly down a bone amulet on a golden chain at her neck. She let out a deep sigh, her body relaxing, and her glamour dropped.

The magistrate lifted her face to the morning sky, a hint of a smile on her lips. Magdud looked similar to the high fae, except she was taller, broader, and with purple skin and tusks. Half her white hair fell in soft waves to her shoulder blades; the other half was shaved, revealing a rune tattoo on her scalp. The early morning shadows didn't hide the myriad of scars on her face, chest, and one arm. The other arm looked untouched, probably regrown *after* the wars, as orc magic accorded.

"It's good to see you, Magdud." Orion tapped his heart twice, a symbol of respect among the orc.

"I'd like to say the same, but you always bring trouble."

"You're the one with a cockatrice." Either no one had seen it, or Magdud's guards turned a blind eye to the magical creature that could and would kill them if left unattended.

"Princess is only a baby." Magdud tickled the creature under her chin. "Aren't you my wittle ittle baby."

Orion raised a brow. The cockatrice was at least a year old—already strong enough to pin fair folk in place. And easily capable of paralyzing, poisoning, and devouring a human. Orion knew how to escape her magical hold, but few in this realm would have the same skill. "How long until there's an accident, and you receive a summons to the fae court for judgment? You want to end up in a fae dungeon?"

"You worry too much." Maggie stroked the cockatrice's head, and Orion noticed two fingers missing from the magistrate's hand. They'd regrow, but Princess wasn't as tame as the magistrate suggested. "Besides, the court has bigger problems than worrying about a sweet, little fair creature in the human world."

"If you think I'm coming to your rescue from a dungeon for something this foolish, you're mistaken."

"But you'll rescue me if I'm sentenced for doing something *wise*?" She smirked at him. "Good to know."

She set Princess on the ground, and the cockatrice wound around Magdud's ankles. The feathers on the end of her reptilian-turned-birdlike tail quivered as she thwacked it back and forth. A drop of acidic spittle from Princess's lips dropped into the dirt, and the ground sizzled.

"Orion," her voice turned serious, "I've never seen this

many Seekers in one area, let alone in Carrus. This attack was noticed. Take care of it before the ruling king sends an army of gargoyles into my city. Carrus is a refuge, and we live in peace with humans. Some of them even know fair folk reside here. I cannot risk the high fae's involvement."

No one wanted that.

Magdud continued, "Some fae folk choose to reside in Carrus because we're outside established fair society's oversight. We don't want the fae meddling in our lives more than necessary. Praise Alysatraee, but I'm sure the high fae are not meeting her lofty expectations."

"I'll send a report soon. I can send one today with your blessing from here in Carrus."

"Wait, you're telling me you haven't sent word to the court yet?" The magistrate drew herself up, her chest swelling. "Orion, rumors have reached Carrus about the Seekers in Unaria. If the Winter King hears of this from someone else and reacts ..." Her purple skin turned darker as she sputtered, trying to find the words " ... if even one gargoyle shows up here, I swear I will let Princess ..."

Magdud took a deep breath, composing herself before she finished her treasonous sentence.

"I hear you're looking for a smokey-golden horse and the two suspects riding it," she said, changing tacts. "The elder elf who died here, did you see the scarring on his hands? Remnants of mineral growths."

"They were filed off?" Orion asked, surprised, then remembered that Brecc's hands had been covered in dust when they'd met.

The Seekers who survived were unlikely to remember killing Brecc. They wouldn't remember much of anything since becoming corrupted. And their minds would quickly drift, falling deeper into their own inner wasteland. The whole wretched ordeal made Orion ill. Seeds were at the center of all the ugliness.

And seeds were an elven responsibility. Magdud felt like the high fae were not doing their best, but the elves were clearly allowing far too many seeds slip into human hands.

"The Minerals elf was once quite powerful, it seems," Magdud said, her expression grim. "Should I assume his partner was elven as well?"

"Did you find her?"

"We weren't that lucky. But we tracked down the elves' horse, and well, the stable boy didn't hear anyone take it, but the horse is gone."

So far, the elf was impressive. She survived the Seekers, slipped into the stables, smuggled away Brecc's horse, and disappeared.

As Magdud provided more details from the night's events, Orion couldn't help but think the most critical piece of the puzzle was Ivy herself. The formidable elf could risk the tenuous peace between both realms.

Dread began building inside him as the nature of his report became more pointed. And it would be incomplete. Unacceptable. Orion began to brace for the reaction from the influential members of the court. He'd have to make up for it, though precious little impressed the king.

"Will you pull back your guards so I can make my report?" Orion asked. "You know how dryads can be."

Maggie nodded. "Persnickety little introverts. But they're consistent."

She scooped up Princess, preparing to go, but she paused. "Orion, there is always a place for you with my city guards here in Carrus."

"That's generous. I appreciate the offer." He was as likely to live in Carrus as Magdud was to return to Aggord, the orc lands in the south. Orion had worked too long and hard to shrink away from his years of training.

"I don't care about your parentage," Magdud added, matter-of-factly. "You have skills that we could use. Besides, I trust you. And that's a rare commodity in either realm."

Not expecting an answer, Magdud ran her thumb down her bone amulet, and her glamour slipped back into place. She stroked the top of Princess's head and casually added, "Make peace with your mother. One never knows how long we have with family. She is what she *is*. You know her nature. She was generous, as far as dryads go."

Magdud had lost her parents and brother in the war, so instead of snapping back at her impertinence, Orion grit his teeth. It wasn't her place to advise him on his mother, especially as the orc could never understand his childhood. Orion's life had been planned out before he was even conceived.

He was born to fulfill a bargain—a calculated, strategic purpose.

The dryad sent him away without tears, heartache, or even empty promises. Orion, her son, was a leaf she'd dropped in autumn, nothing more. He'd heard she'd had another child, a coveted daughter. Meanwhile, Orion was raised and trained as a warrior who could spy on humans and report to the ruling court. A tool for the Winter Court.

Magdud gave him a pitying look. "Attend to your duties. You know the way."

Orion stalked through the forest toward a massive oak tree, wide enough that a dozen dryads couldn't reach around it. There was no worn path, and few knew its purpose.

It'd been two years since Orion had reported to the court. Per their duty, the fae court brought those who broke fair law to justice—including elves like Ivy. Orion didn't make it a habit to hold back information from the king. He fiddled with the bit of parchment in his pocket. Though he was yet to meet an elf he truly respected, he didn't want to condemn one, either.

He slowed as he neared the tree. Orion didn't know the name of this dryad—only their chosen mate ever did. Only dryads could send messages and had unfettered access to the portals between realms.

With his mother's dryad blood, Orion had inherited her ability—a valuable skill.

After waiting for a half hour, the dryad spoke so softly that some might assume it was in their minds. Dryads rarely showed themselves, and this one was no different.

Orion began his message, his mind spinning. He paused, Ivy's name on his tongue. But Orion kept it within, telling himself even with her name, his report was far from complete. There was so much he didn't know.

But how to get what he needed? Track the elusive Ivy or find the mysterious elder elf who'd come to Orion all those months ago. He weighed the options as he finished speaking with the dryad.

He sensed her presence linger, along with a hint of concern. She didn't chastise. Didn't warn.

He was already keenly aware of the timeline. After midnight on spring equinox eve, Summer Court ruled the fair realm. It was one moon cycle plus thirteen days away.

And Summer had no love for Orion.

9
THE HOUSE OF TIDES

Sunlight bounced off the white snow and flooded through the tall windows of Nylann'or Palace, bathing the marble floors in ethereal light. Kolvar Phiro strode the halls, surrounded by advisers as they finalized preparations to leave the city. The treasury adviser stiffened as Kolvar's sister came into view, storming down the corridor to greet them.

Nym always walked with a purposeful stride, but today her tight braids swung violently by her ears with each step. Their mother always said Nym was born a shaft of lightning caught in a bottle, and if the lid shattered, she'd strike.

And she'd burn.

Tense anticipation grew between the advisers, but Kolvar's friend, Lial, ran a hand down his perfectly combed hair, trying unsuccessfully to hide a superior smirk. Kolvar knew that look; Lial was hoping for a verbal spar. Kolvar ground his teeth, bracing himself to soothe the wounded pride of anyone caught in their crossfire.

"Kolvar," Nym said, "the naiads are renegotiating their contract. Today of all days."

Other than the braids, Nym's short, dark hair was pulled

back, her hazel eyes shining with indignation. She looked ready to murder someone, and Kolvar preferred it not be him.

"But, but we're to leave for the mainland in a few hours!" the treasury adviser sputtered.

Nym's nostrils flared, as they did right before she practically gobbled up someone for lunch.

"As a communication and contract expert," Kolvar quickly spoke, "Nym has handled the naiads for years. I'm sure she worked through any complications."

Or so he hoped. Without the naiads to escort them, their ships were more vulnerable to attacks in the northern channel. And the vessels had to leave today; according to the Tide's Councilors, the winds were favorable.

"I had to promise eight extra baskets of silver mailiak fish," Nym said hotly. "I negotiated them down from twenty. Honestly, I'm not surprised at the higher price, but I'd expected a new demand weeks ago. Waiting until this hour is churlish."

"Absolutely unconscionable," Lial added sarcastically, but the advisers didn't seem to notice.

Nym shot him a warning look. Lial had been Kolvar and Nym's closest friend since they were children. Though not officially an adviser himself, between his father, who was the right hand of the House of Tides Council Representatives, and his many influential friends, Lial often ended up in the thick of any drama.

Lial always styled his hair in a slick low-tail and wore tailored layers of clothing, as if expecting to be called before the council at a moment's notice—which rarely happened. In the evening, he typically accepted the best dinner invitations, which Kolvar suspected were likely far more valuable for gathering information than the stuffy meetings he usually attended.

"The naiads claim elves are getting harder to protect," Nym continued. "There have been more elven deaths on the mainland, true. But not increased attacks on the water. None here in the northern islands."

The advisers' questions began pelting them both like hail in a blizzard.

"Will they wait for payment until the next silver mailiak run?"

"Yes," Nym answered.

"When do they wish to depart?"

"Soon. I suggest those leaving the city," she narrowed her eyes at her brother, "board immediately."

"Are more naiads planning to seek safety in the fair realm?"

"They didn't say. However, they spoke of their general fear for the fair folk."

"How many naiads will travel with us?"

"Two protectors per ship."

Lial gave a low whistle, and several others gasped.

"And you accepted such a deal?" an adviser blurted.

Nym drew herself up taller, and even Lial stilled. "Yes, Adviser Daecyne Obsin, I did." Her every syllable was as hard as an ax smashing against a frozen lake. "The alternative was zero naiad protectors and damaging our relationship. Be grateful we can attend the Gathering at all this year."

"We have less time than we'd anticipated," Kolvar interjected. "I suggest we heed Nym's advice and prepare to leave. Let's adjourn our discussions until we return."

With slight nods, the advisers dispersed, their graceful, slippered feet soundlessly hurrying to execute their duties.

"Next year is going to be a dragon to negotiate." Nym folded her arms across her chest, glowering at Lial, who was inspecting his nails.

"Ah, yes, the Centennial year," Lial said, pointedly not looking at her. "It'll be my first."

Every spring, multiple saplings transformed into Gathering

trees throughout Trinth. Only the House of Seeds knew which trees and the location. The elves split into groups, scattered across the human realm; it was a necessary precaution to avoid detection.

Except for once every hundred years.

For a Centennial year, every elf gathered in one location. Kolvar looked forward to this great Gathering; he couldn't be sure who was still alive, and he would celebrate each long overdue reunion.

"It's too dangerous for us all to meet next year." Nym pounded a fist into her open hand. "We must talk to the Council, but we don't know which council members will be at our Gathering this year."

"You know one who will be there," Lial said in a light, conspiratorial tone. "You don't even have to wait for the Gathering. You could talk to a Councilor for the House of Tides at any time. Special perks of being her daughter."

Nym's lips pressed together, turning white, but Lial pushed further.

"You know, Councilor Phiro is the best negotiator in the city. Perhaps you should ask her to join you next year with those mean naiads. Sounds like you need the help."

Nym looked like her eyes might shoot fire.

"We have a bigger problem." Kolvar cut off their argument before they made a scene and led them further down the palace corridor. "If the naiads leave the human realm, we may need to petition the fae council for assistance. We must travel to the mainland to retrieve seeds, so if the fae want elves to survive here, we need their help."

"That's not a bad idea," Nym said. "It is Alysatraee's will that we remain in the human realm. It's our duty."

"The high fae will do whatever is best for them," Lial grumbled under his breath and elbowed Kolvar in the arm.

The pointed nudge hinted that they needed to speak privately, so Kolvar picked up his pace. Nym raised her brow and followed them into Kolvar's chambers. The timing was terrible, so whatever Lial intended to propose must be critically important.

Or salacious gossip. One never knew with Lial.

Outside Kolvar's bedchamber was his personal receiving room. The lead and glass circular roof soared two stories overhead and served as the only window in the room. The muted light revealed walls filled with scrolls, books, art, maps, and a massive stone fireplace. Kolvar's desk was near the center of the room, near two plush chairs, one of which Lial had practically claimed as his own.

The fire was already out, but Kolvar checked his rooms to be sure no servants lingered. Nym pressed her palm to one of the stones on the hearth, and a faint pop of magic signaled that the room was soundproof.

"Spill your secrets and be quick about it." Nym spun to face Lial. Her voice sounded just like their mother's in moments like these, when she was singularly focused. "I have a ship to catch."

Lial ran a knuckled fist across his lips before taking a breath and speaking. "Rumor is that only certain elves are dying. The Seeds Protectors."

Kolvar's blood ran cold. Ivy. Was she alive?

"Protectors are nomadic," Nym said, "and they interact with humans more than the rest of us. Therefore, logically, elves from the House of Seeds would suffer more deaths."

"Still, it's suspicious," Lial said.

Kolvar spoke slowly, thinking aloud. "Without Protectors, can we even access seeds? Without Protectors to lead the way, we don't know where the trees will be each year."

"Alysatraee would never put us in such a precarious position." Nym's words were more confident than her tone.

"We should invite those from the House of Seeds to stay in the north," Kolvar said. "We can protect them."

Nym raised a brow. "You mean Ivy, I presume. That's not a good idea. If you bring her here, elves will talk."

Lial shrugged. "We haven't had anything juicy to gossip about in a while. If you bring a Protector to live in the castle, I'll receive *loads* of dinner invitations. Everyone will want to know your relationship status."

Nym slugged Lial in the arm before turning to her brother. "Our mother won't like it."

Lial gingerly rubbed his arm but teasingly added, "Kolvar, your mother has a very nice northern girl with ties to the wyvern business on the mainland in mind for you."

Nym sighed. "Mother would marry you to a mermaid if she thought that would bring stronger magic to our family."

"I don't care who says you're a stick in the mud, Nym. You *do* have a sense of humor." Lial dodged Nym's swinging fist and started talking in a mock voice, pretending to be her mother, Councilor Phiro. "Children, our family is *special.* From the beginning of time, when Alysatraee planted the tree, giving birth to all fair folk, we were the superior-est."

Lial danced around the room, staying just out of Nym's reach because she wouldn't deign to actually *chase* him. Which was fortunate for Lial because Nym would pummel him if she had a mind to.

"One root of the tree dared reach deep into the earth and found water," Lial continued in his airy, theatric voice, his perfectly combed hair coming loose from its tie, "which gave birth to all water creatures. And a drop of that water mixed in our special Phiro veins. Never mind that all Tides have this power within. No, no. My children must carry on our noble, *noble* legacy."

"You have a death wish." Kolvar rolled his eyes, and Lial pretended to stab himself with a non-existent knife.

Kolvar walked closer to the stone on the fireplace, ready to drop the sound barrier and kick the bickering pair out of his room.

"Your children could be rather dashing," Lial continued, his focus on Nym. "If your mother married you to a merman, your offspring might have green scales and pointed teeth. Quite a fetching look, especially paired with your regal nose."

Nym feinted left but spun around in the opposite direction and kicked Lial in the thigh. The impact pitched him sideways, and he slid to the floor, laughing too hard to try and scramble away. Nym threw up her arms in exasperation and marched toward the door.

"I'm not holding the ship for you, Kolvar," she spat over her shoulder. "And I'm not covering for your tardiness with the councilor, either."

Lial pulled himself up and limped over to his friend, his voice sobering. "Kolvar, in all seriousness, I am concerned about the Protectors. I know you'd extend an invitation to the others, not just Ivy. And if you think offering Nylann'or as a haven is best, I trust your judgment."

"I appreciate you sharing the information." His friend was a master of gathering up rumors and reports.

It was no secret that Kolvar's mother was training him to take over the Council position. But strictly speaking, it wasn't Kolvar's place to know half the things Lial brought him. Then again, it wasn't Lial's place to know any of the things he did, either.

"Your mother protects the House of Tides," Lial said. "If she is considering an alliance with a family with connections to wyverns, she's likely looking for alternate transportation so we don't have to rely on ships or naiads. She's a smart elf. She understands the importance of protecting our access to the seeds."

From birth, Kolvar was taught that the needs of the House of Tides came before himself. The principle made perfect sense, and Kolvar and Nym had sacrificed their aspirations many times for the greater good of their House. Even so, when it came to Kolvar's friends, it was difficult not to blur the lines between what he wanted and what was best for the community.

A servant burst into the room, and her jaw dropped. "Kolvar, you're still here? I thought you'd left for your ship. The councilor will be furious that I failed to deliver you on time."

"Get out of here," Lial said as he clapped his friend on the shoulder. Lial had volunteered to stay behind with several others while most of the Tides elves traveled over the water channel to claim their seeds.

"Stay out of trouble while I'm gone," Kolvar said.

"Not a chance." Lial laughed and winked at the servant as he re-tied his hair and ambled away with only a hint of a limp.

Kolvar double-checked that his things were in order and then rushed to the ships. As he crossed the docks, he slowed as he approached one of the three massive boats, heavy with supplies. From the railing, far overhead, Kolvar's mother stared.

To others, she probably appeared to be calm, but Kolvar knew better. She was disappointed; a Phiro should set a good example through punctuality in all affairs. Deeper still, Kolvar suspected his mother was angry; the Realm's War had left Councilor Emmyth Phiro with simmering bitterness.

Despite what Lial believed, Kolvar knew his mother—the councilor wouldn't approve of Ivy staying in the palace. But it didn't matter. If he saw Ivy or any of her family members, he would offer them a home in the north.

But finding Ivy was a gamble outside his control. He hadn't crossed paths with his childhood friend in years—they hadn't attended the same Gatherings. But more alarming, none of Ivy's family had been seen at *any* Gatherings in almost ten years.

The House of Seeds was smaller than the other two houses, with only one Council representative, Ialant Balrel, Ivy's father. If he didn't appear this year, a nomination would be put forth, and Ialant would be officially replaced by another at the Centennial Gathering next spring. His House needed direction, which Ialant hadn't provided in too long. All the same, Kolvar felt close to the Balrel family.

If Ivy was Ialant's only surviving child, she deserved protection, didn't she? If Alysatraee willed them to meet at the same Gathering this year, he would convince Ivy to shelter in the north.

10
ELVEN GATHERING

Ivy rode Brecc's horse, Sunshine, into a valley as the ash-spewing dragon glided overhead, a mere speck in the sky. In the last two weeks since Brecc's death, Ash had stayed with Ivy but never *near* her. Ash had kept the enchanted glass vial and the precious seed well out of Ivy's reach.

The further they'd traveled south, into the heart of the human stronghold within Trinth, the higher Ash stayed in the sky. Ivy didn't blame the flying rodent; though fair folk were at peace with humans, they were not welcome. In a city like Unaria, an elf could blend in. Outside Easthill, she was a suspicious stranger traveling alone in the woods.

Though she wouldn't be alone for long.

As a Protector, she sensed the pull of the year's Gathering tree, for which she'd been trained. Protectors could live independently, not requiring special instructions from one of the Seeds Ambassadors to guide them. In the past, elves in her House lived and traveled with their families. But more and more seed protectors were like her—alone—the solitary House of Ivy.

Before Ivy reached the tips of where the Gathering tree's

branches shadowed the earth, Ash zipped down, slicing past Ivy's ear as she darted in the opposite direction. It was as if the dragon sensed this was an elven occasion, and she wouldn't be participating.

"Is that your good-bye?" Ivy mumbled to herself. A near smack-in-the-face was progress; at least Ash didn't just disappear without a trace.

Ivy passed under the gnarled branches overhead, feeling her anxiety drain away as she entered the year's Gathering domain. She left Sunshine to graze, continuing on foot. The trees thinned, allowing room for the hundreds of elves arriving for the three-day event. At the center, a wide swath of tall grass surrounded a massive tree with purple leaves and silver fruit. The branches soared above the tallest trees in the area, reaching out and covering the surrounding canopy with a protective embrace.

Taking a deep breath and soaking in the emanating calm, Ivy's chin still quivered with the anticipation of receiving her fruit.

This year will be different. Ivy tried to assure herself, but she couldn't bring herself to approach the tree. Not yet.

Besides, it was respectful to honor the dead, first. She pulled a blue box from her satchel, the one she'd found in Sunshine's saddlebag. Ivy moved to an area littered with blue boxes, each one projecting the image into the air—the ghosts of the dead.

Ivy sat down and pressed Brecc's box, triggering the image of him with a woman. A human. His Sariah. For a moment, Ivy stood, transfixed by the natural smile on Brecc's face. At one time, he had been happy ... even satisfied. He probably didn't even have a fine feather bed in the cottage seen behind him. His whole life had become a performance, perhaps more for himself than for others. But he'd shed all that on the day he'd died, remembering his previous self. This elf, who cared about humans.

The elf who'd asked Ivy to speak on behalf of the Seekers. Seekers like the one Sariah had become.

Ivy's stomach churned as she stepped away, leaving Brecc's projection for his family. Leaving the closure Ivy had never found. And Ivy walked around the rest of the trees, hoping and dreading the vision of a ghost she recognized.

At the end of the path, Ivy let out a sigh of relief and frustration. Walking toward the Gathering tree, mentally preparing to receive her seed, Ivy heard her mother's voice. She froze, hearing it again in the distance. Her heart leapt with joy before she turned and only saw blue boxes.

Ivy's heart hammered in her ribs as she carefully picked through the images, listening for the familiar voice.

"Callium Balrel Rowe," the woman said in a mock-serious voice, speaking Ivy's niece's name. "Leave that toad alone!"

Ivy drew closer to the image, cocking her head. The voice sounded like her mother, but it wasn't. The elf and a little girl played near a pond, thick with lily pads and blooming flowers, with a wild orchard of blossoming fruit trees beyond. From all her travels, Ivy didn't recognize the location. The female elf was too old to be Ivy's sister, Iris, but the child's name was so unique, she had to be Ivy's niece. Where was Calla when this projection was created, and who was with her?

Leaning closer, Ivy watched her niece. She hadn't seen Calla since she was a baby, and her body ached with loneliness. A reminder of the time lost wrung out the last drop of hope she'd held deep inside. Moments she'd never experience.

The elf picked up the little girl, extricating the toad from the child's fingers. The body movements were familiar, and when the elf looked up, her eyes confirmed it: it *was* Ivy's sister, Iris.

The ground seemed to fall out from under Ivy, and she

stumbled forward, onto her hands and knees, unable to take her eyes off the blue projections.

Tomas, her sister's husband, jogged into the image, laughing. "I told you, Calla loves fresh toad. A delicacy."

Ivy's vision blurred.

A heavy hand fell on Ivy's shoulder. She looked up to see a sympathetic expression on Ambassador Wirenth's face, deep wrinkles etched between his brows.

"I've held on to this projection for five years, waiting for someone to claim it," he said with deep reverence. "Iris, Tomas, and little Calla ... they're gone. Killed by Seekers in a village outside Ne'edrei. The blue box was found with their things, after their deaths, and passed on to me."

Unable to feel the ground under her feet, Ivy barely processed Wirenth guiding her back to Sunshine. The ambassador refilled her water and cared for her horse before disappearing. If she'd asked for his company, she knew Wirenth would have granted it. Older than her father, his magic was easily strong enough to sense when Ivy had entered the valley and had come to comfort her. But she was even more grateful he'd left her to mourn alone.

For three days, Ivy stared into nothingness as elves flooded into the valley. They passed like a stream of bodies around a cold stone. Ivy had known her family was likely dead, but the confirmation was both a release of fresh pain and the beginning of relief that only closure could bring. Ivy's hood covered her face—her emotions warring within. Her family was well-known, so Ivy waited until the pre-dawn on the last day, before the stars faded, and fetched the blue box.

Later that morning, the Council would give final remarks, and the elves would disband, disappearing back into their corners of the kingdom. Any elf had the opportunity to speak, but the only real focus was paid to the Council's words. The Gatherings always had an element of joyful reunions and sad stories, but this year, Ivy's sadness sunk her.

Furthermore, she was running out of time to fulfill Brecc's last wish. Speaking to the elves here promised to be difficult, but addressing *all* the elves at the Centennial was far more daunting. Ivy made her way to the tree as the sky was just beginning to lighten. Despite the hour, the line was long—elves had waited all night for their turn.

Spotting her, Wirenth gave her a nod from where he stood near the tree. As the Protector responsible for facilitating the seed gifts, he spoke quietly to an elf. At the same time, a branch from the tree lowered, creaking just slightly as it bent toward the waiting elf, with a silvery fruit dangling within reach. The elf pressed a fingertip into the bark, her shoulders relaxing. Touching the tree often brought a fond memory to mind. Sometimes a vague, comforting image, perhaps a whiff of fresh bread, or a favorite flower. A flash and it was gone. Then the best part of all—the elf plucked the fruit.

Some elves had a look of disappointment after opening their fruit and one looked elated, but most kept their expressions neutral. By the time Ivy's turn arrived, the sun had risen over the trees. A crowd was gathering in front of a grassy mound from which the councilors would address them. Ivy fidgeted, worried about how many seeds she'd be given.

As each elf took their fruit and departed, Ivy's anxiety grew. Brecc had saved her from certain death by teaching her about the tainted ink, but Ivy still desperately needed seeds. She couldn't imagine going longer than a month without a vicious attack.

"It's good to see you, Ivy," Wirenth spoke quietly when it was her turn. "I am truly sorry about your sister. She was a fine elf. Not everyone understood her decisions, but she was respected. She would have been an ambassador one day. Perhaps even the council representative of our house, like your father."

Ivy lifted her chin. "Iris lived her life doing what she felt the Mother wished her to do. I hope I become half the elf she was."

The question of her parents hung unsaid between them. Their deaths were unconfirmed, but it was foolish to assume they still lived, especially considering that her father would've gone to great lengths to retrieve the image of his granddaughter. Ivy sucked in a breath, holding her emotions in a tight ball deep in her stomach.

"I'm ready for my seed, Ambassador," she said.

Wirenth gave a slow nod and gestured Ivy forward. Ivy approached the trunk and pressed her palm against the thick bark as it gnarled into deep swirls.

Images slipped into her mind.

In her vision, Ivy flew into the sky, as if she were a dragon looking down on the earth. She sucked in a breath, shocked at the vivid world around her. She soared north, over trees, the human castle passing below in a blur. Images flooded her mind. Humans. Hundreds of them. Happy and joyful. Laughter and love. Then elves. The tree. Flashes of fair folk, with leering expressions and cruel eyes. The images dimmed, fading, bleeding together. Dread filled her, anticipating some unknown terrible event.

And she fell from the sky.

Fast and hard, she plummeted to the earth. Her heart exploded into her throat. A hundred Seekers screamed in her ears.

Her knees slammed into the earth. She realized, distantly, that the scream was her own.

Wirenth was shaking her shoulders. Ivy wrenched open her eyes, her breathing shallow and fast.

"Ivy?"

Wide-eyed elves around her were talking in loud whispers. Councilor Emmyth Phiro was among them, icily staring at Ivy sprawled on the ground like pig slop. *Fantastic.* Emmyth, likely the highest-ranking official present, was witness to Ivy's outburst. This did not bode well for her little speech later.

Mother of Magic, if Ivy could portal straight into a thousand-degree pixie bramble instead of this, she definitely would.

Wirenth winced as he got to his knees and leaned close. "This is a trial for Protectors. We travel alone and then we're suddenly surrounded by others for three crowded days. And adding the confirmation of your family's murder. It's too much for anyone to bear, even for a Balrel."

Ivy felt the stares, hating every one of them. She pushed herself to her feet, carefully schooling her expression, before helping Wirenth up. When he tilted his head toward the branch, holding the fruit a few steps away, Ivy's breath caught.

The skin of the fruit shimmered at Ivy's touch, the branch shuddering as she tugged it free. The branch swirled past her, almost in a caress, before twisting back into the air above.

Swallowing, Ivy pressed her fingers to the flesh. Then her nail dug into the core, feeling for the seeds hidden within. Ivy hadn't admitted to Wirenth that she needed another vial. But she would before the Gathering dispersed.

Her fingertip found a seed, and she grinned. On a good year, an elf could gather twenty seeds or even more. It was rumored that receiving none portended certain death. It was an idle, unproven tale, but even so, Ivy felt a rush of relief at having at least one seed.

Ivy carefully parsed the fruit in half, searching for more. But she found none.

She forced a calm look, giving Wirenth a nod before walking into the forest to clean her seed. Out of sight, she crushed the fruit, frantically looking for another. She had to have at least two seeds.

Mother of Magic, she wouldn't survive the year with only one. Panic and fear battled inside her, making her head spin. Her hands shook as she strained each portion of the fruit, just in case. Horror dawned.

She had to survive the entire year with one seed.

"Ivy Balrel?" A voice demanded from behind her.

She didn't have the energy to care who wanted to talk to her. Nothing mattered anymore. The Mother had doomed her *and* her family.

An elf with dark red hair and a matching complexion stormed over, demanding attention. "You're the reason my brother is dead."

The female elf's words jarred Ivy, and she fisted her only seed, ignoring the sugary fruit juices that squeezed between her fingers.

"Breccia was careful," the elf shot at Ivy. In her hand she clutched a blue box. "He never would have been caught by Seekers."

This elf is Brecc's sister? Ivy couldn't find words as the stranger closed in.

Nym and Kolvar approached, friends from Ivy's childhood, interrupting the red-faced elf's tirade. The siblings looked similar with their walnut hair, dusky skin, angular features, and height. But where Nym's face was framed by long braids, Kolvar often kept a shorn head, making it impossible to miss the unusual blue color of his eyes.

"Do you know who you're addressing?" Nym from the House of Tides demanded. Ivy had always been a little intimidated by the forthright northern elf. She didn't want Nym fighting for her, but on the other hand, it was far better than having Nym fight *against* her. Nym's eyes narrowed at the red-headed elf. "Who are you?"

"Gneiss Feldspar," she snarled, her attention shifting to the other elf accompanying Nym. "No need to introduce yourselves. You're the offspring of Councilor Emmyth Phiro, Nym and Kolvar." She gave Kolvar a slight nod of respect, before turning her attention back to Ivy. "And you're Ivala Balrel, daughter of the missing House of Seeds Councilor."

"Then you know you could be addressing the future councilor for the House of Seeds," Kolvar said.

Ivy nearly snorted at the idea, but Gneiss beat her to it, adding, "Ivala? Everyone knows the Mother gives many seeds to those she wishes to oversee the peacekeeping—they must live a long life if they want to gain the wisdom needed to help the ridiculous humans. How many seeds did you receive this year, Ivala? Ten? Five?"

Ivy sobered, her nails digging into her palms.

Seeing Ivy's reaction, Gneiss' face darkened into a wicked smirk. "Even fewer? Alysatraee gives you a fitting punishment, then."

"That's enough." Kolvar stepped between Ivy and Gneiss.

Ivy stepped around Kolvar, her voice firm despite her shaking hands. "You should go, Gneiss, before we both say something we regret."

"My brother's glass vial." Gneiss pointed to her own chest, where her magicked vial lay. "It's a family heirloom. We want it back."

"Then you'll have to fight a dragon for it," Ivy said flatly.

"Find Ivy after the Gathering to discuss such things." Nym

grabbed Gneiss' arm, pulling her away. "It's in poor taste to make demands when emotions are high."

Gneiss yanked her arm from Nym's grasp. For a moment it looked like Gneiss would come after Ivy again, but Nym growled and Gneiss cursed and stormed away. Surprisingly, Nym gave her brother a knowing look before leaving Ivy and Kolvar alone. It probably wasn't a coincidence that she headed in the same general direction as Gneiss.

"I'm sorry for stepping in," Kolvar said. "I know you are perfectly capable of taking care of yourself."

"I appreciate the apology, Kol, but forget about it." His action bothered her, but her emotions had been worn thin, and she didn't want to take it out on him. He had a helpful nature, to a fault.

Ivy had known Kolvar for decades. She had been at the ceremony when Kolvar's mother was chosen to become a Councilor. Back when they were younglings still learning how trees breathed, when the moons would cross paths in the sky, and where to find water in an unknown forest. It seemed like another life. Back then, it was just Ivy, Iris, their parents, and her father's brother. Happier years, before the humans had gotten their hands on elven seeds.

"I saw the projection of Iris' family two years ago at our Gathering. I'm so sorry." Kolvar's face softened. "Remember that time we snuck into a feast early? When was that, fifty years ago?"

"Nym was there, too. Don't let her pretend otherwise. It was probably her idea."

"Nym has a way of wrangling others into doing what she wants."

"She wanted that honey'd cheese on butternut bread." Ivy found herself grinning.

"Iris said it was a terrible idea. Against the rules. But she was the first one through the door."

"I think she made herself sick."

"She was a complicated elf."

Ivy's grin fell. "Iris always wanted to do the right thing. But I think in life, she realized following the rules wasn't always the *right* thing."

Ivy and Kolvar stood in silence, and Ivy couldn't help but be reminded that the *right* thing for her was to honor Brecc's wishes and speak.

"On the topic of rules," Kolvar said slowly, "there's another reason I wanted to find you. I want to extend you an invitation to live in the north."

"What?" Ivy realized after the words were out of her mouth how rude she sounded. "I mean, Protectors don't simply move to Nylann'or."

The idea seemed to go against the fabric of nature. No one just *moved* to the icy palace—resources were too scarce. To live with the Tides, one was born there, married into the house, or was a servant. And, besides, if Protectors didn't carry around deadly-ink-beacons, they could generally avoid Seekers.

"Just as a matter of safety. I know it is unusual, but there are rumors and ... well, I walked through the projections, and most of the ghosts are Protectors."

"Rumors?" Ivy asked.

"That elves in the House of Seeds aren't dying by accident. You're being targeted."

Brecc had essentially said the same thing after finding the metallic dusting in the writing on the back of Ivy's drawing. Ivy hadn't known if the attacks were focused on her or on her family. But if Kol's suspicions were correct, perhaps the danger was greater than she'd imagined.

"I think there might be truth to the rumors." Ivy shook her head. She had few seeds and fewer clues as to who was manipulating the Seekers. While she'd prefer to work on her own, Brecc had desperately tried to convince her to work with other elves. He'd died trying, but he'd also given her far more information than she'd ever had. So perhaps Brecc was right. And, she had few friends more connected than Kolvar.

"I must confess, the last elf who tried to help me wound up dead. By bringing me, you could be inviting danger to your sanctuary."

Kol hesitated. "Leaving you behind is riskier than bringing you along. I know you prefer the mainland, and it'll be temporary. Just until we figure out what's going on."

Ivy wanted to know who was behind the attacks, but Kol had only offered to hide her, nothing more. "If I come to the north, will you help me figure out who's killing us and why?"

"If someone is behind this, they're depraved. They must be stopped." Kolvar stared, unfocused, into the forest. "Of course I'll help you—we'll bring this matter to the Council, together."

"Perhaps, but not yet. Let's keep this quiet until we know more."

Whoever had given the ink to the midwife was resourceful. Calculating. Deadly. Ivy wasn't sure who she could trust. But she had to trust someone, and Kolvar was like a sweet puppy. Nym was the wolf.

"Before I agree to join you, there's something I must do." Ivy still had to speak in the elf forum. After her screaming incident at the tree, the elves were unlikely to take her seriously. In fact, chances were she'd embarrass herself further when she spoke. She didn't want Kolvar to agree to attach himself and his pristine reputation to a scorned elf. After crossing the northern channel, he'd be stuck with her in the north for an entire year. He needed to know what sort of trouble he was claiming.

An hour later, Ivy finally gathered up the nerve to speak. Her heart pounded in her chest, and she tapped her satchel. Inside was her only seed, tightly wrapped in a cloth. Usually, elves half-listened to the speeches; the desire to converse before they parted again was understandable. But as Ivy walked up the mound, the elves quieted.

"I'm Ivala Balrel, daughter of Ialant and Tehlarissa." She shared her official name, per custom, though without need. Everyone had silenced for the daughter of the mysteriously absent Councilor. "For many years, I have run from Seekers. My sister, her husband, and her child were all killed by Seekers. The corrupted humans have destroyed the life I loved."

Elves nodded. Ivy swallowed, hoping not to see Brecc's sister.

"But I met another elf while I was in Unaria. Breccia Feldspar."

The moment Ivy said his name, whispers began. Ivy's gaze was drawn to Gneiss, whose eyes had narrowed, her face turning a deeper shade of red.

Ivy's mouth dried, yet she forced her words. "Breccia pointed out that Seekers only exist because of *our* seeds. Elves have some responsibility for what has happened to the humans. If we work together, perhaps—"

"Brecc was delusional," someone shouted. "He fell for a human."

Ivy's brows furrowed. Most elves knew her sister had married a human, traditionally considered shameful and against the Mother's will. But Iris revolted. Still, elves had started to come around when Iris stayed true to the elven ways. Still attended Gatherings. Still loved her people. So for elves to judge Brecc for loving a human felt like a particularly painful stab at the precious memory of her sister.

"Is it not our responsibility? Our sacred duty from the

Mother to watch over humans?" Ivy asked the pointed question. "We are only given these seeds to elongate our lives so we can be wise peacekeepers." Ivy looked at Gneiss, wondering if the elf recognized her own words in Ivy's speech.

Gneiss pushed through the crowd, leaving.

She definitely remembered.

"Not when humans break the rules of magic," someone else shouted. Other elves nodded and started arguing the points among themselves.

Several influential elves stood in the crowd, including Lonsdale, a councilor from the House of Minerals. If an elf didn't know who he was, the medallion he wore on a chain around his neck announced his importance. Of the five council members, two were at this Gathering. And, unfortunately, they were both witnessing Ivy's humiliation.

"If they don't know the rules, are they breaking them?" Ivy asked.

The chatter grew louder, the calm mood from the tree evaporating. Elves started shouting more arguments at Ivy. But the more Ivy listened, the more ridiculous they sounded. Like they were grasping at a spider's web for truth, caught in the snare of their preconceived notions.

Just as Ivy had been.

Was this how Brecc had felt, watching as his elven community abandoned the core of the Mother's responsibilities? The weight of the realization crashed down on her. Everything felt wrong, but Ivy didn't know how she could possibly fix whatever *it* was. Ivy shifted and took in the sight of the tree—Alysatraee's gift. What would she advise?

Ivy paused. The tree *had* given her a vision. Ivy had no idea what it meant, but she needed to figure it out.

Movement below snatched her attention—Kolvar pushed

toward the mound. Ivy wasn't sure if he was going to support her or pull her away in shame.

Shouts sounded from deeper in the forest. Ivy's attention jerked to a hooded figure stumbling from the trees and into the clearing behind the crowd. Most of the elves were so involved with their arguments, they didn't notice the disturbance. Kolvar paused and turned, following Ivy's gaze.

The hooded figure leaned against Wirenth. The elder elf grabbed at his own chest, his eyes widening. The stranger pulled back his hood, and Ivy gasped. Without thinking, her feet propelled her down the mound. Pushing bodies to the side, Ivy could think of nothing else except reaching the newcomer.

Her father.

Ivy rushed forward, arms spread, embracing him. He was thinner than she remembered. He was breathing hard, leaning more heavily on her than he ever had in the past. She pulled back but didn't see joy on his face. Only panic.

"They're already," he coughed, "at the periphery. Run."

A crash and a scream echoed through the trees. The arguing elves finally quieted, realizing something was very wrong.

"Who? H-humans?" Wirenth stuttered.

"Seekers," Ivy's father wheezed. "They overcame the protections."

Through the trees, a human appeared, his hair and clothing dirty and ripped. But it was his eyes that sent a jolt through Ivy. Her hand flew to her satchel, to her vulnerable, exposed seed.

Two more Seekers appeared. Then another. How did they overcome the Protector's repelling magic? No Seeker had ever appeared at a Gathering. How many more were converging on them at that moment?

Shoving her bag behind her hip, she grasped her father.

"I'm getting us out of here."

Screams filled the air as elves scattered, and armed elves

rushed to the perimeter, Nym among them. Ivy pulled her father close as a face she recognized emerged from the trees. Even without the soldier's long, crisp jacket and captain's insignia, she recognized him. The intensity of his gaze she remembered all too well.

It was the Captain of the Unarian Guard. He'd tracked her right to the heart of the elves, along with a horde of Seekers.

II
COLD COUNCIL

Councilor Emmyth Phiro gripped her staff as Seekers flowed into the meadow. She strode toward the struggling Councilor Balrel as a small volley of arrows rained down from the trees, piercing intruders at the edge of the forest. Warriors darted past her, engaging their enemies. She could fight as well as any, but she needed to tend to Ialant.

The crowd of elves who'd gathered to hear her speak moments earlier became a mass of undulating chaos. Parents grabbed their younglings; others calculated the best evacuation routes over shouts and frenzied commands from the Seeds Ambassador and Councilor Lonsdaleite. Kolvar pushed through, moving toward Ivy and Ialant.

Emmyth intercepted her son, urging him back. "You must lead our House to the ships."

His gaze swept to Ivy, but he gave his councilor a curt nod before turning to lead the retreat.

Emmyth pivoted in time to see Ivy wipe tears from her blotchy face, her expression turning to one of grim determination. Emmyth reached out with her senses to Ialant. His body was failing; he wouldn't survive long, even without the stress of a Seeker attack.

Ivy tugged her father deeper into the heart of the meadow, away from the skirmishes. An arrow whizzed past Emmyth, and a Seeker cried out a few steps away. Emmyth pushed her sight northward. She sucked in a breath at the distant Seekers. The numbers thronging the meadow now were but a trickle compared to the coming wave. She took a protective stance, ready to fight off any attacks, unwilling to leave the councilor's side.

"I've made a terrible mistake," Ialant wheezed his admission to his daughter.

Emmyth gripped her staff tighter. Ialant had made many mistakes. Attempting to explain them while Seekers attacked would only spell disaster.

"Anything you've done," Ivy said, gripping her father, "let me help fix."

If only Ialant's mistakes could be so easily repaired. Emmyth needed to know where Ialant had been hiding, what he'd been up to. Few knew the path he'd taken. Emmyth only hoped she had time to rectify his grievous errors. His actions had the potential to doom the fair folk. The fae courts would be furious to know Ialant had been surviving in the shadows all this time. Furious with the entire Council. Furious with Emmyth.

Emmyth took a steadying breath. To salvage the situation, she needed information from Ialant. But she couldn't leave elves to suffer, either. She searched for Nym along the wooded edge. As if sensing her mother's gaze, Nym yanked her spear from a Seeker's chest before bolting to her mother's side.

"Councilor," Nym said, her breathing steady, "what would you have me do?"

"Protect your brother. He must get our House to the ship. You two will lead the way. I'll bring up the rear."

"And those who didn't receive their seeds?" Nym looked over at the pale Seeds Ambassador, as others from his House began to ring the massive tree trunk.

"It's Alysatraee's will that they not receive them this year. The House of Tides must return home."

"And the remaining fruit in the tree?"

"It's not your place to concern yourself with the seeds. Go!"

Nym ran, her spear at the ready, toward her brother who was shouting directions for the Tides. The House of Minerals had sent their strongest to fight while the rest frantically packed. Emmyth ignored them all, stepping closer to the dying councilor.

Ialant coughed and pushed away a seed Ivy attempted to give him. "This is the Mother's will."

Of the several encroaching Seekers, one of them shambled toward Ialant. Ivy grabbed the knife from her father's belt as the attacker closed in. But it wouldn't be enough.

Ivy threw the blade, her aim true. But the Seeker marched forward, the dirty ribbons in her hair fluttering in the breeze, discordant with her jerking motions. Emmyth stormed forward, swinging her staff, slamming the Seeker in the side of the knees. The creature fell. Emmyth grabbed the knife still lodged in the woman's chest, and in one smooth motion wrenched the blade toward the collarbone and ended her pitiful life. Emmyth's entire assault took place in less time than a corrupted could blink.

Emmyth's instinct was to snap at Ivy, but she held her tongue. Why wasn't the youngling, Ivy, prepared with her bow and arrow? She had been gifted a fine set from a late Seeds ambassador. She'd either lost it or worse, traded it to some low-bred human.

"Ialant," Emmyth said, holding her staff in one hand and the bloody knife in the other, "where have you been all these ..." The rest of her question died on her tongue as she spotted a tall, cloaked figure fighting the Seekers.

"Is that a human?" she demanded.

Ialant collapsed, pulling his daughter down with him. Emmyth ground her teeth. What fool had allowed a human among them? Though the stranger was several paces away, he was staying close to Ialant. Even on the verge of death, a councilor shouldn't be so barking foolish. Their sacred elven traditions could be recorded and shared with the entire realm by a single, aware human. Everything from the distraction spells to how many elves existed could be laid bare.

"Your mother was killed just two years after our family split up," Ialant whispered as Ivy held his hand. "She couldn't stay away from her grandchild. Not once we'd learned of your sister's location. Your mother was killed as she was returning home. Oh, my Tehlarissa, you didn't deserve such an end. And I'm to blame." His voice caught in his throat. "We had settled east of Neidrei, hidden in the forest. I'd heard that you were at Gatherings. I dared hope you'd found peace without us. Without your mother, I buried myself in my work."

But where? Who else is involved? Emmyth listened, confident there was still time to correct his errors. Perhaps Ivy didn't need to know about her father's betrayal of their kind.

"But recently, I heard Seekers were hunting you," Ialant continued. "I had to find you. No matter the cost. I-I am so sorry—it should've been me they'd stalked. Seeing you alive is a joy. I don't deserve it. But I'm grateful for it."

Ialant patted his daughter's damp cheek as a male Seeker broke free of the fight at the periphery. He was large and moving quickly. Emmyth cursed under her breath.

This one had found a seed.

A Seeker with freshly ingested seed was unpredictable and dangerous. An elf jumped down from a branch overhead. He dropped his empty quiver and bow to the ground, pulled a sword from the sheath, and attacked the Seeker. An enraged corrupted was still no match for a trained elf with a blade. Even so, Emmyth threw Ialant's knife down, and it sunk into the earth at Ivy's feet.

As Emmyth anticipated, two more corrupted humans emerged, their movements quick and fluid, a wild bloodlust in their eyes. She glanced at her retreating House of Tides, fleeing through a protected channel formed by nimble warriors.

Keeping her ears attuned to Ialant's words, Emmyth sprinted to the periphery, her staff swinging back and ready. To the human eye, she would've been a blur of motion, but Seekers with seeds fresh in their bellies could track an elf's movements. Approaching a group of three Seekers, she swung her staff into the ankle of the nearest corrupted. The woman's bones cracked, and she fell hard on her hip.

The second Seeker had his head low, running in an attempt to ram Emmyth. Spinning in the opposite direction while lifting her staff over her head, she maneuvered out of his path, then slammed her staff down into his spine. She jerked the staff directly back, hitting the third Seeker square in his chest.

Running several paces to give herself room, Emmyth twisted her arms to the side in an arc, then swung them to add to her momentum as she leapt in the air and circled back to meet her attackers. She slammed her staff into one's ear, knocking him to the ground. His eyes rolled behind the lids. The second one had fallen, an arrow in his chest. The woman limped forward, her foot tilted at a grotesque angle, an arrow protruding from her arm.

"Councilor Ialant Balrel," Kolvar's voice sounded from

behind Emmyth. Her son had come back for the pair. "Let me help you to our ship."

That was certainly *not* going to happen.

Emmyth slammed her staff into the ground and kicked out, hitting the Seeker in the chest, knocking her back. The woman grabbed the hem of Emmyth's robes as she stumbled to the ground. Emmyth balanced on one foot and fabric ripped as the woman collapsed. Emmyth cursed under her breath. Formal robes were tedious to repair.

Ialant's voice rasped in response to Kolvar from behind Emmyth, "It's not the Mother's will for me to leave this meadow."

Emmyth slammed a knee onto the fallen woman's body, pulled the arrow from the human's arm, and buried it in her neck. Before Emmyth could return and stop the conversation from spinning too far, light glinted off something in the Seeker's fisted hand. Peeling back her fingers, Emmyth found a glass vial with more than a dozen seeds.

"Go," Ialant urged his daughter.

Emmyth swallowed her surprise at the Seeker's resourcefulness, then slid the vial into her pocket before jumping to her feet, alert for the encroaching wave of Seekers.

"Come with us to the north," Kolvar said to the Balrels. "We'll protect you."

Emmyth turned in time to see Ivy shake her head, pulling her father close.

At least the youngling still had some sense. As much as she pitied Ivy, her presence would be a political nightmare. Besides, it wasn't Emmyth's fault that Ialant had foolishly split up his family—no one suspected he would do such a thing. It had only caused complications for everyone, including Emmyth.

"Ivy is right to be hesitant," Emmyth said, striding back to her son. "Her House is needed on the mainland as our bridge to the trees. How else are we to reconnect with Alysatraee's magic?"

The cloaked human who'd arrived with Ialant approached but stayed out of reach of Emmyth's staff. So, he wasn't a complete fool.

"My name is Captain Orion of the Unarian Guard." He dropped his hood, turning his attention to Ivy. "I'll escort you wherever you need to go."

Emmyth tilted her head, scrutinizing his features. He had the look of a human, but something about him was distinctly fair folk. Dryad perhaps—the aloof creatures abandoned their male offspring. His clothing was human, which meant his father likely was, too, and he'd probably raised the child among his people. Which meant Orion wasn't to be trusted.

Ivy opened her mouth to argue with Orion, but her father's coughing fit interrupted her.

Shadows seemed to reach for Orion, as if darkness wanted to close in. Was he fae touched? Emmyth shuddered at the thought. Who exactly was this stranger, and why was he at the Gathering?

An elf cried out from beyond the tree line. Emmyth's attention shot to the forest. She pushed her vision past the tree line. The wave of Seekers had split, most still coming from the east, but others flanking north. The Tides would be cut off from their ship if they didn't flee immediately.

"How many should we leave behind to protect the tree?" Kolvar asked.

"None." Emmyth lifted her chin. "The House of Minerals aren't cut off from their stronghold in the south. They can fight and retreat after midnight."

"You think they'll last until then?"

"They'll have to."

"Ivy, you can return next year. Travel to the Centennial with us." Kolvar gave Ialant a reassuring look and placed a hand on Ivy's shoulder. "Everyone will be there, and you can figure out your next steps at that point."

Before Emmyth could object, Ivy spoke up, her hand protectively pressed against her bag. "Perhaps that would be best."

Mother of Magic, Emmyth didn't have enough patience for the gossip this would stir. But if her suspicion was correct, Ivy had few seeds and fewer options.

Orion spoke up. "I can escort you to any city on the mainland."

Why was he so eager to help? Emmyth didn't want Ivy traveling across the channel, but it might be better than traveling with Orion. This stranger had proven too resourceful, and Emmyth didn't like unknowns.

"Our paths may cross again, and I will take you up on that offer." Ivy dismissed Orion's invitation.

Ialant coughed; every breath labored. How had he even traveled this far? Emmyth sensed he barely had the strength to form two syllables.

Orion stepped back, giving Ivy privacy for her last goodbye. Emmyth took Kolvar's arm, pulling him close.

"Make sure Nym is guarding our ship," Emmyth urged. "I'll be right behind you with Ivy. Go. Our House needs your leadership. This moment will be remembered."

"You should lead. I'll stay with Ivy."

"No, son, I am the past. You are the future. Today is the day our House will begin looking to you."

Kolvar pressed his lips together, but jogged toward the ship, stopping to help a young family scurry past the last sentries. Emmyth took some consolation after the day's events in that she may have stayed rumors about Kolvar.

A last surge of energy emanated from Ialant, the elf who had once been one of her most trusted comrades. She turned just in time to catch a movement—his hand gesturing to his neck. Ivy pulled a leather strap around his neck and drew up a pendant. Emmyth expected an empty vial but instead saw a solid object of ivory. No, it was bone.

Understanding flooded Emmyth. That's how Ialant had stayed hidden for so long; he'd acquired a glamour amulet. It must have cost him dearly. His head fell back, and Emmyth sensed him slip away, back to the Mother. In the end, he was more clever than all of them. The Councilor gave him a solemn nod. He'd earned it, even if he had lost his way.

Orion's attention was on Ivy. Was the stranger angling for the amulet? Ivy crouched over her father, oblivious to Orion's attention and the encroaching Seekers.

Emmyth took a deep breath and ripped the half-empty quiver from a nearby fallen elf's back and plucked the bow from the ground. "Your father wouldn't want you to die today." Emmyth stormed back to Ivy and shoved the weapon into Ivy's arms. "Let's go."

She yanked Ivy away from her father, and for a half-hour, Emmyth rotated between tugging Ivy forward and fighting off Seekers. Finally, the ship came into view. Rowboats were quickly ferrying waiting elves to the anchored boat. As they neared, a half dozen elven warriors rushed to Emmyth's side.

"Bring a blanket," Emmyth commanded. "Ivy Balrel is in shock."

Within moments, a woolen blanket was in Emmyth's hands. She wrapped it around Ivy's shoulders, using the movement as cover to slip her hand into Ivy's satchel. Hooking the necklace, she discreetly palmed the pendant before they stepped into a waiting boat.

After the short ferry to her ship, the moment Emmyth stepped aboard, she took command. "Where is Kolvar?"

"Getting everyone settled below decks," the first mate said.

A bit of tension drained from her shoulders as she strode to the bow. "Perfect."

She glanced in her pocket at the pendant—a bone amulet. Likely a glamour, but she couldn't test it out until she had complete privacy.

"Councilor," Ivy said, approaching.

Emmyth dropped the necklace back into her pocket and jerked her head up. "Ivy, I'm sorry about your father. He was passionate about his work."

"Yes, yes, he was." Ivy seemed a bit more settled despite her red eyes. "I will always be grateful I was able to be with him when he died. Just as I'm grateful for Kolvar's invitation."

Unexpectedly, Ivy fell on Emmyth in a tearful embrace. Not even her own children hugged her. Some elves were affectionate, but not Emmyth. Uninvited physical touch was disrespectful, at best. At worst, a violation.

"Kolvar can be overly emotional." Emmyth regretted her words immediately. An uncharacteristic slip. She shrugged out of Ivy's embrace.

Ivy smiled, not seeming to notice the rudeness. "I'll return to the lower deck."

Emmyth rocked back on her heels, stiff and uncomfortable. She reminded herself that Ivy's father had just died, and feigned a sympathetic expression as she dismissed the youngling.

She turned her attention back to the skirmish on the shore. Seekers clawed after the elves and their seeds. Elves boarded the ferrying boats as the warriors fought back the attackers. Once the elves were on the ships, the Seekers would turn on each other for the seeds they'd already found. Destruction would follow. Then the fire would eventually burn itself out.

Emmyth's attention caught on one of the boats returning to shore. It held a third elf, instead of just two. One elf had their head down, a half-filled quiver secured to their back. As they turned their head toward shore, Emmyth saw her profile—Ivy. Emmyth's hand flew to her pocket.

The bone amulet was gone.

Emmyth slammed her hand on the ship's carved bow. That's why Ivy had embraced her. The youngling was an emotional mess, but she was calculating. An unacceptable risk. She needed to send someone that Ivy would trust but who was ruthlessly loyal not just to the House of Tides, but to Emmyth.

She spun to the nearby first mate. "Bring me Nym."

12
LAST SEED, LAST CHANCE

Like a fish thrashing against the current, Ivy fought to run in the opposite direction of the fleeing House of Tides elves. Tears streaked her cheeks, and she struggled to breathe, her chest heaving with sobs. She'd mourned the loss of her family, year after year; the unknown was a slow, insidious torment. When she'd received confirmation of Iris and her family's deaths, Ivy thought she was incapable of more tears. But to find her father and then have him die in her arms was fresh anguish.

His death split open festering wounds and shattered her soul. Part of her wanted to lie down and let the Seekers destroy her; to rejoin her family.

But her father had hinted at another path; a mission to uncover his secrets. He'd hidden his desire from Emmyth, which alarmed Ivy. Though she didn't understand her father's reasons, Ivy had pretended to trust Emmyth. Ivy estimated that she could slip away at the shore and disappear without the Tides knowing where she went. Or with whom.

But when Emmyth stole the bone pendant, Ivy had to pull herself together long enough to steal it back.

Ivy clutched her satchel against her side as she plowed through the thinning crowd. The amulet, the blue box of her sister's family, and a single seed were tucked safely at the bottom. She understood the councilor's distrust of her father, but to steal the last thing he gave his daughter ... it was beyond cruel. Why the deception? Though, did Ivy treat her friends any better? The lie she'd told Kolvar didn't sit well. He'd always been good to her, and Ivy had spurned him without a word.

"Wait!" a Tide's elf cried out as Ivy ran past the line of warriors clashing with Seekers who had followed the Tides. "The corrupted are flooding in from the north. You won't make it back to the tree."

Ivy ignored the warrior and bolted into the forest. The Seekers were too close to use her bow and arrow. Her knife wouldn't stop them, either.

But no one was better at evading Seekers than Ivy.

Her father had sacrificed his remaining health to reach her. She didn't know what secrets he took to Alysatraee, but she gambled that Orion knew one or two. Enough to get her started on unraveling whatever had haunted her father.

Ivy didn't have to push her sight far into the distance before she spotted another group of encroaching Seekers, and she skittered up a fir tree. The silver fruit overpowered any scent from the seed in her satchel. With speed and a lot of luck, she might catch Orion. He'd likely fled the moment Ivy followed Councilor Phiro. And why would he wait? She couldn't have risked giving any hint of her true intentions—to go with him.

Brecc had taught her one thing above all else: elves hoarded information. She needed an outsider; Orion was her best bet. Even more poignantly, as her father lay dying, he'd indicated for her to travel with the newcomer. And Ivy wanted to know why.

Timing each opportunity, Ivy silently maneuvered through the forest, her heart thrumming.

Ivy pushed her sight further, through the northern forest, but didn't detect Orion. He was wise to hide. If she could get to Sunshine, she could journey north and catch Orion before dusk.

The cries of the fighting near the Gathering tree pierced her. If she fled, she'd be abandoning fellow elves, leaving them to protect the tree alone. From her location, the distance to Sunshine was about equal to that of the tree, but in the opposite direction. Ivy had lost her father that day, but the Seeds had lost their councilor, their leader. Ivy gritted her teeth and moved toward the tree.

As long as she survived the night, she could track down Orion later.

Ivy pushed her sight to the tree, and her stomach twisted at the dizzying number of Seekers. She ached for her father, his body lost in the press. The House of Minerals would deploy orcs to kill the remaining Seekers and perform proper burials. Still, it was cold comfort.

The Seekers converged under the canopy of the Gathering Tree, hindering Ivy's progress. Sweat trickled down her back as she formulated a new strategy. Focusing on the tree again, she scrambled to formulate a strategy. Her small House encircled the trunk, battling back Seekers. Rocks protruded from some of the fighters' hands—Minerals' warriors who had stayed behind to hold back the horde.

A steady stream of Seekers ambled below Ivy. She turned her attention in the other direction, searching for the next gap in the Seekers. There was none. She was stuck.

At midnight, the few remaining fruits would shrivel to dust, and the tree would revert to the size natural for this realm. But it was clear that the Seekers would overtake the tree, even with the help from the Minerals. In her hidden perch, Ivy's mind whirled. How could she save the seeds *and* her kind?

A Seeker screamed up at Ivy. Her heart jumped into her

throat as several Seekers gracefully spun to see the lone elf in the tree. An easy target.

Ivy grabbed an arrow from her quiver. A handful of focused Seekers could and would break the tree in half to get to her.

Twenty Seekers moved toward her location. Ivy's heart thrummed a warning. She shot the first arrow down, missing her target by a hair. She pulled out several arrows, adjusted her grip, and shot them off in a volley—in a single line leading to the Gathering tree. Without overthinking, Ivy leapt down on the nearest injured Seeker. He was maimed, but certainly not dead. Still, the distraction was enough.

Ramming her way through the injured with her knife, Ivy cut, spun, and jabbed her way toward the tree. The protective line of elven warriors was steps away.

Something slammed into her back, and she fell forward, colliding with a Seeker. Pain exploded in her side. She tried to lift her arm to cover her face, but her body didn't respond.

A Seeker trampled over her arm, his attention completely fixated on the tree. But another one loomed over her, his eyes filled with wild anger. Ivy tried to curl her fingers into a fist, but they merely wriggled. He gripped a knife. Ivy recognized the ornate hilt. Her father's knife. She'd lost her weapon.

The Seeker would kill her with her father's blade.

Ivy screamed as the knife plunged into her side. Energy flooded her, blocking the pain. Horror shot through her when the blade sucked and pulled against her ribs as the corrupted yanked it back out. The shock jostled her senses into action. Ivy kicked upward, aiming for the Seeker's groin, but hit him in the thigh.

He roared, outraged. He brought down Ialant's blade again, but before he could stab Ivy a second time, a dark figure thrust a sword into the Seeker's heart.

Ivy blinked. Orion burst into focus. He gripped Ivy's forearm and pulled her to her feet in a fluid movement that was far more gentle than she'd expected. Wrapping his arm around her waist, supporting the bulk of her weight, he rushed her past the outer ring of falling elven warriors and to the tree. To safety. Revolt at assistance from a human guard was swallowed in a rush of emotion. The warmth of it flushed her cheeks. Gratitude. That's all it was, gratitude that he'd saved her.

"You waited," Ivy said, breathless. She shook off the strange emotions besetting her. This was shock. Still, he could've easily outpaced the Seekers if he'd run south. He could've escaped.

His brow furrowed, and he pulled to a stop. Steps from the trunk, Orion released her, leaving Ivy feeling even colder, which shook her all the more.

"I had a feeling you'd return. What happened?" Orion's voice was gruff. Probably with annoyance.

She blinked, and the image of Orion in his captain's Unarian uniform flashed in her mind. She shouldn't care about him or what he thought about her.

Human soldiers had pushed her kind out of this realm, then kept "order" by harsh means, including questioning and imprisonment of her kind.

Was it a rash mistake by coming back ... for him?

Ivy hesitated to share information with this human guard. Someone who'd risen to the rank of captain had to be the worst of them all. But her father had hinted at his trust in Orion. Wasn't that why she'd returned?

Her arm still tingled where their skin had touched, but she ignored the delusion and pressed her palm to her wound and explained.

"When Councilor Phiro was fighting, my father pulled me close, pointed to you, and said, 'go.'"

And he'd pointed at Orion when Emmyth's back was turned, so no one but Ivy saw with *whom* to go. Or was that a coincidence? Had Ivy read too much into her father's gesture? Her father had been in great distress. He had pointed south, so perhaps he'd simply wanted her to evacuate? Ivy's thoughts and emotions jumbled together, a mess she couldn't unravel fast enough.

"Why did he want me to talk to you?" Ivy muttered as she fumbled for the healing stone in her satchel.

Orion turned to face her, staring down at her with an intensity reflecting the growing skirmish around them. But, before he could speak, a bloodied Seeker with long, oily hair broke through the protective circle of elven warriors, and Orion spun to contend with the attacker.

Ivy dropped her healing stone, readying for a blow. But Orion cut the Seeker down before she could strike Ivy. As more corrupted ambled into the clearing, elven warriors protecting the tree devoured seeds to increase their strength, stamina, and healing.

"Long story." Orion started to answer Ivy's question about why her father had advised her to go with a human soldier, but his attention was riveted on the clashing around them. "When I was tracking you, I found a ripped-up image in Carrus. I was shocked to see the face of the elder elf who had sought me out months ago: Ialant. That's when I knew you two were connected. But unlike you, Ialant wanted to meet. So, I decided to find him. I never guessed it would lead me into a battle."

Another Seeker rushed past the line of warriors, cutting off Orion's explanation. Ivy was desperate to fight, but pain started to bloom. The stone might've worked if she had more time and care. But she'd die here, just like her father, without a seed. She glanced overhead at the silver fruit, bitterness souring her stomach. The Mother granted one fruit per year; a payment for remaining in the human realm. But only one. Condemnation awaited the greedy.

Orion grunted, parried, and killed the Seeker before striding to Ivy and mouthing, "Neidrei."

Her father had lived in Neidrei. Her vision at the Gathering tree had also taken her northward. That's where she'd get answers. Ivy's periphery darkened as she fought to stay conscious.

"We must travel quickly, though. I don't have much time left to investigate." Orion dropped to his knees and fumbled through Ivy's satchel. "Where's your glass pendant? Your seeds?"

"Broken. All gone, but one."

The fighting seemed to dim around her as the memory of Brecc throwing his seeds came back to her. He'd died saving her, but Ivy refused to be buried here without a fight.

Orion found her last seed and held it up between pinched fingers. Ivy grasped it tight but didn't take it. Not yet. She needed to critically leverage her peak strength.

"Help me up," Ivy requested.

Orion pulled her to her feet. Pain screamed through Ivy's ribs. Clutching her side, vomit stung the back of her throat. She swallowed it down—anything not to painfully retch. Orion again supported her weight, providing unfamiliar comfort. She longed to lean into him, but the instinct alarmed her even more than the bleeding stab wound.

She pushed away from Orion and limped to Ambassador Wirenth. Despite his hoarse voice, he shouted warnings and directions to the nearby fighters. He seemed to have aged a hundred years in the last few hours.

"Ambassador," Ivy gasped, warm liquid running between her fingers, "pull all the elves back and flee south."

Wirenth's brows creased, and his mouth went slack. Ivy had felt the same way just weeks earlier. But now she knew another path.

She appealed to his logic. "The sun hasn't set, and already the Seekers are breaking through the line. Our House will perish if we don't concede this battle."

Seekers pressed harder, but Orion stayed at her side, likely wanting to hear the entire conversation. A nearby elf fell, and a Seeker rushed to the tree. Orion jumped forward to stop more from flowing to the elder elf and Ivy.

But another elf went down. Ivy winced, her arms flying up to protect her face as another Seeker charged toward her. A flash of darkness, like a bird, darted through the air, striking the Seeker in the back of the neck.

Ash, the dragon, screeched as she rose into the air, flitting around the massive branches. The Seeker cried out, a hand pressed to his bleeding neck before his knees crumpled.

The Ambassador blinked, unable to find the right words. "Did you ... there's a ..."

Ivy placed a gentle hand on his arm, drawing his attention from Ash. "Wirenth, please trust me. I've witnessed a similar Seeker attack."

When Brecc died, only a fraction of the Seekers had struck, but it was the same situation, *in theory*. Ivy hoped her plan would work on this massive scale. She pressed Wirenth again. "We can live or we can die. Either way, they'll get the seeds."

"We can take as many of them down with us as we can," a nearby injured elf spoke up. The familiar voice caught Ivy's attention. Gneiss, Brecc's sister, was one of the Minerals who'd stayed to protect the tree.

Gneiss shoved a seed in her mouth. She closed her eyes, relief calming the creases in her brow before opening them with renewed fire. Strengthened, Gneiss jumped into the fray, only to be confronted by four Seekers. In Gneiss's enhanced state, she'd dominate the fight a short time before she returned to her normal, elven strength.

A shock of pain reverberated from Ivy's wound. She winced, the injury fogging her ability to form words to the ambassador. "For every elf capable of taking a seed, how many more die before they have a chance? Is this what the Mother intended?"

"Ivy, none of this is what the Mother intended," the Ambassador said, his voice thin. "I don't know how to fix it. Perhaps we are doomed either way. Perhaps I'm too weak to take the path I should."

Ivy bit her lip, fearing Wirenth's meaning.

Wirenth lifted his voice, calling the elves' attention to him. "Retreat! We must retreat south. Follow the House of Minerals."

With his statement, he transferred leadership to the southern House. He lowered his voice to a whisper, speaking to himself. "I will stay to the end."

"You'll be crushed," Ivy said, "like an insect under their feet."

Orion grabbed Ivy's shoulder. "We need to move! When the warriors fall back, the Seekers will surge forward."

Ivy caught the look between Orion and the ambassador. They didn't think the last elves to retreat would survive.

The warriors created an opening on the northern side of the tree. The Seekers flooded in like a dam had been broken. They began to crawl up the tree like ants, clawing and crying in anticipation of the seeds.

The unquenchable call of life.

A mixture of jealousy, disgust, and relief formed a sickening swirl in Ivy's gut. Similar to Brecc tossing out his seeds, Ivy paved a path for the Seekers to grasp their sanity, if only for a moment.

But unlike Brecc, Ivy pressed her last seed to her lips and

swallowed. A warmth trickled from her head to her toes. Her lungs expanded, gulping a deep, invigorating breath. Her mind fired, dozens of ideas and past experiences coalescing into truth and strategy.

Her sight easily pushed to the sailing House of Tides. Pivoting, she scanned to the far northern edge of the forest. She moved again and saw young elves retreating south. Orion's steady heartbeat pulled her attention right next to her. He smelled of earth, steel, berries, and ... snow? And there was something else about him. Her eyes widened.

Orion stepped back, but it was too late. She knew what he was—a fair folk creature. And he wore a glamour. She focused her attention, looking for the edges of the illusion. Looking for the truth.

"Stop wasting your time." He shook his head, a warning in his eyes. "You'll miss your chance to save your kindred."

Around her, the elves seemed to fight in suspended slow motion.

She turned back to the stranger. "This isn't your fight."

Instead of responding to her, Orion moved to the nearest elven warrior and aided him. Understanding his intention, Ivy moved in the opposite direction. They fought as if in a frightful dance, blocking attacks from the Seekers and assisting the elven warriors in their escape. Ivy was only vaguely aware of nails raking, bodies slamming, rocks cracking. Orion seemed to move like liquid around the tree, fighting in a whirl.

Gneiss fought on the edge of the opening, her strength waning. Mud caked Gneiss's hair and a crimson stain blossomed on the thigh of her trousers. Ivy fought beside her and the two of them took the brunt of the force on the eastern side. Orion and another elf on the western. When only the four fighters remained, Ivy signaled to Orion: run.

Ivy intended to protect Gneiss, but also bring the ambassador with them. Orion protected the flank of the last elf as they fled south. Ivy opened her mouth to ask Brecc's sister to help with Wirenth when Gneiss snapped.

"Don't think this makes up for what you've done." Gneiss flashed a glare at Ivy that would melt ice. "Stay away from me." She gripped the vial at her neck and jogged away, a limp more pronounced with each retreating step.

Ignoring Gneiss's sting, Ivy spun to grab the lingering ambassador, but her legs collapsed beneath her weight. Her head spun. Her body was heavy, yet she *had* to convince Wirenth to run. She pushed herself into a standing position but crashed even harder to the earth.

She pressed her hand to her stab wound, but it had healed. Her head throbbed, her vision blurring. Warm liquid oozed down her temple. Ivy sensed eyes on her before she locked her gaze with that of a Seeker. The corrupted lowered her shoulders, a broken arrow in her hand, and ran at Ivy. If the Seeker didn't maim and crush Ivy, the others certainly would.

Orion ran toward her, but he was too far away to help. Ivy's sluggish body felt like molasses. Orion stopped short and dug his fingers into the soil.

Like lightning, one of the tree branches shot down and encased Ivy in a swirl of leaves and bark. The Seeker smashed into the wooden barrier, grunting at the impact, sending leaves and twigs flying. The wooden cage lifted Ivy into the air, swinging nearer Orion who leapt onto the outside of Ivy's enclosure. Orion shouted for Wirenth to jump, but the elder elf stepped back, refusing to leave.

The branch-enclosure shot through the air. Pines and naked trees blurred below. The indigo leaves flapped in the wind, giving Ivy glimpses of Orion.

Who was he?

His expression appeared nonplussed by the fact that the

Gathering Tree did his bidding. This was madness. Not even a Councilor of the House of Seeds could command the trees. She hadn't even known such a thing was possible. Despite her exhaustion, Ivy's mind whirled with questions.

The tree sat them down not far from Sunshine, near the edge of the Gathering. Orion gingerly touched the branch, whispering something in a tongue she didn't understand. Then the tree branch lifted away, leaving the two of them alone.

Orion's gaze moved over Ivy, lingering at her temple. "You've lost a lot of blood. We should find a safe place to rest."

"The Gathering Tree ... can ... it carried ..." Ivy ran a hand across her throbbing head. Her fingers came back slicked with blood. "I've never ... That doesn't ... Why didn't the tree just lift us all out?"

"It isn't a dryad's place to interfere. Besides, it was hard for her to pull enough magic from the fair realm to transport the two of us."

"Who are you to command her?" Ivy clamped her mouth shut before she asked another personal question.

Orion bit his lip, seeming to weigh the question. "I just witnessed an army of peacekeeping elves fight hundreds of Seekers. Elves should have a cordial relationship with humans, at the very *least*. Yet humans are falling victim to the seeds you claim to revere. I don't fully trust elves, and that includes you."

Ivy considered pointing out that she didn't trust fair folk posing as human guards.

"Then why stay and help me?" Confusion and new anger braided into a knot inside her.

"We each want information the other has. We can travel to Neidrei and figure out what's going on." He gestured toward the distant Gathering Tree. "Then we can go our separate ways."

Ivy was in no mood to be told what to do. But the truth was, she had hoped to join him. He had vital pieces of a puzzle she couldn't begin to piece together. Ivy took a deep breath. Orion was intriguing, infuriating, and a bit frightening. But she needed him.

"My horse isn't far," she said.

Orion ground his teeth, but he followed Ivy to fetch Sunshine as the last rays set over the forest. Ivy couldn't see far, her vision suffering from her energy expenditure and injury.

Orion stayed several paces behind, her progress clumsy and slow. She wished she'd stop thinking about the weight of his arm wrapped around her waist; warmth rose to her cheeks, and she chastised herself. Drat the fair folk. Many of them were naturally enchanting, ensnaring the naïve. She remembered the woman who worked on the Blue Mountain—the one who'd pined after this Captain of the Night Guard. Whatever Orion's trickery, Ivy wasn't some human who would fall for his hollow magic.

The sooner she discovered what her father had been mixed up in, the sooner they could part ways. Without seeds, Ivy would need to hide away until the Centennial.

But, thanks to Brecc, she had a chance of surviving. She'd fulfilled her promise to him by speaking and trying to soften the hearts of the elves toward Seekers. It hadn't gone well. In fact, on the heels of her speech, the Gathering had been infiltrated. And now Brecc's family despised her.

She just wanted to put this year behind her. Uncover her father's secrets. And get Orion out of her life. When Sunshine came into view, unscathed, Ivy's heart lightened.

But then her throat threatened to close when she saw who else was waiting for her: Nym.

13
PRETENTIOUS ELVES

Slivers of the moons' light cast dim shadows across the forest, but Orion guided Ivy and Nym with little trouble. The trio moved soundlessly, avoiding Seekers' attention. Orion had intended to set a punishing pace to Neidrei, but Ivy could barely cling to Sunshine and her healing stone.

Every slow step was an agony. Only one week remained until the spring equinox and the subsequent power shift to Summer Court. Orion needed to report *before* that time. At this rate, they would arrive in Neidrei in four days, giving him only two days to uncover the elder elf's secrets. Afterward, he could travel alone. Without having to hold back his magic, he could be in the Winter Court within hours.

Nym rolled two stones around in her hand, her head on a swivel, constantly on the lookout. Orion appreciated vigilance in his guards, but the daughter of the northern councilor could be a problem. The entire Phiro family was known for their ruthlessness in battle—and in politics. As far as Orion was concerned, they represented the worst traits of elvenkind.

Ivy had acted happy to see Nym, which was logical as their families likely spent time together. But Orion saw through Ivy's lies, just like he had when she'd "agreed" to go with the Tides. Even so, Nym had adeptly inspected Ivy's wounds and remained alongside Sunshine after the three of them had fled two hours ago.

Beyond Nym, pressed a weightier complication. Ivy had sensed Orion's glamour after she'd eaten a seed. He was torn between astonishment and irritation. In another few moments, she might have pierced it. If she discovered what blood ran through his veins, she might flee. As it was, Ivy must've been suspicious because she'd kept herself at arm's length, or further, ever since.

The distrust was mutual. Meeting Ialant and Emmyth had only reinforced Orion's opinion of elves. Traveling with their two pretentious daughters was akin to stabbing himself in the foot with an iron poker. No, the iron would be less painful.

Though wary of his companions, he needed to interview Ivy. And he suspected the bone amulet was critical to his investigation.

"How do you think the Seekers invaded the Gathering?" Nym broke the silence.

Orion glared at her.

"Don't get your tunic twisted," Nym said to Orion. "I don't sense any Seekers or humans within an hour's walk. So, how do you think the Seekers broke past the diversion spells?"

"Probably because of Orion," Ivy said.

"What?" Orion's irritation flared further at her accusation.

"Do you still have the image I tossed by the river?" Ivy asked. "The one of my father?"

"No," Orion said. "Ialant requested to see it and then burned it without my permission." Orion hadn't decided if he'd include that fact in his report.

Ivy opened her mouth but then clamped it shut.

"Odd that a councilor would destroy evidence," Nym said. "But then again, I'd heard he'd gotten paranoid in recent years."

Ivy's face snapped to Nym, then she winced and pressed a clenched hand to her temple, still crusted with blood.

"He was a clever man, though," Nym added. "Perhaps he had good reason."

Ivy's lips squeezed together into a thin line. Again, she was holding back. But why? Ivy was either keeping secrets from him or from Nym. He needed to rule Nym out. What would be the easiest way to leave her behind? He glanced at the northern elf, her braids swinging with her long gait as she tracked the movements of the forest around them.

No easy way. And killing her would be a scandal, unfortunately.

"Why would Ialant ask you about a drawing of himself?" Nym asked.

Ivy didn't prod Orion for information about her father. Nym did. The questions were vague and her tone light, but Orion knew an interrogation when he heard one. He'd bet that Nym's mission from her mother included gathering intel about Orion.

He'd have to give the prying councilor's daughter *something*. Orion didn't have patience for elven spy games, but he'd play. For now.

"Ialant requested a meeting with me. We'd barely started talking when I showed him a drawing I'd found of him. When I told him what was happening with Ivy, he cut our conversation short and hurried for the Gathering. He didn't even stop at home for supplies. Just left."

"You insisted on coming with him, I see?" Ivy wryly added, her voice hoarse.

"Your father feared Seekers didn't randomly hunt you," Orion added somberly. "You were marked."

Nym shook her head. “Who would do such a thing? And how?”

Ivy lifted her head just as a moon broke free of the clouds, revealing the determination in her otherwise delicate features. “I will expose whoever is behind the attacks on my family. And on my House.”

“Fortunately, the same Gathering drew you and your father together,” Nym said solemnly. “Alysatraee willed your reunion, however brief.”

Ivy swallowed but said nothing.

“Did he suffer some injury along the way?” Nym asked Orion. “I don’t understand why he was so weak.”

Ialant had appeared hale the first time Orion met the elf outside Unaria, and the elder elf had traveled a great distance. The second time they met, Ialant was changed: gaunt with a yellow pallor and thinning hair.

“He seemed ill before we even began our travels,” Orion said, not revealing a starting location.

“If he’d been hiding in a human city, it would weaken him,” Ivy said. “I would know.”

Nym leaned away from her friend, and her shoulder rose slightly, signaling possible disdain. The haughty elven reaction matched Ialant’s few rambles during their hurried travel.

“We should stop to rest,” Orion suggested. He needed little sleep, but the faster Ivy healed, the faster they could travel. Most of the forest was muddy, but they neared a thick canopy with dry ground and fallen pine boughs made for promising beds.

“I’ll start a fire. We should be fine for at least two hours.” Nym slid her two stones into a pouch tied at her waist.

“Excellent,” Ivy said. “I’ll gather some leaves for tea.”

“I can work while you rest,” Nym suggested.

"Forgive me, but I know how good you are at identifying wild plants. I don't want to vomit all night." Ivy chuckled.

"That only happened once." Nym winced and pressed the heel of her palm to her stomach.

"By the time you two stop reminiscing, I'll have our camp set up," Orion said.

"You picked this grumpy pixie over Kolvar?" Nym jabbed her thumb toward Orion. "I know my brother has terrible taste in clothing and friends, but ... a human guard?"

"Well, I did bump my head," Ivy joked as she slid off Sunshine and led the horse to graze on new grasses.

Orion ignored their banter. Nym was only goading him into blurting his intentions. Truthfully, he was only taking Ivy north so he could question her. Nothing more. But Nym could speculate; a misdirection toward a non-existent connection between him and Ivy. He took a deep breath, bracing himself for the next six days.

Soon, Ivy was steeping leaves in boiling water in cups that Nym had carved from a branch. Orion pulled three pine boughs into a circle around the fire while Ivy checked the tea. From that angle, he noticed her flushed cheeks. His fingers itched to check Ivy for a fever, clean the blood from her brow, and secure her cloak.

Frowning at his compulsion, he folded his arms tight across his chest. He assured himself he simply wanted to safeguard her health—to keep their pace.

Keeping his distance, Orion settled on the opposite side of the fire. Nym shared elven gossip as Ivy wiped away evidence of the battle. As Nym told a story about some childhood friend named Lial, Ivy's petite frame shook with giggles until she suddenly snort-laughed. Ivy noticed him grinning, and she scrunched up her face in annoyance. Orion jerked his attention away rather than explain he wasn't mocking her. Her laugh was mostly tolerable.

"When will you tell us about your little dragon friend?" Nym asked as she rolled stones around in her hand, searching the sky.

"She'll settle down soon enough," Ivy said. "Just don't expect her to make an appearance."

"Why is she following you?" Nym leaned forward.

"I'm not sure," Ivy shrugged. "She doesn't even like me. Honestly, she's like a rat with wings."

"We just need to tempt her with a warm bed." Nym hopped up, jogged several paces away, and dug in a dry spot of earth.

Ivy grinned and stirred the tea, then kicked several hot rocks to Nym, who buried them in the ground. Orion could understand the fascination. He'd never seen a dragon in the human realm before.

When Nym returned, Ivy handed her friend a cup. "You've always had a soft spot for animals."

"It's a *dra-gon*. Who wouldn't be intrigued?" Nym brushed off Ivy's comment and gulped down a mouthful of tea.

Ivy stretched and laid back. The evergreens and clouds blocked the moons, and the embers did little to push back the blanket of night.

"I'm sorry about your father, Ivy. I have fond memories of him." Nym leaned forward, her shoulders tense. Nym's earlier lightness fell away, replaced with a tarnished edge. "The glamour he gave you, I'm hoping I've earned enough trust that you'll show it to me."

"Nym, I've had a hard day." Ivy closed her eyes. "I need to sleep. I can hardly think."

Nym's fists clenched, and the air grew tense. She pressed to see the amulet again, and when Ivy ignored her, Nym set down her cup, jabbing her fingertips into the ground next to it.

"Was Ialant hiding outside Neidrei all these years?" Nym asked.

Orion internally groaned. Though he didn't want to travel with Nym, she already knew the amulet existed, and she'd figured out they were returning to Neidrei, despite Orion's efforts to insinuate the destination was Blackmore. If she stormed off and blabbed to any fair folk, especially if she mentioned Orion's interest in the matter, the resulting rumors and half-truths would muddy his investigation. That might threaten his eventual acceptance by the fae court.

"Let's discuss this in the morning," Orion said. "Emotions are high."

Both elves leveled him with a glare hot enough to melt iron. Then Nym's gaze moved to Ivy's bag.

Ivy grabbed her satchel, clutching it with visceral protectiveness. "We're not children anymore. If you steal this, I won't forgive you."

"I wouldn't." Nym had the decency to look offended. "But I wouldn't have to if you'd be forthright. Your father left the Council under a shroud."

"My family was hunted. My father had to hide, or he would've been murdered ... *like the rest of my family.*" Spittle shot from Ivy's lips as she punctuated the last words. "But if you *must* know, at this very moment, about the amulet that the last surviving member of my family gave me before they died, so be it."

Ivy yanked the amulet out of her bag and rubbed her thumb on the bone. She instantly transformed into a council member: Emmyth Philo.

~

Orion tensed, ready to restrain Nym if she attempted to steal the evidence from Ivy.

"What trickery is this?" Nym jumped up. "Why would your father have a glamour of my mother?"

"He failed to mention that as he gasped for his last breath." Ivy spat. Her voice was slightly deeper but otherwise unchanged despite wearing the glamour of Emmyth.

Ivy inspected her hands and clothing, her face scrunched. Orion could only imagine Ivy's anger and confusion. Families were complicated and ugly, in his experience.

Feeling strangely irritated at Nym's harassment, Orion redirected her attention away from Ivy with information he hadn't wanted to share. "We'll find answers in Neidrei."

Nym stepped back from Ivy, her back still rigid. "So, you're not making inquiries with the human king at Blackmore?"

He reminded himself that Nym suspected their true destination, anyway. And Ivy needed rest. He was not attempting to do Ivy any favors. She was still a spoiled, reckless councilor's daughter.

"I am curious to know why Ialant has this glamour. Same as you," Orion said. "I don't think the answers are with the humans."

"Humans are behind this mess, I'm sure of it." Nym's lip curled into a sneer. "But, if the next step for inquiry isn't with them, why would we need the help of a human captain? Ivy and I can make our own way to Neidrei."

The glamour of Emmyth dropped as Ivy shoved the amulet back into her bag. Clearly, Ivy loved her father, so when she discovered the misdeeds in Ialant's past, the investigation could get messy. He couldn't let Ivy out of his sight.

"Fine. Go without me," Orion bluffed. "But Ialant gave me a location inside Neidrei."

And he wouldn't share it until they stood in its shadow.

Even in the dim light, Nym's wide stance and raised chest broadcast the same ferocity he'd seen as she fought back the Seekers. Now it simmered, boiling behind a thin, cold façade. But she didn't argue his plan.

"I'll take the first watch," Orion said with finality. "Ivy needs the sleep, so we can split her shift if you're amenable."

"Fine with me," Nym slammed every syllable. "I prefer the morning watch, anyway."

Orion sat on a tree log in the shadows as the two elves laid down, backs to each other. When their breathing deepened, Orion crept along the perimeter, searching for dry wood. Under cover of night, he removed his coat and let his glamour fall. He stretched, his body aching after weeks of holding the form he wore in this realm.

Ash settled on a branch not far away, watching him. A vial swung on a chain from her jowls; a dim light glinted off the glass pendulum.

"What have you here?" Orion whispered, moving closer. The dragon tilted her head, considering him.

Orion stepped forward, the dragon within reach. But Ash twitched her attention over his shoulder, and then she shot into the air. Orion sensed someone coming up behind him. He pulled his glamour in place and spun around just as Ivy appeared through the trees.

"You're supposed to be sleeping," Orion growled.

"You're supposed to be watching for intruders." She smirked before casually dropping back her hood. Orion dared breathe but studied her for hints of the tell-tale fear most showed when they learned his identity.

"I could be half-asleep and still smell you coming." Under the blood still matted in her hair, sweat, and mud, Ivy had a pleasant earthy scent. Like petrichor and linden trees. "You need a bath."

"Don't be a troll," Ivy said. "We don't have much time before Nym's sleep cycle lightens. I put a sleeping root into her tea, but her deepest sleep won't last."

"Sleeping root?" Orion was impressed. And alarmed. "How?" *How did you do this without my noticing?*

"The Svyen bush. The mature leaves stave off infection, and the roots are excellent at inducing a deep sleep. I slipped in a root when Nym was distracted with Ash and disposed of it before she noticed."

Noted. Watch everything I eat and drink.

"Of course, if I were to leave a root in for too long, it could render her unconscious. But I was always good with medicinals." Ivy's voice softened. "It's probably why my father was certain I'd survive alone."

What would it have been like to grow up in a family that actually cared? Would that make parting more difficult?

"You tainted Nym's tea before she even asked to see the amulet." Orion raised a brow. "You never trusted her?"

"I'm not sure what to think of anyone, least of all you. So until I know what's going on, the fewer who hear our conversation, the better." Ivy's voice hardened, and she looked up at Orion, the sharp lines of her face reflecting her determination. "Tell me everything."

Beyond her demanding tone, there was a desperation that Orion understood. He quickly recounted the conversation he'd had with Ialant from the previous autumn. The elder elf had asked questions about the fae court. Orion held little back, hoping to encourage reciprocal treatment.

He took a deep breath, revealing more about him than he wanted to, but hoping to earn her trust. "I carry messages between realms," Orion confided. "I thought your father was building up to ask me to take a message for him to the fae court, but he never did."

"Perhaps he meant to, one day." Ivy paused. "Wait, you're a dryad? That's why Gathering Tree responded to you?" Ivy scanned his face, likely wondering what he *really* looked like.

Let her wonder.

Orion ran a hand down his chin. "Another dryad might have let you die. This one helped because she's eager to please."

Ivy opened her mouth to ask why but then didn't, thankfully. Orion wouldn't have known how to respond because even he was baffled. Luckily, the dryad possessed a kind heart and likely no small loyalty to Winter. And naivety. He'd sensed the dryad's youthful presence the moment he'd arrived, just as she likely sensed his.

He imagined the dryad regaling the others with stories about the Gathering, including his sister. Soon, she would inherit their mother's territory. Embarrassment and jealousy reared inside Orion, and he quickly shut them out of his mind. Yes, he had to fight harder for respect from the fair folk, but bitterness would do him no good.

Ivy touched Orion's arm, immediately pulling his attention to the warm spot above his elbow. It was just a graze of her fingertips, but his skin seemed to burn.

"I lost you to some memory, didn't I?" Ivy asked.

He shook his head, and she didn't press him for personal details. Instead, Ivy told Orion about her precarious life over the last fifteen years and the contaminated ink that had drawn the Seekers to her. She choked up as she explained what had happened to Brecc.

"I can't stop seeing him die in my arms." Ivy hugged herself.

Orion had an impulse to draw her close and console her. Shocked and a bit revolted at his instinct, he stepped back. "I have something for you. Wait here."

Using the opportunity to put distance between them, Orion jogged to the camp and went through Sunshine's pack. The cold night, thankfully, air slapped away his wayward thoughts. Nym grumbled in her sleep and turned over—her sleep was lightening. Orion grabbed the knife and strode back to Ivy.

He handed over the weapon, hilt first, giving her plenty of room to grab it without touching him.

"Oh," Ivy gasped. "You found my father's knife."

She plucked it from Orion's hand and ran a gentle finger down the inlaid handle. "I can't tell you how much I appreciate what you've done." She cradled the knife to her chest and looked up at Orion. Her whole body seemed to cave toward the weapon her father once handled. "I thought I'd lost it in the fight."

Though her humble thanks didn't ensure she wouldn't throw him to a siren in the sea to save a fellow elf, there was a tenderness in her crumpled expression. A vulnerability he'd never seen from her, even when she was about to die by the very blade in her hands. Her unguarded moment stirred something inside Orion.

He didn't like it.

"It was the Mother's luck that I found it before we escaped," he said, ignoring his uncomfortable emotions. His whole task would be far more complicated if he believed the elves had hope of redemption.

Orion ground his teeth, reminding himself it wasn't the time nor place to philosophize about the elves and Ivy. He'd only agreed to get her to Neidrei so he could finish his investigation.

He cleared his throat and told Ivy about his second meeting with her father. "As nervous as Ialant was outside Unaria, he was downright paranoid outside Neidrei. Initially, he indicated that he wanted to show me something important in the city, but I don't know what. When we left, I suspect he knew he wouldn't return. I think he hoped you and I would unravel his secrets, and the amulet is our first clue."

"But you traveled together. He didn't tell you anything?"

"The travel was hard on him. He grew weaker every day." Orion suspected Ialant only survived on sheer will to see his daughter. "He did talk about your family. It tore at him to know that, at times, your sister hid in the fae realm."

Ivy tilted her head. "In Iris's blue box, I didn't recognize her location. Massive flowers and luscious gardens."

"Sounds like a Summer creature took pity and allowed her to take refuge." Orion shuddered.

"I never imagined that she would go to the fae realm." Ivy lowered her voice and looked toward Nym. "It's against Alysatraee's will. And it ages us quickly."

"Like a human, correct?" Orion raised his brow.

Her chin dropped. "More quickly than we are used to, I should say. Initially, I didn't even recognize my sister. I'm mostly surprised because of Iris's daughter. She's half-elf and could age like a full human while in the fae realm."

"According to Ialant, your niece and her father resided in the human realm for long periods. By themselves, they avoided trouble. They had a system. It worked smoothly for years." Orion hesitated, but she deserved the truth. "Until they were all killed by Seekers in the human realm."

Ivy paced back and forth, not looking at Orion. He moved away to give her time alone, but she stopped him.

"What else did my father say?"

"That he'd made a grave mistake years ago. That he'd been trying to undo it. He believed he'd found a solution." Orion cleared his throat. "He was ready to confess to the fae courts."

"To the fae? To confess what?" Ivy's voice cracked. "This doesn't make any sense. My father wouldn't commit any crime against the fair folk, let alone one serious enough to take to the fae."

Not even to protect his fellow elves or his family? Orion kept his thoughts to himself.

"You're not convinced, but you don't know my father." Ivy frowned and turned on her heel to march away.

"You're asking the wrong questions," Orion said.

She stopped but kept her back to Orion.

"Why did Ialant have a glamour of *Emmyth*?" Orion asked. "And how will having her daughter along complicate our investigation? Nym seemed surprised, but was it an act? And who will she protect if we find out her mother is involved?"

"I'm more concerned about who *you're* going to protect," Ivy shot back. "For someone with fair folk blood, you seem terribly interested in digging up elven skeletons." Ivy glared at him over her shoulder before stomping back to her bed.

14
GLITTERING GNOMES

"Be careful in your travels, m'dear," the woman cautioned as she handed Ivy a short cloak and knitted hat. Her house was at the edge of a village outside of Neidrei, and Ivy had stopped to trade. "There be strange sightin's in these woods."

"How so?" Ivy wondered if the woman had heard of the same "mindless" Orion had been warned of by travelers two days ago.

The woman worried her lip, glancing back at her toddler picking dandelions next to their cottage. "Frightenin' li'l ones. *Their* kind."

Ivy stiffened. Was the woman referring to elves? Elves were petite, comparatively. But Ivy reminded herself that this younger generation of humans subscribed to exaggerated tales of fair folks' appearance. They probably wouldn't recognize an elf if one were standing right in front of them, especially if their ears were covered by a hat, like Ivy's.

"I appreciate the warning," Ivy said, backing through the open gate. "And the clothing."

The woman nodded, patting the fresh herbs in her apron.

She turned and swept her toddler into her arms, and Ivy jogged deeper into the forest.

Soon, Nym came into view, her arms folded tight across her chest, scowling at Orion. Or, more likely at Ash, who was sitting on Orion's shoulder. The dragon's blue scales seemed to glow in the morning light in a deceivingly majestic display. She'd become a fixture on Orion's shoulder over the last four days, but the vial was long gone.

Nym inspected the items Ivy handed to her. "This cloak looks like it was knit by a blind troll missing eight digits," Nym complained. "And this cap has a hole. Filthy, nibbling rats."

"It's a fair trade." Orion pinched the bridge of his nose. "Learn to find a balance with the humans. They need to eat, too."

He spun on his heel and started toward Neidrei, not bothering to wait for Ivy or Nym. Orion had boarded his horse in the king's stables at Blackmore, another benefit of his captain status. When he rejoined them in the forest, Nym had asked why he wasn't bringing his horse to Neidrei, and he'd answered by handing over cheese, bread, and silence.

"It's the best I could do with Svyen and a few mullein leaves," Ivy explained her barter with the human woman.

"And the dandelions I gathered," Nym added.

Dandelions that even a toddler could pick.

Ivy plucked Sunshine's reins, who was blissfully grazing and trudged after Orion. By Nym's pace, she wasn't in a hurry to catch their guide. Ivy *definitely* wasn't. And it seemed Orion was equally keen on keeping his distance between himself and the elves.

Which *inexplicably* stung.

She didn't know what to make of the half-dryad and didn't care.

Well, perhaps she was a little curious about him. For a

Unarian guard, some of his edges weren't as rough as she'd assumed. His skill with the blade seemed less born of vengeful hate and more of work ethic and dedication to achieve such results. And he ensured she rested comfortably each night and had clean water for her each morning.

Plus, he'd saved her life. So, of course, she'd be curious about him. Feel gratitude, in fact. Naturally. Anything less would be calloused. Heartless. Unfeeling. Which obviously, Ivy was not. Her feelings of *mere* appreciation were an expected result. Normal.

Ivy brushed the dirt from her sleeve as if she could just as easily brush off the tangle of her heart.

Whatever these feelings were, they would pass soon enough when their paths diverged. The thought should've lightened her step. Instead, her gaze sought Orion, studying his broad shoulders and long stride. The idea of never seeing him again settled between her breasts, leaving a dull ache that she tried to rub away.

Tried ... and failed.

Her face heated, and she chastised herself. She shouldn't be the slightest bit embarrassed by the uncomfortable growth of allied companionship, the logical result of fighting alongside Orion. They depended on each other for survival. Her confused feelings would pass.

They had to.

Besides the fact that he'd shown zero interest in her, Orion lived among humans as the Captain of the Unarian Guard, and Ivy dreaded crowded cities.

"Next time, I'll join you for negotiations," Nym said, poking a finger through the hole in her hat as they walked. "I need practice trading with humans, especially with such low stakes."

Ivy bristled, gripping Sunshine's lead tighter. Nym negotiated weighty contracts that impacted hundreds of elves; however, she didn't understand the basics of human nature.

"Your clothing is expertly stitched on materials too fine for most humans," Ivy said. "Even before you say a word, they'll charge you double."

Nym scoffed, gesturing to her muddy, bloodstained clothing. Ivy had once been the same, taking elven quality for granted.

"When are you going to tell us where we're going, exactly?" Nym shouted to Orion as she yanked the short cloak across her shoulders.

Orion ignored her and picked up his already brisk pace, Ash still gracefully perched on his shoulder.

"What spell did he put on that poor little dragon?" Nym grumbled under her breath.

"Ash is not a helpless creature, I assure you." A phantom itch tickled the back of Ivy's throat.

"Why, then? *Why?* I made her warm beds. I snared rabbit for dinner. Yet she prefers that obnoxious guard."

"Count yourself lucky that flying rodent didn't select you as a companion."

A half-hour later, as they neared the main road to the city, Nym jerked to a halt again, fisting her two sense-stones. "People are hiding up ahead. Probably thieves. Veer west."

"How many people are on the main road?" Ivy asked her.

"Enough to blend in." Nym signaled to Orion, and they swung west, avoiding human interaction.

When the city finally came into sight, anticipation swelled within Ivy. Before they stepped onto the main road, Nym grabbed Ivy and held her back. Ivy reached for her bow, expecting another warning, but Nym's intensity melted.

"I've been nastier than a hungry, Winter fae princeling. I apologize." Nym bit her lip.

Ivy blinked, surprised. Humility was a weakness, in Nym's opinion. Nym fidgeted, her gaze darting to Ivy and then quickly away. The interaction was foreign. Uncomfortable. But Nym was either sincere or desperate. Ivy wasn't sure which.

"All is forgiven," Ivy said. "I've been slow, Ash has terrible taste, and ..."

Your mother has crushing expectations.

Ahead, Orion waited. He jabbed a finger skyward, indicating the day was wasting. Ivy waved him off and turned her attention back to Nym.

"Orion is about as warm as week-old bread crust. Though attractive, for a human—I admit that much." Nym rubbed her temple. "Beyond my valid unease with a human involved in *our* matters, my honest, more troubling concern is you."

"What? Why?" A cold stone slid into Ivy's stomach.

"I cared for Ialant like an uncle. It'll break my heart if we find out he's violated the Mother's laws. But for you ..." Nym's expression softened. "No matter what happens, I swear I won't abandon you."

Ivy's mouth dried at Nym's statement. If Ialant Balrel was found guilty of breaking fae law, Ivy would be disgraced—a pariah at Gatherings, her words forever disregarded. But Nym stood by her, swearing not to sever her completely.

"Your words are true comfort." Ivy squeezed Nym's forearm. Though the northern elf had her flaws, she was loyal and painfully honest. Perhaps Nym had come as a friend, not a spy for her mother.

Ash glided toward Ivy. Once they were near civilization, Ivy had expected the dragon to either fly away or hide in a satchel. Ivy groaned at the latter choice but lifted her bag's flap. Ash's talons dragged against the leather from lip to bottom as she settled herself inside.

My dreams have come true. A scratched-up bag that smells of soot.

Nym's lip twitched, but she forced a smile and pulled Ivy along. "We should go. Your grumpy pixie is waiting."

"He's *a* grump. Not *my* grump," Ivy corrected as they jogged to the main road.

"Whatever you say," Nym teased. "But I see the way he looks at you."

"Yes, like a tedious chore," Ivy said as they merged with others on the road.

Even before they entered the city walls, Neidrei assaulted Ivy's senses. Acrid smoke, stale tobacco, and human excrement permeated the air. Fortunately, Orion's insignia got them smoothly past the gate guards without a bribe or bag search.

Nym wiped her watering eyes as they entered the city, and when she spoke, her voice dripped with disdain. "I've read stories of old Neidrei. Seen the drawings."

The squat structures sat like toads on buried ruins; nothing remained of the once glittering fae stronghold. Even as a child, Ivy had always felt wrongness about this place; a purposeful ugliness, blotting out every whisper of beauty that might spark a fondness for anything fae.

Orion boarded Sunshine as the horse's beauty drew too much attention, and the captain's insignia was an unspoken warning for the hostelers to take extra care. Orion wove an irregular path through the city, and Ivy's fingers tingled, ready to grab her knife as she studied the vendors and movements in her periphery. When Orion ducked down an alley, Nym and Ivy followed. Then, doubling back, they stopped before a narrow, dim passage, a dead rat pushed against the wall.

Orion checked over his shoulder, then disappeared around a crate. Ivy hesitated, but Nym nudged her forward. As Ivy squeezed around the first crate, the alley seemed to widen. The trash vanished, and a fat tabby cat appeared, sitting on a box near a single door, licking her paw.

A glamoured passage.

A hidden, ramshackle structure was smashed between two buildings. The tilting roof sat like an eyebrow over the peeling, burnt orange door. Along the top of the frame, someone had painted an ornate, swirling '777.'

"Well, well," Nym said, scowling at Orion. "I'd bet my sense-stones that only those with fair blood can enter here."

Orion knocked. Footsteps sounded inside, and a slit opened in the door, revealing a shadowed face.

"I'm on an errand for Ialant," Orion said.

The slit slammed shut. Something grated against the floor inside, and Nym gave Ivy a sidelong look. Each elf slid a hand to their hidden blades. The door swung open, and inside, a hooded child signaled for them to enter.

Ivy ducked in after Orion and Nym, nearly bumping into one of two long tables in the cramped room. Each table was laden with boxes of varying sizes; most had a spindly tree in a different stage of disease.

The child slammed the door behind them, and the dilapidated building trembled. The youngling threw back their hood, revealing glittering topaz eyes. Ivy's body relaxed, and Nym grinned.

"What's a gnome doing in the middle of Neidrei?" Orion asked him.

The gnome blushed. "It's not difficult to hide among humans."

"No glamour?" Nym asked as Ivy took in the eerie sight of the dying trees. The trees were incongruent with everything she knew of gnomes, the protectors of cultivated plants and crops.

"Just a razor." His accent plodded like heavy boots. "You'd be surprised the places a child can sneak into with only a threat of a whipping. Plus, I'm pretty quick for a gnome. Have to be. The name's Zelbim. But everybody calls me Zel."

While Ivy dimly listened to Nym introduce them both, she peered into the nearest box; brittle debris littered the soil. Across the room, one doorway had a curtain drawn across. A second doorway was open, and the edge of a dingy straw bed caught her attention. Whose was it?

Zel cleared his throat, awe in his voice. "It-it is an honor to meet you both."

"I'm Captain Orion Arya, here to investigate Ialant's work."

Zel gave Orion a bow. "Of course."

Ivy leaned forward, anxious to see more of the room. A book came into view; she'd know the faded green spine anywhere. Did her father sit in this spot studying xylem, stomas, and light while hiding in a filthy city. Taking a step closer, a glint in an open box drew her attention to a familiar medallion. Her heart twisted, the amulet confirming her suspicion; her father had slept, worked, and focused his energy on his life's work in this space.

Orion continued, "Ialant sent for me, then directed me here."

"Will he be here soon?" Zel asked. "I expected him days ago."

Ivy's words caught on the sudden lump in her throat.

Orion stepped forward. "Unfortunately, he didn't survive his recent journey."

Ivy swallowed. "You knew my father?"

The gnome was silent for a moment as he rubbed the back of his neck, staring at the wall with a blank face. "Genius, he was," the gnome finally uttered. "His goal was untraditional, to be sure. I resisted his ideas, in the beginning. But he convinced me. I've been working with him for near ten years."

"What was Ialant working on?" Orion asked.

The gnome dropped his hand from his neck. "The trees. That's why you're here, isn't it?"

Ivy ran a finger across a leafless sapling's sickly bulges and sniffed the dusting of white on the bark. She swallowed, not recognizing the potent disease.

"What's killing these trees?" Ivy asked.

"You mean *who*," Zel said. "Ialant."

Nym's brow creased as she rocked back.

Ivy was sure she misunderstood. "What do you mean?"

"Councilor Balrel nearly completed his mission," Zel clarified, "to end all the Gathering trees."

Ivy blinked, the ruinous accusation slicing through her.

Lies.

Anger sparked in Ivy's gut. She marched between the tables, her attention flying from one dying tree to the next. "My father would sooner save these plants, I'm sure of it."

"No, you don't understand." Zel's face seemed to reflect the alarm Ivy felt. "Your father was once part of something ... something you have no business judging."

"Part of what?" Ivy shot as she closed the distance to the open doorway.

"About fifty years after the war," the gnome said, "some fair folk realized that weakening a few important humans would weaken their stronghold on the entire realm."

Orion rubbed his chin. "Resourceful traders, influential leaders, and key military personnel? Take out key humans, and their kind become weak. Makes sense."

"But, the war is over," Nym stated the obvious.

"Yes, well, some elves, including Ialant, believed that giving humans seeds would gradually destroy their kind."

"Ialant was putting sacred seeds in the hands of humans?" Nym's lip curled, avoiding eye contact with Ivy. "Targeting specific humans for death? To what end?"

"You didn't bleed while watchin' our cities burn. You don't know true pain," Zel said. "Ialant discovered revenge was simple. With a few promises, greed quickly blinds humans."

Ivy thought back to the Seekers she'd seen—their once-fine clothing, ribbons, or shiny leather boots—clues to their lives *before*. Hints of wealth and influence. Ivy's head spun as the poison of the gnome's words stole her breath. He was *wrong*. Misinformed. Her father was exposing this madness, not the cause of it.

Her gaze darted from the dying trees to her father's book on the floor. The world beneath her rolled. She gripped the table, needing some buttress to support her through the chaos.

She didn't even see Orion approach. Not until he stood before her, blocking her from the gnome and Nym's stares. She blinked up at him, willing him to say something that would refute the gnome's claims.

Because if the gnome spoke the truth, her family name was ruined.

"Despite what you might feel, you are strong enough for this," Orion said, his fingertips resting on her arm.

As fast as the comfort had come, Orion withdrew. His hand dropped to his side, but the tether between them remained.

Ivy wrapped her arms around her waist, bracing for the rest.

"When your sister fell in love with a human," Zel continued. "Ialant feared Iris would discover his deeds and shun him. But even more, when Iris had a child, a half-*human* child, he loved her. He realized his error."

"Calla," Nym said. "Iris's daughter's name was *Calla*."

"Yes, yes, of course," Zel added. "And Ialant convinced me to help him."

"So Ialant forgot the Mother's directive, our sacred duty to keep the peace between the realms." Judgment filled each of Nym's words.

Ivy stepped away from the anchor Orion had offered and neared the bed where a tree sat. In the room, notes scribbled in her father's hand sat in a pile next to a healthy tree. Though immature, the branch's buds were beginning to unfurl their leaves. *Purple* leaves.

These were not just any saplings. They were Gathering trees.

Her beloved father, the respected council member, had misused elven seeds. Taking a single fruit beyond what Alysatraee gifted each year was offensive. Taking seeds and planting a whole new tree violated the very foundation of elven ways. Each of these trees was an abomination.

Tears pricked her eyes as she stared at the condemning evidence, defying everything she knew of her father.

"He tried to abandon the trees. Walk away from his revenge." Zel ran a hand across the edge of a box. "That's when Seekers started attacking him. Ialant realized his *friends* had turned against him. So, he split up his family, hoping to save you."

"Why would Ialant's cohorts attack Iris?" Nym interrupted. "Because she married a human?"

"Because she was poised to become the next councilor for the House of Seeds," Zel said. "*And* because she'd married a human. They knew she'd never support their cause."

"Mother of Magic," Nym cursed.

"Ialant couldn't figure out how Seekers tracked his family," Zel continued, "In *the* fatal attack, his home burned to cinders. He should've died. He pretended he *was* dead. He had every reason to believe you'd be left alone, Ivy, while he worked in secret."

"When your father found out you were still hunted, he dropped everything to find you," Orion spoke low, just for Ivy. Somehow he'd returned to her side without her awareness, offering a small island of comfort in her sea of pain.

"In the end, his experiments worked," Zel said. "He found a way to kill Gathering trees."

"Don't worry, Ivy," Nym said. "I don't believe this blasphemy."

But I do.

The poison of lies was not from the gnome. Ialant was the source, and there was no antidote. It soured her stomach until it clenched, and bile crawled up Ivy's throat. Covering her mouth, she darted for the door.

"We'll need proof of these accusations," Orion said, his voice like a knife.

Ivy grappled with the handle.

"I insist on joining any further investigation," Nym demanded.

Ivy threw open the door and retched at the threshold. Ash thumped against the satchel, then pushed up the flap.

Not now!

"Of course, Nym." Zel's voice carried from inside. "No one in the facility would think twice about you being there—"

Zel stopped short as Ash darted into the room.

"An omen from the Mother," Zel gasped.

A bad omen.

Ivy pressed a shaking hand to her stomach.

A cloth appeared in front of her face, and Orion whispered, "What can I do?"

Four small words that meant so much. Not because Orion said them now, but because he'd said them over and over and over again. Sometimes spoken, but more often not. Not because Ivy was a chore but to bolster her.

Orion was a rock.

Ivy swallowed the rest of her tears and wiped her face. She refused to wallow in her father's mistakes. Ivy needed to be strong and make things right. And she would.

Orion wrapped his arm around her waist, and Ivy soaked up the warmth he offered. Even if their end was inevitable, Ivy needed his strength and his belief in her now. There was no shame in his friendship.

He put a gentle hand on Ivy's back, and together, they returned inside before Orion kicked the door shut behind them.

But once inside, the friendly familiarity took on a new meaning as Nym's brow furrowed as she watched them.

"Why won't anyone think twice about my presence?" Nym snapped at the gnome.

Ivy jerked away from Orion's touch and gripped the door frame, forcing her attention to Zel.

"Hmm?" Zel absently admired Ash as she jumped from box to box. "Oh, because the Council is involved. They're a clever bunch, too. Double-crossing them is no easy feat, believe me."

"*All* the elven council?" Orion asked, his voice sharp once more.

"What?" Nym shrilled.

Zel shot up taller as if finally recognizing Nym's alarm and switched to sympathy. "If it's any consolation, I believe Emmyth planned to tell you. Um, eventually."

Nym's breathing quickened, her chest heaving.

Zel muttered under his breath, "On her death bed, or the end of all time and space. Whichever came later."

"This is a test." Nym seemed deaf to Zel's words. "A sick test of the fae, isn't it? To see if I'm fit to become a councilor. Well, I'm not interested. Kolvar deals with political manure, not me."

"I need proof for the court," Orion said.

From her satchel, Ivy yanked out her father's amulet. "I'm guessing this will help us get it?"

Ivy ran her thumb down the bone, shifting into Emmyth's form.

Zel's eyes widened. "It seems Ialant wanted you to finish his mission at The Tree House."

"If anyone pretends to be Emmyth, it'll be me," Nym spat. "Besides, I sound enough like her."

"No, Nym, you're the daughter I'm finally ready to include in my scheme." Ivy refused to be left behind.

"You can't give one of your polite elven nods and expect a tour." Zel disappeared through a curtained door, then re-emerged, holding two glass vials. "We must prepare. One mistake and not even Emmyth could arrive quick enough to spare your lives. You must gain access to the facility and poison the trees inside."

"I'll be there with you," Orion said, the warmth in his voice plucking the strings of Ivy's soul.

Ivy spun, banging into Orion in the process. "They'll never let *you* in."

A slow half-smile pulled at the side of his mouth. Orion gripped something at his chest. A bone pendant? Ivy didn't have long to wonder before Orion shifted into Kolvar Phiro, Nym's brother.

15
DIRTY WORK IN NEIDREI

Nym's skin felt stretched tight, holding in her rampant emotions. But, a Phiro didn't lose control; she bit down and tasted blood. Ivy might believe Zel's rubbish, but Nym doubted she could trust the gnome any more than she could trust Orion.

Which meant, not at all.

As they followed the gnome through the streets of Neidrei, Nym watched Ivy through the corner of her eye. Her friend looked like Emmyth but slunk carefully like a thief, not like a queen who owned the city. Ivy wouldn't last long without help. Nym couldn't leave her friend to fend for herself, not in her state of distress.

"Stop staring at Kolvar," Zel hissed at Ivy as they maneuvered through the streets. "Emmyth never looks worried or confused, even if she is."

He's right about one thing.

"Lift your chest. Phiros don't slouch." Nym gave the same advice she'd heard numberless times from her mother. "Don't be afraid to take up space. And you," she turned to Orion, who hadn't sufficiently explained how or when he'd procured a glamour, "shorten your stride. Kolvar is used to others following him and doesn't try to outstrip them."

Zel rubbed his temple as they turned down a quieter street. "Nym, *your* pent-up nerves are our biggest risk."

Nym's desire to throttle the gnome was marginally overruled by his singular knowledge of the facility's location. She tightened her grip on her stones, senses heightened, preparing for an ambush. Or, at the very least, to stumble into a decrepit, crumbling back-alley cave with trolls mixing poison vats.

They turned a corner, and a sense of foreboding washed over Nym. She didn't hear or see any attackers, but even Ivy and Orion slowed.

"We shouldn't be here," Nym said.

Orion-Kolvar's hand gripped his sword. Leather covered the entire hilt, which Ivy had mentioned was the Unarian style. Nym had begun to wonder if the strange fashion had begun before or after Orion had arrived.

"This way," Zel marched forward. "Push past your fears."

"It's a dissuasion spell," Ivy-Emmyth informed them.

"A powerful one," Nym said.

Ivy nodded. "My father couldn't have created it alone."

Assuming Ialant was involved at all. Yes, the House of Seeds cast strong dissuasion spells before every Gathering. And, yes, Ialant was highly proficient. However, other Seeds elves could've created the spell.

Or perhaps Ialant's mind had crumbled after his wife's death, or he was the scapegoat for some other fair creature's foul deeds. It didn't matter. Nym had already stayed beyond the scope of her task. She intended to leave this cursed city as soon as possible and take Ivy with her.

Orion had stated he'd be parting ways at sunset. Good riddance.

The moment Orion had passed through the glamoured alley

to Ialant's hidden workplace, Ash's behavior began to make sense. The guard had fair folk blood. Therefore, he had ties to both the fair *and* human realms. His background also explained why Ivy trusted him.

But the Captain of the Unarian Guard kept too many secrets, and he could keep them. Orion chose to live among humans. He'd chosen his side, and it wasn't the peacekeeping elves.

The soldier had his report, and Nym had hers.

Emmyth had dispatched Nym to retrieve the amulet and determine Orion's connection to Ialant. That was all. Nym figured out that Orion and Ialant barely knew each other, so she could've stolen the pendant and disappeared long before they'd reached Neidrei. But Ivy had lost everything, and Nym wouldn't leave a friend behind.

Unfortunately, Ivy was stubborn. She believed the delusional gnome and was determined to find her father's dirty secrets. This whole situation was turning to utter insanity. Nym would deal with Emmyth's displeasure at staying past her objective because Kolvar was right; Ivy needed to recuperate in the safety of the north—gain her wits before she did something ridiculous.

Like fall in love with someone who reeked of trouble.

"This is where I leave you." The gnome had already explained that his appearance would raise suspicion.

Due to Zel's chronic headaches and inconsistent work, the Council replaced him at the Tree House. Zel could've returned to his family in the fair realm, but he was embarrassed at his failure. Ialant accommodated his needs, giving Zel purpose. Obviously, Ialant had taken advantage of the gnome's fragile state.

Zel held out two vials for Ivy. "You know the trees best—one drop of poison per branch. Ialant did a lot of damage before he went into hiding. We suspect none of the original trees survived, which forced the Council to start again with new seeds."

Ivy-Emmyth gripped the vials, her face pale. "Why not report the crime to the fae court? They could dispatch orcs and clear out the facility within days."

"I agree," Nym said. She had zero intention of poisoning anything. "Besides, time passes differently in the fae realm. Why rush?"

"With the glacial pace of the rulings in a dangerous, complicated fae court?" Zel stopped rubbing his temples long enough to glance up at Orion.

"Let's just get this over with." Nym adjusted her belted blade under her cloak and the spear slung across her back.

"Leave your weapons," Zel offered again. "Most visitors aren't armed."

"Most visitors didn't arrive straight from a Gathering attacked by Seekers," Nym shot back.

Zel shrugged. "Your decision."

Nym patted the satchel at her hip, where she had secreted away two items. The first, only she knew of, and she'd stitched it into a faux lining of the bag. Ivy's House would need it later. The other item was Ash, who napped silently, thank the Mother. Ivy had wanted to leave the dragon at Ialant's workshop, but what if Ash nibbled on a poisoned branch? Bad idea.

The glamour had changed Ivy's body and altered her clothing, but it would only hide the stained bag, out of reach within the glamour. In case they needed to check on Ash, Nym wore the shabby bag. So Ivy put the precocious dragon into a slumber, promising the medicinal was harmless, and Nym carried her.

"Will you return to the fae realm after the courts finally make their judgment?" Ivy asked Zel.

"Yes, I'm pleased with my honorable work." Zel took a deep breath and placed a hand on his chest, relieved. "My part is nearly finished."

Zel gave final instructions and lumbered back toward his workshop. The trio strode deeper into the empty portion of the city, surrounded by an eerie quiet. A prickle of warning ran down Nym's back; she couldn't be sure if instinct or the ever-present spell twisted her insides. She rolled her sense-stones around in one hand, straining for any noise. But it was almost like other magic dampened the stones.

As they neared the final turn, a stranger came into view. He sat on an empty crate with a deck of cards, ice-blue hair falling across his face. He raised his chin, revealing purple skin and tusks. An orc. The fair creature sat in broad daylight in a human city. The strange sight was more alarming than an entire human military unit. Between the orc and the dread that had grown since she'd entered the empty streets, Nym's free hand closed around her dagger's hilt, hidden at the base of her spine.

As Zel had instructed, Ivy signaled the watch guard with a double-tap to her shoulder, and he mirrored the tap in return. Even so, Nym didn't drop her guard as they passed. The next street came into view, revealing their surprisingly underwhelming destination.

Ahead, a tall, crumbling structure loomed: the Tree House. The faded mud walls slumped under the weight of the aging roof. Loose sections threatened to slough off and leave random holes for windows.

More like "The Tree Shack."

As they approached, a mountain of weight lifted off Nym's shoulders. At her side, Ivy let out a long breath of relief. The dissuasion spell had lifted.

Nym wiped her sweaty brow at the base of a tall, wooden

door. What was on the other side? Dead trees? Outcast fair folk? An orc army?

The hinges on the door grabbed Nym's attention. Her jaw clenched. A small detail, but a derelict structure with robust hinges of *dwarven military design* alarmed her even more than the orc watch guard. Nym shifted her weight, preparing for an ambush. The last thing she wanted was to waste a seed because she'd trusted the gnome.

"Relax," Ivy said through gritted teeth.

The sense-stones bit into Nym's palm. She hated the precarious situation. But she either had to trust Zel or run. And Ivy wouldn't run. Nym slid the stones into her pouch and shook out her hand, feigning calm.

The door swung open, and an elf in a simple, clean dress and apron stood in the doorway. Her braided hair flaunted her uncovered, pointed ears. Ivy-Emmyth pretended not to be surprised. In fact, she lifted her chin with an air of boredom.

Perhaps Ivy could pull this off after all.

"Councilor Emmyth Phiro," the elf's eyes widened, "what a surprise."

Nym grinned at her victory; her mother was unknown in this place. Why had Nym allowed any doubt?

The elf gave a respectful nod. "But as always, we welcome you."

Nym's smile cracked.

"This way," the elf said.

Nym froze, her mind stuck on the elf's statement: "as always."

Ivy-Emmyth nudged Nym across the threshhold, snapping her out of her daze, just before everything around her seemed to twist, melting into a different place entirely.

16

THE TREE HOUSE

Orion didn't rein in his awe as the shabby clay walls transformed into marble veined with gold. At their feet, massive flowers and meticulous gardens grew along winding paths of colorful, crushed, polished glass. Trickling fountains soothed, and the scent of spring blossoms replaced the city stench.

Birds chirped in the massive oak trees in each corner, their branches reaching out like a lattice, supporting the soaring glass ceiling.

"Classical Neidrei style," Nym whispered, her eyes watering with unshed emotion. "Just like Nylann'or, but not modified for the harsh weather."

How could something so beautiful still feel so wrong? There was a presence in this place, but Orion couldn't pinpoint it unless he put his feet in the soil.

A step ahead of him, Ivy held herself together, her head up, impersonating the snobbish councilor perfectly. Nym wouldn't have been able to feign calm, not like Ivy whose life had taught her to compartmentalize her emotions. Unfortunately, he'd learned to do the same. Though, acting as Kolvar, he could show his surprise and ask all kinds of questions that Emmyth should already know.

"Was there anything, in particular, you'd like to inspect?" their elf escort asked Ivy-Emmyth, but her gaze settled on Orion. "My name is Valjyre."

Orion replied, his voice passable for Kolvar. "Emmyth battled Seekers a week ago at the Gathering. She's saving her energy and her seeds."

Ivy held up her healing stone on cue. Nym had stained a portion of Ivy's lip red, indicating injury to her mouth.

"Wise and prudent." The elf nodded, her hand gliding to her glass vial resting against her apron.

"Emmyth spoke of a workshop?" Orion prompted.

"Of course. This way," Valjyre said.

Orion's attention swung between Ivy and Nym, alert for signs of distress. Creating Kolvar's glamour had been easy. Like breathing. More and more, he wanted Ivy to know the truth about him. He'd hoped perhaps she'd figure it out when she was ready. But, perhaps he'd need to sit her down and explain. But not in Neidrei.

They passed under a wide archway, and Nym gasped. The marble walls and glass ceiling remained the same, but instead of an ornamental garden stood a small *orchard* of purple-leaved trees. Dozens of elves and gnomes tended the trees, all dressed in simple clothing and matching aprons. After Ialant's attack a decade ago, the Council had obviously gotten to work: new seed plantings, and a *lot* of them. It would take every drop of poison to destroy these trees.

To Ivy's credit, she didn't react.

A gnome jogged over, his face flushed. "Councilor Phiro. What an honor to have you here again. I'm happy to report we're back on track."

Nym's fists clenched at her sides. Orion wasn't surprised at the evidence of her mother's betrayal piling up. How long would Nym believe her mother's involvement was a lie concocted by Zel? He wanted to stay at Ivy's side, but Nym was a risk that needed managing.

"What's the updated schedule?" Orion-Kolvar asked, wanting to gather information and get out of this place.

"It will be close, but the seeds will be ready before the next Gathering," the gnome replied.

It's always been about the seeds.

Nym swallowed, her breathing quickening. He moved next to her, giving her a warning glare.

"We received word about the Seeker attack," Valjyre said, looking at Orion again. "We are grateful you're all safe."

Did Kolvar know this guide elf from somewhere? The clothing at his neck felt tight.

The gnome continued, "The attack is another reminder of why our work is so important. A thousand seeds are difficult to procure but worth the effort."

A thousand seeds?

"For what?" Nym blurted.

The gnome let out a nervous laugh, glancing at Ivy, who had stiffened. "I'm sure I don't know. Only the Council is privy to the master plan."

Nym tried to force an innocent, curious expression—and failed—when her stomach gurgled loud enough for the entire room to hear. Great, Nym might vomit.

"I'm sure Councilor Phiro has good reason to keep sensitive information quiet," Orion said, redirecting their attention.

Zel had already claimed the Council used the seeds strategically to hurt humanity. But was that just one step in their unknown plan? The Council likely had a more elaborate next step in place. A plan Emmyth knew. The *real* Emmyth.

The gnome's tone turned grim. "We worked and overcame, despite the difficult circumstances a decade ago."

Ivy nodded with false compassion as her hand slid into her pocket where she kept the poison. Ialant was the reason for the "difficult circumstance," and his daughter had come to finish what he'd started.

"We ended up grafting from the Centennial tree," Valjyre casually added.

Ivy's head snapped upward, her back rigid, her only strong reaction since they'd entered. Nym looked confused, so whatever the guide elf was referring to, it was something only a House of Seeds elf would understand.

"Centennial tree?" Nym asked.

"Oh, yes, I forget the House of Tides doesn't study these details." The elf flashed a condescending smile at Nym. "During the war, the House of Seeds planted Gathering trees.

In the beginning of time, Alysatraee gifted a single tree—the Centennial Tree—that elves visited once every hundred years. Can you imagine?"

"So, the Centennial tree," Nym said slowly, "is the *only* true tree from Alysatraee?"

The guide elf's nose scrunched. "I guess that's one way of looking at it?"

Ivy had paled. Not good.

"You think these - these *experiments* have the Mother's blessing?" Nym asked, gesturing to the orchard.

Nym was about to lose her temper, but Orion moved to Ivy's side. He braced her elbow like the dutiful son of an injured mother.

"Of course? How else could we survive the dangers of the human realm?" Valjyre said in a saccharine tone. "How could we have survived the war at all? There have been hurdles, yes.

But elves overcome. Replant. Graft. And now expect a plentiful supply."

A supply for what?

"Would you like to inspect the seeds, as usual?" the elf asked Ivy-Emmyth.

Ivy nodded, and Orion shot Nym another warning look over his shoulder. Nym ground her teeth but followed as the elf led them into yet another room.

The tall ceilings dwarfed the single table in the center of the space. Two elves hunched over it, inspecting seeds. Behind them was a tower of shelves lined with velvet cushions. The elves straightened from their magnifying glasses as the Phiros entered, and one elf handed Ivy-Emmyth tweezers.

Ivy silently inspected the seeds, likely understanding far more about them than Emmyth ever would. While Ivy worked, Nym and Orion glanced at the shelves. Each cushion held a single seed labeled with names and cities. Intended victims? Ivy set down the tweezers, her face unreadable. Determined.

Good.

Orion drew the elves' and gnomes' attention with an amusing story about the trek north after the Gathering attack, allowing Nym and Ivy to communicate without notice.

"Will you tell us more about the grafts from the Centennial tree?" Nym interrupted.

"Let me show you," the guide elf beamed at Orion-Kolvar. But, instead of returning to the orchard trees, she led them down a different path. The walkway ended at a wall of wavy glass with matching doors guarded by four orcs.

The wrongness he'd sensed when he first entered increased as they neared. But it wasn't an evil as much as deep mourning. Whatever was happening beyond the doors made the dryad magic in his blood simultaneously cry out in warning and curl up and weep.

17
CUTS AND GRAFTS

Ivy felt frozen as if cockatrice-stunned.

"This tree still fills me with awe," the guide elf, Valjyre, cooed. Fortunately, she was looking at Orion, or she would've seen the complete shock on her fake-Emmyth face.

In the center of the room loomed a tree wide enough for twenty elves to reach around. The grooved, gnarled branches bucked against the glass roof, constructed even higher than the others with added buttresses. A ribbon of withered bark, blackened as if burned, wove a wide swath up the trunk, nothing growing from its wake. But the healthy branches caught Ivy's attention, covered in green buds ready to burst forth.

"You mentioned setbacks a decade ago," Nym's voice cracked, "yet this tree appears much older than ten years."

"This tree survived that … mishap, and accepted the Centennial graft." The guide elf, Valjyre, gestured to the tree. "A gift from Alysatraee."

Nym gripped her hands behind her back. "Kolvar would *love* to hear all about your efforts to save this tree."

The guide elf's face lit up, and Orion opened his mouth to

object. But the guide started chattering as she pulled Orion away, not noticing the murderous look he leveled at Nym.

"We don't have enough poison to kill the orchard and this tree," Ivy whispered. She frantically wiped the sweat from her face and fanned the neck of her dress, hoping she didn't have armpit stains. Emmyth never showed her nerves.

"Which do we choose?" Nym asked. "The orchard or this massive beast?"

"I sensed this tree the moment the dissuasion spell lifted," Ivy said. Actually, the ground had pulsed hard enough to be felt down the street. This close, Ivy's heart thrummed in tandem. "I'd assumed the feeling was from the young orchard, but—"

"Which one?" Nym pressed as she gestured to Orion, who was rushing around the tree. "Someone is clearly not enjoying the sparkling company."

Ivy ignored the flirtatious guide elf and focused on the scars marring the trunk where cuts had allowed for bonding the fresh grafts. "This tree. The power it emanates ... it'll easily produce enough fruit to harvest a thousand seeds next spring. All the trees in the orchard combined couldn't match it."

"We'd assumed they were referring to the orchard for harvesting," Nym frowned.

Ivy wasn't sure what to make of the grafts. What would Alysatraee say? Ivy closed her eyes and reached with her senses.

A mournful lament reached back, a deep melancholy that sunk Ivy.

"I don't know if I can ... I don't know if ..."

Ivy longed to press her fingers to the trunk, but something deeper warned her back. She remembered the tree had already given her direction. Beyond the path north, the tree had shown her more.

The cruelty of fair folk. Dread had cut Ivy—a sense of an impending, terrible event rumbling forth like a dark storm cloud crashing down the mountain. And Ivy was at the center of the tempest, delivering one tragedy with poison's rage but stopping a greater evil from coming to fruition.

"I'll do it," Nym offered in a rushed whisper.

Ivy shook her head and gripped the vials. Her stomach roiled at the idea of destroying a tree that bore the branches of the *one* true Centennial gift. But, if anyone were condemned, it would be Ivy.

"Orion is practically running around the tree," Nym muttered under her breath as Orion and Valjyre neared.

"I'd like to see the orchard again," Orion called out.

"But we want to admire *this* tree." Nym's nostrils flared.

Orion's gaze dropped to Ivy's pocket. His pulse feathered in his neck. Something was wrong. They needed to get rid of Valjyre.

Ivy pivoted to Nym and tapped her throat.

Nym's brow arched, but she understood. "Emmyth is parched and desires tea. Then we should leave for the long journey back to Nylann'or."

As Nym followed Valjyre, she winked over her shoulder at Ivy. Ivy only needed moments to finish what they'd come to do. The roots mirrored the branches, growing right under her feet. All Ivy needed to do was dump the poison where she stood.

The door shut, and Ivy gently removed the vials from her pocket. Before she could uncork them, Orion grabbed Ivy's wrist, far rougher than he'd ever been.

"A dryad has already claimed the vessel. If this tree dies, so will she."

18

PICK YOUR POISON

The aproned guide fetched tea while Nym waited in a section of the garden enclosed with boxwood, yew, and another dense plant that her tutor would be horrified she didn't remember. Any northern elf might have relished the soft petals and pleasant scents in the garden, but Nym's body buzzed, anxious to escape.

Without a chaperone, Ivy wouldn't need long to poison the tree. Not even orcs would dare intrude on Emmyth Phiro. As much as Nym hated to admit it, Ialant was clever to select Emmyth for the glamour. Though, how had he acquired it? Multiple creatures could create glamours, including Winter fae with their innate magic and human witches with their skilled charms.

Perhaps less important than "who" was "what" Ialant had offered in return. Desperate creatures made rash decisions.

Nym lingered near the path leading back to the orcs and the grafted tree, monitoring for potential trouble. But the workers seemed happy to attend to the orchard further away.

Wondering what was taking the guide elf so long, Nym moved to the next section of the garden and then the next. The guide had shared her name, but Nym promptly forgot it. Through the wall of thick stalks topped with vibrant blooms, Ivy couldn't see anyone on the other side, but she slowed when she heard voices. She recognized the guide's familiar, nasally tone and inane chatter.

"Are you sure?" The thick stalks muffled the guide elf's voice, but Nym could still make out the words. "The orcs will arrive by morning?"

"It's an inconvenience we can manage," a soft male voice responded.

"I'm a bit nervous about having more orcs here," the guide elf said.

"Strange things are afoot," the male voice responded. "But not to worry. 'Tis lovely to imagine that next year, orcs may travel by day in Trinth without fear of repercussions."

Half-listening as the male voice explained the preparations, which included hunting for wild boar and collecting straw for beds, Nym's mind stuck on the timing. How did the orcs travel so quickly to Neidrei from their home in the far south? They were fast, especially at night. But, not *that* fast. How long would it take if the Council had sent one unit to clean up at the Gathering and another straight to The Tree House?

Calculating, Nym shook her head. It should've taken them at least another six days to arrive, assuming their leaders dispatched units within mere hours of receiving word of the attack. Who was that efficient?

"Too bad you can't take the councilor's daughter to help in the hunt," the guide elf said, grabbing Nym's attention again. "Did you see her weapons?"

"Hush now," the male said. "We don't want to offend—"

Nym leaned closer to the stalks, straining to hear.

"What's going on?" the guide elf asked.

A new, unfamiliar voice spoke in an excited tone, "Kolvar is addressing us before he leaves."

Nym straightened. What foolish plan was this?

"I'll fetch Nym," the guide said.

Nym bolted away, not wanting to be caught eavesdropping. Back where the witless guide had deposited her, Nym took a calming breath.

Ash shifted in the satchel.

Nym cupped her hand over the bag, her mind swimming. Was Ash just stirring in her sleep? Two gnomes hurried along the path, headed toward the orchard where Kolvar was supposedly speaking. They gave nods, and Nym nodded in return, a bead of sweat running down her spine.

The little dragon was easily distinguishable, especially in the human realm. If Ash had chosen Orion as her companion, the two would eventually be linked. The death of the grafted tree and the appearance of a vibrant blue dragon would be memorable—too memorable—and connect Orion to the impending incident.

Furthermore, hundreds of elves had seen Orion with Ialant. Then with Ivy. Of course, her friend would never reveal Nym's involvement, but her insides twisted at Ivy's likely punishment from the elves and fae.

Ash shifted again.

Forget the fluff-for-brains guide.

She had to find Ivy and Orion and evacuate. But was Ivy with the massive, grafted tree? Or in the orchard? Their plans were unraveling.

Nym spun on her heel and followed the gnomes. Why was Orion making some grand speech as Kolvar? This was *not* the time for some last-moment "lesson" he wanted to impart—a secret explanation for future questioning when the workers realized all their plans had been destroyed.

Blood pounded in Nym's ears as she followed a gnome through the orchard and into the seed inspection room. What had felt cavernous earlier was now crammed shoulder to shoulder. Even a few orcs stood inside, a head taller than the elves.

Orion stood on a stool, and everyone circled around, faces wide with curiosity. Nym tried to catch Orion's attention, but he was busy speaking with admirers.

Nym didn't dare move through the press of bodies for fear of disturbing Ash further. Instead, she found a place at the back, near the door, ready to wave at Orion when he looked in her direction.

Where was Ivy? Nym scanned the room, not seeing Emmyth's face. Through the open door, Nym caught a glimpse of Ivy-Emmyth emerging from the flower gardens. Nym moved to the door, catching her friend's attention. Ivy tapped her pocket as she strode into the orchard.

Nym swallowed. Ivy still had the poison; she planned to poison the orchard.

"Nym and I appreciate the kind welcome in The Tree House," Orion-Kolvar said. "This has been an enlightening experience. We have learned much about Gathering trees."

Orion continued, riveting the crowd. When Nym was satisfied no one else was coming, she closed the double doors to the room and stood in front of them, muttering an excuse that Kolvar had asked for privacy. Privacy from whom, Nym would have to fabricate an answer if asked. But no one stopped her.

Being a Phiro had its perks. Well, until the trees died. Or the eventual fae court summons. Whichever came first. Then, being a Phiro would become very, *very* not-fun.

Ash shifted, her talons scratching the bottom of the satchel. Nym's hand flew to the flap. The gnome in front of her turned around, searching for the source of the noise. Seeing Nym, his eyes widened, and his head whipped back to stare at Orion again.

Nym slid her hand inside the bag, desperate to soothe the frightened dragon. She stroked the top of Ash's head, and a row of razor-sharp teeth slammed down on Nym's finger. She gasped, unable to stifle herself in time.

The two elves next to her gave her quizzical looks. Was her finger bleeding? How would she explain that? Nym forced a smile despite the warm liquid running down her finger.

Orion droned on and on. Nym's finger throbbed. It wouldn't be long until Ash shook off her drowsy state and insisted on stretching her wings.

Orion continued, "Grafting the Centennial Tree was a bold plan."

Ash's head pressed up against the flap of the satchel. Nym stiffened, looking for a place to hide. She needed to escape, but Ivy might be caught and restrained if she opened the door.

"That grafted tree, brought so low, will soon produce the thousand seeds requested." Orion's gaze found Nym. She pressed down on the Ash-sized bulge and shook her head, her braids flying.

No, I'm not fine. No, I don't think Ivy is done. No, I don't think this was a wise plan.

Orion continued stalling, talking about the duties of elves. Then Orion spoke up for Ialant. "We must assume that whoever poisoned the original orchard must have been desperate—felt they had no other choice."

Not subtle at all. Nym gritted her teeth, knowing everyone here would know who was behind this orchard's demise: pretend-Kolvar.

Ash pounded her head against the flap and scratched harder. Attempting to cover the sound, Nym cried out and bent her knees as if faint.

Orion continued talking, ignoring Nym's fuss. The elf next to her grabbed Nym's arm.

"Steady," the stranger said. "You've traveled a long distance. I'll help you find a place to sit in the garden."

Nym leaned against the doors, sweat beading her brow and her bloody hand still shoved in the satchel, hoping not to receive more abuse.

"A walk through the orchard will set me right," Nym said. "But stay for Kolvar's speech. He loves the attention."

Nym clutched the top of the bag and squeezed through the door, slamming it behind her.

Ivy spun around, eyes wide.

"We must leave, *Emmyth.*" Nym rushed toward her friend as she wiped the blood off her finger inside Ivy's satchel. "Our little friend is waking."

Ivy tilted the bottle upside down, the last drops hitting the soil. Behind Nym, the door burst open, and voices sounded. Nym grabbed Ivy's arm, hurrying her toward the entrance doors. Behind them, a nasal voice sounded, and Nym cringed.

"My apologies, Councilor," the guide elf said, giving a small bow to Ivy. "I thought you were with your son. I couldn't find you, and now I'm afraid your tea is cold. I'll fetch you a fresh cup straight away."

"We have a long journey. We must leave." Nym glanced back at the orchard and imagined, for the briefest moment, the disease ravaging each tree. Grief struck her, sudden and chilling. Nym couldn't get out of the cloying guilt of the Tree House fast enough.

Nym and Ivy moved toward the door like molasses in winter. Everything seemed to slow as several workers strained for a last look at the visitors. The elf guide giggled and Nym figured Orion had just joined them. Ivy signaled, and an elf moved to open the door.

Nym shuffled along the glass pebbles, covering the sound of Ash's insistent scratching. The dirty city beyond beckoned. Sanctuary.

Ash's body tightened inside the bag. Nym's heart pounded, anticipating a dragon's screech. Or for the bag to start on fire. Or some blaring indicator that they'd traveled with a secret dragon, an event salacious enough to prompt too many questions.

Please, no. Please, no, no, no.

Ash shifted, knocking into Nym's thigh. Then soot flew out of every crevice of the satchel. Silent condemnation, worse than any roar. A literal cloud of suspicion shot up around them as an inky haze formed around Nym ... with fluff-for-brains standing right behind her.

19

GRUMPY PIXIE MESSENGER SERVICE

Ivy gasped as dark ash exploded, and the nearby workers' eyes widened.

In one smooth motion, Orion ripped off his cloak and draped it over Nym's shoulder and satchel. Somehow, the covering swept up most of the soot. But not nearly enough to hide that the Phiros had secreted *something* inside The Tree House.

Valjyre was two steps behind Nym, her jaw slack. She'd clearly figured out they'd brought an unknown dangerous magical element into the Tree House: potion, artifact, or animal. The real Emmyth wouldn't break the law over something so easily avoidable, like sneaking a magical creature into the human realm—and into a stinking elven-controlled facility.

Their hosts would ask questions.

If Ash didn't stop scratching at the bag's walls, the elves would demand to see inside. Would they discover the bone glamour at Orion's neck? Ivy's neck? The poison-tainted bottles in her pocket?

She envisioned standing in front of the fearsome fae court.

Sharp teeth lashed. The Gathering Tree had warned her, hadn't it?

Ivy sickened. Invisible prison walls closed in. Her body thrummed, and she struggled to breathe. Orion grabbed Ivy's shoulder and whispered something she couldn't hear over the pounding of her ears.

She read his lips as Orion mouthed, "Go."

Ivy snapped out of her stupor, grabbed Nym, and yanked her toward the exit. As they approached, an elf opened the wooden door. His brow raised when Nym coughed, ash floating behind them. Glancing back, Ivy noticed Orion hadn't followed. He was talking to Valjyre and another gnome.

"Did someone recently add ash to amend the soil?" Orion asked as he brushed Valjyre's forearm.

Other nearby elves murmured, their attention flitting from Ivy-Emmyth to the lingering cloud.

"It's possible." Valjyre cocked her head. "Yes, ash was added today."

Orion nodded. "Perhaps someone kicked up the soot as they passed by."

Valjyre's attention flitted to Nym. "Someone must have accidentally disturbed the soil."

Nym gripped Ivy's arm and practically shoved her through the open door. Ivy managed to give the elf near the door a nod as they passed, but Nym didn't slow until they were past the orc-guard, who barely looked up from his dice game.

In an alley, Nym shrugged off the cloak and brushed off her clothing, though it did little good.

"You said she'd sleep until the stars shone," Nym threw open the satchel, and more ash billowed. But not the dragon; the creature rested her head over the side, relaxing as if she hadn't just thrown a complete fit.

"Because she's a mangy cursed creature." Ivy pressed her

hands against a mud wall. "The winged-rat must metabolize faster than I'd estimated."

Ash's tongue flicked out. Apparently, she'd merely wanted a bit of fresh air. And she'd thrown a tantrum to get it.

"What happened with the grafted tree?" Nym pressed her eyes shut. "What should we do now?"

"I realized the orchard was the better option." Ivy didn't mention the dryad as Orion's skills weren't hers to reveal. "I never doubted that the caretakers would figure out the trees failed at our hand. The question is, will they connect Ash to Orion?"

Ash jumped out of the bag and flew to greet Orion when he appeared. She landed on his shoulder and seemed to glare at the elves.

"Are orcs coming for us?" Nym asked Orion. "Should we run?"

A shudder ran down Ivy's spine at the thought of getting dragged into a fae court. Only Ivy had physically poisoned the trees, and she'd receive the sharpest punishment.

Ivy planned to travel alone until the Centennial, but being hunted by orcs was worse than running from Seekers. Orcs were faster and more intelligent, and some were skilled trackers.

"We have time to escape the city," Orion said.

"What?" Nym blinked. "How?"

"They believe it was a simple gardening accident," he said. "I spoke with all elves and gnomes with a direct eye-line of the incident."

"They witnessed my bag turn into a ball of ash!" Nym threw up her hands. "Someone will realize the story is highly suspicious."

"Not before we're through the gates. We should go." Orion

whispered something to Ash, who then tapped her head against his chin and shot into the sky.

"I cannot believe our luck." The corner of Nym's lip twitched into a grin as they marched forward.

Ivy contemplated what she'd just seen. Orion had manipulated the elves' and gnomes' thoughts. That wasn't dryad magic. Had he tried to protect her and Nym, or was he only looking after himself? She wanted to believe they'd become friends, but how well did she really know Orion?

"They were bound to question Nym's family, regardless," Orion spoke in hushed tones as they passed the delineation line of the dissuasion spell. "Many elves are good liars, but I suggest you avoid questioning altogether. Let Emmyth answer to the Council. Dozens of elves can account for her and Kolvar's whereabouts over the last several weeks. But no one can account for you."

"Let me worry about my family." Nym set her jaw, quieting as they passed through a busy street before continuing.

"You both realize," Ivy said, "what we saw changes things. We now officially depend on the fae court to save humankind from the elven seeds."

Elves were peacekeepers between realms; they'd utterly failed. Humans didn't realize it, but now it was up to the fae, the humans' blood enemy, to save them. The trio fell silent at the morose concept.

After waiting in line at the gate and the subsequent bag search, they hurried into the forest to meet Zel. Alone, Orion and Ivy dropped their glamours. Ivy took a deep breath and stretched, feeling lighter.

Sunshine grazed in a clearing near the pacing gnome. When Nym told Zel about the orchard and the Centennial grafts, he flopped down on a trunk, rubbing his temples.

"I suspected Ialant hadn't killed all the trees. But to graft branches from the Centennial ..." Zel paled, his brow dotted with sweat.

"It's a violation of Alysatraee's law," Nym finished his sentence.

"Ialant's plan failed," Zel spoke more to himself than the others. "*My* work was a waste. I risked everything for nothing."

"Not for nothing." Ivy sat next to him. "You told me the truth of my father and family."

"Ialant mixed the poisons, you know," Zel confessed, his expression pinched. "He handled them so often. All his experiments. They caught up with him."

Ivy crossed her arms, attempting to hold her emotions in as she remembered how pale her father had been when he'd arrived at the Gathering. How long had he been sick?

"Ialant did the right thing in the end. And so did you," Nym said. "The Council is working to disrupt the peace between the realms. Even if you and Ialant couldn't completely stop the Council's plans, you slowed them. Because of you, the Winter Court might be able to stop another war."

"Perhaps. But in the meantime, the Council will trace this incident back to me." Zel dropped his chin, hiding his watery eyes. "I'll destroy our research and leave the city, too."

"Will you return to the fae realm?" Ivy asked.

"I-I don't know," Zel said.

"The fae courts will likely call on you to report on the Council's misdeeds," Orion said.

"Ah, fair folk politics." Zel rubbed his temples.

Nym pressed a hand to her stomach, her finger coated in dried blood. Ivy could only imagine what was running through her mind. Once the truth came out, the Phiro's were ruined. Kolvar would never be on the Council. Nym would be stripped of her duties, too.

"I need to go," Zel said.

"I'll escort you back through the gates." Orion tapped his insignia, which would gain them quick entrance.

The elves bade goodbye to Zel before he stomped away with Orion.

"Zel is an odd one," Nym said. "I hope never to see him again."

Ivy didn't ask if it was because he knew of Nym's involvement in poisoning the orchard or because his testimony would damn the Phiro name. Either way, Nym lost.

"Nym," Ivy said, "I would rather be an outcast with a friend than rule the realms alone."

Nym spun on her heel and grabbed the nearest branch like it was her salvation. Her shoulders shook, and the limb bowed under her weight.

"Nym ..." Ivy didn't know what to say.

Nym wiped her face and faced Ivy. "I'm not sad. I'm angry. Earth's-core-magma-angry." She paused and let out a slow, shaking breath. "I have to face my mother."

"I know," Ivy said.

A part of her desperately wanted to go north, but her presence would only anger Emmyth and complicate things for Nym and Kolvar. Still, Ivy dreaded being alone. Though she had suffered as her battle wounds slowly healed and she'd learned of her father's disgrace, she'd also enjoyed the warmth of friendship and shared goals.

"I promised not to abandon you," Nym crossed her arms, shoving her hands in her armpits. "If you want to come with me, I will welcome you."

"If we travel together, Emmyth might interpret that as an alliance. A threat." Ivy shook her head.

"We can be strategic. The decision is yours."

Ivy leaned back, tempted by the prospect of affable support from Kolvar and Nym. But was that better for them or her?

Ivy fisted the bone amulet. "Will you do me one favor when you arrive home?"

"I'll tell Kolvar you're sorry for abandoning him and making him look like a pitiful love-struck clotpole." Nym grinned, wiping her eyes again.

"Find me," Ivy said. "When all this is done, and we're both ruined, don't hide as I did. Don't try to weather the hurt alone. We'll get through this together. I promise. Seeing you again, well, you know my once-innocent childhood heart. Being around you reminds me of so much *good.*" Ivy's lip quivered. "I've missed you."

Nym burst into tears and wrapped her arms around Ivy. "You're not good for me, Ivy Balrel. Respectable elves don't cry."

"We're no longer respectable, remember?"

"You're horrid, you know?" Nym gripped Ivy tighter before stepping back and wiping her nose. "I came here on a mission. A refined, spy-kick-arse-mission. And you've turned me into this puddle of slush. No one likes *slush*. They want snow, or they want sun. Not this." Nym gestured to her snotty, definitely blotchy face.

Ivy took a deep breath. "And, another favor."

Nym rolled her eyes. "Why not?"

"If you could give Kolvar my apology ..."

"Look, Ivy, I only jest—I know there's nothing more than kinship between you and my brother."

"I don't think he'll be upset, honestly. I simply want him to know I appreciate his offer, and I am sorry I lied."

"I'll tell him. Meet you at the Centennial? It promises to be very *interesting.*"

Ivy grinned and handed over the glamour pendant of Emmyth. "Wouldn't miss it. How are you getting home?"

"I'll run north to the coast, then take a wyvern across the channel."

"But, you hate heights." Ivy bit her lip, realizing Nym would need to keep her identity a secret. Which meant not leveraging her family name. "Do you have enough coin?"

"I'll figure out something."

Ivy dug through her pockets, finding little of value. Her gaze fell on Sunshine. Brecc desired to help humans—so did Nym. "Sunshine will fetch a good price. Just be sure she has a doting owner. She's part unicorn, after all."

"She's what?" Nym's jaw dropped.

"Well, that might not be strictly true, but she *looks* like she has unicorn blood."

"Speaking of bloodlines," Nym paused, listening for anyone approaching, "Orion reports to the fae realm. The Grumpy Pixie Messenger Service is probably part dryad."

Ivy rolled her eyes.

"What aren't you telling me?" Nym asked.

"I don't want to betray his trust."

"So, you trust him?" Nym frowned

Ivy held up her hand, hearing someone approach—Orion, judging by the gait.

"Listen, Ivy," Nym pressed, "we don't know Orion, except that Ialant used him to report to the fae courts—something your father couldn't do on his own. Orion was his witness, his messenger. Now it's done." She gripped Ivy's shoulder. "He isn't one of us."

"Trust me, I know." Ivy forced a half-grin. "But I appreciate you worrying about me."

"I've seen the way he looks at you. And I understand why you're drawn to a tall, dark, mysterious stranger." Nym grinned. "With really great shoulders and a jawline an artist would covet. And his sullen attitude ..."

Ivy raised a brow.

Nym cleared her throat. "I'm just saying, when he threw his

cloak on me, it should've scattered the ash, making the cloud bigger. But it was almost like ... he made the ash disappear. I-I don't know. Furthermore, why would the elves and gnomes believe a random pile of ash was sitting on their shiny path and that I happened to blunder into it? Yet, they *did*."

"What are you saying?"

Nym lowered her voice. "I'm saying, he turned into Kolvar. Convenient, don't you think? And illusions are Winter fae magic. And Grumpy Messenger insists on returning before the equinox when the Summer Court convenes."

Ivy's shoulder's tightened as Orion's footfalls grew closer.

Nym spoke quickly. "It's possible that one of his parents made a bargain with the fae. In the process, Orion could've gained fae magic, perhaps a special amulet."

"Is that possible?" Ivy asked as Orion's form became visible between the trees.

Nym turned her back to the approaching captain, quickly whispering. "We've never been to the fae realm. Anything is possible. But the simplest answer is often correct."

Ivy pressed her lips together, signaling for Nym to quiet.

Instead, Nym stepped forward and hissed in Ivy's ear. "I'd wager that a dark debt binds Orion to the Winter fae."

20

FAE TRUTH IS A LIE

Orion escorted Zel inside Neidrei's city gates, then rushed back to find the elves one last time. His tenuous partnership with Ivy and Nym was over now that he'd finished investigating the influx of Seekers. He'd uncovered Ialant's secret work at his workshop and the Tree House a day earlier than expected, but the sooner Orion returned to the fae court, the better. The fae held the fate of the humans in their hands.

Still, he wanted to see Ivy one last time. The elves weren't what he'd expected—cold, heartless creatures who'd turned their back on Alysatraee. Though the elves had been wrong about many things, so had Orion. As Orion neared, Ivy was already watching him, her eyes red, and Nym was checking Sunshine's saddlebags.

"Until we meet again," Orion said to Nym, giving her an elven nod.

"Pray it not be too soon." Nym flashed a crooked grin and mounted Sunshine.

Orion looked from Sunshine to Ivy, surprised she'd let such a precious mount go.

"It seems fitting," Ivy said, seeming to read Orion's thoughts. "I started this path alone, and I'll end it the same way. At least this time, Seekers aren't tracking my every move."

Ivy stood in a wide, determined stance, but the veins of grief in her voice fissured through Orion like cracked ice.

How had he missed it? Though Nym was returning to a hostile home, she had her brother and her House. Ivy had no one. Part of him had been jealous that she wandered the forests alone, away from court, spying, and crowded cities. But with Nym leaving, Ivy's protective guard slipped, revealing her loneliness.

"If you're willing, Ivy," Orion spoke before considering his words, "the court would benefit from your testimony of the Gathering and The Tree House."

"Are you asking me to speak? In front of the Winter Court?" Ivy's voice squeaked.

Orion told himself he invited Ivy because she would be useful. Not because she intrigued him. Not because she challenged his beliefs. Not because he found himself wanting to protect her from the cruelties she faced alone.

Ivy stuttered, "I-I—"

"That's not a good idea," Nym interjected. "Ialant will be accused. As his daughter, won't his shadow fall on her?"

"I wasn't involved with the illicit creation of the trees," Ivy said.

"But you were involved with destroying them." Nym leaned forward in the saddle. "It'd be safer for you in the north than in the fae realm. For many reasons." Nym's attention slid to Orion.

Orion ignored Nym's biting remarks and focused on Ivy's furrowed brow and furtive glances. He'd wanted to help her, not cause further distress. "Of course, if you're used to traveling alone and—"

"It's not that," Ivy interjected. But she bit her lip and fell silent.

"I promise, you'll be under my protection until you return." A jolt shot through Orion as he spoke the specific, defined words. He straightened at the magical reminder; his word was his promise. So, Ivy really *would* be his responsibility. Yet, oddly, he didn't regret his statement.

Ivy cocked her head and searched Orion's face, her gaze so penetrating that Orion reminded himself that without a fresh seed in her body, she'd never unravel his glamour.

"You should go," Ivy said to Nym. "Either way, it's best you don't know my decision."

Nym stilled, hesitating, before finally giving a sharp nod. "I trust your judgment. Whatever you decide, be careful. Send for me if I can provide any aid."

At Nym's coaxing, the horse seemed to fly along the animal track through the trees. Ivy fiddled with her father's knife as she watched her friend disappear through the forest.

"It'll be nightfall soon, and the equinox is tomorrow night. Your horse is boarded to the south, and mine is galloping north. How do you expect to get to Winter Court before midnight tomorrow? How far to the nearest portal?"

Orion had boarded his stallion outside of Blackmore as he'd readily kept pace with Ivy when she was injured, and more importantly, he'd planned to return to the fae realm via magic.

He crouched and pressed his fingers into the earth. He reached with his senses, searching for the dryad overseeing the domain. The response pricked against his skin in warning. Orion yanked back his hand, shaking off the familiar sensation; some dryads had long stopped recognizing him, especially those more closely aligned with the Summer Court.

Everyone played favorites.

This dryad wouldn't deny Orion, but she might delay for a

day or two. Time he didn't have. Usually, Orion traveled with ease with or without dryad portals. But Ivy changed everything.

Ivy slid the knife away with finality, studying him. "It seems that my presence complicates your situation. You're the only witness they'll need, and as you said, I'm used to traveling alone. It's probably for the best."

Orion realized he was pacing and stopped. Ivy had a point, though he was loathe to leave her. Orion had been rash to invite her; he would either have to slow his pace dramatically or reveal more of himself than was wise. Prudence dictated Orion should report, and then return to the human realm to find Ivy. He could whisk her to the court after the autumn equinox when the Winter Court ruled again.

"Where did you plan to hide—" Orion's words caught in his throat, and dread filled his limbs. He carefully reviewed his wording. With a groan, he realized he'd promised to protect Ivy until she *returned* to the human realm.

Meaning she had to *leave*.

Orion couldn't leave Ivy unprotected unless he wanted to lose control of his magic, possibly wholly, along with his sanity.

Orion heard Ash before she darted down from the sky. Black smoke unfurled from her jaws. Ivy jumped back, waving her arms in a vain attempt to keep the haze away from her. The dragon lit onto Orion's shoulder, tucked in her wings, and nuzzled his cheek.

"Look, you two can go on your merry, smoke-filled way," Ivy said, backing away from the ash-cloud falling behind him. "I don't wish to be a burden. Again." She turned to leave, and Orion practically jumped to grab her arm.

"Don't go," he said.

Ivy raised a brow, her lips pursed, and Orion's neck heated. He dropped her arm as if she'd singed him. "I mean, I promised to bring you, and so I shall. Just, please, I need a moment to plan."

Not planning had gotten him backed into an Ivy-responsibility-bargain. Orion paced, weighing the importance of his secrets against the needs of the humans. In Neidrei, Ialant had risked his health and, ultimately, his life to help humankind. But Orion's stomach clenched at the idea of revealing his magic to *anyone*. He'd kept one particular secret hidden; divulging it was akin to walking himself into a noose.

He could either return before the equinox or keep his secret. Not both. He raked his hands through his hair and returned to Ivy.

"Do you have more of that root you gave Nym and Ash?" Orion hoped that since they'd trusted each other to stand watch for the last week, this wouldn't be too much of a stretch.

"Yes. Why?" Ivy folded her arms.

"We can travel by foot to a suitable portal and arrive after dawn. But, if you trust me, I can take us there much faster."

"I'd run, and you'd use the trees?" Ivy raised a brow.

"I'd use my magic." Orion didn't elaborate. "And if you're asleep, it'll be less complicated to bring you with me."

"You're asking me to trust you to take me to an unknown location while I'm unconscious?"

Orion shifted his stance, itching to go. "Yes. We can arrive in the fae realm within the hour or not until tomorrow. It's up to you."

Ivy huffed. She wasn't fully healed, and he didn't know how far she could realistically travel. Still, Orion half-expected her to insist on running. Instead, she glared at Ash and then rummaged through her satchel.

"You find the firewood," Ivy said, finding a small, ash-coated piece of root.

It didn't take long to warm the water in Ivy's cup. While

they waited for the root to soak, Ivy settled next to Orion. The setting sun reflected warm notes of amber in her hair, and he found himself leaning closer. Ivy gazed at him, and he noticed the flecks of gold in her brown eyes.

"Why are you bringing me with you to the fae realm?" she asked.

Orion's heart thumped. Honestly, he wasn't sure anymore, but now he was bound. Part of him was grateful he had an excuse to bring her, but at the same time, that longing alarmed him. He couldn't afford distraction. Not when he was so close to finally receiving an invitation to reside in the fae realm.

"If it's only out of pity ..." Ivy worried the edge of her sleeve. "Listen, I don't want to be a millstone. Truly. My family didn't sacrifice everything for me to impede you now."

"It was initially out of pity, but there are other practical reasons," Orion wasn't sure how to broach his *other reasons,* so he glazed past them. "By trusting me, I'll barely lose an hour."

"Well," Ivy paused as if debating her next words, "I'm glad for the company."

He gave her a halting nod, frozen between wanting to cup her cheek in his hand and flee from whatever was happening between them.

"Thank you," Ivy spoke slowly, followed by a soft smile. She broke eye contact, nervously reaching for her drink.

With a jolt, Orion realized her specific choice of words.

Thank you.

It was the promise of a future favor. Ivy tied herself to him, indebted.

Guilt snaked through Orion. Ivy entrusted her life to him, not only tonight, but she'd bound herself to him for an unknown future favor. Her words allowed Orion to decide the terms. She trusted him completely, and what was she getting in return? A visit to the most vicious court in existence.

Orion's tunic seemed to squeeze his neck. Sweat beaded his brow. He bolted from the fire, the cool air cutting through his open cloak. He wanted to smack his forehead against a tree for his misstep.

He'd simply wanted to help Ivy, but he'd foolishly made a promise without thinking. And Ivy didn't understand the significance of his wording—a bargain. He hadn't tried to deceive her, but he had. Ivy had entangled herself with someone she barely knew.

Nym was right—the court was no place for Ivy.

But it was too late. Orion's stomach churned. The only thing he could do now was prepare her. Did she know the basic rules of the fae? What did elves teach their children?

Panic started coursing through his veins. The shadows called, beckoning him to disappear. The weight of Ash on his shoulder helped tether his runaway fears. No, he could make this work. He'd bring Ivy to the fae realm, report, then bring her straight back.

Orion took a deep breath and turned to Ivy as she tossed the spent root and tucked her empty cup back into her satchel. Determined, he sat and coached her while the root settled in her system.

"I know about the fae courts." Ivy yawned. "Even the Winter fae. My parents told us the stories. Besides, my sister survived there for years. I'll only be there a day."

Or hours.

"The court is intimidating," Orion warned.

"I'm up for the task. I'll be convincing."

"I'll carry your bow and quiver," Orion suggested, seeing her eyes glaze.

Ivy slid off her weapons and handed them over to Orion, her hand brushing his. Her warmth pushed back the cool evening, a tension lightening between them.

The realization that Ivy was beginning to mean more to him than his report to the king concerned him. But he'd weathered worse challenges, hadn't he? Once Ivy was back in the human realm, their connection would wain—disappear.

Orion shrugged on the bow and secured the quiver. Ivy lingered close enough for him to feel the radiating heat. Her gaze moved to his lips, and her chin tilted up. Without thinking, he lifted a calloused hand to her cheek. She leaned into his touch. The tender warmth was foreign; Orion welcomed it. He nearly lost himself and ran his thumb across her lips, but he stopped.

Ivy was out of sorts, so he had to keep enough sense for the both of them. Besides, he couldn't torture himself nor continue to mislead Ivy. He needed to tell her the truth *before* they entered the fae realm.

"Ivy," his voice choked as he dropped his hand away.

She winced and rocked back. "You don't need to explain."

"This isn't the right ..." Orion struggled to find the right word, " ... time. There's too much to tell you."

"No fae bargains. No fae food. And most of all, don't trust the fae, even though they can't lie." Ivy's lids drooped.

Ivy swayed, and Orion steadied her. She leaned into him as her legs gave way. Despite her compact, muscular frame, Orion effortlessly swept her into his arms.

"I think I hear travelers. About two miles away." Ivy swallowed, her head bobbing. "Horseback. Headed this direction."

Orion should tell her the truth about his connection to the court, and he would. But she wasn't in any condition for that discussion. Besides, knowing wouldn't change her desire to testify. It would only alter how she felt about *him*.

Orion dreaded seeing the expression on her face when realization dawned. Would she be disgusted? Distant? No matter her reaction, he owed her the courtesy of discussing his affairs, privately. He gripped Ivy tighter, bracing himself for the fae realm.

Ivy's lids closed, and her head fell against his chest. Orion called the shadows, allowing them to swallow him, Ash, and Ivy. The dragon dug her talons into his cloak, instinctively responding to what was coming. Orion closed his eyes; if they were open, only pitch black would surround him. But with his eyes closed, his other senses sharpened. He pushed himself forward, Ivy tucked against him, as trees blurred past.

"What magic is this?" Ivy rasped, shivering. "I can't see."

Orion shifted Ivy in his arm and pulled his cloak around her against the coolness of the falling night.

"Don't worry," Orion said. "You're safe."

"I know." She wrapped her arms around him, burying her face in his neck.

Orion's heart and mind warred, tearing him inside as the darkness carried them from shadow to shadow until they finally crossed into an amenable dryad territory north of Blackmore castle. Setting Ivy on the ground nearby, Orion negotiated with the dryad before scooping the elf back up. He walked into the tree as easily as a human would walk from one room into the next. His body felt squeezed, but he mentally pushed back, keeping a protective cushion around Ivy and Ash.

Moments later, he stepped into blinding sunlight bouncing off sparkling snow. Ivy groaned, squeezing her eyes shut, and Orion shifted his cloak over her face and torso. Orion sensed someone approaching. A portal guard, most likely. If Ivy were alert, she'd warn him and likely urge him to hide.

But there was no more hiding. Instead, Orion dropped his glamour and moved to intercept the advancing guard, desiring an official escort to the Winter castle. The portal guard came into view, and his hand dropped away from his sword, though he eyed Ivy with suspicion.

"Orion Arya," the guard said, "The dryads reported that you would be returning. Welcome. King Eldrin awaits your report."

Ivy stirred, and Orion tensed. He needed to get her tucked away before she woke. It was only fair that he speak with her alone as soon as she recovered. The last thing he wanted was for her to see him in his true form before he could explain. Or even worse, before Princess Selleth discovered her.

21

HALF-DRUNK PRINCE

Ivy awoke to arguing voices. She blinked open her eyes, and the room came into focus. From her simple, soft bed, Ivy faced a rough-hewn, white stone wall with a single, dusty shelf. She shifted her attention, following the shaft of light from a narrow window to where it illuminated a modest, unlit fireplace mere steps away. Ivy wasn't sure what she expected in the fae realm, but it wasn't this plain, ordinary room.

Orion paced near the empty fireplace while a stranger lounged in the only chair, a leg over the sidearm and his hand swinging a goblet as he spoke. Ash fidgeted on the back of the stuffed chair as the loud conversation continued.

"Can you at least *act* sober for an hour?" Orion asked, running an exasperated hand through his dark locks.

Ivy propped herself up on her elbow, inspecting Orion. Something about him was different, and it wasn't just that his hair was loose.

"You can trust me," the male stranger replied dismissively as a bit of wine sloshed over the rim and splattered onto the white granite floor. "She'll be our little secret. You won't even owe me—the entertainment of this whole affair will be payment enough."

Orion huffed, about to reply, when he noticed Ivy was awake. In two bounds, he was at her side.

"How are you feeling?" he asked.

"I'm fine." Ivy glanced from Ash to the stranger, not surprised by the fae shape of his ears, which were still short compared to hers. Then again, fae ears were elegant compared to Orion's rounded human ear.

"Ivy Balrel, let me introduce you to Rime Zrin'arya, of the Winter Court," Orion said.

As Rime stood, the light reflected off black feathers. He had wings. With her attention on Orion, she'd assumed the extra mass was part of the furniture. The fae stretched and adjusted his magnificent black wings, which extended below his knees, before tucking them back. Even tucked, they were breathtaking. Each feather glistened like a raven's. No, the shape was akin to a swan. Her heart thumped, her mouth dry, reality setting in.

Though Rime was clearly inebriated, he stood tall and regal. She was in the fae realm, standing before a fae, probably an esteemed member of their court.

Ivy was too nervous to speak. Not because of his handsome features but because he was fae. Besides, Orion was the more attractive of the two, and she never had trouble speaking with him.

Rime was fae. Even in the human realm, they instilled fear. In their land, fae could exercise their full power. Who knew what malevolent magic he held: memory manipulation, glamouring, or other deceptive skills? The Winter employed the most subtle, cruel magic of all the fae.

Of course, Ivy knew she'd see his kind—in theory. In actuality, a single fae made her palms sweat, and her tongue stuck to the roof of her mouth. Suddenly, Orion's rules that he'd repeated ad nauseum seemed less frivolous.

And Ivy couldn't remember any of them, her mind suddenly a sieve.

"Rime, will you bring me fresh clothing?" Orion asked the fae.

"What is this? Commanding me about like a servant?" He winked at Ivy and sauntered past the mantle. As his wrist neared the wall, some stones became semi-translucent, revealing a circular stairwell beyond.

Ivy had never seen similar magic, but she kept her mouth from falling open like some human fool. Even so, at Rime's words, she realized what was different about Orion. His attitude had shifted. While he'd seemed self-assured before, here he was commanding and direct. Yet somehow more comfortable, too.

"Be quick, Orion." Rime's mirth waned. "The king is expecting you straightaway. A quarter-hour delay could cost you." He gave Orion a meaningful look before stepping through the translucent wall. Then, the wall solidified in a snap, concealing Rime as he ascended the stairs.

"Are you presenting the crimes of the Elven Council?" Ivy asked. "Should I join you?"

"I presume the king will delegate his adviser to interview you," Orion spoke quickly, "but, in the meantime, I want you to stay in this room."

"Where am I? Why—"

"You're in the castle. I brought you through a secret entrance. Rime can answer further questions, but I must tell you some things before I leave."

Ivy glanced at the only door, wondering where it led. "Wait, you're keeping *me* a secret?"

"For safety."

"Should I be worried?" Ivy sat ramrod straight on the edge of the bed, wondering if she'd made a mistake in coming. Orion was already leaving her alone with a fae and a drunken one at that.

"Rime will look out for you." Orion bit his lip, searching Ivy's face.

"You're making me nervous. What aren't you telling me?" She wished Orion would touch her arm or even simply lean closer. A reassurance that everything was fine.

"Rime is my half-brother."

Ivy blinked, unable to understand how that was possible. "Your mother is a dryad, and your father is human ..."

Orion's face pinched.

Ivy swallowed, realizing Orion had never said his father was human. She'd assumed it based on his appearance and prestigious captain position.

Ivy pushed off the bed, backing away from Orion, dreading the answer she needed. "Who are you?"

"I'm Orion Arya, captain of the night guard, son of a dryad, and a Winter fae."

"Oh, Mother of Magic." Ivy's legs buckled, but she caught herself on the edge of the bed. How had she been so blind? Now, she was stuck in the fae realm, unsure how to get home, dependent on a fae she hadn't fathomed was *fae*. The ground beneath her rolled, and she gripped the corner of the bed.

"Ivy, it's still me," Orion spoke softly.

The bed sheet's threads strained under her tightening grasp as she struggled to make sense of her situation. Orion hadn't lied to her. Not once. Yet, he had deceived her. He'd warned her to be careful; she just hadn't understood he meant to be cautious of *him*.

She forced herself to stand, pleased her voice was steady and cold. "You said your report was your priority. And my testimony supports your report. I understand. That's why I'm here—that's all you've wanted since the beginning."

Orion opened his mouth, his face reddening, then clamped it shut again. His lack of response to her accusation cut deeper than any blade. Her breathing quickened. Was there enough air in this room? She wanted to flee, but where would she go? As much as Orion infuriated her, he was still her best chance at survival.

More importantly, she wanted to testify. It was still the right decision. So, for the moment, she and Orion were aligned. But as soon as she told the truth of what she'd witnessed, she'd leave. She didn't know how, but she'd disappear.

"It's in my best interest to get you to the king's adviser, who will hear your statement and then take you home," Orion said. "I would ask one favor, though."

Ivy frowned, her body tightening. She owed him. She'd told him *"thank you,"* and he was collecting. He could ask her anything, and she was bound to honor the request.

"What favor?" Ivy's pulse quickened.

"That you keep all knowledge of how we traveled to this realm a secret."

"For how long? And from whom?" Ivy was terse, though the request seemed small. She repeated the wording in her mind, analyzing for any consequence of agreeing.

"For a thousand years or until I die. Whichever comes *later,*" Orion said. "And you must also keep the secret from every creature other than Ash." The dragon perked up at hearing her name.

"That's reasonable." Too reasonable to be trusted. "I'll consider it."

"The offer expires when Rime returns." Orion stepped toward her—close enough to feel the heat rolling off him.

They stared as if waiting for the other to break. Ivy pressed her lips together, though questions mixed with fury inside her, roaring to be spilt. But she refused to give Orion another piece of herself, even broken shards.

Contrary to Nym's suspicions, Orion wasn't bound by debt to the Winter fae. He *was* Winter fae. Ivy closed her eyes, blocking out Orion completely. She'd deluded herself into thinking they'd become more than allies of necessity. However, Orion had never actually stated any goal other than gathering information for his report. He'd never intended them to be friends, let alone anything more. From the moment they'd met in the Gathering, he'd worked toward this—his victorious return to his court.

Ivy's lids shot open, remembering something else from the Gathering. When she'd taken a seed during the battle, when her body was in a heightened state of healing and sensing, she recognized his glamour. Yet now, besides the hairstyle and the attitude, he was exactly the same.

Which meant he was still wearing a glamour.

Anger flashed through her, and she closed the distance. Her fingers grazed his neck and chest, searching for a necklace. An amulet. She hated that her fingertips seemed to spark with every touch. Not finding any talismans, she cursed under her breath.

"You never had an amulet for Kolvar's image." She shook her head. "Winter fae have the power of illusion. You *create* amulets." For all she knew, Orion created her father's amulet of Emmyth.

"I never reveal myself in the human realm."

"It must be exhausting to hold a form for years on end." Ivy couldn't keep the bitterness from her voice. "Yet even now, you still keep yourself hidden in your own realm. I can only assume it's because you wanted to deceive me for as long as possible."

"I didn't want to frighten you."

"Why? Because you wanted me to be coherent in case I was called to court? Or because you never intended to tell me the truth?" It was impossible to know Orion's intentions; fae could talk in circles without revealing a thing.

"Rime won't be much longer. Make your decision because time is running out." Orion crossed his arms across his chest.

"Show yourself," Ivy demanded.

"Stop being so stubborn. I ask a simple boon."

"Show me."

A sorrow flashed across his face an instant before massive dark grey wings appeared at his back. His features shifted slightly—his eyes brighter, his face more chiseled. Did he get a bit taller? Ivy gasped. She hoped he assumed she was horrified, not impressed.

Behind Orion, the wall shimmered.

"I'll take it. I'll take your deal." Ivy sputtered the words as the wall became transparent.

"Good. Our deal is sealed," Orion gave her an elven nod of approval. Part of her melted.

Manipulative goat.

Rime stepped through the wall and handed Orion a stack of clothes. Standing next to each other, the resemblance was uncanny. Orion's skin was tanned, his cheekbones more pronounced, and his patterned wings were lighter, but the familial resemblance was unmistakable.

"Hurry to my chambers. Change," Rime said. "The king won't wait. And I hear our adoring sister is with him and looking forward to seeing you."

Orion raised a brow.

"She adores the crown. Not us. Was that not implied?" Rime grinned as he shoved Orion toward the stairwell. "And she looks forward to seeing you get pummeled with difficult questions."

"Wait, why would your sister be with the king?" Ivy asked.

Rime looked at Orion. "You haven't told her? And you brought her here? You seriously have mush for brains."

"Tie your tongue, Rime," Orion said. "It's not for you to discuss."

"Told me what?" Ivy's heart thumped, realizing that Orion had *more* secrets.

"Selleth Zrin'arya is likely to win the throne," Rime said to Ivy, a grin spreading. "And she's our sister."

Ivy stepped back, confusion and fear mingling with growing fury. She asked another question, though she already suspected the answer. "And why is she likely to win the throne?"

Orion elbowed Rime in the stomach, and his brother doubled over.

Still, Rime gasped an answer. "Besides her winning personality? Because she's been taught every ruthless trick by our father, Eldrin Cor'arya, the Winter King."

22

Have a Baby, Gain a Crown

Prince Rime leaned against the wall as the elf paced in the tiny room, cursing Orion under her breath. Her behavior intrigued Rime; all fair folk were taught to respect the fae as children. And lore taught them to tremble before the Winter Court.

As the son of the fearsome Winter King, Rime was accustomed to others' trepidation; with a word to his father, one could disappear without a trace. But this elf was fuming instead of fawning over him. Nor cowering. It was obscene. And her frantic pace made him dizzy.

"Let's go, elf," Rime said. "I'm thirsty, and you're ... smitten."

"I'm anything but *smitten*." She spun, her hands fisted.

Rime stifled a grin, oddly entertained by her display. Elves were usually little more than wet rags, but this elf had some vinegar. That, or she *had* fallen for Orion. Perhaps both.

"Follow me. I have a warm fire in my rooms." He moved to the wall and waved for the elf to follow. She folded her arms and stared.

Moons, she was as stubborn as a centaur. Well, prideful creatures were all the more fun to goad.

"Your feelings are only natural," Rime baited her. "A shallow attraction, of course, but predictable. Orion is half-fae, after all. He can't help who he is. Half the Winter Court is obsessed with him, so don't be embarrassed."

The elf said nothing, but the crease between her brows deepened.

"If our father extends a place for him in the court," Rime pressed the barb deeper, wanting a reaction, "every noble family will petition the king to wed their daughter to Orion. Apparently, most families find him more suitable than I am. Can you believe that nonsense?"

"The precious, courtly fae daughters can have Orion," she fumed. "I'd rather be bitten by a venomous snake."

"Ah, true love, then. I wish I had that."

She turned her back to Rime, muttering, "You are deranged."

"I heard that. And I know. But at least I *know*."

"I'm not sure how that's of benefit."

Rime mulled, his sluggish mind turning. If Orion reciprocated this elf's feelings, even to the slightest degree, his brother would be vulnerable. His sister would leverage this elf in an instant. But as Orion was a rare ally, Rime intended to figure out her threat risk.

Rime, realizing the elf was staring perplexedly at him, relaxed his expression.

"I don't understand you," the elf said. "Aren't you a prince? Shouldn't you have ... standards for yourself? Your family rules *all* the fair folk for half of our lives. You are justice. You represent Alysatraee. Yet, you act like a child."

Indignation should've burned at her words, but he'd given up caring about the law long ago. What choice did he have?

"You look cold," Rime said, though he couldn't care less if

her toes were frozen and falling off. "There's a warm fire in my rooms."

He dragged himself to the circular stairs out of the nursemaid's quarters. The room had been vacated two decades earlier. Even if he'd wanted to cry on his nursemaid's shoulder, which he didn't, she wouldn't remember him. His father had seen to that.

Rime's fingers itched to hold a goblet. He glanced back long enough to see the elf frowning, but she followed, thank Alysatraee. Yet her hand drifted to the knife at her hip.

"Lesson number one is free," Rime said as he climbed the steps and entered his receiving room. "Don't be a threat. Don't act like you're *thinking* about becoming a threat. Because your eyeballs will be plucked out by gargoyles and left out for pixies to play with before your body freezes on the mountainside."

The elf grimaced, giving him a wide berth as she moved to the balcony.

Rime continued, "This is one lesson Orion thinks he knows, but he doesn't. Not quite."

The elf ignored him. Stubborn centaur-elfsitting was less amusing than he'd envisioned. Not for long. He grinned as he grabbed a fresh goblet and prepared to pour her a drink.

Then Rime paused, the decanter hovering over the goblet's rim. He pictured Orion's inevitable fury when he discovered his little brother had bespelled the guest before she reported on dreary human realm gossip. Though, if Selleth were here, she would've enslaved the elf six different ways by now.

Rime poured the drink.

He began to hand her the goblet, then reconsidered. As much fun as watching the elf clean the fireplace with pocket lint might be, the entertainment wouldn't be worth Orion's ire.

"Best to stand back from the ledge, elf," Rime begrudgingly warned as he kept the Brandywine-filled goblet for himself.

"Ivy. Call me Ivy," she said as she stepped back, her body stiff.

Rime meandered to her side, admiring the expanse of ice and barren trees surrounded by looming, jagged mountains. Clouds hung, low and heavy, hiding the mountaintops. But they wouldn't be for long. When summer ruled, the clouds turned to wisps, and the sun dared shine. Even so, the highest reaches were never without their blanket of snow, no matter who ruled the realm.

"It's so ..." Ivy's words trailed off.

"Magnificent? Awe-inspiring? Cold?"

"Mournful."

Rime sipped his drink, unhurried. "I suppose the air itself dreads the equinox. But I don't mind it. Everything has its place. Life and death. Blossom, decomposition, and rebirth."

Rime rarely waxed philosophical and never publicly. But this ruffian wouldn't be around long enough to oust him for thinking past wine or his next tryst.

"Lights are moving below." She pointed to the trees.

Rime squinted, seeing nothing, then remembered her superior elven sight. "Pixies, I imagine."

"I've never seen one before."

"How fortunate."

None of the few elves Rime had ever met dared arrive with a bow and arrows or wearing hunting clothing. Orcs carried weapons. Elves wore billowing, pale tunics with delicate, woven crowns. Where did Orion pick up this unrefined creature?

Ivy shivered, moving back into the room, past the wall of abandoned books and his neglected golden harp.

"You promised a warm fire," Ivy complained. "These embers are on their last breath."

"Warmth is relative."

"Even Ash is cold," the elf said.

"Who is what?"

"The dragon." Ivy pointed to the velvet chair across from the fireplace. Curled up in the corner sat the blue-scaled creature. The Lenonius Draco lifted her head, seemingly scowling in disapproval.

"What a useless companion dragon," Rime teased, the elf proving to be passable entertainment. "I'll make you a bargain. If you can get the fireless dragon to spark a flame, I'll personally bring in more firewood."

The elf huffed, marching toward the double doors leading to the royal wing. "You're impossible."

"Good luck finding your way out of the castle. Oh, and I hope you survive long enough to find a dryad willing to portal you home."

"I'm not running away. I'm simply done with *you.* I'll ask a human servant to take me to the king's adviser."

This elf could definitely *fit in with stuffy centaurs.*

"Sounds like you have a plan. Perhaps not a good one, but a plan nonetheless. Hopefully, a Winter fae won't find you. One quick nefarious spell and," Rime snapped his fingers, "you'll be licking their boots for the rest of your life. And as you might remember, fae are pouring into the castle because of the coming equinox festival. The chances of you flitting by unnoticed are, well, infinitesimal."

She gripped the door latch but paused. Good.

Elves weren't Winter's subjects, so she wasn't compelled to listen to Prince Rime's demands. Nor was she bespelled to serve him, nor was she a prisoner. However, Rime had promised Orion to keep her in his sights.

"I'll make it worth your while," Rime said. "I'll answer three questions. It'll be fun."

For me.

The elf thrummed her fingers on the latch before spinning. "I choose the questions?"

"Of course."

"Agreed."

Good. Because I'd have to chase after you. Mortifying.

The stubborn-centaur spun and stormed back to the fireplace, sorting through the paltry kindling supply. "I have my first question." Ivy shoved bits of wood into the fireplace. "Tell me about Orion."

Rime rubbed his temples. This bargain was too easy, and he needed a challenge. "Lesson number two, elf. Be specific," he taught. "I could tell you Orion's favorite color, which would fulfill the requirement."

The elf stopped stoking the fire and inspected Rime's expression before continuing. "Tell me about Orion and who he is to the court. I don't need to know his secrets," she rushed to amend. "Just the general knowledge amongst the court."

Oh, moons above, fae would eat her alive. No wonder Orion had hidden her and bargained for her strict safety.

"I'll answer your first question as I *think* you intended. Consider it my welcome gift to you." Frankly, it was more a gift to himself. A satisfying answer for her meant she'd be more likely to answer him, too.

Ivy's kindling flared to life, and Rime suppressed a groan. With spring coming, just *thinking* about a stuffy fire made him sweat. Instead of whining, he unraveled his older brother's past.

"After the last battle with humans, fair folk retreated into this realm. The fae wanted spies in the human realm, messengers that could easily slip from one realm to another. Someone with dryad blood. But they also needed someone they could trust—a fae. So, my grandfather, the former Winter King, struck a deal with the dryads. Ultimately, they selected Prince Eldrin to mate with a powerful dryad."

"Your father." Ivy pressed her fingers to her lips.

"Yes. And the bargain helped Prince Eldrin secure the Winter crown from his sickly father, gravely injured in the war, without waiting for the Winter Crown Trials. Prince Eldrin and the dryad conceived Orion, born of strategic need."

Rime watched the elf grip the branch in her hand tighter, her mouth agape. He didn't need to share that bit of gossip, but the politics of the crown had always irked him. And Ivy's reaction made him feel like he wasn't insane for thinking court politics were complete rubbish.

"The fair folk determined Orion's destiny before he was born," Ivy whispered.

"Whether male or female, the child would be raised to spy on behalf of the fair folk. I'm told the dryads were relieved the babe was male."

Ivy grimaced

"They're quite pitiless and cruel toward non-females," Rime pressed.

"As an elven peacekeeper, it's not for me to condemn, just to understand the fair folk."

Stubborn *and* self-righteous—Ivy was part-centaur, at least.

"What are you grinning at?" Ivy asked.

"Nothing. I'm grinning at *nothing.*" Rime's smile widened at his wordplay. Ivy shoved two branches into the fire, and they immediately burst into flames, highlighting the lines of irritation across her face. He sobered. "Once of age, Orion served in the human realm, sending messages to court."

"You mentioned the king might invite Orion into the court," Ivy said. "What does that mean? Could that happen soon?"

Rime sighed. Had this elf learned nothing? "Are you asking your second and third questions?"

"No ... well, my second question. Do you think Orion will stay in the fae realm?"

"First, answer me this," Rime said. "Are you related to Ialant Balrel?"

Ivy folded her arms. "That wasn't part of the bargain."

"I said I'd answer your questions but didn't say when. I'll answer them after you answer my questions." He didn't gloat, not wanting to lose his momentum.

"Ialant Balrel is my father." Ivy spat, her eyes tracking the fire as she seemed to debate her next question. "I can only assume you know him."

"You're learning," Rime said. "Good. You posed your question as a statement. Still, it's not clever enough to get an answer."

Ivy's nostrils flared. "Did you ever meet my father?"

Did? "Did" was past tense. Was Ialant dead? Rime sat his goblet on the table, wine splattering his sleeve.

"Did you know him?" Ivy's tone turned serious.

"I decline to answer that question." Ialant pictured the elder elf, his purposeful stride as if what he had to say actually mattered. Fool. And now he was dead. "Pick another one."

"You can't change the rules. You must answer my question."

"I agreed to answer three questions. I didn't guarantee which ones."

Ivy let out a yelp of frustration and threw a log into the growing flames.

Rime stepped back toward the balcony, wracking his memory to recall Orion's message from Carrus—the partial report sent via dryad to the king. Orion hadn't mentioned the stubborn-centaur nor her father. But logically, elves were involved. And Orion was too clever not to have known it then. Why had Orion kept quiet about *her*?

Surely his brother wouldn't risk his father's ire over this centaur-elf. Would he?

Rime needed to clear his head. He itched to call for a servant to bring lunch, but where to hide Ivy? Rime wasn't in the mood to explain her presence, and she didn't seem the type to obey.

"Did my father ever come to the Winter Court?" Ivy shot.

"It would be strange for an elf to come to the fae court," Rime hedged. Truthfully, Ialant had approached the king months ago. Unfortunately, Rime's lack of response told her plenty, though not specifics.

The double doors began to open. A flash of servant's clothing, and Rime reacted.

"Get out!" he threw his goblet, and it clanged against the door, splattering wine across the room. The dragon shot upward, and black ash exploded.

"Mother moons!" Rime screamed. "Leave me, woman!"

The servant squealed and slammed the doors. Those humans had fog for brains. Best case scenario, she was bespelled and would barely remember Ivy or the dragon.

"What is wrong with that dragon?" Rime fumed over the bits of dust. He'd be bothered by servants in his rooms for a *week* while they cleaned. He'd probably need to call in an actual fae servant for this level of toxic removal.

"Ask Orion. She's *his* companion." Ivy smirked as she brushed ash from her shoulders.

Disgusting. I doubt it. "Fine, keep your little secrets."

"Believe what you want." Ivy folded her arms and thrummed her fingers. "What do you know of the Elven Council?"

"Only what I learned from my tutors. A council of five members represents three elven houses. Long ago, they traveled from city to city as peacekeepers and mediators. Now elf houses are isolated from each other and the humans. Elves were supposed to help the humans, but instead, they hid."

Ivy shook her head. "Strange, you know so little, yet so much."

"Your kind keeps the peace between fair folk, and mine judge them." Rime faced her but didn't approach the hungry flames. "Alysatraee gave us all responsibilities."

Ivy shoved the largest log into the maw, and the flames threatened to overflow across the hearth.

"It's my turn to ask a question." He licked his lips, eager for the answer. He couldn't pass up the opportunity to gather information from outside the castle and his sister's network. "Do you know of fair warriors living in the human realm? Any skilled fighters. Someone unattached to court politics."

Ivy's forehead scrunched in concentration. Finally, she stood, her expression turning as cold and hard as the mountain outside the window.

"I'll answer your question on one condition." She stepped toward him.

A bubble of excitement dared to form inside Rime's gut. Finally, a bargain. A game worth playing.

"If I answer you," Ivy continued, "you'll answer my next question fully and without hesitation. *Any* question I ask."

23
CRUEL WINTER KING

Orion's footsteps echoed as he stormed down the corridors, repeatedly fisting and relaxing his hands. His well-practiced, hardened shell already swallowed the flicker of vulnerability he'd allowed himself.

After learning Orion's identity, Ivy's expression had shattered as porcelain slammed against the rocks. He'd expected her reaction, yet her disappointment and revulsion cut like a dull blade between his ribs.

And Orion couldn't attempt to explain or console her. Not with Rime listening. The prince's loose tongue was a risk—a calculated risk Orion had taken. Even so, exposing his feelings to any fae would be foolish, even to his most trusted brother.

Away from Ivy, the chill of the castle brought him back to his senses. Begging Ivy to understand why he'd kept his father's identity concealed would be a mistake. Even after she had time to process what she'd learned, one unavoidable snare demanded they treat each other with cool regard.

The vicious Winter Court.

Though Ivy was disgusted with Orion, he couldn't allow her

to be hurt. If Ivy garnered attention from the fae, she'd become a target. A game.

After all, he'd promised to keep her safe. He had an oath to fulfill. It had nothing to do with how he felt about her. She was simply a witness he had escorted to the court.

Orion fisted his hands again, questioning himself. He'd allowed himself the occasional shallow relationship in the past. Never long-term. Never serious. And yet, Ivy had gotten past his defenses, despite how he'd felt about elves.

When he'd confessed, and she'd winced, he'd wanted to snap back a sharp retort—that Ivy was *only* necessary to verify his report. But he couldn't get a syllable out of his throat. She'd become far more. Unable to lie, he'd refused to speak the truth. So he said nothing at all. Why bother trying? She'd rejected him.

Everyone in the human realm did. Orion's best chance of acceptance was in the fae realm, with his father's kind.

Seeing Orion near, the guards heaved open the massive, carved doors to the Winter King's vaulted throne room. Orion gritted his teeth as he crossed the threshold. Of course, instead of greeting his son in a private receiving chamber, everything had to be a grand show of power. Orion strode across the patterned, blue floor slabs inlaid with gold and passed the elegant fountain, the water frozen in place. A water droplet fell, echoing in the cavernous room, signaling Winter Court's rule melting away.

The king would not be in a pleasant mood.

Overhead, beams of sunlight cut through the wavy glass, and Orion's thoughts turned back to Ivy. How long would she haunt him? The sooner they separated, the better.

He'd given her an easy opportunity to repay the favor she'd granted him. Easy, but *essential.* Either her silence would protect him, or one wrong word would doom him. Anything Ivy sensed, felt, or saw as they traveled to the portal could get Orion killed. And his sister would be the first in line to stab him in the back. No, she wouldn't hide her intention. She wasn't of the Summer Court. No, Selleth would come straight for his throat.

He'd acted like a youngling, blindly trusting Ivy to keep his secrets—based on what? Friendship? Something more? After seeing how quickly she'd pushed him away, he was grateful for her binding oath as a secondary method to secure the knowledge he'd kept hidden all his life.

A magical fae skill no one knew he possessed.

Not even the king.

His ability to control shadows was a rarity even among the Winter fae. And while Orion wasn't a prince and never would be, anyone who showed magical competence tended to disappear. Or, in the case of one unfortunate, charismatic cousin, she mysteriously lost *all* her memories. Selleth interpreted many things as threats, and she eliminated them.

Along the balcony of the second floor, two pairs of guards stood, staring down at him with grizzled expressions. Orion climbed the wide staircase leading to the dais. To either side, carved pillars of the kings and queens of the last age held up the towering ceiling, reminding them all of whose shoulders they stood on. The railings were coated in ice, and a dusting of snow appeared on the upper steps. Passing the guards, he strode to the throne.

On the king's left stood his oily adviser, Rithmat, with mousy hair, a narrow face, and beady eyes. Princess Selleth stood on the king's right, her skin so pale it appeared blue. Her gossamer wings twitched and settled behind her back. Few fair folk knew Selleth's hair color because the strands were covered in layers of ice, but Orion knew it was black, like their father's.

She wore a crown made of ice so finely chiseled it mimicked stacked diamonds.

Bending a knee, Orion knelt to the Winter King. With every report over the last decade, Orion had hoped to warrant an invitation from his father to return to the fair realm permanently. Orion despised hope because a bit of it insisted on blooming in his chest. Every time.

His new report proved the elves had broken the peace with the humans. No other creature had uncovered the Elven Council's devious plot. If the news impressed the king, would this be the day Eldrin welcomed his son home?

"Rise, Orion," the king said, his voice a deep rumble.

His father didn't look much older than his children, with obsidian hair, broad shoulders, and a sharp tongue that would cast judgment a thousand times faster than a kind word. He wore a simple, thick gold crown and held a scepter with a glowing blue crystal in his meaty hand. The backless throne, allowing for the king's massive black wings, sat against a backdrop of long, silver spikes that glistened like ice. On the curved wall further behind, carved words of the ancient law stretched to the ceiling. Whispers spoke of age-old judgments of when bygone kings had levied justice by impaling those who broke Alysatraee's law, throwing them on the lance-like silver.

"Report," the king's adviser, Rithmat, demanded from Orion. "The king received a vague message via the dryad in Carrus, but that was months ago."

Yet only four days here.

Orion bit back the terse reminder. Rithmat was baiting him; the adviser was in Selleth's pocket, and arguing would only hurt Orion's goals.

"I heard alarming rumors from Ialant Balrel, the House of Seeds Councilor." Orion watched his father for a reaction, but there was none. However, Selleth shifted.

That was unexpected. Selleth knew of Ialant, at least by reputation; her habit of disguising an errant wing twitch gave her away.

Orion continued, explaining how he'd arrived at the Gathering just as Seekers attacked. "Before he died, Ialant gave me the location of his laboratory in Neidrei. I found it along with two elves, and we uncovered—"

"You traveled with elves?" Selleth interrupted. "This is a change. After reporting on their lackadaisical attitudes for decades, you deigned to associate with them?"

"Some do misappropriate seeds," Orion turned to the king, "which I'm prepared to discuss."

"Go on," the king waved a hand, signaling for Orion to continue.

Orion explained what they found in Ialant's laboratory, The Tree House, and how the trio worked to destroy the orchard. Orion kept the discovery of the dryad to himself; Eldrin and Selleth would perceive his refusal to poison her as weakness.

"Only one tree remains, but it is mature and will be fruitful in the spring. The elves plan to distribute the seeds to human nobles, military captains, well-connected merchants, and any other key human whose corruption will crumble and weaken our old enemy's society."

"Interesting development." King Eldrin considered Orion for a long moment. "If you're correct, the Council's move will create chaos in the human realm."

"Do you think this could restart the war?" Rithmat asked Orion.

"Yes," Orion said. "This added strain could fissure the peace between realms."

"This is a substantial claim to lay against the Elven Council," Rithmat said, lifting his chin. "They are the peacekeepers."

"Their actions directly violate their own rules and the Mother's laws," Orion said.

"That is for the Winter King to judge." Selleth narrowed her eyes. "Furthermore, the only proof is your word."

"Orion's word has always been true," Eldrin said, his expression still like stone. "And accurate."

"I brought Ialant Balrel's daughter to corroborate my findings," Orion said, now even more committed to keeping Ivy out of sight until he could arrange for her to privately meet with Rithmat. Selleth would want a chance to interrogate her, which Orion wouldn't allow. "This is why I requested a closed meeting. The findings are salacious, and I thought it best to keep them quiet."

The king rubbed his hand against his bearded chin. This was usually when he dismissed Orion to return to his post in the human realm. Orion held his breath, waiting.

"My son," the king said as he rested his forearms on the icy throne. Eldrin ran his thumb down the gold scepter staff, pausing. "You have toiled in the human realm for over seventy years."

Almost ninety.

The king continued, "Your work is exemplary. Essential. However, the time has come for you to come home. You will return to the human realm long enough to insert another fae in the Unarian guard. Then you will have new duties here. You've earned your place in the court."

The king slammed his scepter against the arm of the chair, the sound humming in Orion's chest. He could hardly believe the invitation.

"W-welcome home," Rithmat sounded as stunned as Selleth looked. Her gaze slid to the king's profile, and her lips twisted as if she'd eaten an unripe berry.

"It is my honor to take my place in the Winter Court." Orion bowed deeply to the king before giving his sister a polite bow and ignoring Rithmat completely.

"I'll request his rooms be properly appointed," Rithmat said.

"In the royal wing," the king added.

Rithmat scowled but hastily wiped it away. "Yes, of course."

Selleth raised a brow and nodded. "Welcome, brother. I look forward to your return."

Orion didn't trust himself to speak, knowing that the only thing Selleth looked forward to was building power. Living in the human realm had afforded him the luxury of not taking sides between his siblings or anyone else. Now Orion needed a new strategy.

Orion nearly turned to leave, wanting to disappear while in the king's good graces, when he remembered he still had one duty. "Shall I send a report to the orcs through the portal, letting them know you'll be dispatching them? If I send a report now, they'll have a week to prepare before your official command tomorrow."

The king leaned back. "This close to the reign of the Summer Court, it would be unwise to send such a weighty request. It's not in our interest to fluster the Summer Queen. When her representative arrives, we shall give them a report with my recommendation but leave it in Summer's capable hands."

Orion kept his face plain, though inside, he reeled. It wasn't like the king to step away from a strategic, impactful decision, no matter the hour, especially when it concerned Alysatraee's law.

"I am here to serve you," Orion simply said. "Shall I escort Ivy Balrel to Rithmat to give testimony? I can bring her straight away." The sooner Ivy gave her statement, the sooner he could take her home.

"I trust your report," the king said. "She can be a second witness to the Summer Representative tomorrow night at the equinox celebration."

Tomorrow?

"Of course," Orion said, fighting to school his expression. Not only did that delay his plans, but it was oddly uncharacteristic of the king. He never allowed sharing sensitive information with other courts without at least verifying it first.

"I will see you at the celebration tomorrow night," Selleth said to Orion.

Orion had no intention of leaving Ivy's side until she was gone, which wouldn't be until after the equinox, the most troublesome night of the year.

"How exciting," Selleth continued, her voice flat. "The equinox ball will be the first event where you'll be officially introduced as a member of the court."

Orion paused, torn between wanting to keep Ivy in sight and the glaring absence at his first official announcement. He'd longed for this day. His sister couldn't understand precisely how much the words would mean.

But he couldn't leave Ivy alone. Besides, there would be future functions. As a boy, his father had trained him in dances, etiquette, and all formal expectations. Over the years, he'd have other introductions.

"And, you should bring the elf, the Council member's daughter," Selleth said casually.

Orion stilled. Selleth did nothing casually.

"An auspicious occasion. Quite an honor for an elf," Rithmat added, not bothering to hide his malicious tone.

Orion fabricated an excuse. "I hardly think an elf is appropriate company."

"Come now," Selleth grinned, sending a jolt of warning

down Orion's back. "The moment the king promises a court appointment, you become too sophisticated for other fair folk?"

Orion avoided the king's gaze, knowing his father's high value of the law meant impartial judgment of all fair folk. His father would handily bar him from the Winter Court for blatant prejudice. And Selleth knew it.

"While the equinox celebration welcomes all fair folk," Orion kept his voice steady, "generally only the fae celebrate in the castle ballroom. As we must protect our witnesses, putting her in such a vulnerable position is unwise. Her word impacts the safety of her kind and the entire fae realm."

Orion avoided her name, hoping to hide his personal attachment. But simultaneously, it could reinforce Selleth's claim that Orion was too highbrow. Selleth's lip twitched, and Orion grounded his teeth, waiting for the king to speak—his final command.

The king took his time studying Orion. "Bring the elf," the king finally said. "It's expedient to have her on hand when the Summer Representative arrives. Besides, you can protect her well enough."

The king, Selleth, and Rithmat paused, the quiet weight of their expectations falling in judgment on Orion's shoulders. *Always agree with the king.*

The last thing Orion wanted was to dangle Ivy before the court. And he *really* didn't want to give Selleth access to her. With Orion's return, Selleth would stop at nothing to exploit Ivy to manipulate him.

"I see the benefits of bringing the elf," Orion carefully selected his words. "However, I doubt she'll agree to a fae event."

She definitely won't. She would resist entering the vortex of a fae equinox celebration, *especially* after he'd broken her trust.

The king gripped his scepter tighter, his barrel chest slowly expanding as he sucked in a breath.

"The king demands it." Rithmat leaned forward, a glint in his eye. "Persuade her."

Below, footsteps scuttled up the steps. Orion pivoted to see a human servant hurrying toward the dais.

With a pointed glare and a wave of his hand, the king dismissed Orion, and he was grateful to escape.

"A visitor from the human realm," the servant said.

Orion slowed, but before the servant spoke again, the king dismissed Selleth and Rithmat. Orion frowned, hurrying before his sister caught up; he'd had enough of her games for one day.

Furthermore, now that Ivy was required to attend the spring equinox ball, he needed to prepare her. Not just with a dress but with rules, warnings, and anything else that would help armor her for the event. Only after they'd survived that gauntlet and she'd given her report could he portal her back to the human realm.

He only wished he didn't yearn to hold her again on the return trip.

24
FAE BARGAIN

Ivy schooled her expression, ready to dig in her heels if Rime refused her offer. He looked almost impressed before he began emanating a frightening intensity.

"If you promise honesty but give a lie," Rime began, "there will be consequences. You're entering into a fae bargain. And if you attempt to wriggle out of it, your connection to your magic will be altered. Perhaps lost completely. Alysatraee's immutable law is as sharp as it is just."

Underneath his act of nonchalance, the prince was far less lazy kitten than a clever fox. Ivy steeled herself, her parents' dire fae warnings blaring. Another feeling flashed inside her—concern for Orion. Did he know the ferocity that simmered inside his brother? Was he in danger?

No, Orion was fae and could take care of himself.

And so could Ivy. She hadn't come this far to be cowed.

"If you're afraid," Ivy said, "I'll sweeten the bargain by answering your two questions before you answer mine."

"Fine." A ghost of a grin played on Rime's lips. "I agree to your terms."

Though not the dullard she'd first imagined, Rime didn't

seem murderous. However, would he cast her into the dungeon if he didn't want to answer her question? Yes.

A fae would bury their bargain rather than break it. Rime had made no threat, but he was a prince of the infamous Winter Court. None of them would think twice about making their problem "disappear." Orion wouldn't even know she was held captive.

If he even cared.

Ivy folded her arms, hiding her trembling hands. She'd been a fool, blinded by Orion's fae charm. After a drop of companionship from Brecc, she'd craved more connection. And Orion's constancy, though gruff, had seemed trustworthy. Ivy hadn't logically questioned his motives. She'd followed her instincts.

No, she'd followed her desires. Orion became a thread of hope in an ocean of running, and fear, and loneliness. When Orion looked at her, her heart sang. And when he touched her ...

Ivy's heart swelled.

And she hated that she reacted just thinking about Orion. Curse the fae and their beguiling tricks. She'd been so focused on *him* that she'd ignored the things he didn't say.

Her misstep was a harsh reminder that she could only rely on herself. Part of her wanted to shrivel up and disappear. The other part of her, the one screaming in her head, told her to run. But to escape this place, she needed to know where to flee.

Even so, trepidation trickled down her spine as she stepped into something her family and even Orion had warned her not to do; her first fae bargain.

"The deal is struck, then." The words rang in her head. "To answer your first question, you want to know of warriors with fair blood in the human realm." She forced herself to look at him, her chin up. "You're looking for someone like me."

"Not quite. I'd prefer someone without pure elven blood."

Ivy raised a brow at his admission. Part-elves couldn't

tolerate seeds but *could* reside in the fae realm. Did Rime need a protector in the Winter Court?

Though she hated to admit it, she had few connections since she'd separated from her family, and furthermore, elves rarely mated outside their kind. And outside her kind, she only knew Zel.

"Ash is the most fearsome, non-elven magical creature I've met in the human realm. She is perfect for distractions and inflicting coughing fits."

Rime dropped his gaze and poured himself more wine. Instead of drinking, he pursed his lips and tapped on the rim, staring blankly out the window. "My next question, then. What happened between you and Orion?"

Ivy balked, her mouth dry. "N-nothing—"

Her throat constricted—a magical warning. Her word wasn't strictly true. Startled by the power of the bargain, Ivy started with the facts of when she "met" Orion in Unaria. She continued through each event and wasn't interrupted up until the Gathering.

"Wait," Rime said. "How many Seekers attacked the Gathering? Hundreds? How would so many converge on your location?"

Ivy cocked her head at the question. They *wouldn't* all show up in one location by unlucky accident. The Seekers had help.

She squeezed her eyes shut, realizing with growing horror that something could lure them like a wolf to a wounded animal—the azurite mixture. The same mixture that was inked on the back of her family drawing. Likely, someone from the House of Minerals pounded the stone to dust and combined it with ground seeds to draw the Seekers.

"You know," Rime said. "Don't you."

"I only suspect. And it has nothing to do with Orion." Ivy's mind raced, thinking of places elves could have placed the "ink"; the mixture would've been nearly invisible on tree trunks or the mud. Once an elf knew the Gathering location, they could have tainted the forest within a day.

But who? Ivy swallowed, remembering that two of the five council members had been at the same Gathering. Three, actually, counting her father. With a three Gatherings happening simultaneously, it was illogical that more than half the Council was at the same location.

Unless they'd known. Ivy's stomach roiled, the truth evident; the councilors had come to witness the spectacle. How many elves *had* sealed the Council's sordid plot for revenge with their blood?

"Orion saved my life in the fight." She kept the involvement of the dryad a secret, sensing it was Orion's story to tell. "Then we traveled to Neidrei."

Rime's eyes glazed as Ivy retold the events of The Tree House. But, he leaned forward as Ivy spoke of Orion's invitation to Ivy to report to the fae realm.

"But Orion didn't need your report," Rime mused. "Why did he *really* bring you? Were you in danger?"

"Elves aren't mind-readers. That's a Winter fae trick. *You* ask him why he brought me." *And then let me know.*

"You don't seem to understand the implication of Orion bringing you here," Rime said, his expression wary. "He's *never* brought a witness to the fae realm. He's never brought anyone. It'll garner attention."

A warning pricked her neck, but she couldn't run. Not yet.

"I'm here to report to the king's adviser. I won't abandon my duty, but I think it's best to slip away shortly after."

Rime blinked and seemed to shake off his brooding thoughts. "And your question is?"

"I need to find a dryad who will portal me back to the

human realm. Where do I find one that is nearby and amenable?"

"I will answer that. And I'll do you one better. No bargain required."

Ivy hesitated, suspicious of Rime's helpful attitude. "Go on."

"First, I can show the king's adviser your testimony before the equinox festival. I can project our conversation about the seeds and the Seekers into his mind."

"And the second favor?" *The one where I don't owe you anything in return.*

"I'll not only tell you the nearest dryad's location, but I'll take you there myself and command she sends you through. But it must be before the equinox festival because, at midnight, summer rules the realm. A dryad could ignore me for the next six months."

Ivy gazed out the window, threads of wistful regret encircling her. With the entire realm to explore, she'd expected to see more than Rime's rooms. At least he had a view; she'd seen the snow-covered mountains of Winter.

When she caught movement out of the corner of her eye, she jumped, her hand finding her hilt. Across the room, a fae crouched with a hand on her hip, too. Ivy shifted, and the figure mimicked her action. Ivy's jaw dropped, realizing she was looking into a massive mirror.

"What did you do to me?" Ivy asked, moving closer. Cool silk material swished around her legs. "You gave me horns?"

Rime grinned, and the mood shifted. With their bargain nearly completed, the prince relaxed.

"Respectable goat horns. I will not get caught sneaking an elf out of the castle." Rime grimaced like he was looking at rotten food. "Better that they assume I'm attempting to hide an affair."

"Well, thank you for saving me from being caught with a

prince who can barely walk in a straight line," Ivy said sarcastically. "Embarrassing."

"Rude. I can walk just fine." He straightened and strode to the door. "I'm more worried you'll give us away because of your stench. When did you last shower?"

Now who is rude? But he was right. She needed a bath. Plenty of cold rivers awaited in the human realm.

"To be fair, I don't mind tongues wagging, but the Elven Council machinations mean trouble. It's best that you disappear." He dropped his voice, but her elven ears heard him mumble "political muck" and "avoid Selleth's attention."

Was Rime attempting to protect himself? Not Orion? She hadn't wanted to cause trouble for anyone. Discomforted, she changed the subject. "My dress is green? Isn't that a bit cliche?"

"It's a popular color for Spring fae. Just giggle like a brainless pixie, and no one will question your disguise." He looked appraisingly at the dress. "You almost look fit for a prince ... from a distance. Ready?"

Before Ivy could retort, her attention fell on the blue dragon, and her heart sank. She crouched beside Ash on the chair, reluctant to leave the creature. Of course, the flying rodent had chosen Orion.

Even so, Ivy had nothing left of Brecc. She had no family left. No one watched for her.

"Ash," she said softly, "I'm returning to the human realm. You're welcome to join me. My satchel has room, and I have the strength."

The petite dragon shifted, assessing Ivy with a single, beady black eye. Her tongue flicked out and brushed Ivy's hand. It was barely an acknowledgment, but Ivy warmed all the same.

"Until we meet again." Ivy ran a finger timidly down the dragon's side, emotion swelling at her last good-bye. "Keep Brecc's seed safe, wherever it is."

Ivy stood, stepped over spilled wine, and followed Rime. As the door clicked behind them, the last string connecting her to her life *before* snapped, leaving only memories.

In the wide hallway on the right and the left stood fae guards. Rime extended his elbow, and Ivy lay her hand in the crook of his arm. Rime wore a jovial expression, but his eyes were cold.

Orion was stern yet held a whisper of warmth. Ivy couldn't help but want to see him again. To study his face without a glamour. He'd said he would accompany her back to the human realm, but this was better. Less messy.

She'd shared so much of herself, and he'd shared so little. Nothing real. Why torture herself by seeing him once again?

Ivy gripped Rime's arm tighter. "Get me out of the fae realm."

Guards lined the royal corridor, their stone-like expressions matching the marble columns. As Rime passed, they gave a fae salute; an arm extended outward, below the waist, palm facing down. At the guards' backs, ice-covered walls were melting into sheets of water. Streams cut along the edges of the hall, rushing past in the opposite direction.

A glass-domed ceiling soared overhead, and bright afternoon light bounced off the dripping walls. The corridor ended at a balcony overlooking an atrium below. But on the other side of the atrium, an expansive window soared several stories tall, framing distant twin mountains, a deep canyon between them.

"That's the main road to the Summer Court," Rime said.

Ivy's attention was drawn to a line of fae stretched along the road leading to the castle. Above the crowd, bright blue glass-like orbs flashed as if lightning threatened to escape from within. The spherical sentinels mirrored the fae dressed in fine gowns and shimmering jewels, raw power confined within seemingly delicate forms.

Rime swept her down an elegant staircase. While they descended, Ivy whispered additional insights she'd gleened from the Gathering and The Tree House; details needed for the king's adviser. As they neared the bottom of the stairs, voices sounded, and Rime quickly ushered Ivy down a narrow side hall.

"There are more fae here for the festival than I'd expected," Ivy said.

"It's torture for introverts," Rime joked. "Over the last week, Autumn and Winter fair folk have descended on the premises to mark the end of Winter's rule. The castle grounds are crawling with fair creatures. Everyone from stoic centaur representatives to satyrs and their raucous parties are here. After the Summer contingency leaves, I'll sneak out of the castle for some real fun."

Ivy chewed her lip, grateful she hadn't fled into the forest with so many unknown visitors. She opened her mouth, tempted to ask Rime questions about Orion. But what did it matter now? Instead, she focused on the atrium's earthy scents of rich soil, trees, and flowers to distract her; at least the escalating sound of rushing water piqued her interest.

As they crossed the threshold into the atrium, she inhaled a deep breath, an immediate affinity despite the unfamiliar vegetation. She visually swept the expansive space, quickly realizing that only a fraction of the atrium had been visible from the royal balcony above. It could easily fit a thousand elves.

Stepping along a stone path, rivulets of water rushed around Ivy's feet, urging her forward. Blackened trees were dripping, revealing tiny buds along their spiny branches. In nearby raised beds, green shoots dotted the dark soil. The entire atrium oozed a sense of wild release.

"Not what you expected?" Rime asked. "In the palace, the atrium has the biggest physical shift each season. Alysatraee's laws supersede all, forcing the ground to blossom."

The rivulets gathered together, forming streams. Rime jumped over one, and Ivy followed. They passed an interwoven willow fence with tangles of sleeping browned vines clinging along the curves. Behind it towered a budding deciduous tree with unique silver bark, skirted by a smattering of crocus shoots.

"Just ahead." Rime picked up his pace.

As they neared a narrow side door, a servant jumped and opened it. A breeze rushed through, giving Ivy goosebumps. Though her elven clothing was sufficient for cold weather, the single layer of silk supplied little warmth.

Following the prince, Ivy entered a wide hallway of swirling lead and glass. Two servants straightened and opened a set of double doors leading outside. The chill cut through Ivy's clothing, pricking her skin. She wrapped her arms around herself as she maneuvered to stand in the sunlight.

"Prepare Starless," Rime commanded one of the servants.

"Who?" Ivy asked.

"Starless Night. My horse."

The prince led Ivy down a series of steps from one balcony to the next. Ivy wanted to enjoy the view, but her eyes watered.

"C-can I get a coat?" Ivy's teeth chattered.

"Oh, yes. Well, you *are* a thin-skinned Spring fae." He winked as a white wool cloak appeared in his hand, and he lowered his voice. "Don't act tough around the servants. Act *Spring.*"

Whatever that *means.*

Ivy shoved her arms through the slits of the cloak, wishing

Rime had produced a coat with sleeves. As they reached the castle's lower level, servants delivered a horse as black as pitch. Rime glamoured his wings away as he mounted, and a servant helped Ivy settle behind the prince. She clutched Rime's tunic, and then forced an awkward, chittering giggle.

Was that "Spring" enough for him?

By the flat stare Rime shot her over his shoulder, that was a big "no." But what more could Rime expect when her frost-bitten lips could barely move?

Snow kicked up behind Starless as they wove through the trees. Glowing pixies trailed after them, giggling and gnashing their pointed teeth. Ivy's face and fingers grew numb as she clung to Rime's back and cast nervous glances behind. Finally, the pixies grew bored and fell away.

She blinked away the tears in her eyes, straining for signs of fair creatures through the trees, but had little luck. Finally, mercifully, they stopped. Rime dismounted with fluid grace, but Ivy barely kept her feet under her when she stiffly slid from the mount.

"I could've helped you," Rime said, though he stared at the trees. He grimaced and rubbed his chin. "Um, this way." He tromped through the snow. "Almost there. I think?"

Great, the prince is lost in his own woods. The fair realm is in wise hands, indeed.

"Wait here." Rime signaled for her to stay put. His wings reappeared as he jogged forward and stopped at a magnificent cedar. When he started speaking to the unseen dryad, Ivy tried not to eavesdrop by turning her attention back to the castle.

And Orion.

When he'd promised to bring her back safely, she'd looked forward to it. Orion's words had seemed poignant at the time. No, she'd deluded herself into thinking there was anything between them. His fae magic had drawn her in with false allure.

She'd willingly closed her eyes and danced to his tune. The rumors were true; fae were churlish, insensitive louts more likely to throw one into a siren's lair for entertainment than to snatch an elf to safety.

Though, to be fair, Orion had helped Ivy many times. He'd saved her life before they'd even had a real conversation. He'd been gruff, yes, but also kind when he didn't *have* to be. She'd convinced herself it was better to leave quickly—a clean break. But was Ivy a coward, slinking away without a goodbye?

Rime spoke right behind her, and Ivy jumped.

"It's just me," Rime said. "Calm down. I thought elves had good hearing."

"I w-was actively ignoring you, that's all," Ivy's words slurred.

Rime gingerly patted her on the shoulder. "Best of luck in avoiding all the council members who probably want to kill you. Or *will* want to when they find out you hung their dirty underthings on display. Welp, until we meet again, Ivy Balrel."

Rime sauntered back to Starless.

Ivy tucked her hands into her armpits, debating. "Wait!"

"Yes?" Rime's black wings twitched. His ominous, imposing, magnificent fae wings.

She nearly asked to stay but stopped herself. What was she thinking? Ivy belonged to a Trinth-bound elven House. Orion was the son of the dreaded king of the fetid *Winter Court.*

Ivy reminded herself that she did *not* agree to get sucked into the middle of Winter's machinations. And apparently, Orion existed at the center of dangerous, high-stakes fae politics. So, if Orion cared enough to explain himself, he could track her down easily enough in the human realm.

"I d-don't know how to u-use a portal." Ivy made up an excuse for stopping Rime.

"Oh, yes, of course. Just touch the tree and think of your

destination," Rime said as he gripped Starless's saddle horn. "The dryad will deliver you to the nearest portal in the human realm."

"Wait!" Ivy shouted again.

Rime groaned. "What?"

"Will you g-give Orion a message for me?"

Rime looked at her like she was half-crazed but nodded.

"Promise?" Ivy dared to press.

"I will deliver your message if it doesn't compromise my brother or me."

"Fair enough." Ivy shoved away the embarrassment of sharing her thoughts with Rime, trying to prove to herself that she wasn't a coward. Ivy tried to straighten, in case Rime put her image into Orion's mind. "I appreciate you h-helping me find out the truth about my father. And for bringing the f-follies of the Elven Council to the feet of King Eldrin. You helped me fulfill my duties to Alysatraee, which brings me great c-comfort. I hope you got what you wanted and that you are welcomed home."

At least one of us should be so lucky.

Ivy stepped toward the tree, and her thoughts swirled. She'd finished what her father had started. Hadn't she? So why did she feel like she'd left something undone—or perhaps some*one* behind?

25
GOING, GOING, GONE

Orion rushed to the nursemaid's room where he'd left Ivy, only to find it empty. He took a deep breath, reminding himself not to panic. Rime wouldn't let her out of his sight; he'd promised. Just as Orion had promised to safely transport Ivy back to the human realm. If he didn't escort her personally, his magic would be impacted. Robbed.

Unable to bring down the barrier to the stairs to his brother's rooms above, Orion stormed through the servant's hallways.

"Have you seen Prince Rime?" he asked the first servant he found.

The man bowed, keeping his gaze down. "Not I." He gestured to a serving girl. "But she did just an hour ago."

Orion took one look at the girl's puffy red eyes and wine-splattered dress, and he sprinted toward the prince's quarters. Rime was long past his tantrums. Wasn't he? Orion had entrusted his magic and, more importantly, Ivy, thinking his brother had matured. Sweat broke out along his brow, and he chastised himself for not locking Ivy in the nursemaid's quarters alone. Alone was safe.

He spread his wings and flew up the open stairway to the royal corridor. Ignoring decorum, Orion landed and grabbed the nearest guard, questioning him.

"The prince left not a quarter-hour ago," the guard explained.

"Was he alone?"

"He had a fae with him."

His brother left with a visitor? No, Rime would keep Ivy within sight. Had Ivy run?

"A Spring fae," the guard added.

His brother could barely tolerate Spring fae. Leaving Ivy to spend time with one didn't make sense. Orion's heart jumped into his throat as he formed the most probable scenario. Rime's glamouring skills were excellent—better than most presumed. But where was he taking Ivy? And why?

"Which way did they go?" Orion asked.

The tapping of approaching footsteps up the stairwell made the hair rise on the back of Orion's neck.

"The stairs," the guard said.

The footsteps grew louder, along with the jabbering. There were few residents of the royal wing, and Selleth was among them. Chances were, his sister and her admirers were moments away.

Suffering the princess's barbs was better than getting caught looking like a nervous child attempting to elude her. Orion strode toward her, pausing on the landing for her to pass. He ignored the fluttering lashes of the three female fae accompanying his sister and Rithmat's pointed glare.

"Already pining after your rooms, brother?" Selleth said with false sincerity. "It seems your new station makes you impatient."

A fae with white freckles that contrasted with her otherwise dark skin grinned at Orion, a spark of mischief in her eyes, while the two others flashed each other amused, knowing looks. Orion hadn't bothered to learn any of their names, but he supposed that would have to change soon.

"If you're looking for your brother, he's likely still abed," Rithmat sneered.

"Or in the wine cellar," one of the fae giggled.

Anxious to find Ivy, he ignored them, willing them to hurry along.

"I would like to meet this elf of yours," Selleth said.

"Elf?" One of the fae's eyes widened, the ice in her hair tinkling as she looked at Selleth. "In the Winter Court? This is something I must see."

"You will soon enough, I'm sure," Selleth said, a grin forming at the corner of her lips. "Orion invited her to the realm."

Determined to pretend Ivy meant nothing to him, Orion didn't react. If he became flustered or offended, Selleth would recognize the elf's importance. The princess would dig her claws into Ivy just for the joy of making Orion squirm. But he wouldn't offer Ivy up on a silver platter, with or without his promise.

"Oh, she must be an Elven Councilor," the freckled fae said.

"No," Selleth replied. "She's the daughter of a disgraced outcast."

Orion's temper flared at Selleth's mockery. His sister cared nothing about injuring Ivy and everything about making Orion appear weak.

"The elf is well respected," Orion forced a flat tone, though he wanted to snap at his sister and bolt after Ivy. "She is here, serving the fair folk. As we all are. If you'll excuse me—"

"Bring the elf to Rithmat," Selleth interrupted, "to report before the equinox celebration."

Orion pressed his lips together. Seeing his reticence, Selleth quickly waved him away before Orion could embarrass her by refusing. "You may go."

Orion's wings tightened so quickly that the muscles in his back threatened to spasm. Not only was he the king's son, but now he was a recognized member of the court. As of an hour ago, only the crown had the authority to dismiss him, which Selleth knew. Rather than waste his time slinging insults, Orion marched past them down the stairs, his wings itching to fly.

As soon as he was out of sight, he rushed to the atrium. When he questioned the servants, they confirmed his hunch that his brother had taken his favorite escape route. But why would they leave when Rime was simply tasked to keep Ivy safe? Whose idea was it to leave the castle?

Orion didn't take long to track Rime and Ivy into the woods. With all the fair creatures and the bright afternoon hour, traveling by shadow was dangerous; the erratic lines of darkness made it impossible to hide himself consistently. Nor could he use his wings along the narrow path, and flying overhead would draw attention.

Orion jogged after the hoof prints, telling himself that Rime was merely giving Ivy a tour. Yes, a friendly, safe woodland excursion. However, his brother wasn't known as a generous host. He *was* known as a profligate rake. Orion found himself pushing harder; in these woods, he was more concerned about Rime's wandering hands than a rogue pixie or troll attack.

Shaking off his irrational concern, he realized the direction of the path: to the nearest dryad portal. Shock thundered through his veins, realizing Ivy was galloping toward *his* doom.

He ripped off his boots and ran, pressing his thoughts

through his toes. With every step, communicating into the root system below the soil, Orion pleaded for help.

Halt the portal to the human realm. Stop the elf.

Orion's mind raced. He had to escort Ivy to the human realm. Not Rime. Not unaccompanied, either. With him.

He should've told Ivy the truth about his unintentional bargain. As much as Ivy hated him, she wouldn't purposefully break his promise. The elf was tougher than a dragon talon on the outside, but inside, she was tender. Even so, she would inadvertently ruin him if she left the realm.

Hot iron seemed to slam into his chest. Orion stumbled, crashing into the mud and snow. Through the agony, he registered Ivy's touch on the dryad portal—she was leaving.

And she was ripping away his magic in the process.

Ramming his fingers into the roots of a nearby tree, Orion begged the dryad to wait. He could feel her, torn between two brothers. Orion and Rime. Two masters.

His heart wrenched. If only he had Ivy's sight, he'd know who was watching. But he didn't.

Traveling by shadow was the quickest. Orion had to risk exposure or lose his magic forever.

Jumping up, he grabbed the nearest wisp of darkness, shrouding himself. In the stark differentiation of light and shadow, Orion clumsily dove toward the dryad's tree. Transforming into shadow where fair creatures gathered was risky, but what choice did he have?

He flew in fits and starts, his stomach knotted, knowing any creature would notice him as his form appeared wherever the shadows didn't touch. In the afternoon light, the barren, leafless canopy left him exposed. Between the shadows, his wings pumped, slamming into tree limbs and breaking branches.

Barreling ahead through the air, he sensed his brother.

Clumsily dropping, a tremor of pain shot up Orion's legs as he crashed to the ground, one knee slamming into the mud.

"Orion!" Rime's horse, Starless, shifted to kick.

The prince's eyes flicked over his brother like he'd seen a wraith. Ignoring his brother, Orion ran for the portal. But Rime caught him, fisting Orion's tunic.

"W-what did—"

Shoving his brother away, Orion stumbled to the tree. His quick request and apologies were ragged on his tongue, and the dryad moved just enough for him to reach through. But instead of pulling Ivy out, the dryad pulled Orion *in*.

26

TROUBLE WITH TIDES

Nym dismounted the wyvern at the caverned stables, curses spewing from her mouth. The same string of vile words she'd slung across the entire Northern Channel. Pins needled her fingertips as she shook out her hands.

"What a slug," Nym muttered at the beast as she glared at the sunrise. "If you're the fastest in the realm, I pity the rest of the herd. Incompetent breeders."

Without the cover of darkness, any chance of surprise was forfeit. Good thing she never depended on luck.

"It's majestic," the young stable elf cooed at the wyvern.

"Please make arrangements to have this creature returned to the mainland." Nym shuddered, pitying the rider. She rattled off instructions for the wicked, winged beast as the stable hand nodded profusely.

"Yes, of course," she said, though her eyes didn't stray from the horrid animal. "I saw you approach and sent word of your arrival."

Nym sucked in a sharp retort; the child was merely following protocols. Though Nym still longed for a bath and more time to gather possible allies, Emmyth would expect an immediate report. Nym had to work quickly.

Her body ached as she dragged herself through the covered terrace, then off to a side entrance into the palace. Her hip screamed in protest, but she hid the limp anticipating at least one spy was studying her approach. Of course, Lial bound down the path to greet her.

"Good to see you this morning, Nym." Lial grinned.

"Go away, Lial. I'm not in the mood."

"We must celebrate! Returning victorious after not dying at the hands of the Seekers? Everyone's calling it the Battle of the Gathering." He mockingly swept his hand as if brushing the mountains in the distance. "Of course, the stories of your bravery are already becoming legend."

Nym stopped short, her temper sharp after her frigid, thirteen-hour ride at an unnatural height. "What happened is not a joke, Lial."

Lial sobered. "I know. I just ..." Lial's chin fell. "Humor is the way I cope. Childish, I know."

Nym stormed forward, leaving Lial behind.

"I really am glad to see you alive and well," he called after her. "Perhaps not *well,* but—"

Nym lifted a hand without looking back, and he was wise enough to shut his mouth. Shoving open the door, Nym marched to Kolvar's rooms. Between curt greetings as she traversed the halls, Nym searched her pocket, grasping a stolen piece of root. By the time she arrived at Kolvar's door, her muscles had loosened up, and her limp disappeared. She entered without knocking, finding Kolvar at his desk with his usual cup of steaming hot tea while scribbling on parchment.

"You can't come to greet your sister?" Nym asked.

Kolvar dropped his quill and closed his eyes in relief. "You're back. Finally. I've been worried."

How had Lial known she'd returned but not her brother? But she had bigger problems to discuss. Nym slammed the door shut.

"We need to talk." Nym glanced at the walls, guessing how many spies were listening. She pressed the She hadn't raced across the channel in the most miserable way possible for someone to warn Emmyth of Nym and Ivy's discoveries. She didn't even want to hint at trouble, so she didn't engage the soundproofing. Nym leaned against his desk, her finger brushing the lip of the teacup. "I've been sitting far too long on the back of a wyvern."

Kolvar tilted his head but didn't question her. Instead, he got up and grabbed a glass of spring water and a cloak before leading her outside. The strip of exterior stone barely qualified as a balcony, but it was private.

"A wyvern?" Kolvar whispered, handing her the drink and setting his cloak around her shoulders. "You must have been desperate. What's going on?"

Nym recounted what they'd discovered in Neidrei. She confessed that Orion had glamoured to look like Kolvar in the Tree House, but Kolvar was too kind to complain that his appearance had been used. He only paled as she explained their mother's involvement in the Council's unlawful plans.

"We'll approach Emmyth together," Kolvar said.

"No," Nym said. "If things go poorly, you must keep your distance from this whole mess."

Kolvar frowned, saying nothing. Nym knew he wouldn't comply, but he was too appeasing to outright refuse.

Nym forced a smile and backed into Kolvar's receiving room. "I hope to see the councilor shortly."

"I'll join you. I'd like to hear the report, too."

Stubborn elf. Kolvar's refusal to follow her directions almost made Nym feel less guilty about what she'd done. Almost.

Predictably, Kolvar would never let her walk alone into the jaws of certain political annihilation. But she'd told him anyway because an honest elf with authority needed to know the truth before Nym jumped into the political volcano. She handed her brother the empty water glass and his cloak. While he turned his back, Nym fished out the sleeping root she'd drop into his tea.

"Finish your tea while I wash up," Nym said.

"Use my basin. The water is fresh."

Nym nodded, her heart tightening. She'd never tricked her brother before, not like this. They were no longer playing children's games. But the deception was essential for the House of Tides to transition smoothly. She scrubbed her face and hands until she heard a thump, then she hurried to Kolvar's side. He lifted his head from his desktop, and a pang of guilt siezed her.

"I'm dizzy ..." Kolvar's distant eyes barely focused on her.

"Lie down." Nym practically carried him to the couch, his weight heavier than she'd expected.

She placed a pillow under her brother's head and squeezed his hand, impressed by how he'd taken the news of their family's downfall in stride. He was the most humble elf she'd ever met, which meant he was unlikely to scramble for the council seat. She reminded herself that she'd lied to protect him and their House; she'd do whatever she could to help him secure control.

"You're the only one we can depend on," Nym whispered.

Oblivious, Kolvar breathed heavily and stared at the ceiling in a daze. Nym rushed to fetch a healer and continue with her plan when she noticed a note had been slid under the door.

She bit her lip, tempted to read it. She clutched the letter to her chest and strode back to Kolvar's desk, debating. She'd never disrespected her brother's privacy before.

She'd never done a lot of things before.

Cracking the black wax, Nym opened the message:

Ship arrived in the night, north of Nylann'or Palace. Anchored. Ship is dwarven design.

The note shook in Nym's hand as she closed the suspicious message. An old ship had anchored in one of the inconvenient northern harbors. Only those who wished to arrive unnoticed skipped the Nylann'or port. The question was, did they plan to leave as quietly? Doubtful. Was it the fae court here to issue an arrest for Emmyth? Or was it an elven council member here to arrest Nym?

Nym's heart raced. She needed to act. Striding into the corridor, she found a servant and demanded they bring a healer for Kolvar. At least he'd have a witness as to why he wasn't present for the coming confrontation.

Instead of going straight to Emmyth's council chambers, Nym marched to the office of the Tides Councilors' right hand, Omasys Darcassan, Lial's father. He hadn't been implicated during her visit to the Tree House, and though that didn't mean he was innocent, she needed to attempt to find an ally. Omasys wasn't an adviser, but he had his own kind of power—connections and influence.

Nym lifted her hand to knock on Omasys's door. Her heart thumped, knowing once she spoke against her mother, there was no turning back. Her friendships would dissolve. A sadness bubbled up, with Lial at the center of it. She realized she'd miss him, and the emotion caught her by surprise. Though Lial was annoying and more ambitious than he cared to admit, he'd always been her safe place. Part of her wished to stay silent, clinging to the window of peace and respect before the fae court intervened, disgracing her family.

No, Nym needed to speak out before her mother could do more damage. And, as the dreaded messenger of bad tidings, Nym's reputation would implode via the whole gossip-ball-of-doom that was coming. If Nym faced this problem head-on, controlling the narrative, perhaps she could shield Kolvar's reputation.

Nym knocked and was admitted. In Omasys's stark, organized office, Adviser Bellas sat in the chair across from his desk. Nym groaned, seeing the law adviser, the elf that Lial nicknamed "ethereal." In Nym's opinion, "stick-in-the-mud" was a better fit.

"Welcome back, Nym." Omasys gave Nym a gracious nod.

He and Lial had the same blond hair, but Omasys pulled his into an unfashionably tight braid that trailed down his back. Though no longer a warrior, he rigorously trained and insisted Lial do the same.

"I'm glad you are hale after the Battle of the Gathering." Bellas looked Nym up and down as if she felt exactly the opposite.

Rumored to have fae blood, Bellas was an effortless beauty. Other elves were jealous of her flawless appearance, but Nym was envious of her mind. The elf remembered everything she read as if it were seared into her memory.

Nym quickly calculated Bellas's likelihood in supporting the claim against Emmyth. The adviser used to scold her and Lial when they were children, with long-winded reminders of the rules. Bellas wasn't an adviser then—just the bossy big sister Nym had never wanted.

Begrudgintly, Nym admitted to herself that the reasons she disliked Bellas were the very reasons the advisor might be trusted to follow the law she touted.

Nym stepped forward. "I have news from my mission on the mainland. I wanted to speak with you before I report to the Tides Councilors."

"You'll only be reporting to Emmyth," Omasys said. "Councilor Mormaris still hasn't returned."

Nym hid her glee at the second councilor's absence. "That's unfortunate."

"Mormaris and I attended the same Gathering. We were only a half-day north of Heikton," Omasys explained. "Our Gathering was located on the path between yours and Yllalen'al."

"Alysatraee is gracious," Bellas said, touching her heart with her withered right hand, a defomormity she'd been born with that no seed could fix.

"As the House of Minerals fled home to Yllalen'al, they stumbled into us," Lial's father explained.

Two weeks ago, Nym would've believed the convenient locations were a gift from Alysatraee. Now that Nym knew of the council's duplicity, she wondered if they altered the Gathering locations. Was that even possible? Nym didn't know what to believe anymore.

"Councilor Mormaris offered to alert the orcs in the south and bring them to the Gathering for aid," Omasys continued.

"As was proper." Bellas gave a sharp nod of approval.

Nym considered the timeline for the orcs arrival at the Tree House. The councilor's actions *could* explain how the orcs arrived earlier. But six days earlier? No.

What was she missing? Could councilors send messages via the dryads, like Orion? Even if they could, which she doubted, elves need the fae court's approval to dispatch orcs. Wouldn't they? Nym sucked in a breath, tempted to ask Bellas, the expert in the law.

But, questions on rules and orcs had to wait. Every moment Nym delayed, Emmyth's suspicion grew.

"Could you excuse us?" Nym asked Bellas.

Bellas's gaze could've burned a hole in Nym's forehead at the request. It was rude to dismiss the adviser, but Nym's trust had limits.

Bellas quickly smoothed her expression and spoke as she stood. "With the attack at the Gathering tree, how we do things may need to change. Nym, I've always respected you and Kolvar. I want you to know that, no matter what happens."

Hiding her unease at Bellas's words, Nym nodded. She'd need to visit Bellas soon; the adviser was sitting on potentially important information, and Nym was done trusting existing lines of communication. When Bellas shut the door, Nym handed Omasys a folded note that she'd written during her journey to the northern channel. Though unaware of any spying stations into his office, she couldn't take a chance. Omasys's brows raised, reading Nym's accounting of the last two weeks.

"Where is Ivy now?" Omasys asked.

"I don't know. We parted south of Neidrei." That was true, but Nym didn't mention that she intended to meet Ivy at the Centennial. "I need to report to Councilor Philo. Will you be joining us?"

"Of course, I was planning to attend the Tides meetings today, anyway." He tugged at the neck of his tunic. "Let me go first and clear everyone except the advisers from the chambers. This is a sensitive matter."

"I appreciate your discretion."

Though Nym had contemplated this moment, now that she'd begun to unveil the treachery of her mother, it felt *real.* The note she'd written days ago for Omasys had felt like a distant confession. However, going before her own flesh and blood unraveled Nym. She was about to rip away precious titles, authority, and respect from the elf who'd birthed her.

"Go ahead." Nym lifted her chin. "Clear the room. I'll be there shortly."

Recognizing his brief window, Omasys hurried away. Nym's plan was in motion. There was no turning back. Emmyth needed to be caught unaware. Though Nym hated destroying her mother, Emmyth was the master of twisting situations back in her favor. Nym was a warrior, not a politician; now she must be both.

Nym's hands shook and she clutched them together. She almost wished Lial would show up and distract her with some ridiculous joke or observation. She shook off the notion and poured herself a glass of wine, the neck of the decanter clinking against the rim of the goblet.

From that angle, a bit of broken black wax on Omasys's desk caught her attention. The tiniest sliver of loose parchment was visible under the book on his desk. Nym bit her lip, telling herself it was too risky to look at someone else's mail while spies likely watched.

Then again, who would care about *that* when Emmyth was evicted from her council seat in an hour? Nym slid the parchment from under the book, revealing a note with a broken seal.

She scanned the words. It was the same message by the same hand that she'd seen in Kolvar's office. Who was spying and reporting to both her brother and the council's right-hand? Were they also reporting to Emmyth?

Nym tucked the missive back where she'd found it and left the office, taking the long route to the council chambers. Too soon, she reached her destination. She pressed her hand to the door and sucked in a deep breath. This was the last time she'd enter this room with Emmyth as the councilor. Last time the Philo name wouldn't be a curse word on everyone's tongues. The last time her mother would look upon her with any degree of fondness.

Nym would denounce her mother, then call for Kolvar to become the new councilor. He would work with the fae. Together, they'd stop the war before it roared back, biting them with a curse of iron blades and blood.

With both hands, Nym shoved open the doors. In the council chambers, Emmyth waited on the raised platform in the elegant council chair. As usual, her mother's hands were folded in her lap, her jaw set. On her right was Omasys. On the floor, eight advisers awaited Nym's report.

The treasury adviser, Daecyne, puffed up his chest, like a cat anticipating gorging on milk. Nym forced a proud stance, though his expression didn't bode well. He'd never liked Nym; not since she became the ambassador and negotiator with the naiads, a position his nephew had desired.

Nym's footsteps were silent on the stark, marble floor as she passed massive pillars holding up the painted ceiling. Approaching Councilor Philo, Nym gave her a low nod.

"Welcome home, Nym Philo. We are all anxious for your report from the last three weeks." Emmyth's voice was harsh. That's when Nym noticed her mother's hands were not gently clasped together, but gripped tightly. "I've already informed the advisers that I sent you to track what Ialant was involved in these last few years." A thread of warning laced her mother's voice.

Nym's jaw clenched. Her mother knew a trap had been laid. Did she know Nym had set it?

"Speak up," Daecyne spat.

Nym took a deep breath, her knees weak. Feigning calm, she unfolded the story of the Gathering, the fighting, and of the stranger, Orion. Nym explained how Ivy's injuries slowed their progress, then she paused. Dreading what came next. But she pressed on and explained what she found in Ialant's research lab.

The room silenced.

Bellas shot a meaningful glance over her shoulder at Omasys. Yes, Ialant had broken the law. Yes, it was ugly. And unfortunately, Nym wasn't done. Her lungs constricted, but she swallowed and pushed through what the companions had found next: the Tree House.

When Nym slipped Ialant's glamour of her mother over her head, a collective gasp sounded. Half the advisers stared at the ground, a few scowled, their faces crimson, and the rest stood slack-jawed.

She dragged her gaze to Emmyth. Nym's heart thundered, wishing her mother would deny the claims. Shout that she wasn't involved. At least to feign surprise. Of course, the councilor acted impassive, her face a mask. Her expression only changed briefly when Nym spoke of tricking the elves; her mother looked almost impressed.

Almost.

Though Nym already knew her mother was guilty, Emmyth's silence still felt like a betrayal. A final, condemning obliteration inside Nym's core. Through Nym's accounting and after she removed the glamour, the councilor never once took her attention off her daughter—unnerving. How could her mother be so unfeeling? So calm.

"This is quite a claim," Daecyne said, though he looked pleased. Nym half expected him to lick his lips in anticipation of his nephew snatching her position.

"Do you deny it?" the law adviser demanded, turning to Emmyth.

The councilor lifted her chin. "And if I don't deny the claim?"

Nym stiffened. Emmyth knew her trial could be forfeit if she admitted to treachery. What game was she playing?

Lial's father straightened and nodded to Daecyne, who jogged to the entrance doors behind Nym.

"You stand accused of treason against Alysatraee's law," Bellas announced. "While this is investigated, I move to remove you from your position as councilor. You will be replaced by an interim adviser."

"And who will replace me?" The corner of Emmyth's lip ticked up. "You?"

Nym nearly spoke in favor of Kolvar, but something in her gut wriggled—Emmyth's reaction felt off. The trap Nym set for her mother was going as it should, so why did she feel a warning deep in her core? The door opened behind her and the captain of the guard strode inside. Several other guards flooded in behind him and surrounded Emmyth.

The advisers whispered, shared furtive glances, yet Emmyth didn't seem to notice any of them. Her complete attention was focused on Nym. The intensity wasn't angry or panicked but felt full of curious anticipation.

Nym squirmed, and she told herself her discomfort was due to witnessing her mother's helplessness. Arrested. Humiliated. Not because Emmyth acted *nothing* like she'd expected. Her mother was calm under pressure, but this was a new level of cold calculation. Even Emmyth had a breaking point, didn't she? Nym clutched her hands together behind her back.

A hand rested on her shoulder, and Nym jumped. Jerking to the side, she realized it was Lial.

"Whatever you need, I'm here for you." He gave her a sad smile.

What was he doing here?

His father cleared his throat. "I move that Lial Darcassan become the interim councilor."

27

TORN BETWEEN REALMS

The dryad didn't speak, but Orion sensed her fury.

"Orion?" Ivy sounded muffled. Distant.

"It's me."

"I can't move." Ivy's voice rose, panicked.

"I apologize ... for everything," Orion spoke to both Ivy and the dryad. He softened his voice. "Ivy, I will take you to the human realm if you desire. But, the king wants you to deliver your message to the Summer Representative."

"Can't Prince Rime convey the evidence on my behalf?"

"Yes," Orion practically choked on the single word. His training told him to use manipulative language to convince her to stay, but he owed Ivy the plain truth. "However, the king requested *you*."

"Your *father*," Ivy added.

"Yes, my father," Orion paused, regretting that he hadn't told Ivy the truth sooner, "King of the Winter Court."

Ivy fell quiet. Meanwhile, the dryad pricked at him; to keep creatures in her home for any length of time wasn't natural. Beyond her annoyance, he sensed the dryad's strain—holding Ivy between realms.

"Ivy." Orion reached for her but caught nothing. The elf was deep in the portal, suspended on the cusp of the human realm. With a simple earthly thought, Ivy could be gone. "We are separated. I can't reach you. If you enter the human realm ..." Orion could barely speak the words. "Ivy, I've led a life of secrets from before I can even remember. It's who I am."

"Elves keep secrets, too. It's gotten us nothing but pain. We should share knowledge. Not scramble for power by hoarding information."

"I'm trying. I am." Orion hated his helplessness, completely dependent on the elf and the dryad. "The truth is, if you go through the portal without me, I'll lose what makes me fae."

The dryad's prodding ceased, replaced by turmoil. Fear. Why?

And what makes you dryad, she whispered. And the realization hit him. Not only would he risk his fae magic, but his *dryad* abilities. His command of the portals and his easy communication with his sisters could be lost. The dryad shuddered, seeming to sense his thoughts. She pressed on him to hurry—her grip on Ivy was failing.

"I don't think abilities *make* you fae," Ivy said.

Orion blurted a dark laugh. He wasn't sure if he was more stunned knowing the dryad cared that he'd be cut off, or recognizing that he did, too. He'd lost most of his dryad ability already, and now that he'd been invited to live in the Winter Court, he'd always planned to let go of the rest in order to reach his full fae potential.

The dryad's anxiety tightened around him, and Orion's breathing grew shallow. She was bound to send Ivy wherever she chose, dooming Orion to lose his dryad *and* fae magic.

"Ivy, please. I need you." The utter truth of his words pierced him. "Return to the fae court."

The dryad cried out as Ivy slipped.

"How do I return to your detestable court?" Ivy spoke slowly, her tone indecisive.

"Think of the area right outside of this tree." Orion feigned calm though the invisible vice around his chest tightened.

"You first," Ivy said.

Terror shot through him. What if she didn't return? He fought his instinct to demand that she follow his instruction without question. Instead, he forced his eyes closed and stepped out of the cedar. Snow crunched under his foot, and he held his breath, waiting for Ivy. The shadows had lengthened considerably, but Rime still waited.

"What happened?" Rime stepped toward him.

Orion shook his head, every heartbeat stretching slowly, as Ivy failed to appear. Where was she?

Rime took another step. "How did you travel to this portal so quickly? Without a horse? And why did you fall down from ... from the trees? Not above the tree line. *Below.*"

"Don't push, Rime. Not now."

"Please tell me you haven't kept certain *skills* from me," Rime's nostrils flared as his gaze inspected Orion's rumpled feathers. "I've never kept anything from you. Even secrets you could blackmail me with. Or get me killed."

Orion winced, knowing Rime had completely trusted him. "We all deal with our family in different ways." Orion's words spilled before he registered them. "You drown yourself in drink and distractions."

"Better than hiding," Rime shot back. He spun and grabbed Starless's reigns. The prince mounted, every line on his face filled with fury. "Congratulations, brother. I got word that you're invited to take your place at court."

Orion had only left his father's throne room an hour ago. "How did you—"

"Don't think you can play the neutral party any longer.

You'll have to get your hands dirty, down in the muck with the rest of us."

Orion wished he could say he'd throw his support behind Rime in a bid for the throne. His brother was the closest thing he'd ever had to a friend. And Rime needed the support. Desperately.

But backing the prince would end Orion's welcome the moment Selleth took the crown. She would lord over Rime, reminding the prince of her victory. But to her half-dryad brother, she would inflict *so* much worse. The future crown's punishments were only limited by her imagination.

Rime cursed under his breath, but Orion's thoughts were obliterated as Ivy stumbled from the tree.

Orion caught the elf in his arms, relief spilling off his shoulders. For a moment, Ivy tucked into Orion before shoving him away. She fell to her knees, gripping the sides of her head with both hands, a soft moan escaping her lips. Her body curled inward as if attempting to protect herself. Confused, Orion knelt next to her, wanting to comfort her but unsure how.

"We will talk. Soon." Rime glared at them both as he tugged the reigns. "By the way, you both entered the tree *yesterday*. The equinox ball is mere hours away."

Ivy's hands dropped away from her head, her body relaxing as she took a deep breath. Blinking, she lifted her face, noticing Rime. He frowned before galloping away, disappearing through the trees.

Ivy shivered and tugged her white cloak around her. Her breathing evened out, and she stared at Orion's bare feet. "Nice brother you have. He could've left the horse and flown himself back. What got his feathers twisted?"

"The cold won't kill us." *But my father might.* "We need to hurry." Orion unclasped his cloak and layered its warmth over the white cape Rime had likely glamoured for her.

"You avoided my question. What's going on between you?" Ivy asked, staring after Rime's path.

"It's political. Nothing to do with you."

"Brotherly fight? Then, it's not my place to ask." Ivy clutched Orion's cloak as she stood.

Ivy's horns, ears, and clothing would've been stripped away when she'd entered the earth realm; Rime was obviously too distracted to notice he'd left it in place when she returned. Few fae could hold glamours at a distance. Rime was one of them, though he'd miraculously kept the extent of his ability a secret.

"Your glamour will drop as soon as my brother remembers it. So, prepare yourself to be revealed as an elf."

"I'll try not to embarrass you," Ivy said, trudging after Starless's hoof prints.

"Ivy," Orion grabbed her wrist. She looked up at him through her thick lashes. For a moment, he hoped she'd forgiven him.

Then she yanked her arm away and kept marching.

The gulf between them stretched, the chasm widening. It would continue to crack and grow until he explained. Perhaps his honest excuses wouldn't repair the damage, but he owed her. Orion jogged to her side. Before he could speak, Ivy did.

"Why did you bring me here?" Ivy blurted, her voice tight. "You didn't need my witness. Was I just a nice ... bonus? A tool to impress your father?"

The early evening breeze whistled as it whipped through the branches. Orion didn't know what to say. Ivy wrapped the cloak tighter as she stormed forward.

Orion jogged up to her side. "You looked so forlorn saying goodbye to Nym. I couldn't leave you alone when I had a better solution. Or, I thought I did. I'm a half-dryad surrounded by fae. Perhaps, part of me liked having another non-fae in the court." He dropped his voice, struggling to articulate his feelings. "I want to feel less alone. Or, perhaps I'd hoped we could be alone, together."

Spilling his deepest insecurities made the ground tremble under his feet. It was just his paranoia, but still, his knees felt weak.

Ivy stopped walking, her brow scrunched. His gaze moved from her dark eyes to her rose-petal lips, which she was biting, seemingly uncertain.

"Orion," she said, "I didn't know. There's a lot of things about your life I still don't understand."

Orion struggled with what to say, knowing Ivy deserved a truthful piece of himself right then and there. "Few others like me exist, and none in the Winter Court."

Ivy pivoted, squaring her shoulders to him. It was almost as if she'd dared curl her toes at the edge of the canyon, asking him to leap. Blinking back emotion, she whispered. "*That,* I understand."

"If you give me a chance, I will attempt to unravel who I am." Orion wanted to try, though his life was layered, with some things so tightly held it felt as if parts of him were behind a granite wall.

Ivy took a half step closer and reached for him, her thumb brushing the back of his hands as her palm began to whisper up his forearm. Then her hand shot to her hip as her head tilted, and her attention darted to the woods.

"Someone is coming." She frowned, patting where her knife usually rested, but it was glamoured away. "A fae. Severe-looking creature."

"Gossamer wings that look like a dragonfly?" Orion swallowed.

"Not that I can see, but she does have antlers."

Orion relaxed. Not Selleth.

"Can you fly us back?" Ivy evaluated his wings.

"Not today." He'd hardly used his wings in the last decade, and he'd used what strength they had while he'd battered them trying to catch Ivy.

"I'm weak from the portal," Ivy said, "but I can still evade creatures on foot. You can fly, and I'll meet you back at the castle."

Orion shook his head and evaluated the shadows, refusing to let her out of his sight on the eve of the equinox. "Who else might be able to see us right now?"

Ivy scanned the forest. "Pixies between us and the castle. Satyrs. Oh, a centaur, headed to the front gates. He's moving fast. But none are near enough to see us."

"Anyone else? Any creatures with sharp vision, like elves."

"No others."

"You wanted to know me, Ivy? Hold on, and I'll *show* you my biggest secret," Orion said, grateful for the setting sun. "Dusk comes quickly. The king is undoubtedly wondering where we are." *And furious.* Orion left that part out. "He probably ordered someone to hunt us down. However, even more pressing are the preparations for our presentation at the ball."

"A ball?" Ivy's jaw dropped. "I thought it was a celebration."

"I'll explain everything, just not here."

"At least Rime already made me a dress." Ivy flashed a grin, but it seemed forced. Nervous. She gingerly wrapped her arms around his neck, her warmth seeping through his tunic.

"I need Rime to drop your ridiculous glamour."

"But I'll embarrass you." Ivy didn't meet his gaze, her words soft, but weighted. Orion winced, remembering how gruff he'd been about elves when they first met.

"You're superior to any courtly fae," Orion wrapped an arm around her waist. Ivy started to look up at him, but a branch cracked and her attention jerked back to the forest.

"We should leave," she warned.

Orion pulled the shadows to him, encasing them both in darkness. The ground dropped away beneath their feet. Ivy gasped, her grip tightening. But she stayed silent as they raced back to the castle. They easily dodged all fair creatures, mere blurs along the way. If his magic was known, creatures might've been on the lookout for the telltale signs of Winter magic. But no one was the wiser.

Though Orion dared rejoice in having Ivy in his arms and his magic intact, his thoughts were tempered by the night ahead—a gauntlet of fae debauchery. Rime hadn't been cruel in taking Ivy to the portal. His gesture was a misguided attempt at kindness. For the Winter, the spring equinox brought bruised fae egos, shorter tempers, and sharper retributions. Alliances and enemies were both wrought in abundance, and Ivy was a shiny new creature to provoke.

While powerful, the king had little desire to play games. His reign ended soon, and he had no intention of marring his last season of rule by unnecessary provocation. Selleth, on the other hand, probably schemed in her sleep. Orion needed the king's protection for Ivy, plus the good graces of the princess. However, there was only one way to guarantee Selleth would play nice for a single night. Unfortunately, if Orion gave Selleth the one thing she wanted, his loyalty, he'd lose his brother, the only friend he'd ever had.

28
An Unexpected Sapling

Ivy thrilled at the darkness swirling about her, bits of the forest visible through the surrounding storm. Despite the long shadows cast by the setting sun and Orion's intimate darkness, Ivy guided Orion to the edge of the forest undetected. As they flew, Orion explained the oath he'd inadvertently made. His unguarded confession crumbled the thick wall she'd built between Orion and herself. She tried to concentrate on his every word, but she didn't know what exhilarated her more, flying through the forest or being wrapped up with Orion.

Finding a quiet copse of trees near the castle, Orion gently planted his feet on the ground. The shadows fell, unveiling them both, but Orion's arm stayed wrapped around her waist. For a moment, Ivy clung to him, trying to unravel her anger and desperation to leave the realm from the feelings Orion stirred. His arm shifted, but instead of withdrawing completely, his palm pressed against her lower back. A bit of Ivy melted, and then she remembered *exactly* why she wanted to flee; despite his promise of plain honesty, she was wary of fae charms.

Ivy stepped back, but her attention stayed fixed on his face.

Though she didn't want to blindly rush forward, Ivy couldn't deny the magnetic pull toward him.

"May I escort you to your room to prepare for the evening?" Orion asked her, holding out his hand. It was unnecessarily formal but deliciously comforting.

Ivy lifted her chin, matching his tone though not hiding a grin. "Why Orion, I would very much appreciate an escort. Especially as I have no idea where my lodgings might be in your maze of a castle."

"Point taken." The spark in his eye signaled his mood had shifted from anguish to ... was that humor?

Ivy had no sooner grazed her fingertips on his palm when he gripped her hand, drawing her close as he led her into the open. Warmth emanated through her fingers and up her arm. She would've sworn it was magic, except she'd studied Winter fae abilities, and creating heat wasn't one of them. Nor was it dryad. It was Orion. Though she didn't want to feel anything but friendship for him, fae charms or no, if she wasn't careful she'd wind up falling.

In the portal, Orion had asked ... no, he'd begged her to stay, hinting at his distressing situation. She would've returned just for that reason alone, but he'd also promised to be open. Unvarnished. Vulnerable. And though Nym would think it completely insane, part of Ivy needed to know this half-fae, half-dryad she'd spent two perilous weeks alongside. She needed more than a glimpse of his true character.

Orion guided her along the same route she'd taken with the prince. For the first time, Ivy took in the whole of the Winter citadel. The stronghold curved and stretched toward the sky, buttresses and crenellations bladed and fanged as if hungering for blood. Pale light emanated from the towers, calling its kind forward to pay homage as the season closed, and casting the gargoyles on the lower ledge into eerie silhouettes. The procession through the expansive main gate was shorter than earlier. The orbs hovered, casting a blue hue over regal centaurs, giggling groups of satyrs, fae carriages, and other fair creatures.

A guard spotted Ivy and Orion from afar and jogged to intercept them. "My lord, I didn't realize you were on the grounds." The guard's gaze briefly caught on Orion's grip on Ivy's hand. "I'd be honored to clear the way for you to the main entrance."

"I don't wish to make a fuss until my position is officially announced," Orion said. "But please lead the way to the north balcony entrance."

"Yes, my lord." The guard saluted and marched quickly ahead.

Orion and Ivy followed but at a distance, allowing for private conversation.

"It must be an honor to have the king's guards already aware of your appointment," Ivy said.

"It is," Orion paused, his hand tightening on hers before he relaxed it again. "It's surreal to be invited home."

"You've been working toward this honor for most of your life," Ivy said as they climbed the stairs. "It's natural to feel a little overwhelmed at finally attaining your goal."

Orion quieted as they passed guards who gave crisp salutes at the entrance to the lower balcony. As the pair strode forward, he continued in a low tone. "It's the timing of the whole affair. I'd like to think I earned my position, but why now?"

"You didn't think sharing the news of the Elven Council's misdeeds would elevate you in the king's eyes?" Ivy asked.

Orion slowed, his attention turning to the view. Ivy hadn't appreciated the vista while running to the portal, but with Orion's cloak, Ivy comfortably drank in the sight. The mountains encircled the back of the citadel, enclosing it in a jagged embrace. The blackened branches of the trees blanketing the valley seemed to claw at the evergreens dotted among them as the sun plunged into the western mountains.

"I did hope to be welcomed home, yes," Orion said, his gaze skimming the treetops. "Yet, the invitation felt rushed. I anticipated my matriculation into court life to move at a tentative pace, but the king has already announced my return to the guards, and he's introducing me to the court tonight. I wouldn't be surprised if he gave me an official duty within the week."

"Isn't this a good surprise?" Ivy asked.

"Perhaps. But, I also thought the king would quickly move to call the Elven Council members to judgment, not casually pass the information to Summer. In some ways, the response from the king is the opposite of what I'd expected."

Orion shook his head as they moved up the next flight of stairs. Ivy let him stew while she enjoyed the feeling of his hand encasing hers. In the years before her family fractured, she'd had childish infatuations, but the experience was nothing like *this*. Orion's hand was calloused from sword work, matching her own which was rough from living in the forest, climbing trees, and constant running.

"There was another oddity, too," Orion interrupted her thoughts, "I nearly forgot. I was excused from King Eldrin's presence before he discussed a visitor from the human realm."

"Emmyth?" Ivy tightened her grip on Orion's hand.

"Doubtful. She wouldn't have had time."

"But in the human realm, time moves differently, correct?"

"For every day in the fae realm, ten pass in the human realm." Orion nodded. "Once I'd entered the fae realm, it was a mere two hours until I greeted the king. No one could've informed Emmyth of anything suspicious within twenty hours of our departure. Nym might not even be back home yet. However, the visitor could be an elf or a southern orc reporting on the Gathering attack. I'll find out once I've been given an official position in the court."

Long after I'm back in the human realm. Ivy's heart twisted.

The clothing against Ivy's body shifted from silken robes to rough material. She opened Orion's cloak to see her familiar elven clothing. Her free hand flew to her ears, and she smiled. "I'm back to myself."

"Just in time," Orion said as he led her up the last set of stairs to the entrance into the palace. "Will you tell me what happened when you exited the dryad's portal? I was worried. You seemed pained."

Ivy chewed the inside of her cheek at the memory. Before she reemerged into the Winter forest, a vision exploded in her mind. The same divination she'd seen at the Gathering played in her mind, but the vision was longer this time.

"If you don't wish to share it, I understand," Orion said. "I'm here to listen when you're ready." He released her hand, moving it to the small of her back as they reached the double doors to the castle. Striding forward, the warmth of the atrium enveloped them.

Shedding the warm cloak as they navigated over the rivulets of water, Ivy relished the plants' energy. Though in the human realm, seeds extended her life, she felt the connection to the living earth just as easily in both realms.

As they passed the silvery tree, Ivy gasped.

"What's wrong?" Orion stepped closer to her.

Ivy blinked, unsure if the sapling before her was real. She stepped gingerly past the willow fence to the base of a large tree with silvery bark. At her feet, the ground had been freshly dug up and mounded around the young tree with healthy, purple leaves.

Orion cursed under his breath as he moved to Ivy's side. "How is a Gathering tree in a fae atrium?"

"The tree wasn't here before," Ivy said. "I remember passing by here yesterday—someone planted it recently."

"But we poisoned the orchard," Orion said. "Zel and your father were testing younger trees, but they were dying, and Zel had planned to destroy what was left. This tree appears healthy."

"Have you seen Gathering trees in this realm before?" Ivy asked, desperate for clues.

"Never," Orion said.

"Gathering trees shouldn't be cultivated at all, nor should they exist in the fair realm," Ivy explained.

Only elves residing in the human realm received seeds, and for good reason. Seeds didn't work in the fair domain.

"Perhaps the Tree House held young saplings we weren't aware of," Ivy said. "An elf or gnome could have brought this one to the Winter King for protection."

"If so, Eldrin granted their request." Orion frowned. "Or is this evidence?"

"It's fortuitous that you have an official place here," Ivy said, more to convince herself than Orion. "You can uncover the reason. Advise your father to intervene before the Centennial and stop this madness. In the last war, tens of thousands of fair folk died. He can't let that happen again."

"We should go before anyone notices our attention on the tree," Orion took Ivy's hand, but she ripped it away.

"Why? Let's find a gardener and ask questions."

"The gardener will alert whoever planted this tree that we know about it. Ivy, you have an opportunity tonight—listen to gossip and ask about visitors. We might learn information we can leverage before those involved realize that we're investigating them."

Ivy nodded, reaching for him. He caught up her hand in his, the simple action sending a jolt through her; Ivy felt taller, stronger—as if her feet had grown roots. Her heart seemed to swell, knowing that Orion supported her purpose—he'd taken it upon his own shoulders, too. Orion cocked his head, inspecting her. Ivy breathed a smile, and the concerned lines along his brow smoothed before he guided her through the halls.

Orion led her down an ornate hallway, a guest wing. Water gently trickled down the walls, compared to the torrent in the royal wing. When Orion passed by, guards saluted, and as they neared a set of doors, a servant straightened and threw them.

"We've been expecting you," the servant said formally to Ivy.

Inside the room, a human servant and a smartly-dressed fae paced. The human bowed, wringing her hands. She was short, even for her kind, and shallow wrinkles framed her eyes. The tall fae's nostrils flared as she flicked a glossy curl over her shoulder.

"Where have you been?" The fae's words were more of a chastisement than an actual question.

"Prepare our guest, Ivy Balrel, for the evening," Orion said, ignoring her tone. "Do as she requests, and deliver her to the Great Hall."

"We've little time, so if you'll excuse us." The fae shooed Orion out the door, and Ivy keenly felt the separation.

"Ivy, I'll see you soon," Orion promised before leaving. The fae slammed the door behind him, muttering about leaving her too little time to work with such a poor canvas.

Ivy rolled her eyes, and the nervous human's shoulders relaxed. The bossy fae was a tailor, and she didn't pretend to care a whit about comfort, nor did she ask for opinions as she worked, which was fine with Ivy. Elves knew little of court fashion, and the tailor seemed overly motivated to make sure Ivy looked presentable.

As Ivy stood in front of a mirror, the human servant nodded approvingly with every shift of the fae tailor's glamour. Plunging neckline or high neck, lace or chiffon, trailing train or short skirt, the human smiled dimly at them all. The fae tugged at the material and shifted Ivy about like a rag doll so the fae could see all angles.

The woman was bespelled, but she seemed somewhat aware, signaling her spell was waning. She was probably a girl when she'd struck a bargain that tied her to the Winter Court. The magic had likely lightened over the years, as fae entrapment spells often did. By the time the spell broke, anyone the woman knew in the human realm would be long dead.

When she and her sister were young, their parents taught their daughters about fae magic; they gave extensive lessons on many subjects. As elves, becoming liaisons between the realms was their duty, which required lengthy training. And though Ivy didn't know it, she was trained for wartime communication. But Ivy planned to use every bit of knowledge and every trick her parents had taught her to keep the peace from fracturing.

"Somehow, in all my elven training, I've not learned much about fashion," Ivy said, barely keeping the mockery out of her voice.

"Fashion is *everything.*" The fae tailor shot her a flat stare.

"Pft, ask the cook, and he'll tell you that food is everything," a familiar voice said from the doorway.

The servants dropped into a deep curtsy as Prince Rime strode forward. His black, shiny feathers dominated the room, and his fine clothing and ornate crown emanated royalty with every step. Ivy gave him a respectful nod but held her breath.

What was the prince doing here? And where was Orion?

29

EMMYTH'S LOYALTY LIES

Nym stared in shock as Omasys held out his hand, inviting his son to join him on the council seats' dais. "Lial, please join me."

Next to her, Lial froze in place. The captain nudged his shoulder, and Lial's attention flew from his father to the Tide's legal adviser, Bellas.

"Lial?" Emmyth chuckled. "Your primping, every-merry son is an interesting choice. You imagine him reading dull budget reports? Overseeing food distribution? Sitting in mediation meetings?"

"If you were merely deceived by those in the Tree House, you'll avoid the dungeon," Lial's father said, changing the subject. "If you were naive to the machinations or driving them, it doesn't matter. You've lost your council seat."

Bellas stepped onto the platform. "Emmyth Phiro, your actions have gone against the sacred law of Alysatraee."

The turmoil in Nym's gut turned to acid. She'd expected shock from the advisers. Denial. Not immediate, harsh action. The succession was too coordinated to have been thrown together within a half-hour of Nym's return.

Omasys gave a nod to Daecyne, the treasury adviser, before speaking again. "After I was informed of odd expenses, signed off by Emmyth, I had spies follow our councilors. That's when we discovered the Tree House. You're finished, Emmyth. And when your fellow Councilor, Mormaris, returns he'll be dismissed as well."

Nym's breathing quickened. The advisers knew? They *knew*. And they did nothing about it until the timing was right for *them*. Not for the humans they hurt. Not according to the Mother's laws. The advisers were selfish, grasping children.

"Impressive game you played, Emmyth, but it's over now," Bellas said, a hint of pity in her voice.

"The same five elves have sat on the council since the end of the war." Adviser Daecyne puffed up his chest. "It is time for a change."

"And who will replace Councilor Mormaris?" Emmyth asked, giving Omasys a cold stare. "You?"

Lial's father gripped the back of the council chair. "Emmyth Phiro, step down."

The guards moved to surround Emmyth, and the captain held a magicked rope to bind her wrists.

"The seeds," Nym blurted. "There are enough to poison a thousand humans." Nym wouldn't allow the coming avalanche of disease to be forgotten.

"The equinox is tonight," Bellas spoke in a reassuring, practiced tone. "We will send a message to the Summer Court. They'll listen to reason."

"Your grip on the Tides is finally at an end," Daecyne grinned, looking from Emmyth to Nym. "Your daughter will be the first to go. I have already suggested a replacement."

"Your loyalty is bought at a meager price. I'm glad to know its worth." Though seated, Emmyth still managed to look down her nose at the treasury adviser.

Nym scanned the room, expecting someone to come to Emmyth's aid; the councilor wouldn't go down this easily. But the only person riveted on Emmyth's every move was the captain. Behind Nym, guards stood at the doors, blocking the exit. Nym's stomach roiled. A trap *had* been set.

And Nym was the trigger.

Emmyth was caught in the net, along with all the Phiros. Omasys never intended to give Kolvar a chance. Despite her own desolate future, it stung infinitely more that Kolvar's prospects had been snatched away, too.

"Put Kolvar in the dungeon until we can sort out his part in this," Bellas said to Omasys.

"How dare you," Nym growled, her body buzzing. Her brother was unaware and helpless. He'd wake up in a cold cell, confused and possibly sick.

"That's for the new councilor to decide," Lial finally spoke. His every syllable made Nym want to punch his teeth in.

Omasys looked pleased. "Well said, Lial. Swear him in, Bellas."

Nym itched to make Bellas bleed for sending Kolvar to the dungeon. Instead, Nym gripped her hands tighter behind her back, the glamoured pendant digging into her palm; she wouldn't be tossed out before she witnessed this fateful moment—Omasys's pivotal gamble to command the council seat.

How long had Omasys been colluding with the advisers? Had Lial conspired in this coup? Were any still loyal to Emmyth? Nym was torn over her last question, knowing her mother had acted wickedly. But at the same time, this was her *mother*.

More than any battle, Nym splintered inside, her bones aching as she watched wolves ripping Emmyth's authority to shreds and fighting over the scraps of her power.

Lial cleared his throat. "Shouldn't the advisers vote before swearing me in?"

Bellas signaled to a guard, and she marched forward with a bowl. The ceremonial water dish was kept in a locked corridor with other magical relics, meaning Omasys and Bellas had planned this months ago. Nym's return with damning evidence had likely created an opportunity for Omasys, so the advisers moved up their orchestrated timetable.

As the eight advisors lined up to place their vote, Lial leaned closer to Nym.

"This isn't how I'd envisioned this day going," he whispered.

Nym bristled, her hands fisting. "You envisioned a celebration? Me smiling and nodding in approval?"

At the base of the dais, Bellas dipped her finger into the bowl of water, sending ripples to the edge, signifying her vote for Lial as the new council member.

"My father has always wanted me to rise higher in the ranks than he could," Lial said as Daecyne voted for him. "But, Emmyth's seat? I assumed it was unofficially reserved for Kolvar."

"My brother hasn't been mentioned ... beyond carting him off to the dungeon," Nym hissed.

Lial had known. Beyond the chaos, guilt, and pain, his betrayal cut the deepest.

Another adviser voted for Lial. The trade adviser stepped to the bowl, but before voting, she asked, "Who dispatched the orc guards to the Tree House?"

Omasys had mentioned that Tide's Councilor, Mormaris, had alerted the orcs after the Gathering. And while sending orcs to aid after a Seeker attack was allowed, sending them to protect illicit seeds in Neidrei was a violation against the Mother's law. Nym bit her tongue, wanting to demand answers she was in no position to ask.

The existence of the Tree House threatened the peace between realms. Only fae courts held the authority to dispatch the orcs in *protecting* something with such long-reaching potential devastation.

The grumpy pixie messenger, Orion, intended to report everything he'd learned of the seeds to the Winter King. An influential fae in that court had dispatched the orcs to act against the law. Nym pressed her eyes shut, desperately hoping that Ivy was nowhere near the fae lands.

"I did not request the dispatch of the orcs, so I can't say for certain," Emmyth spoke slowly, her words heavy, portending danger. Nym's body stiffened, wondering at Emmyth's calculations. Omasys and the advisers assumed they had Emmyth cornered; Nym's instincts warned otherwise. Emmyth dropped her lashes, her attention flitting to her hand for less than a moment. Nym noticed her mother was clutching something shiny, mostly hidden up her sleeve. Her medallion—a symbol of her rank rarely worn outside of formal affairs. The metal wasn't catching the light, it was dimly glowing. Emmyth shifted and the medallion slid completely under the fabric of her sleeve, out of sight. It was unlikely that anyone noticed the medallion in the heartbeat it was visible, other than Nym.

The trade adviser stepped back from the bowl without touching the water. A withdrawal. She didn't vote, but Lial only needed the support of five of the eight advisers to take the council seat. He already received four votes, not to mention his father's authority to decide in the case of a tie.

"I'll do whatever I can to help you and Kolvar," Lial whispered to Nym. "I won't support sending him to the dungeon."

Disgusted, Nym snorted. "Very magnanimous."

"I swear, this isn't what was supposed to happen." Lial glanced up as another adviser stepped back from the bowl.

Did the artisan adviser vote or withdraw? Did it even matter? She had to focus and be a witness to this lunacy. She'd played her part; the rest was out of her hands.

And she hated how the situation had spun out of her control.

She'd expected to turn her family's life upside down, yes, but now grief and pain threatened to suck her under. Emotion bubbled. The fury she'd pushed aside threatened to surface. It would've been better if she could scream, fight, destroy—anything to expel the brimming rage. Instead, her eyes burned. Emmyth's last image of her daughter would be one of apparent tearful distress.

Nym would rather jump into a vat of poison than cry. If anyone assumed she was sad, she might run them through. She dropped her gaze, ignoring the rest of the vote, terrified someone would notice tears lining her eyes.

If she slipped out, only one elf would notice. Her mother. Despite everything, Nym wouldn't abandon her. Nym gripped the glamour pendant and braced herself for the announcement naming Lial as the new councilor.

"We have a tie," Bellas said.

Surprised, Nym swallowed the lump in her throat but kept her face down. Omasys stepped off the dais.

"I admit," Emmyth interrupted, a touch of menace in her voice, "I suspected an attack by the Seekers was bound to happen."

Omasys stopped in his tracks, and the room silenced.

"Fortunately," Emmyth said, "when it did happen, our strongest Tides warriors were present, defending our kind. Otherwise, the *inevitable* attack would've been a slaughter."

Was her mother admitting her twisted reasoning behind her coordinated attack on her own kind at the Gathering?

Emmyth continued, "The Seekers have been a growing threat."

Because of you. Nym wiped her eyes, stunned that Emmyth would speak lies of omission after Nym had just explained the full horrors of the council's actions. Emmyth's words danced ridiculously around half-truths. Did she expect to rewrite history?

Emmyth continued, "Fortunately, Mormaris was just south of the attack and was able to alert the orcs."

Because you'd placed him there.

The edge of Emmyth's lip twitched. An almost-victorious grin. Omasys flicked a finger, signaling for the captain of the guard to take Emmyth into custody.

The captain didn't move a muscle.

"And Councilor Mormaris returned just last night." Emmyth lifted her chin.

The dwarven-made ship in the northern harbor—the note Kolvar received had said it arrived last night. Dwarves had been driven out of the realm, but the warships they'd crafted remained behind with the orcs.

"Fortunate, don't you think?" Emmyth's accusing gaze raked across Omasys and the four advisers who had voted to install Lial.

Emmyth signaled to the captain, and his attention swung to the back doors. On cue, the guards pulled them open, allowing in a stream of orcs. Pounding through the main aisle of the chambers, they marched two by two. Most of the orcs' long hair was braided, portions shaved to show their rune tattoos. Their skin ranged from dusky pink to lavender to periwinkle, and most had prominent tusks protruding from their lower lips.

Lial grabbed Nym, yanking her out of their path. She shoved him away, and he lifted his hands in surrender, but his eyes never left the newcomers streaming past. The lead orc tapped his shoulder with two fingers as he approached the council seats.

Emmyth returned the salute, signaling trust and camaraderie. Part of Nym felt a swelling of pride at her mother's duplicity. Her advisers had attempted to usurp her, but with the arrival of the orcs, Emmyth had snatched back control.

But then a realization shuddered down Nym's spine—her mother wasn't one for gracious forgiveness. She was a proponent of decisive *example.*

Councilor Mormaris swept through the open doors, his robes and long, black locks flowing behind him, his medallion prominently displayed on his chest. He gave Emmyth a respectful nod, but his lips were pressed into a thin line. Emmyth had taught her children to check the tension in Mormaris's jaw to gauge his mood; the muscles were so taut that Nym wondered if his teeth might shatter.

With a wave, Emmyth signaled whom to secure.

The wrists of three advisers were bound, and the captain secured Omasys with the very rope Lial's father had intended for Emmyth's wrists. Unsurprisingly, the councilor from the most prestigious family was left alone. She'd be reprimanded another way; Bellas might prefer banishment to Emmyth's punishments.

"Take these four to the dungeon," Emmyth commanded. "I'll deal with them later."

In a decade or two. Nym pitied their fate, even Daecyne's, as they were dragged away.

"What of my son?" Omasys asked as he was shoved toward the doors.

"What of him?" Emmyth flicked her hand, and the orcs dragged Omasys away. A merciless response considering he would be trapped with no communication, worried about the unknown for years.

The captain of the guard grabbed Lial's arm.

"Leave him," Emmyth commanded.

Sitting next to her, Mormaris tensed. "You wish to strip his titles, of course."

"What titles? He's earned nothing. He is nothing. Let the pawn be a pariah, a scourge on anyone who speaks with him."

Emmyth's cruelty sliced Nym. Lial was a fool, but he didn't deserve to be a living reminder of the consequences of crossing the councilors. He was annoying and naive, but Nym believed him when he'd sworn to have no knowledge of his father's devious plans.

"Let him witness these events. He can write to Kolvar about it in his little notes." Emmyth frowned, and Lial stopped breathing. "Yes, I know about your little communications. The black wax was a nice touch."

Lial was the spy? He reported to his father and his best friend, and *not* Emmyth. Nym wanted to smack him for being so thick-skulled.

"How did the orcs arrive here so quickly?" Nym asked, taking the focus off Lial; besides she wanted the answer. No one could've traveled from the Tree House faster than Nym. Yet the orcs did.

"I have multiple means of communication." Emmyth kept her tricks vague. "The trees began failing the day after you left, and the elves began to question everyone, starting with me."

Nym squirmed but said nothing and let her mother talk.

"At first, I assumed that impostors had glamoured as our family. However, I'd sent you on a mission to track down Ialant. And he knew of the Tree House. I had to admit you might have been involved."

Nym racked her mind, recalling her studies on travel and

fair folk communication. Ships were fast, but not faster than Nym on a horse and wyvern. She could only think of one means faster: dryads.

But how did Emmyth have dryads at her disposal? The more Nym figured out, the more questions she had.

"Then, it occurred to me that we haven't had any of the Mother's warriors here since the war," Emmyth continued. "We were due for a safety inspection of the palace."

A peacetime visit wouldn't need permission from the fae. And a visit that *happened* to intervene during a questionable council vote? Fortuitous, indeed.

"The councilor's perfect timing in arriving within a day of your own return," Emmyth said, "is another sign that Alysatraee is on our side."

"How can you say that?" Nym blurted. "We are Alysatraee's peacekeepers. If we can't do that, we don't deserve the seeds."

"You've been taught a very narrow view of the Mother—the old beliefs, from the years before the war. Your whole life has been naively climbing a lattice, oblivious that it's built with the bones of elves killed in combat."

Nym tucked her arms across her chest, holding back a venomous rebuttal.

"When I sent you to track Ialant and the Unarian captain, I knew you'd retrieve the glamour pendant. I knew you'd figure out where Ialant had been hiding. And finding out his companion is half-dryad ... brilliant work, daughter. But finding the Tree House? Beyond my expectations." Emmyth's face softened into the proud smile Nym had always worked diligently to earn. "I believed in you. But did you believe in me? No. You destroyed the orchard. You've made our kind at the Tree House doubt me and my will. But the mission continues, as Alysatraee wills it."

"This is insanity," Nym said. She glanced at Bellas who'd

been allowed to remain, but the adviser had lost all signs of rebellious spark.

"For me to show you a new path and expect you to blindly race down it is impractical. I realize that now. Yet pains me to see you fail this minor test of loyalty. Though, you were faithful to the teachings given to you. The teachings I allowed. Encouraged. So I won't execute you. Not yet."

Nym's throat constricted, and her arms squeezed around her ribs. Her mother's statement was as painful as any kick to the face Nym had ever experienced.

"Y-you threaten to execute your own ... your own daughter," Lial stuttered, "after she followed the rules you've given her, her entire life? After she accomplished everything you'd asked?"

Lial moved to stand between Nym and Emmyth. Making a desperate choice, Nym grabbed his collar with one hand and slapped him with the other. In that split moment, before his body spun, Nym slipped the glamour of Emmyth down his tunic.

"How dare you speak for me." Nym shoved him for good measure.

"Take him away, before he says something else he'll regret," Mormaris said through gritted teeth.

Two guards grabbed Lial's arms and dragged him away. He shouted something, but Nym didn't hear it. She was too focused on her mother.

"I'll give you time to decide where your loyalty lies, Nym." Emmyth's voice was cool, as if she hadn't just threatened to have her daughter murdered.

Hands tightened around Nym's arms.

"But until you do, you'll sit in the dungeon." Emmyth gestured to the guards at Nym's sides. "Search her for the glamour."

Nym ripped her arm out of their grips and snatched the root

she'd already used on Kolvar. She flashed it to the crowd and then shoved it in her mouth, swallowing it. "Come and get it."

Nym's taunt crossed a dangerous line. And she'd pay for it.

Mormaris's grip threatened to splinter the arm of the chair, and Emmyth's cheek twitched. Mormaris wouldn't dare suggest they gut Emmyth's child like a fish, but her mother might.

The root hit Nym's stomach like a rock, and she thought she'd be sick. For a moment, Nym wished she'd paid attention to her herbology lessons, then she'd know what happened if one ingested the root. Then again, perhaps it was better not to know.

"Get her out of my sight," Emmyth snapped.

Perhaps Nym's tiny victory would bring her solace as she stared at the same stone walls for years. Not even Kolvar could save her. Eventually, the guards would figure out Nym didn't have the glamour, finalizing her utter and complete failure.

Emmyth used her daughter's arrival to ferret out who was loyal. She'd known about Omasys's plans all along, and she'd set a trap for the dimwitted advisers. Now that they'd confirmed who'd spearheaded the revolt, the Tides Councilors would re-establish themselves, stronger than ever.

"Why?" Nym's lips moved, but no sound came out as the guards yanked her backward. She'd been so careful, but Emmyth had outmaneuvered them all.

Emmyth's eyes were as cold as the icy northern channel as her daughter was dragged from the chamber. Nym's vision tunneled as another realization dawned. Emmyth was hiding her away because the Council couldn't have anyone interfering with the elven designs. They were determined to poison the humans and re-ignite the war. And they were destroying anyone who stood in their way.

30
BASTARD HALF-BROTHER

Orion dreaded confronting Selleth, but he wouldn't be kept from his own rooms. He stalked through the palace, preparing himself for a verbal spar. Why avoid it when the princess would respect him more if he showed backbone, anyway? He'd held back for years, not wanting her to interfere with an invitation home. But now that he'd received it, he had to establish his place or be crushed under her heel.

Emerging from the guest wing of the palace, Orion crossed the massive hall. The paintings and tapestries had been removed centuries ago, except for the cold marble sculptures; splatters were more easily cleaned off stone. The vaulted space fit as many fae as the ballroom. Many still lingered after watching the brutal fight between a cockatrice and a hydra. Orion shuddered as servants wiped up the gore in the center of the room. The spring equinox festivities bordered on the horrific.

Tonight, Ivy was fair game; Orion was determined to protect her from becoming prey.

As Orion wove through the crowd, fae whispered, their

gazes drifting in his direction. He glanced up at the balconies where three stories of fae mingled overhead. Several observed him as he moved across the space toward the royal quarters. Ignoring the spectators, he pushed through the crowd.

At the end of the hallway near the entrance to the royal wing, two orcs chatted. A familiar face startled Orion. He swallowed his surprise at seeing Magdud, the magistrate of Carrus. Here in the fair realm, she'd thrown off her human glamour, and she jested with her companion.

Before Orion could approach Maggie, she broke off her conversation and strode toward Orion. She looked past him until she was a step away. Making brief eye contact, she gave him a quick orc salute, a double-tap to the shoulder, but then she added a subtle, third tap. Ever so slight, the gesture might've been mistaken for a sloppy greeting. But it was their code: she needed to talk. Urgently. Orion returned a nonchalant triple tap in return.

The two indifferently passed each other without a word, but Orion's mind churned. Why was Magdud in the fair realm at all, let alone on the spring equinox? Maggie had essentially cut herself off from every fae court when she and others had splintered from their kind in the human realm. Their kinfolk still dwelt in Aggord, one of the few strongholds still controlled by the fair folk. She'd broken no law, but had shattered the unsaid rule: thou shall not find contentment *outside*.

Orion strode past two fae guards and into a narrow hallway. The din faded, and his muddied thoughts cleared. For Magdud to be here and signal him meant she held sensitive information. Would she be at the ball? If so, Orion had to arrange a place to meet.

The flapping of wings announced Ash's arrival and snapped Orion out of his thoughts. She landed on his shoulder with a soft thud and nuzzled his chin.

"Well, hello, my long-lost companion," Orion jested as he climbed the winding staircase. "Did you eat yourself into a comfortable nap in Rime's rooms while I was away?"

Indignant smoke puffed from her nostrils, and she crouched down on Orion's shoulder. He assumed Ash was irritated with his teasing, but at the top of the stairs, Selleth came into view.

Orion vacillated between pride and worry that she'd waited for him. Either way, he approached his sister with caution.

"Good evening, princess."

"You're finally gracing us with your presence." Selleth looked him up and down in distaste. "I heard you were returning, and I wish to escort you to your rooms for the first time."

"Kind of you." Too kind. She'd either been blocked from his rooms and wanted to inspect them, she wanted a favor, or she simply intended to intimidate him. As they strode together, Orion decided that whichever it was, at least she was using honey rather than vinegar—no, rather than poison. Though, he guessed she had a blackmail threat or two up her sleeve as a backup.

"How do you know the orc?" Selleth asked.

Orion kept his pace even, but inside a warning screamed.

"What orc?" Orion asked, assuming nothing; doing otherwise was a sure way to give away information his sister might not know.

"The one you greeted a moment ago," Selleth said.

Definitely Magdud.

"I know many creatures that reside in the human realm, and she is a political asset," Orion said.

"You don't know her well?" Suspicion laced her voice.

How much of their exchange had Selleth noticed? Orion remained calm.

"I know her well enough."

"She either dislikes you," Selleth said, "or she's hiding something. Which is it? Or is it both?"

"When I need information from her city, she is helpful. She's loyal to the fair realm, if that's what you're asking."

Selleth was fishing for information on his allies—likely her future targets when she wanted to manipulate Orion.

"When I'm queen, I may need your assistance with the human realm," Selleth said. "A queen needs insights on the affairs of their kind. So you'll need to forget this lone dragon lifestyle and strengthen your connections. That sort of thing will make you useful."

I'm not a slave you've bespelled to control.

Orion bit his tongue, reminding himself that Selleth one day could become queen—Alysatraee save them all. He needed her respect, not her resentment.

Two guards stood at either side of his wide wooden door, featuring a tree. Each leaf was painstakingly carved into the wood. He pushed it open and entered the rooms.

"Rime whined about not getting these rooms," Selleth mused as she ran a hand across the stone wall. "I think father wanted him surrounded by books—but Rime must crack a binding if he wants anything to sink into that thick, wine-addled skull."

Selleth gave the crackling fireplace wide berth as she inspected the room. Ash lifted off Orion's shoulder and settled on a cushioned perch inset high above the fireplace. The room was larger than Rime's, though Orion might've misjudged the size; the prince's overstuffed furniture and pillows, clothes, shoes, and wine bottles filled every crevice.

Orion's desk dominated the room, a heavy chair tucked behind it. Orion imagined his future responsibilities meant many an hour in that very spot. After being an active guard for decades, he wondered how he'd adjust to court life.

Selleth opened a set of double doors, leading to a comfortable, four-poster bed covered with fur blankets. Orion was pleasantly surprised by the rooms. His father hadn't spared any expense.

"This room is far too hot for a pure-blooded fae." Selleth lifted her chin "And you have a small balcony."

Her barb might have pricked a month ago, but somehow her words had lost their sting. Selleth still bruised him, but since meeting Ivy, something had shifted. He respected himself more, as a dryad-fae. He didn't know how or when it had happened, and Orion hadn't even noticed the change until that moment—all fair folk deserved respect. He'd been taught this all his life, but now he *believed* it.

Selleth rambled insults about dwarves being mole rats. She chuckled, her mood dark. In public, the princess was pretentious about honoring all creatures. But Orion knew her prideful bias. Alone, her true beliefs were revealed—that fae were apex predators, and all others were prey to play with or to destroy.

If Selleth harmed Ivy, Orion feared what he might do. Yes, his oath bound him to return her safely. But before she left, was there a chance Ivy might enjoy the evening? Want to stay longer?

The room had fallen silent, and Orion blinked. Selleth stared at him with a knowing smirk. He definitely had to keep Selleth away from Ivy.

"Do you know?" Selleth asked, but Orion hadn't been listening to her babble. He had no idea to what she was referring. She waited, but Orion stayed silent. Her grin widened. "Dare I ask what has you so distracted? Or should I say *whom*?"

"Selleth, I've had a trying day, and I need to prepare for the evening."

Instead of leaving, his sister stepped closer. "Do you know who met with the king after we were dismissed?"

Orion paused. "I suppose you do?"

She grinned, the spark in her eye returning. "So you don't know."

Orion stayed silent.

But Selleth wasn't fooled. "Dear brother, humans may flit around their realm without consequence, but here information moves quickly. Keep up."

"I've done as you and our father have asked, which is to entreat our elven guest to stay in the realm."

"Well, then," Selleth smiled again. "As you've been a good half-fae, let me help you. You'd never guess who arrived—even I was surprised. And you wouldn't believe what they brought as a gift."

I have a guess. It has purple leaves and is sitting in the atrium.

"Remember, dearest brother, you need allies in the court. I can help you."

Orion was in an impossible position, forced to choose between the princess and the prince. But if Selleth forced him into a corner, Orion knew who he would pick: Rime. Selleth and her games could rot.

He'd find out who had come to visit the king. Whoever it was had arrived from the human realm. Chances were, they brought the Gathering sapling, or they knew who did. And Orion would find them without Selleth's help.

"Perhaps you will replace Rithmat as my most trusted adviser."

Orion would rather serve the human duke than do Selleth's dirty work. Besides, Selleth had never trusted him. Orion slowed, realizing there was one reason his sister would actually do exactly as she said. She would gladly flaunt Orion's loyalty. Rime had many good qualities, but humble wasn't one of them. If Orion and Rime's brotherly relationship cracked, Selleth would take advantage—she'd break it.

Orion's presence next to Selleth would be a daily kick to Rime's ribcage.

"Besides, you know that elf isn't your future." Selleth inspected her fingers.

Orion jolted at her sudden change of subject. "Ivy. Her name is Ivy Balrel."

Selleth flicked her hand as if waving off the name before it reached her ears. "That elf might not be the cleverest creature, but she's not a complete dimwit, either. She'd never sacrifice nearly a thousand years of her life in exchange for a tenth of that time in the fae realm."

Ash jutted her head off the cushioned platform overhead, her body angled and tense. The last thing Orion needed was a dragon attack.

"I wouldn't be so selfish as to ask such a thing of anyone." Orion kept his voice even. He'd longed to be with his kind, welcomed into the light of day. How could he ask Ivy to stay in a realm where she would age quickly without the aid of Alysatraee's seeds.

"She's smitten with you, clearly. You are the son of the king, after all." Selleth admired herself in the mirror, running a hand down her icicle strands of hair. "You'll grow bored of her. By the time she's realized it, she'll have wasted her short life. That's not fair, is it? Better to break her heart and let her hate you. Get her out of the realm as quickly as possible."

Selleth cared about no one but herself, however it didn't make the princess's solution invalid. While Ivy was the last creature to ever bore Orion, Selleth's proposal was logical. Though, the mere thought of separating from Ivy pained him.

"Dear brother," Selleth smiled, and Orion half-expected her lips to crack, "I must seem cold and calculating. But that's exactly why I need you. I need someone with compassion to guide me; someone I trust. I'd prefer your proven loyalty to our family over any groveling, ladder-climbing creature. When I'm queen, I will trust your word as our father did. Though the Winter Court may not appreciate you, I will."

Did Rithmat know of this proposal? Doubtful.

"What would you want in return?" Orion asked.

"Nothing."

"Just my sworn allegiance to support you in your bid for the throne?"

She grinned, and Orion could've sworn her teeth sharpened into points. "You'll need to pick a champion; it's expected. I'm a valuable ally. I will elevate Ivy by requesting the most respected families engage with her tonight."

Selleth was probing for a weakness, wanting to know if Ivy was a tender spot. Seeming to sense his unease, Ash shot down from her perch, landing on Orion's shoulder. Her taut neck reared, and Orion whispered for her to calm. Though his sister could cover any soot stain with glamour, the insult wouldn't be forgotten; Orion would find himself served dragon stew one evening. His mouth dried, knowing his duplicitous sister wasn't above such a malicious deed.

A knock came at the door, then opened. A servant stepped in and curtsied. Orion signaled for her to speak, grateful for the interruption.

"King Eldrin expects you," the servant said. "You will be the first royal family member presented."

"I'll be in the antechamber shortly," Orion said.

The moment the servant left, Orion glamoured himself in evening attire. Selleth grabbed his shoulder. He felt her glamour overtake his own, but he didn't resist the effort. Sensing no spiteful aggression, Orion let her glamour form. Now was not the time to test the limits of her power; nor reveal his own. His tunic changed from a midnight blue to deep emerald green, and his hair lengthened to his shoulders.

"I suggest this style for tonight." Selleth released him and stepped back, appraising her work.

She didn't ask what he thought. She didn't say it was the fashion. It's what she wanted. She might hate the look, but love the control. Even if he did champion her, it didn't guarantee her manipulations would ease. It was no wonder that Rime had given up and hidden away.

But Orion wasn't ready to be cowed.

"The green color is a subtle, approving gesture toward our elven guest." Orion kept his voice light. "And the hairstyle is similar to many elves I've met." He swept a hand over his long locks, simultaneously pulling it back into a low tail and shortening it to just below his neck. "But I prefer it shorter."

"As you wish." Selleth gave a tight-lipped smile.

If Orion promised to throw their brother out the window, Selleth would take Ivy under her wing. As a bonus for his allegiance, the princess would spill every detail on Eldrin's mysterious visitor. But Orion had given no promise. He would accomplish his goals without debt.

Tonight, he'd officially be a welcomed member of the court. He needed to make a good first impression, arrange a secret meeting with Magdud, and protect Ivy. The night was about to get complicated.

31

FAE TAILOR'S RESTRICTIONS

Ivy avoided eye contact, but she watched Prince Rime's every tick. She was in his court when his power was its greatest. Was he angry that Ivy hadn't left after he'd graciously taken her to the portal? Had she broken a fair rule? Would the prince take out his frustration with his brother on her?

"Are you sure you don't want me to glamour you for the ball?" Rime said to Ivy. "You can pretend to be a visiting fae from an outlying city. Or even someone debuting at the court?"

"Excellent idea." The fae tailor looked genuinely pleased with the suggestion.

Rime stepped closer, and Ivy scrutinized his mood. He could glamour her into a frog on a whim ... and toss her into the snow.

"I'll make you plain; no one will notice you," Rime said.

A safe camouflage? Why?

The tailor frowned, but before she could argue, Rime poked Ivy's back. Her reflection morphed into a ridiculously fluffy, sparkling, gem-encrusted, pale pink dress. Her skin shimmered along the cheekbones and up her shorter, fae-looking ears. The reflection looked like her, but with glass-smooth skin and every scar erased. Did fae sit around perfecting their beauty spells all day?

At least I'm not a frog.

Instead of mocking the frivolity, Ivy flattered. "You have incredible skill."

"Do what you will with her hair and make-up, but you can't send her out in that dress," the fae tailor huffed. "It's yesterday's fashion."

"Prince Rime," Ivy interjected, daring to push for adjustments, "I'm an elf. I don't want to hide what I am." She shifted, lifting the heavy, beaded material. "And, I do like the dress, but can you lighten the weight?"

The jewels hampered agility. In a fae ballroom, one couldn't be too careful.

The tailor stepped between Rime and Ivy. "Though I appreciate your clumsy attempt, let a master work." She snapped her fingers at the human servant and pointed for her to fetch the wine before turning to Rime. "Sweet berry red wine? Or woodsy white?"

"White," Rime said.

The tailor grabbed Ivy's shoulders, her fingers digging into the elf's flesh, and pivoted her subject toward the mirror. The tailor's forehead scrunched in concentration, and Ivy's bodice morphed into green velvet, structured with invisible boning, constricting at Ivy's waist like a vice. Dark beaded tulle overlaid the green satin skirt, extending to the floor in a divine swish of material and sparkling gems.

The human servant's hands clasped together, her eyes filled with admiration. "Beautiful. Simply exquisite. Your best work of the night."

"Diamonds?" Rime raised his brow, holding a goblet of wine in one hand.

"Emeralds." The fae tailor pursed her lips, inspecting her

work. "It would be better to hide the brawny musculature of her back, but she wishes to stand out as an elf." Disappointment laced her statement, but Ivy didn't mind showing her strong stature. Perhaps the fae would think twice before testing her.

"My turn," Rime said, jabbing the back of Ivy's skull.

Ivy's lip color deepened, but otherwise, her face remained the same. Her braided hair transformed into elegant curls, pinned behind her head and cascading over her shoulder. She couldn't help but admire their work. Turning, she noticed the un-glamoured edge of her scar that wrapped from her shoulder blade to her ribs. Rime had secured her hair with golden, leaf-shaped pins, putting her elongated ears on full display. Though Ivy didn't appreciate being handled like a doll, she conceded that the duo exceeded her expectations.

"Give us a moment?" Rime asked.

Ivy fiddled with her fingers as the fae tailor and human servant left, knowing Rime wanted *something*.

"How do you like the dress?" Rime's tone was light and without malice.

"Other than the fact that I'll freeze? Just fine."

Rime gave her a rueful grin. Without witnesses, the prince glamoured her without a touch. Sleeves appeared, but they were unhelpfully sheer.

"Heated pockets?" Ivy pressed.

He set down his nearly-full wine glass. "Fine."

Ivy slipped her hands into the warmth and smiled. "And a cloak?"

"You're *so* fussy. Worse than humans."

"So that's a 'no?'" Ivy kept her voice jovial, matching the prince's tone. But Ivy suspected that whatever Rime was angling for, she wouldn't like it. "Whenever I'm glamoured, my bow and arrow conveniently disappear." *Conveniently for everyone else. Not for me.* "It doesn't give an elf much confidence that she's trusted."

"Fae leave their weapons at home. It's uncouth. Other than guards, anyone found with a blade longer than their hand gets a lovely trip to the dungeon. And the food down there is terrible." Rime made a face. "Furthermore, as far as most fae are concerned, elves are austere ruffians. Don't give them more reasons to disdain you. And definitely, under no circumstances, run around like a lunatic warning of an impending war."

Ivy raised a brow.

"Yes, while I was waiting for Orion in that portal-tree, I heard about his report to the king."

Ivy wanted to ask exactly *what* Rime knew, but she already had a different, more important question. A familial question she didn't dare ask. Not yet.

Instead, she returned to the topic of weapons. "So, I'll be vulnerable when I meet the Summer Representative? I'll have nothing."

Rime gave an annoyed sigh and moved to her side. "Your elven sight and hearing isn't *nothing*. However ..." His words trailed off as he pressed his hand against the back of her waist. Beneath the glamour, Ivy felt a shift near her hip. Rime lifted his hand, revealing her father's knife in his grasp.

"It's a beautiful blade," Rime said, handing it over, hilt first. "And a sign of my trust."

Ivy grabbed the knife, comforted by the weight in her palm.

Rime gave her a leather strap. A scabbard. "I'd glamour this onto your thigh, but somehow I think Orion would make me regret it."

Ivy turned away from Rime and lifted her dress to secure the sheath. "You're wrong about Orion," she said while sliding the dagger into place. "We worked together to accomplish a mission. And now it's over. That's it."

"So you say, but I'm not buying what you're selling."

Could Rime be right? Ivy's heart swelled at the thought. Then she quickly quelled her reaction.

"There's nothing between us," Ivy said. *There can't be.*

She dropped the hem of the dress, sensing Rime's "request" coming. This was her last chance. Did she dare ask a question that risked Rime's good humor?

Yes. Yes, she did—it was now or never.

"Rime, did you make a glamour for Ialant Balrel, my father?" Ivy asked.

Rime narrowed his eyes, silent.

"A simple 'yes' or 'no.'"

"No."

"Did Orion?"

Rime's lip twitched. "He can't. Or at least I didn't think he could. But, who knows what Orion can do."

Ivy paused. "What do you mean?"

"Most Winter fae can create glamours for others. But Orion can only make glamours for himself, or so he says."

"Has he ever lied to you?"

"A ridiculous question. You should know better." Rime looked at Ivy like a dirty smudge on a pristine cloth. "The iron-clad law restricts fae from speaking falsehoods. But we can bend the truth or leave it out. However, dryads have different rules. So who knows what Orion can speak."

"I just want to know what happened with my father. He must have come to the fae realm for a glamour. I have little time to find answers before I leave."

"Even if Orion asks you to stay?" Rime paused. "My brother wouldn't have brought you here just to speak to the representative; he's shared important messages in the past and never brought anyone."

Because of his accidental promise, he had to bring me.

However, his later admission came to Ivy's mind, *I thought we could be alone, together.*

Ivy selected her words with care. "Orion probably felt sorry for me. He's feeling charitable."

Rime chuckled. "I don't think so. You're important to him."

A warning rose inside Ivy. Would Rime use her to manipulate Orion?

"No, I'm temporary," Ivy said. "Elves can't stay in the fae realm."

"So, Orion isn't worth shortening your life by several hundred years?" Rime barked a laugh. "I agree."

Seeds only worked in the human realm. She'd age quickly while the fae around her didn't. Though fae could live a thousand years in either realm, elves could not.

"Well, I'm feeling charitable, too. And not just because you're likely to earn your father's council seat," Rime said. "I won't take advantage of your naivety at the festivities."

How kind of you.

Rime had a spark of mischief in his eye as he gestured to the door. "It's time to leave for the celebrations."

Ivy hurried to the door, hoping to end the questioning.

"In the spirit of cooperation," Rime continued from behind her, "I advise you to avoid the princess and her lackey Rithmat. My sister delights in elevating herself by stepping on the broken backs of others. Don't bow to her."

"I appreciate the warning."

Rime placed his hand on the door latch. Ivy anxiously waited for him to open the door, but he didn't.

"Ivy, can Orion shadow-travel?"

"I've never heard the term." Ivy blanched, guessing at *exactly* what the prince meant.

"Winter magic enables many of us to manipulate shadows. However, relatively few can transport themselves. Not only is it complicated to learn, but one must be born with a large magical reserve. Half-fae cannot perform this magic. At least, I've never heard of anyone who could."

The reason for Rime's visit became crystal clear. He wanted to know Orion's secrets. Of all the creatures in both realms, he assumed Ivy would know.

And she did.

"Who knows *you* can shadow travel? Or that *you* can glamour at a great distance?" Ivy already knew the answer to the latter.

The prince had expected her to be in a different realm by now, and he'd been sloppy. Ivy knew too much. Even if she hadn't promised Orion to keep his magic a secret, she would have. She'd wouldn't deliver such a cutting betrayal. "Tonight, I will not be revealing anything about *anyone's* magic."

Ivy's tone signaled the finality of her words. By keeping Orion's secret, she'd prove her trustworthiness to Rime, too. Would Rime see her as a possible ally or a threat? It was a risky gamble. Frogs didn't do well in the snow.

Rime's nostrils flared. He opened his mouth to speak, but then he snapped it shut. He threw open the door and stormed down the hall.

Ivy stared at the ceiling, calming her frayed nerves. "At least I'm not a frog." She took a deep breath. "Not a frog."

A servant cleared her throat, and Ivy realized the same human servant was waiting for her in the hall, giving her a curious look. "I'm to deliver you to the ballroom. You may hop if that's your preferred way to travel."

Ivy swallowed, but the servant flashed a grin before leading Ivy down the hall. Ivy forced herself to raise her chin, pretending she was a welcomed guest. But inside, she was anxious to find Orion.

Only because I'm in an unfamiliar place with creatures who would gladly test the sharpness of their claws by sinking them into my back.

Once she returned to the human realm, her life would become far less complicated. Ivy was meant to fall in love with an elf—a peacekeeper. Orion was a half-fae born to spy and manipulate. He wasn't the one for her.

Even if he was willing to live with humans, Ivy wouldn't ask Orion to give up his dreams and his family. Though she wasn't sure what spurred Orion's brotherly fight, it was no coincidence the argument had started with her arrival. Her mere presence caused contention. Ivy would do anything to get another day with Iris, her sister. She wouldn't be a stumbling block in Orion and Rime's relationship.

The servant guided Ivy into the Great Hall, and the magnificent space nearly stopped her in her tracks. The overhead glass dome framed the moon. Motes of light danced between the glass and crystalline frosted walls, bathing the room in soft shimmer. Fae and orc guards dotted the wrap-around mezzanine overhead. A wide staircase swept from the mezzanine to the main floor with a grand platform halfway between.

The servant pointed out the food and wine on long banquet tables, but Ivy found herself bouncing on her heels, alone and small.

"Orion will descend the stairs and pause for an introduction on the landing," the servant said. "The honored guests will be introduced first. Then the royal family."

Ah, the platform was for showcasing the influential fair folk. Ivy was happy for Orion—he was welcomed and celebrated. She reminded herself to enjoy this moment because soon it would be gone. She should be appreciative their paths had crossed. This was his home, and elves didn't belong. Ivy pushed away any spark she'd held for him—she'd only get burned.

"Sorry for all the stares," the servant continued as she ushered her to an open spot on the floor. "You're handling it well."

Ivy hadn't noticed, but once the servant drew her attention to the haughty looks, they were hard to ignore. Fae stole glances, their faces cold glares. Ivy began to sweat despite the chilly room. Even the servants scrutinized her every move.

"Perhaps I should've allowed a glamour."

"I like that you remind the snobby fae that elves still exist. Fae think they're the center of Alysatraee's creation. But I know fair lore. Fae are simply a branch, not the whole tree." The servant's tone turned formal, and pity flitted across her face. "You're Orion's guest, but don't expect him to spend much time with you. He'll be officially introduced tonight, and he's meant to spend his time with the high court and dignitaries. It's customary for him to grace you with a single dance, however, so be alert. Make sure he can easily find you at any point during the evening. Do you know the dances?"

Ivy nodded, though she wondered how Orion would find her in the sea of fae.

"Enjoy your evening." The servant flashed a tight smile before scurrying away.

A fae bumped Ivy's shoulder, scowling. Another shot a menacing stare, making Ivy's skin crawl. She dropped her attention to the non-threatening brownies as they moved massive trays of food to the banquet tables. About half the height of an elf, brownies were barely visible under the folds of linen, earthy-toned clothing that piled up their neck, resting under their noses.

The room quieted, and everyone pivoted to face the stairs. Ivy glanced up as the high commissioner began to announce names. The first was a striking fae with dark skin, white freckles, and smooth horns. Another with wings. Another with antlers.

Ivy lost track of their names, and her attention wandered. A tall brownie without a tray wove through the crowd, his back to Ivy. Before he disappeared into the crowd, she caught a glimpse of his pale blue tunic, fine trousers, and long cap. It wasn't typical brownie attire, and something about the creature seemed familiar.

"Lord Orion Arya, of the Shadowmoon bloodline," the high commissioner announced, "Portal Keeper of the Realms."

A hush fell as the half-dryad stepped down the stairs to the landing. Ivy felt as if the room faded. Orion's grey feathered wings framed his broad shoulders, where Ash perched and somehow managed to look regal. Orion looked every bit the royal son of the fae king, dripping in confidence and impossibly attractive. His sharp gaze scanned the crowd. It was unrealistic for her to expect him to spot her, but when he looked in her direction, he stopped. His eyes fell on her; he lingered for a heartbeat, his expression remaining stoic.

Even so, Ivy's heart pounded against her ribs. Her careful planning was for naught. The spark she'd promised to stomp out stubbornly flared brighter. She wasn't sure if she should be infuriated with her treacherous feelings and bolt from the room, or ignore the blaring warnings and blindly let the night wash over her.

No matter what she decided, Ivy knew this night was one she was destined to regret. The real question was, which choice would she regret *less*?

32
DANCE IN WINTER COURT

An unending line of fae waited to congratulate Orion, but his attention kept sliding to Ivy. He'd spent the hour before his introduction trading favors to ensure that only families he'd approved asked her to dance; each were under oath not to bargain, tease, or embarrass the elven visitor. When they asked why he bothered to help her, Orion simply said that she was a guest of the royal family and was to be treated as such. Now that he was a recognized son of the king, it was true. Though, it wasn't the complete truth.

"An honor, as it were," a centaur with a grey-flecked beard continued his long-winded congratulations, "to be given a title of Lord Orion Arya, Portal Keeper." The centaur's haughty tone and constant throat clearing grated on Orion's nerves.

"Yes. Quite." Orion wondered why Eldrin hadn't made him an ambassador to the human realm, a more prestigious position that the king had hinted at on many occasions. It was almost as if his father wanted to restrict him to the fair realm as much as possible.

Again, Orion looked past the centaur at Ivy. She was smiling at her fae partner, and it might have made Orion jealous, but he recognized the slight tightness in her cheeks.

"Of course, the Winter fae are best suited to the courts ..." The centaur let his sentence fade.

Orion yanked his attention back to the conversation, quickly dissecting what had been left *unsaid.*

"When I am scheduled to visit your land, I'll send advanced warning." Orion kept his face a well-practiced mask. He'd rather the centaurs just tell him they didn't welcome his visit. As merely the king's messenger, the fair folk were direct; but now, with his official title, the passive-aggressive comments were already tiresome.

Even Ash had grown bored. Orion could've sworn he'd seen her with someone's jeweled ring, but now the dragon was nipping meat off a banquet table, no ring in sight. With a last rip, Ash flew toward the balcony. Orion figured she'd find a way into his office window and end up cuddled on her new perch. The sneaky dragon had already amassed a glittering hoard.

Steps away, Rime pointedly ignored Orion. But whenever a parent of a single, eligible fae daughter asked Orion to dine at their home soon, the prince rolled his eyes or glared over the rim of his goblet. When Orion finally got rid of the centaur, he couldn't put off dancing. He was almost grateful to escape Rime's barbs and fair folk questions; the conversations might've seemed shallow to a casual listener, but every sentence was riddled with innuendos and subtle traps.

Let's get this over with.

Moving past the press of bodies, Orion asked the first fae to dance. Each partner had been negotiated in advance, a small price to pay in exchange for a safer evening for Ivy. Orion was determined not to look at his elven guest; staring made his affection obvious. He'd tried telling himself they were necessary allies, his loyalty merely the result of the accidental oath.

However, though Orion was loath to admit it, he dreaded parting from Ivy.

But what could be done? As Selleth said, it was kinder to keep a distance.

After Orion endured three dances, his ears ached from gossip and cutting remarks. His collar felt too tight, the room seemed to crush in, and he longed for silence. Or a sincere conversation. At the very least, his partner could discuss the weaknesses of the ballroom security or the qualities of swords versus axes. Instead, Orion plastered on a smile, nodded, and became a shallow, distant shell.

His father would be proud, if he'd noticed. The king had left for the outside terrace where he'd soon perform a showy bit of magic: controlling the weather. Orion glanced out the open, exterior doors. His dancing partner chattered away, blind to Orion's indifference. Ivy's form danced in his periphery, pulling his awareness. As if sensing him, her gaze lifted to his; she was warmth in a cruel storm. For one glorious moment, he allowed himself to study the freckles across her nose, the curls framing her tanned face, and her red lips.

She blinked, breaking his serene oblivion. She turned her head toward the open doors, to the king, then back at Orion. Her expression softened, and the corner of her lips curved in a reassuring smile. If he could wrap himself up in Ivy, he would.

The dance steps took them further from each other, their line of sight interrupted. Orion sighed as his view swung across the crowd. Before he could attempt to listen to his blathering partner, he noticed Magdud. The orc's stare could burn a hole through wood. She gave a quick jerk of her head, then slipped into the hallway that led toward the royal wing. But the same hallway led to a lesser-used entrance to the atrium—an excellent meeting place.

"When will you visit the eastern province," his dance partner mewled.

"When the king sends me." Orion couldn't drum up enough effort to sound interested. His partner still gave him a saccharine smile as she massaged his neck. It was all he could do not to physically shudder.

The dance dragged on, and Orion was anxious to follow Maggie. The dance partners Orion had arranged should afford him a quarter-hour conversation with Magdud. Still, he wished he could ask Rime to protect Ivy while he was out of the room.

Finally, the dance ended. Orion extricated himself and marched toward a side exit. He couldn't help a backward glance at Ivy. Instead of pleasure, horror snaked through him; Selleth and her entourage were surging toward their elven guest. With the princess's intensity, no fae dared approach, leaving Ivy vulnerable. With Orion leaving, Selleth was swooping in, claws extended.

Orion spun on his heel and strode back into the throng. The prominent fae families were mere blurs in his periphery as he cut straight to Ivy. But Selleth was closer. Did the princess have one of her boot lickers prepared to dance with Ivy? The result could be disastrous. Orion's stomach tightened, and he moved faster, forgetting cool decorum. Fortunately, Ivy ripped her gaze away from the coming horde of malicious fae and spotted Orion. The tightness in her face tore at him, but at least she had enough wits about her to pivot and walk gracefully at an angle away from Selleth, meeting Orion in the center of the floor.

If the musicians noticed the pair or if it was luck, Orion didn't know, but the music began.

"Would you care to dance?" Orion asked.

In answer, Ivy placed one hand in his open palm, sending a wave of warmth through him. Orion wrapped his fingers around hers and told himself it was proper and expected for him to dance with his invited guest. It was fine. *Fine.* No one knew how his heart raced the moment he placed his hand on her back. Then their feet moved in rhythm with the music, their bodies effortlessly in sync.

"I didn't know if you'd get a chance to break away from your admirers." Ivy looked up through her long lashes.

Orion dropped his attention to Ivy's dark eyes, wanting to swim in them.

"I'd planned to dance with you at the end of the evening, then escort you directly to the equinox ceremony with the Summer fae." That was the safest plan. Or he'd thought it was. Now he realized he couldn't leave Ivy—not here.

"I'm so pleased you've been given a title. A proper welcome home." Ivy's words were sincere. Orion almost wished for bitterness—it would make it easier to push her away. But Ivy was kind. Despite losing her family, she celebrated Orion's reunion with his own.

Orion pulled her closer, his thumb brushing up against the flesh of her back. He slid his hand down the velvet bodice to her lower back, but somehow the action felt even more intimate. The way they seemed to fit together was probably due to the time they'd spent trekking through the forest. He'd lived among human guards for years, but he'd kept himself at an emotional distance. Honesty was vulnerability—he'd never intended to share so much of himself with Ivy. Now he was torn, wanting her closer, but knowing they were scrutinized. Knowing this could be their only dance. Knowing she was leaving.

"How can I avoid Selleth?" Ivy asked the obvious, practical question.

Orion wanted to tell her to stay by his side until dawn. But he couldn't be alone with Ivy. Everyone would suspect he was whisking her away to a private corner. His attention would put an even bigger target on Ivy's back. He'd begun to hope—foolishly—that Ivy would consider staying for a day or two, but apparently, Selleth and every other manipulative fae had set their sights on her.

"Orion." Ivy's fingers whispered across his neck, sending a shiver down his spine. "I'd like to see the view from the balcony."

Beyond the main terrace, the balcony wrapped around the castle, creating many semi-private alcoves. It might have been a good idea if it weren't *Ivy.* She bit her lip, drawing his attention to their perfect shape. What would it be like to kiss her?

"You'll freeze out there," Orion made an excuse, not trusting himself. "King Eldrin intends to bring snow before midnight."

"I'll be gone tomorrow. Who knows if I'll ever return." Ivy's gaze flicked from his eyes to his lips. "The night won't last and ... no regrets."

It was a terrible idea, but he couldn't deny Ivy's request. He'd get her a cloak. She'd experience the snow. She'd gain a memory. He just hoped he didn't get his heart ripped out in the process.

"Of course." Orion pivoted her, his hand pressed against her lower back, guiding her toward the doors.

33
BARELY CRUEL KISS

Ivy could see little of the dark forest beyond the railing, except for the many bonfires. Overhead, clouds rolled in, diffusing the moonlight and hiding the stars. Ivy would've welcomed blanketing darkness, but blue orbs along the railing bathed the balcony in a soft glow. She'd never cursed light so much in her life. The instant Orion had taken her hand to dance, what had remained of her icy resolve had melted into a puddle.

Orion curled his wings, buffering her from the wind as puffs of snow began to fall. Further down the balcony, other fae mingled in their sheer dresses and frosted materials, impervious to the chill.

"Snow? On the spring equinox?" Ivy asked, relishing how his feathers created a warm cocoon.

"The king flexes his might, *especially* on the spring equinox. When the Summer Representative arrives, he wants to remind the contingency of exactly whose realm they're in."

"It doesn't hurt to showcase his power to all the Winter creatures, as well." Ivy grinned. Her gaze skimmed over his face, his lips, daring to look where her fingers itched to touch.

"Sometimes the best way to avoid battle is a display of strength."

A servant rushed to Orion's side and handed him a cloak. A half-dryad wasn't immune to the cold, yet he tugged his satin-lined cloak around her shoulders. The rough feel of his hands sent goosebumps down her arms. The feathers of his wings barely fluttered in the rising wind, and Ivy wished she could see him fly. Just once.

"May I?" Ivy gestured to his wings.

Orion tilted his head but nodded. Ivy ran her fingertips over the silky grey feathers. She held her breath and wove her fingers deeper, the down beckoning. Orion winced, and Ivy jerked back, concerned that she'd somehow injured him.

"My wings are just sore," Orion reassured her, gently taking her hand.

He pulled her hand to his chest, and Ivy melted closer, into his warmth and singularly delicious scent of earth, winter berries, and snow. She exhaled and studied the feathers, each one grew darker at the tip. She ran a thumb of her other hand gingerly down a single vane. Her flesh glided across the surface like water, yet the touch set her every nerve on fire. Ivy branded this moment into her mind, determined to recall it again and again. Soon, elves from the House of Seeds would travel safely with their families again, but Ivy would only have memories to keep her company. And this would be a favorite.

"Summer won't arrive for another two hours," Orion said. "I'll keep you safe until then."

Ivy was particularly wary of one fae: the princess. Selleth's maliciousness oozed from her pores. While Rime was volatile, he left Ivy in one piece. She guessed the princess wouldn't be so generous.

"I have a meeting I cannot miss." Orion released her hand.

"But, I have a secure place for you. I'll assign your guards, personally."

"Don't put me away." Ivy met his eyes. She'd be alone for hours, days, *years* to come. "I'm safe with you."

"Are you?" His fingers brushed a wayward curl from her cheek.

Ivy ignored all reason and pressed her palms against his chest. She felt his heartbeat quicken. She was drawn to him—perhaps because she couldn't keep him. But she had this moment. Wrapping her fist in the fabric of his tunic, she pulled him closer. His arms wrapped around her, closing the distance.

Orion hesitated, his lips a breath from her. His eyes searched her, his face reflecting twisted emotions of want and concern.

"Orion," Ivy pleaded.

Orion's hands ran up her back, around her shoulders, and took her face in his hands. He paused, poised on the precipice. Then he tipped up Ivy's chin and leaned closer, and her heart thrummed a frenetic beat. His lips pressed to her forehead, and Ivy closed her eyes, letting his kiss seep into her skin.

A sweet whisper of what might have been.

He straightened, but Ivy didn't open her eyes. Instead, she leaned her cheek into his palm cupping her face. Her fist still gripped his tunic, unable to release him. He ran his trembling thumbs across her cheeks. Grateful for every drop of affection, Ivy slowly drank it in.

Orion leaned away. His one hand gripped the balcony railing, and the other lingered on her waist.

Of course, he didn't want to give his whole heart to an elf who wouldn't reside in the fair realm. He wouldn't ask her to stay, though if he did she'd be sorely tempted. And just because she was willing to break her heart for a moment of bliss didn't mean he would do the same.

Orion's voice was rough when he spoke, pulling her attention back to his lips. "A trusted guard will escort you to my chambers. Now that I'm in the royal wing, no one is allowed entry without my permission, except on the king's order. Not even Selleth. I'll send for you when my meeting is over. It will be brief."

"I'd rather stay at your side." Ivy glanced past him at the jovial fae chattering further away. She longed to be near Orion, but at the same time, she knew nothing of his clandestine meeting. Blindly joining could be unwise. "Either way, I trust your decision."

Orion looked upward and sighed. His jaw set, he rested Ivy's hand in the crook of his arm, in a formal manner, and led her to stairs and down to a lower level of the balcony. Servants threw open a set of doors, and Orion swept Ivy through. Orion kissed her knuckles, then released her just as they turned a corner. Orion's appearance changed into that of a fae stranger wearing a guard's uniform. Ivy straightened as they passed another set of guards. Without Orion's distracting touch, Ivy recognized the hall and the scent of the atrium. Orion was headed toward the royal wing.

Ivy's heart sunk. Orion *was* the fae guard delivering her to his office. If he didn't want her near, she wouldn't beg. That's something she'd *definitely* regret. But, instead of turning up the staircase to the royal chambers, he turned down the hall that led to the atrium. Ivy's connection to the earth grew along with the scents of damp soil and the sound of rushing water.

They entered the atrium, greeted by a hundred narrow rivulets. Dense plantings now boasted sprouting leaves. Ivy's mood lightened, relishing the pulsing, growing life. Even with the moon hidden by the stormy clouds, Ivy could easily see green buds and hear nocturnal critters.

"No gardeners at night?" Ivy asked.

"Not tonight," Orion said as his fae guard glamour dropped. "All Winter fair folk are invited to the festivities. Human servants are re-tasked with roles to support the event. You should see the kitchens. The atrium isn't popular, anyway—the summer elements are uncomfortable for Winter."

Footsteps stomped in their direction, and Ivy focused on the trail to the center of the atrium, locating the culprit.

"I hope you're meeting an orc," she whispered.

Orion grinned as an orc with white hair and broad shoulders approached. Rune tattoos were popular among the orcs, but Ivy didn't recognize the symbol on the visitor's scalp.

"Who is this?" the orc asked, her tusks framing her frown.

"This is Ivy Balrel," Orion said. "She's here to do the Mother's will and help broker peace. Ivy, this is Magdud."

Ivy wondered at the specific, and slightly odd introduction. But, Magdud's shoulders relaxed.

"I'm not in Winter for giggles," the orc said. "I was requested."

"I figured you wouldn't leave Princess-death-stare behind just for a stuffy winter celebration," Orion joked.

"Who says I left her?" Magdud pursed her lips.

"Not a bad idea, really. She should be *left* here when you return."

"Pft! I'll leave her with Rime while I'm at it. He needs a familiar."

"Probably not one that will kill him."

Magdud's smile faded, and she glanced over her shoulder. "I have disturbing news. The orcs from Aggord have been sent to multiple locations. A warship was deployed. A *warship.* Something isn't right."

"How long ago?" Ivy asked.

"About two weeks after I last saw you," she said to Orion. "Over a month ago, human time."

"Around the time of the attack at the Gathering." Orion rubbed his chin.

"Perhaps I have another piece of this puzzle." Ivy led them to the Gathering sapling.

"What kind of tree is this?" Magdud asked.

"It's a sacred Gathering tree," Ivy spoke, but her attention was drawn to the soil at the base. "They produce the elven seeds."

Magdud stepped back, her body stiff.

"Someone's been here." Ivy pointed at fresh footprints, too small and wide to be fae or elven.

"Brownie?" Magdud asked.

"Gnome," Orion said.

Ivy swallowed, her mind reeling. It was a gnome she'd seen earlier in the ballroom, dressed in fine blue tunic.

"This tree appeared after I met with the king yesterday," Orion began. "A visitor from the human realm met with him directly after I did. Gnomes assisted in the Tree House. Any one of them could have transported the sapling."

"No, it wasn't just any gnome." Ivy raised her voice, "I know you're here, Zel."

Magdud and Orion silenced, their hands sliding to their weapons. Ivy signaled for her companions to calm. With all the running water, tracking a gnome in the atrium would be a challenge; Ivy wanted Zel to come to them. Orion lifted his hands away from his sword, his palms forward, showing he was unarmed. Magdud frowned but followed.

"How did you know?" Zel's voice echoed, but Ivy pinpointed his location, just thirty steps away on her right.

"This is where I'd have gone tonight, given the chance," Ivy said. "Please talk with us. We swear you no harm." Ivy glanced at Magdud who took a deep breath, reluctantly nodding.

"I had to bring the tree," Zel called. "It was my only chance.

I expected to turn it over to an adviser, receive the appreciation of the fair folk, and return home. I was surprised it earned a meeting with the king. Honest."

"If you received your accolades, why stay?" Ivy asked.

She'd been a fool. Zel had told her many times that he wanted to return to the fair realm. He wanted to remove the black mark from his name. Of course, bringing a gift of this magnitude would tempt him.

"I got a gift from the king himself, and a note with his seal," Zel said, defensively. Then his voice turned sad. "But I couldn't go home."

Ivy shook her head, pitying the gnome's position. "Because deep down, you knew gifting a sacred tree to any fair folk was against the Mother's will. But, we can still work together and fix this."

Killing the tree was the simple solution. Ivy moved to rip the tree out of the dirt; newly planted, it wouldn't be difficult to destroy. As her fingers gripped the bark, a shock reverberated up her arms and down her body, rooting her to the ground. A vision opened up in her mind—of Zel.

The gnome handed something to a flailing Seeker—a hidden object.

"Ivy!" Orion shouted.

Her vision snapped away. Orion was behind her, an arm bracing her against his chest, holding Ivy upright. Her fingers still gripped the top of the tree. She sensed its weakness; with a single tug, she could uproot it.

"Dear Mother, please forgive me," Magdud whispered urgently behind them both. "And also forgive Orion for being a love-blind twit who brought me into this mess."

Ivy released her grip, but not because of Magdud's words of fear. But because within the glimpse of a vision she'd seen, there was a hint of *hope.* Her earlier visions were visceral and close, but this one felt veiled like she was an outsider.

"Zel," Ivy's voice shook as she stared at her hand, "the Gathering tree has a message for you."

She waited for Zel as he paced. Finally, he moved closer. Orion loosened his arm around Ivy but stayed by her side. Zel peeked around a nearby tree, hesitating.

"I just want to go home," Zel's voice trembled. He slid to the ground, staring blankly ahead.

"The Seekers probably want the same," Orion whispered.

"Does the tree speak with you?" Ivy asked. Gnomes weren't required to live in the human realm and didn't benefit from the seeds, but they were connected to plants and the earth.

"Gnomes communicate in their own way. I've tried, but she rarely whispers to me." Zel slumped.

"Try again. Ask a different question. Or perhaps ... be open to a different answer."

Zel raised a doubtful brow, but he lumbered closer and pressed his hands into the loamy soil beneath him, his fingers worming down into the ground.

Ivy looked away, feeling intrusive. Without thinking, she reached for Orion's hand. As she brushed his palm, his fingers grasped hers, firmly grounding her. While she had Orion, she'd take all the strength he was willing to give.

Zel mumbled something unintelligible. She glanced at the gnome, and his eyes were open and fixed on the tree.

"Zel?" Ivy asked.

"She wants me to heal the Seekers," Zel whispered.

"Impossible," Magdud gasped.

Ivy's jaw dropped. The Seekers were her natural enemies. She'd run from them. Feared them. Killed them.

"Did she show you how?" Ivy asked, stunned and questioning.

"I only know that Alysatraee commands it." Zel moved toward the tree, ignoring the others. "I should've destroyed this tree as I'd promised you and Ialant. But, Alysatraee has a better path. I felt the relief of the corrupted, as if I was one of them."

Was Ivy expected to help heal those who'd killed her family?

"I once wanted revenge on the humans," Zel said, as he fell to his knees and began digging around the tree's base. "Later, with Ialant, our attempts to fix what we'd done were thwarted."

Ivy refused to accept that her father had thrown away the last decade of his life for nothing. "Your work. The mistakes you made and the things you learned—you have knowledge no one does."

Magdud punched a hand to her hip, her voice awed. "Between betting on finding an extinct Pegasus or on Seekers ever getting healed, I'd have put my coin on the winged horses. But, if the Mother wills it ..."

"I could be their salvation," the gnome finished Magdud's thought, adding in a quieter voice, "And my own."

"If you'd consider staying, Zel," Orion said, "I can protect you and your work. I'll talk to King Eldrin and find suitable accommodations and a workspace."

"If Zel heals the Seekers, repairing the relations between the realms is possible," Ivy said. Her mind shifted, latching on to new ideas.

"For now, we need to meet with Summer," Orion said.

Ivy released Orion's hand and knelt down where Zel still sat in the soil. "If you'd prefer to work in the human realm, I'll assist you. Whatever you need. I'm not as knowledgeable as my father was, but I'll do what I can."

Zel gave her a timid smile.

"I can assist you both in Carrus," Magdud added, looking at Ivy and Zel.

Zel raised his chin, his voice determined, "First, I'll—"

Ivy pressed a finger to her lips, warning him to quiet. Footsteps sounded. Ivy jerked her attention back to the atrium entrance. With the rushing water, she hadn't noticed the intruder.

"A fae entered the atrium," Ivy gave a low warning. "And he's headed this way."

34

TEMPTING FAE DISTRACTION

Orion helped Ivy to her feet and dropped his voice, "We've been followed."

Magdud scanned the pathways. "I'll circle around to the northern hall."

"Go, we'll buy you time." Orion turned back to Zel, but the gnome had disappeared, forced to leave the tree behind.

"Zel's resourceful," Ivy assured him, "but we must draw the intruder to us to distract from Magdud."

Orion regretted not taking Ivy to his rooms, leaving her out of this. Though if he had, they wouldn't have discovered Zel.

"It's been an illuminating visit," Ivy spoke in a regular tone, then laughed. The bubbling sound of joy rang through the atrium, trumpeting their location and drawing in the spy.

Orion dropped her hand and whispered, "We should act like ..."

"Um, friends?" Ivy teased, but without meeting his gaze.

"I'm only trying to keep you safe."

"Too late." She forced a smile.

The urge to wrap her in his arms was overwhelming, but instead, he led Ivy away from the sapling. He'd keep the target on her as small as possible. Orion hated these political games, but he relaxed his posture and strolled forward. "Next week, this place will be so green, you'd hardly recognize it."

"I'm ever so grateful you gave me a tour of the atrium. But," she raised her voice, loud enough for the intruder to hear, "it seems we have company."

Rithmat slunk into view on their left. "Here you are."

Orion stepped forward, flaring his wings just enough to keep Ivy out of the adviser's reach. "Rithmat, I'm surprised to see you here rather than celebrating in the Great Hall."

"What about you? You're the honored guest of the night, but I see you found your own entertainment." His lips curled into an oily grin.

Ivy recoiled, and Orion scowled at him. At least Rithmat was smart enough to look abashed as he cleared his throat.

"I'm here to fetch the elf for the Aequus Ceremony," the adviser said.

"We're not meeting for over an hour. What's the hurry?" Orion asked.

An uncomfortable silence followed, but Orion let Rithmat fidget. If he was on the king's errand, he'd be impertinent. His nervousness meant Selleth had tasked him to spy on Orion.

Of all the dangerous creatures from across the realm currently in the palace, his sister chose to spy on Orion. He stayed calm, but inside a warning sounded louder than the central Unarian bell. He'd thought he'd avoided Selleth's paranoia. He was wrong. What was the princess worried about?

Rithmat's attention slid to Ivy, scrutinizing her behind Orion's wing. Perhaps Rithmat wasn't spying on Orion after all. But why Ivy?

"Are you escorting me to the ceremony?" Ivy asked Orion, her voice tight.

"Sons of kings don't escort visiting witnesses," Rithmat purred. "That's not a task worthy of their time. But I'd be—"

"I'll escort her," Orion interjected. Though being close to Ivy was increasingly difficult, Orion wasn't about to hand her over to the slippery adviser.

Rithmat raised a brow, shifting to get a better look at Ivy before he continued, "They're meeting—"

"I know the ritual," Orion bristled, his wings flaring further. He'd grown tired of others assuming his father hadn't taught him well. "Now, if you'll excuse us."

Rithmat gave Orion a stiff bow. "As you wish."

The adviser marched out of view, and Ivy tilted her head, listening.

"He's gone." She wrapped her arms around herself.

"We could return to the ball," Orion offered, though he wasn't in the mood to be stared at or fawned over.

"If that's what you'd prefer," Ivy said.

"Did I upset you? Did—"

"You have been kinder than anyone could have expected," Ivy interrupted.

"But?"

"Rithmat is right. You are the king's son, and I am just ..." She paused, glancing everywhere but at him.

Her defeated tone hung like a shroud. Did she think he was pushing her away because she wasn't good enough? The idea took his breath away. If anything it was the other way around.

"May I show you something from when I was young?" Orion held out his arm, sensing Ivy's caution. She took it, but her grip was loose.

Past clusters of trees, Orion led her to the far side of the atrium and through a plain, wooden door. Inside was a small room with a round window on the opposite wall. The faint light permeating the snow clouds outlined shelves of pots, crates, and dry paper.

"A storage room?" Ivy asked.

Orion tapped a small glass dome near the door, activating a dim glow. Containers of labeled bulbs and seeds lined two walls and a barrel of soil sat below the window.

"Winter fae are nothing if not excellent preservers of plants in their dormant, growth phase," Orion said wryly as he walked past the first set of shelves.

On the opposite side of the room, Ivy inspected dried seeds, tucked under a blanket of dry paper, categorized by species and date. "You jest, but I forgot how Winters' work can be so very tangible. So real. It's not just about the glamouring ... nor the trickery."

"We're all complicated creatures. No one is all good nor all bad."

Ivy flashed a grin. "So, you wanted to show off the Winter faes' organizational skills?"

"Well, we're also fantastic at making ice cream."

"I had some tonight. With blackberries."

"I wonder who made a clandestine trip to the Spring court to fetch berries."

"Fetch? Or steal?" Ivy smirked, making the tightness in his chest begin to ease.

"Did you help in the gardens as a youngling?" she asked.

"No," Orion said, simply. Truthfully, the king's anger flared at reminders of Orion's dryad nature.

The transition to the fae court was brutal. His existence from within his tree, connected to the forest, was all he'd known until Eldrin had fetched him. His father began training Orion in open meadows before introducing him to castle life. Yet, the stone citadel itself was an easy adjustment compared to the fae inside. They'd have destroyed him with glee.

"This place was my escape," he said.

Ivy nodded. "There is a comforting buzz of life here."

He remembered the first, arduously long event he'd been invited to: the king's wedding. The crowd of pompous creatures left him wishing he could shrink and disappear into the cracks of the stone grout. He'd broken a sweat, hiding his dryad features, but he'd done it. Eventually, once Orion had mastered glamouring, his father invited him home more often ... always in conjunction with assignments.

"What should I expect at the Aequus Ceremony?" Ivy bit the inside of her cheek.

"Each court brings one official representative and two attendings. Selleth will be the Winter Representative, Rime and I are the attendings, and a few guards will join us. That's all. The king likes to keep the ceremony discrete."

"No one likes drawing attention to their diminishing power," Ivy remarked, then her gaze stopped on an empty portion of wall. In two steps, she stood in front of it, inspecting. "What's this?"

Orion blinked, surprised. "How did you notice the glamour?"

"I didn't." Ivy shrugged. "It's just oddly inefficient."

"It's a door, glamoured by a previous gardener." Orion brushed off her question. Part of him was curious to see the hidden closet again, but he'd already risked sharing too much with Ivy.

She raised a brow. "A secret passage?"

"Nothing that exciting. It's an impractical, little space. The glamour will fade within the decade as the gardener passed away a few years ago."

Ivy absently stepped closer to Orion as she ran her fingers across the stone. With her hair pulled up, he followed the curve of her neck to where it met the cloak she wore. Orion leaned back, the room suddenly too intimate.

"If you want to eat or rest before the ceremony, now is the time. I'll return you home afterward." Delaying the inevitable would only pain him more.

"Before we go, I do have one question." Ivy stepped back from Orion, her face serious.

Orion braced himself, unsure what to expect.

"Did you create the glamour for my father?" Ivy blurted. "The glamour of Emmyth?"

Stunned, he jerked back. He'd already admitted that he couldn't create glamours. "No."

She scrutinized him. "Do you know who did?"

"Where are these questions coming from?" Orion folded his arms across his chest. He would've told her if he'd known who'd created the glamour. Plus, he'd already explained his limited abilities. Even so, she'd had other opportunities to ask. Why now? What had changed? He'd only left her alone for about an hour after the portal fiasco. "Wait. Did you speak with Rime tonight?"

Was Rime angry enough to poison Ivy against Orion?

Ivy dropped her gaze.

"When we first met, I kept my secrets. Of course, I would," he said.

Her lips pulled into a frown.

"Yet, I never lied," he said. "I couldn't." Even now, if he had the ability to lie, he wouldn't.

Ivy's shoulders slumped. Quiet. Hurt.

Orion shook his head, torn between scooping her into his arms or fleeing the cramped room.

"I'm sorry," Ivy said, her face downcast. "I shouldn't have doubted you."

He considered Ivy's question—born of desperation to

understand her family. He couldn't blame her for asking. At least she'd been comfortable enough to dare press him. And to trust his answer. Could he reciprocate her trust? He wanted to, but what good would it do to reveal more of himself? Could he suffer another rejection?

Ivy stepped back and tucked her arms against her chest, her face scrunched with worry.

"I'm not upset with you," Orion assured her. "It's me. I'm ..."

Afraid?

Orion squeezed his eyes shut, hoping his next move wouldn't be a mistake. He unlatched the glamoured, invisible door and pulled it open.

Inside the closet, glowing motes softly bounced off the narrow, empty shelves. It seemed smaller now, of course. In one long stride, Orion could touch the back wall, and with both arms outstretched, his fingers reached the shelves on either side.

Orion pictured his younger self, legs tucked under him as he drew on the wall. The charcoal drawings remained: trees with root systems as elaborate as the branches. This room had meant safety to him. Yet, now, phantom feelings of profound loneliness washed over him.

"Oh," Ivy clutched the cloak at her neck, her voice a whisper. "Your hideaway." She looked to Orion for permission to enter the space.

He should've quickly nodded. He should've casually smiled. He should've pretended he wasn't ripping open an old wound.

Hints of his shame were scrawled across the walls. Ivy's perception might forever change—swinging on a fulcrum, pivoting from respect to disdain. Orion swallowed the self-destructive fears ricocheting around his head and forced a stiff nod.

And Ivy stepped forward into his past.

She knelt, her back to Orion, inspecting the clumsy art without a word. Orion forced a steady breath as she slowly stood back up. She turned, facing him, her expression soft but guarded. Then she reached out, beckoning. He took her hand in his own, and she squeezed it. Her proffered comfort wrapped around him, stronger than magic. With the slightest tug, Ivy coaxed him inside, then reached around and shut the door. The floating lights seemed to transport them to another realm, far away from the pressures of the court, like they had done when he was little.

"I think the fae gardener pitied me a bit—as much as fae can—and he created this place," Orion explained quietly. "Perhaps he was wistful in his old age."

A mote bounced off Ivy's hair and lit her face. His gaze dropped to her lips. He'd wanted to kiss her a dozen times that evening—a risk he couldn't take.

Coming in here was a bad idea. A layered, complicated, terrible idea. He edged back.

"Do you remember," Ivy asked, interrupting his retreat, "when we fought side by side at the Gathering?"

"Of course." He'd put his life in her hands and hers in his.

"I would've died without a seed. So I took my last one. And at that moment," she said as she stepped toe to toe with Orion, "I was as close to you as I am right now. And I sensed your glamour."

"I was hiding my wings." Orion's heart thumped.

"Orion. You're half-dryad ..." Ivy trailed off, her silence blaring as she looked up at him through her lashes.

Orion's palms began to sweat. Did Ivy know? Or was she

guessing? He hadn't fully dropped his glamour in so long that he wasn't sure he could.

"Keeping your boundaries, your protective glamours, I understand why. Even more so after experiencing Winter." Ivy rested her palms on his forearms. "But if you want to share your true self, I'd be honored."

The first trick King Eldrin had taught Orion was to glamour. The primary lesson had spoken volumes: Orion's contemptible dryad features were a liability. Not even Rime knew Orion's true appearance; glamours were ubiquitous and expected. Never questioned, to Orion's relief.

His longing to connect with Ivy warred with his abhorrence of vulnerability. He remembered how quickly Rime had soured when things got complicated. Only a fool would fully bare themselves to anyone. Even so, would Ivy be different? Orion began to tremble with battling emotions.

"We should go." Orion pressed his back to the door, cracking it open. Ivy dropped her hands away, her fingertips grazing his wrist. As she slipped under his arm and out into the now-darkened storage room, he paused. He glanced at the simple, black lines on the painted wall. Then Orion followed Ivy into the dark storage room and closed the door on the light motes.

With scant moonlight filtering through the high windows, Orion moved to re-activate the light near the door, but Ivy grabbed his sleeve, stopping him.

Ivy said nothing, but she kept a steady pressure on his arm. Not a demand, but an invitation.

Orion pivoted, squaring himself against her silhouette. Snow thudded rhythmically against the glass, the window fogging.

"Sometimes, the only way forward is through the darkness,

grasping in an unknown expanse," Ivy whispered, the weight of her hand almost a plea. "A beacon is not guaranteed."

"I am the son of the Winter Court." Orion ached for her to understand, but yet lacked the words to explain. "I cannot help who I am. I'm drawn to shadows and they to me."

"No, Orion. You misunderstand. You are *my* light."

Her soft words shot through him.

Even without seeing her face, he knew what Ivy wanted. Him. Not forever. Just tonight. The problem was, he knew he'd want her tomorrow.

For a thousand years.

Forever.

He swallowed, his muscles taut. Ivy released his sleeve but otherwise stilled. She was giving him a chance. A choice. She'd claimed to want to know him, but would disgust fill her eyes after she saw the *real* Orion? Did he owe her the opportunity to find out?

Did he owe himself?

In the scant light, he pushed his glamour away, his soul bare, knowing Ivy could see him perfectly. His skin turned a shade greener, hints of bark in the shadows. Supple willow branches hid within his locks of dark hair. And a ring of woven leaves crowned his head—not frost-bitten thorns, but one with deep, glossy holly leaves and crimson winter berries.

Ivy's hands moved up his forearms, over his rough skin. Her fingers wound through his loose hair, and nervousness twisted his belly. But her caress was smooth and curious, and he dared hope she wasn't revolted. She rose on her tiptoes, reaching up and grazing her fingers across the holly crown. Orion's wings curled, instinctively protective of Ivy as she leaned closer and took a deep breath.

He yearned to hold her, kiss her. She stayed close, reaching one hand to his cheek. It was a light gesture, but with it, Orion melted, an unexpected lump forming in his throat.

She ran her fingers down his neck and over his bicep, sending sparks down his arm. Though he couldn't see her face, he sensed her longing. It matched his own.

No, they were magnets, drawn too close. They'd crash together, only to be ripped apart. Orion hovered, desperately reminding himself of all the very good reasons to leave.

Yet, he didn't budge. Ivy's hands gripped his elbows, leveraging herself higher and pulling him toward her at the same time.

"Ivy?" Orion whispered the question.

"If you don't kiss me, Orion, I swear I will burn this citadel down."

"Well, it's made of stone, so good luck." He chuckled under his breath as he swept Ivy into his arms. He dipped down, brushing his lips against hers. "How will I say goodbye tomorrow? This could break me ..."

Ivy whispered against his cheek. "You're assuming my heart isn't already shattered."

The last of his will crumbled, and his lips met hers. He could have sworn the room spun. Or that they were falling. He felt nothing under foot. No pain. No past. Just that moment.

His hand snaked under the cloak she wore, bringing her closer as they kissed again. She tasted like blackberries, honey, and the summer dawn. Her glow thawed his heart, the frozen and long-forgotten desire for affection.

He tripped over his own feet, and Ivy giggled as he straightened.

"I must admit," she said. "I couldn't figure out why I kept smelling holly berries. About drove me mad."

"I should've known your elven nose would be my undoing." Orion couldn't help but grin. Revealing his true appearance to

Ivy was a relief, like the entire palace weight had been lifted from his shoulders.

Yes, he was fae, but he was also dryad. Perhaps when he cut off all his dryad magic he would look more fae. But part of him wasn't ready to reject his connection to the trees.

She pivoted, her back against the door, blocking their exit. It was almost a dare, defying his usual wish to be early to appointments. The moonlight illuminated the edges of Ivy's face, the rise and fall of her chest with each deep breath. Orion would always remember this moment, carved out of time, when it was just Ivy and him. Her gaze roved over him, and she bit her lip. He let himself be drawn to her, closing the gap again.

Her fingers gripped his upper arms, then slid up around his neck. "Lord Orion Arya, son of a dryad mother and the Winter King, Portal Keeper of the Realms, and Captain of the Unarian Night Guard."

Orion lifted a brow at his long titles.

"I wish I'd known you when we were younglings," she continued, pulling him closer. Her lips brushed his as she spoke again, her voice barely a whisper between kisses. "I would've liked you then, too."

35
EARTH, BERRIES, AND SNOW

Ivy followed a step behind Orion through the palace as he escorted her to the Aequus Ceremony. He'd taken on the appearance of a common fae guard, which was only slightly less distracting. Even without his wings and dryad features, the curve of his broad shoulders drew her attention. The memory of her arms wrapped around him made her cheeks burn despite the chill.

Orion led Ivy past groups of cavorting fae, but Ivy dropped her chin, and they paid her little attention. Several guards stood outside the entrance to an unfamiliar wing. With a curt nod, Orion marched past the guards and through a set of doors, leaving the crowds of revelers behind. In the cavernous halls, unseen rushing waters disguised the occasional, rotating guards' footsteps. The stark, marbled walls were decorated by woven tapestries. Some depicted landscapes, but most retold past battles or glories of ancient royals. Ivy wondered if one day Orion would be woven into their honored history.

They passed a door as it was closing behind a guard, and in that moment of visibility, Ivy spied a wall of spears. An armory? Was the training yard access nearby? She imagined sparring against the fae. She wasn't half-bad with a spear. What if she sparred with Orion? Her body warmed with the thought. Distracted, Ivy didn't notice Orion slow, and she slammed into his back.

Orion spun and caught her elbow.

Ivy flushed at his touch. She didn't need his help catching her balance, but the fact that he'd reacted so quickly to help her sent heat burning up her neck. "I'm sorry. I was just ..."

Daydreaming.

She tried to brush it off. "Sometimes elves can be clumsy."

"I mean, elves aren't known for their grace," Orion said, with dry sarcasm.

Ivy's cheeks burned hotter at being caught in a ridiculous lie. Even worse, she realized she'd been walking practically on his heels the entire trek across the palace.

"Well, I guess it's a good thing I didn't unglamour my wings just now," Orion joked as he released her elbow.

Despite her foolishness, Ivy basked in Orion's teasing. Under his grumpy-pixie-facade that Nym had warned her about, he was thoughtful and protective. She enjoyed their banter. She wanted to rest her hand on his forearm as she laughed. She liked it when his wings curled around her.

"I promise to pay more attention." Ivy strained to hear footsteps in their proximity. Hearing none, she grinned. "You might as well unglamour your wings and return to your usual fae form. No one is near."

Orion tipped his head toward the next corner. "I didn't know elves could see through walls."

"If you want me to be completely sure," Ivy darted forward, peeked around the corner, assessed, and returned to Orion's side. "Down that hall, fourteen guards are stationed. Just beyond, outside, Prince Rime awaits with fae and orc guards."

"That was quick—" Orion stopped, his eyes wider. "*Can* you see through doors?"

Ivy chuckled. "The doors were open as a guard was entering the palace." Part of her wanted to let Orion believe she *could* see through doors and walls, but she wouldn't have an opportunity later to tell him she was teasing. After this meeting, she'd be leaving. Whatever *this* was between them, was like water slipping between her fingers. Whatever she wanted to say or do, she was nearly out of time. "Anyway, there are no guards nearby. Yet."

Orion's appearance changed, back to his fae glamour. He loomed over her, his wings tucked and his dark hair loose. He looked so similar to the true-Orion that Ivy brushed her own lips, remembering their kiss.

Ivy jerked her hands behind her and forced herself to look away. "How long until Selleth arrives?"

"She's usually the last to—" Orion stopped short. "Wait, there were fourteen guards stationed along the wall?"

Ivy nodded.

His breathing quickened and he glanced back down at Ivy. "She's not here. Not yet."

Ivy wanted him to whisk her away to a hidden corner before the ceremony, but it would set a poor tone to be late to his first official ceremony. Her hope deflated as she admitted the distant, but growing sounds. "Several heavy, rhythmic footsteps are headed in this direction. Probably Selleth and her guards."

"We have a moment, then, before they arrive." A grin touched the edge of Orion's lips. He pressed his palm into the wall next to her ear, leaning closer, enveloping her in heady scents of earth, berries, and snow. Her lips parted, excited anticipation sparking from her head down to her toes. She'd expected a delivery straight to the representatives, but if Orion was willing to delay, she wouldn't argue.

His heart sped like a jackrabbit as he leaned down to kiss her. She could hear every thrum.

She grinned, hooking her arms up around his shoulders as she met his lips on hers. The corridor fell away, and she sensed the exact distance of the trees, even through the thick walls. The green. The growth. The life. The strength. She'd always felt connected with the earth, but this was different. The same thing had happened in the atrium storage room, so she'd attributed it to the nearness of the seeds. But here? Among stone walls and distant rivulets of water?

Phantom whispers called from the trees and energy thrummed under foot, pulsing out to every corner of the fair realm. Her arms slid around Orion's back pulling him closer.

His fingers tangled in her hair as they kissed, and Ivy's hands roamed the planes of his back and ribs. She lost herself, forgetting she was in a stone citadel. Forgetting she was even in the fair realm. If she could stretch out each moment of this night, she would.

Ivy broke away, her shoulders pressed against the wall while gripping his forearms. "What if I stayed another day?"

"I'd like that," Orion said, playing with her locks of hair that had fallen from the clip.

"What if I stayed two?"

Orion ran his thumb over her collarbone, his gaze intense. "We could travel the forest, away from the fae."

A giddiness rose in Ivy, but she tamped it down. She couldn't stay long. Besides the fact that she aged over ten times faster in the fair realm, she needed to check on Nym. Beyond Nym's confrontation with Emmyth, Magdud's warning nagged in the back of Ivy's mind. Of course, it made sense that orcs had been sent around the realm after the attack at the Gathering, but a warship? Why?

No matter what was happening, after Ivy reported the Elven Council, the elves were in for a tumultuous future. Ivy was determined to be with her kind as they grappled with the lies and then had to rebuild their way of life. She couldn't hide in the fair realm.

Though she dearly wanted to.

"How close?" Orion asked, emotion and fire dancing in his eyes.

Ivy greedily anticipated the next two days. "They'll turn the corner in five, four—"

Orion cut off her countdown with a quick kiss to her forehead, then he pulled her toward the next bend. "Let's get this meeting over with."

He gave Ivy's hand a quick squeeze, then released her before they came into view of the fourteen fae guards flanking the double doors. Ivy walked at his side, but kept a proper distance, feigning that she was the unaffected guest of the king's son. She distracted herself from Orion by studying the art on display. Along the wall, a small painting was tucked between two historical tapestries. A painting of a massive tree—with purple leaves and silver fruit.

Ivy didn't want to think about the portal home, but the portrait of the magnificent tree tugged at her. When Orion had fetched her out of the dryad-portal, the tree had given her another vision before she'd been released.

"There's something I think you should know," Ivy whispered as they walked. "You asked me what was wrong after I exited the portal earlier today. The tree gave me a reminder of the vision I'd seen at the Gathering. Only this time, it showed me more. The vision extended and ..." It was so odd to say aloud, "creatures were chasing me."

"Seekers?" Orion asked.

Ivy spoke quickly before they reached the stationed guards. "No, they were elves. And behind them were gnomes, centaurs, dryads, and many others."

Orion's wings flared, and he stopped short. He dropped his voice low, so only Ivy could hear. "What does it mean? Are you in danger?"

"The vision didn't feel like a dire warning." Ivy couldn't even consider another possibility. She'd had enough trouble evading mindless Seekers, let alone healthy elves. "The feeling was more ... determined. I think." Almost as if she were running *toward* something, but what it was, Ivy couldn't imagine.

"How can I help?"

She couldn't explain what his support meant to her. "Perhaps while I stay here for a couple days, the break might give me time to figure out the meaning. And perhaps I could work with Zel, too?"

They quieted as marching footsteps grew nearer. Orion held his hands at his side, not touching her, but his eyes simmered with some emotion before his expression masked. Ivy didn't turn to observe Selleth, but she felt the princess's attention trained on them.

Without a word, Orion shifted his body, putting a wing between Ivy and Selleth's small entourage. Ivy quickly marched forward, grateful for Orion's gesture. Though, it didn't protect her from the verbal barbs.

"My, my," an unknown female voice whispered, too quiet for Orion to overhear. "Lord Orion's overly attentive to the churl."

"One can't blame him," Rithmat's nasally voice responded. "When one lives in the mud, they're bound to come home with a parasite."

Selleth said nothing, as if she couldn't be bothered with

gossip. It wasn't reassuring. Ivy feared the princess's wounds would be more deadly than pointed words.

Ivy concentrated on the doors as guards moved to the handles. For the next hour, she had to shove Orion out of her thoughts. Or at least make a solid attempt. Not that her self-worth depended on the fae's respect, but Orion's life would be easier if Ivy proved to be intelligent and reliable. She began mentally rehearsing her words for the Summer Representative, preparing to explain the elven conspiracy she'd discovered.

Once she reported the misdeeds of her kind, she'd have fulfilled her oath to Alysatraee: bring peace. Also, she'd have done all she could to finish what her father had started.

It was Zel's turn to do Alysatraee's will. He didn't need Ivy's help with his research, though he'd likely tolerate it. So, what was left for her to do?

Ivy marched forward, the answer quick to her mind. She'd do exactly what her parents had hoped she'd do: live her life.

As they passed the armed fae, two broke away from their station and marched on either side of Ivy. Ivy tensed until Orion's hand reassuringly brushed the back of her arm, signaling the accompanying guards were part of the ritual.

Though she felt as if she were walking into a nest of cockatrices, she enjoyed these moments with Orion. She hadn't ever connected with anyone like she did with him. Yes, she was grateful to live the rest of her life in peace, but now she dared want something more. What if she stayed three days? A new excitement put a lightness in her step.

The guards drew open the heavy doors, blasting them with frigid air. Ivy shuddered, despite Orion's cloak. At least it snapped her attention away from the attractive, half-dryad creature at her heels and back to the coming meeting. Outside, Prince Rime, two fae guards, and six orc warriors waited.

"Whatever you do, don't rush," Rime said sarcastically as

they crossed the threshold onto a portico. "It's only your first Aequus as the king's recognized son. No big deal."

Orion ignored the jab.

Rime continued, undeterred, "Good thing Selleth didn't arrive before you. She'd have you gutted for making her wait. Of course, *her* time is more important than everyone else's."

"She has the flame?" Orion asked.

"You didn't check? She's literally ten steps behind you." Rime rolled his eyes. "If she doesn't and the Summer Court attacks, it'll give you a chance to show off your sword skills for your elven *friend*."

"Don't worry," Ivy spoke up. She felt far more confident around Rime with Orion at her side; he'd pluck her frog-enchanted-self out of the snow. "I'll protect you, young prince. Even without my bow and arrow." She shot him a meaningful glare.

"You'd save who?" Rime pressed his hand to his chest in mock gratitude. "Is it just me, dear brother, or is Ivy more concerned about my welfare than yours. She's offering to save *my* life, after all."

"Orion can take care of himself." Ivy smirked, and Rime's lips almost quirked upward.

Orion glanced back over his shoulder, still blocking Ivy's view of Selleth. "The princess is in position. It's time to begin."

"That masculine cloak won't do for the ceremony, Ivy," Rime said. Looking smug, he reached toward Ivy's shoulder as if to perform magic. Before his fingers touched her, Orion grabbed his brother's hand in a crushing grip.

"The cloak is fine," Orion said through gritted teeth.

Rime cocked a brow and jerked his hand innocently into the air. "Touchy, brother. Be careful not to show your true feelings to the rest of the court, though. I mean, unless you want Ivy's head removed from her neck."

Despite the banter, tension wove between the brothers, pricking at Ivy. A reminder that their reconciliation might hinge on her departure.

"Age before beauty." Rime gestured for Orion to lead the way.

Protectors before the weak, Ivy kept the quip to herself. The prince was putting Orion and Ivy in a more vulnerable position, but Ivy wasn't concerned. She and Orion had survived far worse than a few Summer fae.

Beyond the portico, snow flurries still fell. However, clouds were dispersing, and bright moonlight illuminated the area. Orion walked at her side, one wing subtly flared, protecting her from the bitter wind.

Ivy felt her hair magically shifting in her golden clip. She was about to snap at Rime, but she flushed and clamped down on her words when she realized what he was doing. The prince was glamouring her while she was still obscured behind Orion's wing. With Ivy hidden from sight, no one would notice his power to manipulate without physical touch, but Selleth *would've* noticed Ivy's tousled hair at the ceremony. Though Rime was a spoiled prince, at least he wasn't throwing her to the ice dragon—there was good in him. That, or he saw Ivy as a future pawn.

"How did you like your pockets?" Rime asked from behind her.

Orion gave her a sideways glance, but she shrugged.

"All that begging for a place to warm your hands, and you didn't even use them, did you."

The muscles in Orion's jaw ticked, and he marched faster. Curious, Ivy slid her hands into the pockets of her dress."

I should've been taking advantage of these. They're—

Her right hand brushed the hilt of her knife. There was a gaping hole in the bottom of her pocket. A jolt of danger shot through her—she could reach the weapon strapped to her thigh. A weapon only she and Rime knew of.

Yes, Rime was setting her up to be his pawn. It was too great a favor, and fae weren't kind creatures. Though, Orion's heavy cloak reminded her there was one fae she'd fight for. She glanced at him from the corner of her eye. When this meeting ended, she'd fully enjoy two blissful days at his side. Maybe three.

36
PRIVILEGED PRISON

Emmyth stared across the prison chasm at her wayward daughter. Nym stood far too proud, depite her pale, waxy face, another sign she didn't understand her precarious situation. Nym had spent two days of solitude in near darkness, and from what the guards had said, she'd been sick the entire time. Emmyth sensed unease from what was left of her advisers when she'd refused to send her daughter a healer, which irritated the councilor. How dare anyone question how she handled her own child.

The cavern's fissure between them was too wide to jump, even if Nym were healthy. And Nym's little island left nowhere to hide from scrutiny. Emmyth had held back when in her council chambers, but here she could openly address Nym's many failures.

Emotion boiled like a vat of oil in the pit of Emmyth's stomach. Yet, she continued to shove her feelings down, her singular focus on Nym. She could still be saved. Emmyth's life had always pivoted around her family. While her son's soft temperament lent well to becoming a future, post-war leader, her daughter's fire was the one the Tides needed now. Emmyth had thought Nym was ready, but the brief stint with Ivy had proven otherwise.

Nym's weakness threatened to unravel Emmyth's plans. At this point, utilizing odious years of prison to ground some sense into Nym's naive head was a luxury Emmyth couldn't afford; Nym needed to come to heel soon—before the Centennial.

Only this place—The Prison Hand—could humble Nym.

"I don't know what you expect me to say." Nym had edged closer to the lip of her cell with every new question Emmyth had asked.

"Any information is better than, 'I don't know.'" The councilor forced a calm demeanor. She suspected Nym toed the edge of the abyss just to annoy her mother.

It was working.

If her daughter had a dizzy spell, she'd plummet to her death. Her life utterly wasted.

"Well, it's the truth," Nym said. "I don't know Ivy Balrel's location. I don't know what happened to the amulet."

Emmyth signaled for the guards to leave her alone with the prisoner. Nym walked along the rim of the saucer-shaped, floating prison, grumbling at their audience as they departed, "Don't let the iron door burn you on the way out."

Nym neared one of the four ornately chiseled columns along the perimeter. They each extended to twice Nym's height, though they held up nothing but air. At the center of the prison, a fresh water circulated in a massive raised bowl, as clean and blue as the southern seas. But, as magnificent as the columns and pool were, they hadn't inspired the name of this particular cell.

An enormous, granite hand grasped the bottom of the prison, holding it afloat. The fingers were poised as if ready to pulverize the saucer, prisoner, and the pool of water in its crushing grip. The magical feat was awe-inspiring and frightening to behold, as if the hand of Alysatraee, herself, held the prison aloft, the rest of her arm and body invisible. Untouchable.

"I never would've guessed that I'd witness The Hand from this perspective." Nym nudged a loose pebble off the edge and into the abyss below. After a few breaths, she stopped waiting for it to hit the ground. "I guess it's quite a privilege to be considered dangerous enough to warrant an invitation to this little patch of paradise."

"You don't know how fortunate you are, Nym," Emmyth said. "It is a 'privilege,' as you put it, to be isolated. Your weak position is hidden from other prisoners." The image of an imprisoned-Nym would damage her daughter's ability to command in the future.

But not punishing Nym and allowing her to align with a disgraced House of Seeds elf on the wrong side of a war would be far worse.

"By 'other prisoners,' you mean your former advisers." Nym's lips tightened as if barely holding back more accusations.

"If you were housed near the traitors, don't presume you'd somehow steel their resolve against me." Emmyth held back a mocking laugh. "They'll be desperate to earn their way back to freedom within a month. They're not as strong-willed nor as disciplined as I've raised you to be. So, yes, I'm doing this for your own good."

"Do you hear yourself? You are committing crimes against Alysatraee, yet you believe you're helping *me* by sentencing me to The Hand. I'm tasting a bitter layer of irony stuffed in the middle of your scrumptious cake-of-hypocrisy."

Emmyth bit back a sharp retort, refusing to fuel Nym's rage. The youngling's temper needed to cool. Isolation in The Hand would help.

"You showed me no loyalty nor trust," Emmyth said. "And though I find it painful, it's not the worst of your crimes. Your actions go beyond hurting me and your fellow Tides. Beyond hurting all the elven Houses."

Nym dropped her chin, but not in fear. Her braids shifted forward and her gaze bore into Emmyth's as if she could singe the air between them. Emmyth's attention flicked to the pool behind her daughter, wishing there was another way to teach her.

"If you were to *guess*, where did Ivy Balrel go after you parted?" Emmyth studied every minute facial twitch and muscle reaction in Nym's body. Nym didn't react, so Emmyth continued, asking each question slowly and evaluating Nym's response. "To the forest? Alone? Back to Unaria? Is she looking for others from her house, like Wirenth?"

To Nym's credit, she kept her stony expression. She shifted her weight at the mention of Unaria, but Nym had been trained to randomly adjust her stance during questioning.

"What happened to Wirenth, anyway?" Nym moved away from the pillar to the edge of the pool, pressing her fingers against the lip. With a shaking hand, she scooped water to her lips.

"I'm not sure, but Adviser Daecyne said he never regrouped after the attack at the Gathering. My guess is the elder elf was killed by the Seeker horde."

Nym's face jerked back to Emmyth, the braids around her face flying in an arc. "You're terribly cavalier, *mother*." She spat the word like a curse. "As if his death is nothing. It should mean everything, especially to you, the guilt drowning you like a weight tied to your ankles in the ocean. How can you sleep at night with all the blood on your hands?"

In the past, her daughter had always disguised any unhelpful tenderness with anger and hard work. Now it oozed from her pores, wild and unpredictable. Perhaps this was inevitable, but it didn't mean she couldn't be saved.

"It's a war," Emmyth said, fighting to keep her voice flat.

The battle for fair folk lands had robbed too many of their kind. At least now they finally had a way to defeat their enemies and take back the cities they'd lost. Not even the Mother would deny them. Coordinating the Gathering so Wirenth would be at that location was no small feat, only accomplished by Alysatraee's grace.

"Even war has rules." Nym tightened her arms across her chest. "Or there should be."

Emmyth and her parents had once been naive, too. Unfortunately, her parents hadn't lived long enough to realize their folly.

"Did Orion, the Unarian guard, go to the fair realm?" Emmyth asked.

"Why would a human guard go to the fair realm?" Nym's expression revealed nothing, but her shoulders tightened. Emmyth would have to work on that telling reaction later.

"Did you not recognize he was fair folk after spending weeks with him?" Emmyth asked, a hint of mockery slipping into her tone before she caught it. She took a deep breath, recalling everything she gleaned about Orion.

Emmyth still wasn't sure if Orion was fair-born. He'd traveled with Ialant but for how long? In the month since the Gathering, her spies hadn't reported his return to Unaria, nor had the dryads reported him going through a portal. Where was he?

Her mind caught on her first impression—she'd thought he might be dryad-born. If so, a fellow dryad might not reveal his movements, even to an elven councilor. If Orion had slipped into the fair realm, it confirmed his dryad blood.

What business did he have in the fair realm? If Ialant had asked for his help, it was possible Orion reported the Council's actions. If the wrong fae learned of the Tree House, it meant the Council's plans had become unnecessarily complicated.

Emmyth's mood darkened.

Furthermore, Ivy would certainly reappear at an inconvenient time. Emmyth couldn't rely on the Seeds elf staying hidden, or better yet, a Seeker finally catching up to her.

After Ialant's betrayal, his family had been cut away like a diseased branch. Manipulating the midwives was easy. Besides, the deaths within the House of Seeds relieved them not just of the Balrel family, but forced the rest of the Seeds to rely on the remaining councilors. The Minerals councilors had already narrowed down Ialant's replacement to two pliable Seeds elves. Selecting a Seeds candidate would've been the ambassadors' responsibility, but with the elder elf dead, the council would wield their influence in the coming vote.

"Is Kolvar well?" Nym asked, interrupting Emmyth's thoughts.

"So you care about his recovery after you poisoned him?"

Nym's nostrils flared.

"What did you tell Kolvar?" Emmyth asked. "I know you spoke with him." Was Nym's conversation meant to distract Kolvar? Or was he helping his sister?

Nym pressed her lips together, signaling she wouldn't give until she received.

"Kolvar will survive, despite the palace uproar you caused," Emmyth said. "He was put into a deep sleep while he heals."

"I guess he can't scheme if he can't talk."

Nym's slivered words burrowed deep. A throbbing ache threatened to seep through Emmyth's walls, but she'd long ago learned to numb her pain. She slammed the door on Nym's words as if they'd never existed.

"The healers predict he'll be ready to awaken tomorrow." Emmyth planned to question him while he was still groggy.

She'd find out one way or another if he was part of the coup. "Did he willingly take the poison?"

"I love Kolvar," Nym said, sounding resigned. "He's always been a good brother."

"But?"

"He's too soft." Nym turned away from Emmyth, her thumb running along a carved lily in the stone.

"What do you mean?" Emmyth prompted.

"I told him about The Tree House. The short version."

"His reaction?"

Nym glared at Emmyth from the corner of her eye before continuing. "Kolvar was shocked. Of course, he didn't like my plan. Typical. He's like the sand after the tide goes out—malleable. Washed away when the waves return." Nym pressed the tip of her nail into the stone. "He tried to distract me from confronting you, so I had to drug him. He supports you because you're our mother. He seems to think that matters."

Her statement hung, an emptiness that seemed to shout, *but you don't matter.*

Nym's words jammed the shards deeper; a jolt reverberated to Emmyth's core. Nym always knew how to land a punch where it mattered. Emmyth struggled to stay calm. Ripples of pain threatened to uncover the torrent of emotions she always kept buried.

Emmyth forced her feet to stay rooted, and she changed the subject. "I suspect you didn't swallow the amulet, no matter what some believe. If you gave the amulet to Lial, I assure you, we'll find it. Do yourself a favor and just confirm the location."

She needed to leave the dungeon. Not because of Nym's jabs. There were simply more important discussions to be had, of course. Plans to be altered and communications to be sent. With Orion's possible fae involvement and Ivy missing, the Council needed an alternate strategy.

"I lost the amulet over the side of The Hand." Nym pretended to gag, a hand at her throat. "You're welcome to hunt for it, if you can find the bottom of this prison."

Emmyth drew a long breath. She had hoped to bring her daughter into the fold, the inner circle who knew the real truth of the humans. Emmyth helped her children forge a path to greatness. Yet, rebellion was her reward.

"I assure you," Emmyth began, "the orcs are already reconstructing Lial's movements after the scuffle in the council chambers."

Though the glamour wasn't a serious risk, Emmyth wouldn't rest easy until it was found and destroyed. In the scant hour when the orcs couldn't confirm Lial's location, Emmyth suspected he'd slipped into the Healer's rooms to talk to Kolvar. Unfortunately for Lial, Kolvar had been unconscious and secreted away.

But if Lial had the amulet, and Emmyth suspected he did, he'd hidden it. But it hadn't gotten very far. He'd likely panicked and tossed it in the greenhouse or in his rooms. Both locations were being thoroughly searched at that very moment.

"I'll find the amulet," Emmyth continued. "Save me the headache of looking, and I'll release you sooner."

"Oh, good. If I pretend I know where your glamour is, will that be helpful? And what would my reward be? A full year off my two *hundred* year sentence?" Nym threw her arms up in the air as if a year of freedom was nothing. Her daughter flashed a saccharine grin. "But, promise me some fine berry wine, goat cheese, and wafers and we have a deal."

Emmyth pitied her daughter. She always had to take the hard path.

"Nym," Emmyth said, her voice firm, "the adrenaline coursing through your veins is lying to you. It's keeping a secret about something happening to your own body."

Nym rolled her eyes, but Emmyth wasn't bluffing.

"Do you know why The Hand is reserved for the most powerful fair creatures?" Emmyth asked. "Do you know why no one has ever successfully jumped across the crevasse? Even if you had enough room to run, no one has the momentum to cross it."

Nym turned her back on her mother, but of course, she was listening.

"I suspect you'll blame your weakness on a weary ride on a wyvern's back. Or the lack of food. Or whatever illness you brought upon yourself. But I assure you, it's not."

Nym's body tightened. Emmyth had her attention. Good.

"This prison isn't reserved for elves. Any fair creature who breaks Alysatraee's law while in this realm may be sentenced to The Hand." Emmyth paused, calmly clasping her hands. "It's for the prideful. The strong. The ones that need to be taught their own weakness."

Even from across the crevasse, Emmyth sensed the magic. The crystal blue pool in the center of The Hand was deceptive, glamouring the marble-sized sphere affixed to the bottom. Nym would figure it out soon enough, too. But there would be nothing she could do about it.

The blue orb at the bottom of the pool couldn't be removed. Nym drank from the tainted pool, but even without taking a sip, the marble siphoned Nym's power via the connecting iron veins riddled throughout the rock she stood on. Each day, she'd grow less and less capable of using her magnificent gifts from the Mother. She wouldn't be able to see at a distance. She wouldn't be able to hear the guards approaching. She'd be as weak as a human.

Nym lifted her chin and faced her mother, defiance written in her stance. Emmyth shook her head, hoping her daughter would break sooner rather than later.

Emmyth turned and walked away; the rough, cave-like walls led to the iron door. Her mind turned to ways to protect the Council's plans. The spring equinox would put the power in the hands of the Summer Court; Emmyth needed to consult the heavens and calculate the current time in the fae realm. Had she missed it?

She grabbed the latch, impatient to get back to work when Nym's voice echoed through the chamber, as melodramatic as ever.

"Ivy is going to be a thorn in your side. She'll make you all bleed." Nym let her vitriolic words hang before she continued. "And when she finds me, I will help her end you."

37
SUMMER COURT AEQUUS CEREMONY

Orion kept close to Ivy, surveilling the forest out of the corner of his eye as they walked together. There was no cause for worry, but he'd promised to return Ivy home safely. No, he had to stop lying to himself. His promise was no accident—he'd wanted more time with Ivy. And he'd felt driven to protect her long before he'd carried her to the fair realm. Even now, despite the seemingly serene beauty of the coming ceremony, tension coiled in his shoulder blades.

The wide silver carpet rolled out before them, over top of the outdoor marble floor. On either side of them, brown, dormant vines criss-crossed the columns holding the glass roof, which magically never piled with snow. Snow softly fell, obscuring the distant trees, but the colonnade floor stayed dry despite the open walls.

At the end of the long walkway, the ground gave way into a massive, circular stone pit. On the opposite side, the marble path continued, glass roof and all. Four sets of steps led down to a circular stage with an altar at the center.

Ivy gazed at the open pavilion. "Is this the Winter Court arena I've heard so much about?"

Sour memories had spoiled the realm for Orion many years ago, but Ivy's awe-like reactions inspired him to see a splendor he'd never noticed.

"Three thousand fae could watch tonight if they desired," Orion said.

"Ten times that number if needed," Rime spoke up from behind. "It expands into a proper coliseum."

"So I've heard," Ivy said.

Ivy paused at the precipice, alert. Her attention jerked upward, and she gasped at the sky. Following her gaze, Orion spotted the silhouette of a massive dragon passing overhead.

"Majestic," Ivy said.

"Ash's distant cousin, perhaps?" Orion joked, keeping a straight face.

Ivy grinned. "Hardly."

Orion had seen dragons before, but with Ivy, everything was different. He felt more comfortable than he ever had in the court. He wanted to believe it was the long-awaited welcome from the king, but he suspected it was Ivy's presence. What would his life be like when she left?

The air grew dense, grabbing his attention as the pressure in his ears grew uncomfortable. A nearby dryad portal was active. Without his toes in the soil, he could only speculate that it was the arrival of the Summer Court. The snowfall lightened, confirming it.

Ivy dropped her gaze and searched the dark trees in the distance. Her eyes narrowed. "Twenty fae are emerging from the forest."

"Right on time," Rime muttered.

"Both parties bring guards, and possibly aides, record keepers, or servants," Orion explained as he ushered her down the stairs. "Though only six guards and the three representatives are allowed to attend the ceremony."

"How does it feel to be the exception to the rule, Ivy?" Rime teased, but didn't wait for an answer. "You're special. A witness requested by the Winter King himself. Oh, the *honor.*"

Ivy flashed a tight smile while shoving her hands deeper into her pockets.

"The Summer Queen already approved your presence, of course," Orion assured her. "They're expecting you. As a witness, you'll wait with me until you're called upon."

"If there's trouble ..." Ivy bit the side of her lip.

Orion gripped Ivy's elbow. "Retreat to the castle."

Rime rolled his eyes. "There hasn't been trouble at these ceremonies in ... well, ever. Never. Metal isn't even allowed for the representative nor the two attendings. Orion and I are the latter, merely present to trade power and compliments. Maybe braid each other's hair."

Orion continued holding Ivy's arm. Though no elf would need help down the stairs no matter how slippery, he'd take any proper excuse to touch her. With the other hand, he tapped his side, missing his sword. The representative and attendings were barred from carrying metal at the ceremony.

"What are the chances of a ... disagreement?" Ivy asked, moving almost imperceptibly closer to Orion.

"None," Rime scoffed from behind them.

Very little, Orion thought as they reached the bottom step.

Orion signaled to the six orc guards above, including Maggie, and they fanned out around the Winter-side of the ring. Four Winter fae guards joined Rime and Orion near the altar on the lower stage, and two guards stayed behind with Selleth.

He'd been at these seasonal power exchanges in the past and, like Rime stated, they were dull routines. Even so, Orion was cautious. Perhaps with less time fighting criminals and Seekers and more time in courtly doldrums, he'd become as complacent as his brother.

Rime and Orion took their positions at the northern corners of the stark, perfectly square, marble altar, the center hollowed out and ready.

"Where's your sister?" Ivy asked, scanning the empty stairs.

"Never has a fae enjoyed an *entrance* as much as Selleth," Rime said dryly.

Ivy laughed, but seeing a guard's glare, she quickly choked it back.

"Do we have a problem?" Orion snapped at the guard.

Rime raised a brow. "You've been bristling since you arrived. Do *you* have a problem?"

Ivy interrupted any retort. "Who do you expect from the Summer Court?"

Rime's attention slid from Orion to Ivy, then back to his brother. But, he relaxed and responded. "Some pompous Summer fae, I suppose. Probably one of the queen's children. As far as the attendings, usually giggling Spring fae are selected by virtue of their sparkling personalities." Rime chortled. "By 'sparkling,' I mean 'the Summer Queen wants to ingratiate herself with their families.' Keep in mind that this is a simple ceremony. Any drunken fool can perform it, so they're usually not the sharpest arrows in the quiver. Afterward, the Summer contingency returns to their court for a gaudy celebration. Those with The Seasons Heart are hailed as conquering heroes." Rime lifted his nose in the air. "Gits. All of them. As if performing a basic ceremony that has literally existed since the dawn of Alysatraee's creations is some kind of accomplishment."

"If it's simple, why all the guards?" Ivy asked.

"Peacocks. For show." Rime struck a pose, flexing. "A

shallow display of flared tail feathers between the courts. Besides, why should you worry? You're armed."

Armed?

All eyes fell on Ivy, but before Orion could question anything, the vines on the far columns shifted, turning green and bursting with colorful blooms despite the cold.

Moments later, a male fae strode into view, flanked by his two guards. They paused at the edge of the top step, staring down at the Winter contingency.

A Summer guard announced in a booming voice, "Prince Devain Seral'Ray of the Summer Court."

"The Summer Queen's third child," Orion whispered. Ivy could hear, even though she was a full step behind him.

The summer prince wore a bright yellow tunic peeking out from his heavy cloak. His blond hair fell loose, his gait smooth as he marched down the steps.

"He's really taking his nickname to heart, the 'Golden Prince,'" Rime muttered under his breath. "More like 'Prince of Sunshine up your ar—'"

"Arbiter," Orion cut off his brother. "He's known for fairness."

"Complimenting his good looks?" Rime sarcastically uttered under his breath, "You're too kind."

Orion's retort dried on his tongue when the two attendings appeared behind Prince Devain. Rime straightened, his eyes widening. The male and female attendings wore no cloaks, but padded, pale golden vests, gloves, and caps pulled over the tips of their ears. Orion would recognize them anywhere.

"Alyssum and Alion of Spring," the Summer guard boomed their introduction.

Orion dropped his chin and whispered, "Twin children of an infamous warrior."

"They appear no more menacing than the Winter fae," Ivy replied. "Though not even Spring is known for compassion."

Ivy's knowledge of the fae's nature reassured Orion, but even so, he was glad she was somewhat obscured behind him. Spring could be blindly ruthless, especially when defending life. In the war, their soldiers were among the most brutal, their father among them. Why were they here?

Orion reigned in his runaway concerns, reminding himself that there wouldn't be an argument tonight. The equinox ceremonies were simple but sacred. No one would dare stir up trouble. Besides, Spring harshly punished violations. The twins had likely won some sparring competition, and the privilege of attending the Aequus was the reward. There was some obvious, logical reason—Orion was just paranoid after decades of spying.

Even so, the Winter King would be livid with anything other than a polite hand-off. Or worse, disappointed. Orion wouldn't let that happen; he'd keep a level head.

Six Summer fae guards escorted the prince and his attendings to the base of the amphitheater. Mirroring the Winter guards, they stationed themselves near the steps. Orion scrutinized the guards, but they seemed more focused on spacing themselves perfectly apart and less concerned with Ivy and Winter.

"Princess Selleth Zrin'arya of the Winter Court," an orc announced from the lip of the coliseum above.

A hush fell, everyone's attention on the northern steps. Selleth appeared, towering over them all, holding the blue flame in her cupped hands. The princess strode down, her ornate train held aloft by a dozen pixies. How Selleth wrangled them into such a task, Orion hated to guess. Selleth's icicle-hair clinked together as she descended, motes of light floating above her in the illusion of a crown.

Orion's lips pressed together, and Rime mouthed *Peacock.*

Selleth's pomp was a purposeful illusion meant to foreshadow her power. At the very least, he and Rime still agreed that their sister's antics were excessive. Selleth strutted forward and placed the fiery Seasons Heart onto the altar, an arm's length away from Orion. The fire expanded, filling the empty, hollowed marble with vivid blue flames. Selleth and Devain took turns speaking rote lines:

Winter season's end
Growth renewed
Rest brings strength
The season's rhythm
Her command,
into summer's hand

The Summer prince thrust his cupped hands straight into the fire and scooped up a flame in his open palms. The orc warriors, including Maggie, marched to the south side of the coliseum; they were now Summer's to command. Orion glanced back to see Ivy's awe at the literal power shift between the courts. Her attention darted from guard to guard, as if studying each orc's position—a normal, expected assessment after being chased by Seekers for over a decade.

A pop of pressure indicated the dryad portal was in use again. Surprised, he glanced at Summer, but of course they wouldn't have felt anything. Even if he had Ivy's superior vision, they were recessed into the ground and didn't have a line of sight into the forest.

Maggie and the other orcs were on the rim. He caught her eye and flicked his attention just to her side, with the slightest jerk of his head. She glanced over both shoulders and didn't seem alarmed, which reassured Orion. The portal was probably accessed by a Summer servant returning to their realm.

Even so, the Spring attendings seemed off. Their arms were stiff at their sides, gloved fingers oddly extended. Their intense scanning of the coliseum put Orion on edge.

"I see you brought warriors to the exchange," Selleth said, her voice amused.

Another creature might have assumed the princess wasn't bothered by the warriors' presence. But Orion knew her better than most; the only thing she hated more than surprises as Spring fae. Normally, Selleth would either already know why they were in attendance, or she'd *pretend* to know. So, she hadn't been informed, *and* she was just as curious about their presence as Orion.

Good.

"The attendings were switched in the final hours," the prince reassured, his focus on the flame in his hands. "The chosen attendings were unable to join us, but fortunately, the twins were visiting and volunteered to escort me. A blessing from Alysatraee as they're rarely in Summer."

Selleth nodded as if in understanding, but her lips quirked a brief, brittle smile. "King Eldrin has information for your queen. Ivy Balrel will report on events from the human realm."

The Spring attendings exchanged a glance. Keeping his attention on them, Orion signaled for Ivy to step forward. Ivy's face revealed nothing, but, of course, she'd be careful while any fae scrutinized her. Ivy took her place next to Selleth and spoke about misuse of the seeds and the Elven Council's scheme. The Summer prince's eyes grew wider as the story progressed.

The attendings stared at Ivy; Alyssum's nostril's flared and Alion's lips pressed into a tight line. As Ivy spoke, Orion added what he'd seen, supporting her.

Yet, the Spring attendings didn't relax. Behind the prince,

the twins shared another meaningful look. Unease pricked behind Orion's neck.

The brother warrior, Alion, spoke up, "The fighting will start up again. Death will follow."

Selleth glared at him as if disgusted that he dare speak without permission, but a pit formed in Orion's belly, and he really wished he had his sword.

"We share the same concern," Ivy said.

"I will take your witness to the Summer Queen," Prince Devain assured them.

"Very well." Selleth signaled the end of the conversation.

Devain started for the southern stairs, but his attendings stood rooted. Orion stepped forward, his arm brushing against Ivy's back. Selleth mirrored Devain and marched away, either not noticing or not caring about the visiting attendings.

"With Ialant gone, another will be appointed in his stead," Alion's voice rumbled. "Where and when?"

Ivy paused, then slowly spoke. "Why would you care about elven dealings?"

"The Council wants an elf that will vote with them," Alyssum said. "There's a chance to stop the corruption of the humans, but only if the *right* elf takes the Seeds Council seat. A unanimous Council has power."

For fae, they cared a lot about humans and elves.

"It's odd," Alion said, leveling his gaze at Ivy, "that your father was the one to come up with the plan to poison the humans in the first place."

Ivy's gripped her fisted hand behind her back. "We don't know who—"

"But we do know. Ialant Balrel, your father, convinced the Elven Council to comply with his plan."

Orion's temper flared. "Tread carefully, Spring. Believing lies doesn't make them true."

Rime cleared his throat, "Ialant was the only elf who came to our courts for help in rectifying the Council's mistakes. Where were your high ideals then?"

Prince Devain stopped, his head tilted, looking flummoxed by his attendings.

"The courts might have stopped this nonsense," Alion said, "given the proper opportunity."

Proper?

The Prince Devain looked across the platform to Selleth, as if asking for help, but she stood on the first step, her chin raised and an eager glint in her eye.

It's Summer rule. Summer's problem.

Selleth had removed herself—a bad sign. If there was an escalation, she could defend herself by saying she wasn't even on the amphitheater floor. Typical Selleth.

"Our fae courts must consider an elven recommendation, *especially* when the Council presents a unanimous suggestion." Devain puffed out his chest, as if he was the final word on the topic.

But Ivy stilled, and Orion tried to deduce what the warriors were *not saying.* Tension grew thick in the silence, and Rime shot Orion a concerned look.

Ivy slipped her hand back into her pocket. Orion's wings twitched, and he edged closer to her, signaling to the visitors that Ivy was a protected Winter guest. Though, if she flashed her knife, the situation would get *so* much worse; Summer ruled, and they could take her away.

"After the war," Alyssum continued, "all but one councilor pushed for peace. Ialant dissented. Without a unanimous voice, the court had no clear direction."

"You seem awfully well informed for two Spring fae who were younglings at the time," Rime argued. "How would you know about super-secret meetings between fae royals and the Elven Council?"

Orion scowled. His brother had an excellent point.

Prince Devain's nose scrunched, either in annoyance, confusion, or both. Whatever confidential information the twins thought they knew, their prince had been caught off guard. He knew nothing more than Winter. Selleth's giddy expression signaled her anticipation; she relished the friction and salacious gossip.

But Orion hated wherever this conversation was leading. His instinct was to grab Ivy and run, but she'd refuse; Ivy leaned forward, anxious to understand their cryptic words about her father. Though nothing they said sat right in Orion's gut.

"Where are you getting this information?" Ivy asked, one hand still pocketed.

"We had a first-hand conversation with someone who was *in* the meeting." Alyssum looked Ivy up and down, her lip curled. "They reported that Ialant recommended a retreat."

"Not a truce," Alion added.

"You spoke with an elf?" Ivy's voice trembled. "A council member?"

"The Aequus isn't the place for such discussion," Prince Devain said. "The ruling court should—"

"Emmyth Phiro told us everything," Alion interrupted, his face reddening.

Ivy's jaw dropped. Orion gripped her elbow to steady her as he spat, "Emmyth is a liar. Did you not listen to a word Ivy said? She glamoured as Emmyth, which granted us access into the Tree House. The elves knew well!"

Devain's two Summer guards' feet were planted wide, their arms held at their sides, as if ready for a fight. Next to Rime, his guard's hand slid to his hilt. Orion's concerns about his father's opinions disappeared as his focus narrowed on protecting Ivy from whatever these Spring attendings had planned.

"Emmyth was a spy, *pretending* to go along with Ialant's plans," Alyssum said. "But she was reporting to the Summer Queen the entire time. Your attempt to entangle Emmyth in your wicked plot won't distract us from the real culprit." Her gaze fell on Ivy, and the Spring warrior's frown deepened.

"You're completely blind." Orion was disgusted they believed such bold lies.

"Emmyth is clever. Devious," Ivy said, but the attendings remained tense, already determined to assign guilt.

Alyssum bent her knees, her face turning hard. "Emmyth wished for peace. But Ialant recommended a *feigned* retreat. He wanted to fight another day."

"You're saying ..." Rime blinked as his voice trailed off.

Alion shouted as he reached his hand over his shoulder, "The war isn't over. It never was."

The twins pounced as they drew thick, wooden maces and descended on Ivy.

38

FINAL BATTLE

Ivy held her ground; Orion was behind her, unprotected. The Spring warriors held wooden, morning star clubs in each hand, the ends bulbed with carved, polished spikes. Alion charged her, Alyssum a step behind. Ivy lifted her left arm and redirected Alion's blow. The jolt from the club reverberated up her arm, rattling her teeth.

Orion punched Alion in his exposed ribcage. The Spring warrior countered with his other fisted morning star, aiming for Ivy. Orion shifted, shielding her, using his hip to check Alion's swing, cutting the strike short.

Ivy ducked, avoiding Alyssum's kick to her head, and pivoted out of range. Orion's guards engaged—their duty to defend him.

Ivy was on her own, without Winter's protection.

With the guards engaged, the once austere ceremony turned to chaos. Ivy sprinted for the stairs, using her speed to distance herself from Spring. She was thrown forward, pain exploding from her back.

"Ivy!" Orion yelled.

Rime dove for Ivy, his hand extended. He jumped, but not far enough to reach her.

Ivy twisted, ignoring the searing pain that raced along her back. Rime was already reaching a hand toward her, actually trying to help. With a touch, he could shed her cumbersome dress and gain her bow and arrows. She reached, but their hands flew by each other, less than a finger-length apart. It might as well have been an uncrossable gulf. Ivy appreciated Rime's attempt. Even at this tight proximity, her arrows could stab like daggers.

Orion grabbed under Ivy's arms and yanked her to her feet.

"Run!" Orion hissed as he spun to block Alyssum.

Orion was right. She couldn't win against such odds, and her presence enraged the Spring. Shoving aside her frustration at their accusations and the uneven odds, Ivy ran.

Warmth oozed down her back. Her shoulder blade was a flame of agony. Something tore in her back. A muscle? She ignored the injury, her dress catching her attention instead. Her ridiculous gown wasn't tripping her. It was gone, replaced by her elven clothing, satchel, bow, and a quiver of arrows. Rime had removed her glamour, even though they'd never touched.

Hope kindled. All Ivy had to do was reach the palace. No fae was faster than an elf. She leapt past Selleth, only pausing halfway up the stairs to check on Orion.

He was in the midst of the fight.

"What is the meaning of this?" Prince Devain shouted, taking a timid step toward the fray, cradling The Heart flame against his chest.

Alion was too busy fighting Orion to respond. Two pairs of Winter and Summer guards had engaged. With blades. Orion's two guards fought two Summer fae, leaving Orion to fight Alion. Fortunately, Orion was more than capable with his fists, feet, and using his winged movements to his advantage.

Rime must have commanded his guards to fight because they had stopped Alyssum's guards from assisting their attending. Rime gave Ivy a quick fae salute. She couldn't believe he risked revealing his magical skills. Ivy would've grinned, despite the panic pulsing through her body, but Alyssum slipped past the guards, her club raised as she lunged at Rime while his back was turned.

Before Ivy could think, she had her bow drawn and arrow nocked. Ivy bit back the stabbing pain and aimed. She would've delivered a fatal shot, but killing a fae official was too great a risk. She let the arrow fly, her arm tingling. The arrow sank into Alyssum's leg, but not deeply.

Rime spun in time to see Alyssum's face redden in pain or anger. Probably the latter. Fae shouted, but Ivy ignored the noise. Inexplicably, Alyssum smiled. An unnerving, *victorious* smile. The warrior yanked out the arrow, inspecting the tip. Ivy didn't know the reason, but her glee made Ivy's stomach twist. Alyssum's lips pulled into a frown. She threw the arrow on the ground and shifted quick enough to stop one of Rime's guards from grabbing her. She fought the guard, ignoring the unarmed prince. Rime—ever ridiculous—winked at Ivy. His toe was on her arrow.

Ivy squinted at it. Her arrows were all metal-tipped, yet that one appeared to be obsidian. A glamour. Why?

"Idiot elf," Alyssum shouted. She'd broken free, her fae guards contending with Winter. Alyssum bolted for the stairs, her sights on Ivy.

And the Spring warrior wasn't limping.

Fae healed quicker in their own realm, but this was beyond miraculous. Did Alyssum have armor under her trousers?

"A hundred years is nothing for the fae," Alyssum continued as she climbed, shaking her fist in the air. "Fair folk lost the battle, but we never ended the war."

Ivy froze at Alyssum's words. A lifetime to a human *was* nothing to a fae. It was longer than Ivy had been alive, yes, but the sentiment rang true.

The warrior bounded up the stairs, gripping her morning stars. One shone with crimson blood. Ivy swallowed, knowing it was hers. The Spring warriors had come prepared. Armor and weapons. Yet, they hadn't brought metal, which meant that wasn't allowed. Very *not* allowed.

Ivy's hand flew to her pocket, the handle of her knife visible. Rime had never intended for Ivy to actually use her metal blade. Letting her keep the weapon both placated Ivy and pricked at Orion. A win-win for the prince.

Ivy ran up the remaining stairs, determined to gain sanctuary in the Winter Palace. When she was beyond everyone's line of sight, she grabbed her knife and shoved it into her belt, hidden under her cloak. She had zero intention of finding out the consequence for some unknown metal-prohibition. The promenade's columns whizzed by, encased in slumbering vines, but Ivy's gait was slower. Her arm wasn't responding well. The wound must've been more serious than she'd suspected.

Distracted, Ivy didn't sense the earthy changes surrounding her until it was too late.

As quick as a whip, a now-green vine released the column and wrapped around her wrist. Another seized her waist, twining up her torso, small leaves sprouting as it extended along her body. Ivy jerked away, but the vines tightened. Another moved to encircle her other wrist, but she was ready. She gripped the vines that had ensnared her arm and torso and used them to balance as she leaned back.

The vine darted past, and Ivy was already twisting, giving her captured arm enough slack to snatch her knife. Surely the punishment for using metal couldn't be worse than dying at the hands of an enraged Spring fae. Gripping the knife in her free hand, she took aim at the entangling vine and slashed.

Behind her, Alyssum screamed. The vines spasmed, and Ivy cut her way free. But her victory was overshadowed; vines crawled up every column. She would never make it past dozens of them to reach the palace. Spring in the fair realm meant Alyssum was at her peak strength. Ivy was outmatched. She had to do something unexpected.

Ivy pivoted and charged Alyssum. A heartbeat before they clashed, Ivy drop-slid on the marble floors. Alyssum lunged at her a moment too late. Now behind the fae, Ivy jumped up. She grabbed Alyssum's arm, pulling her wrist up and pinning it behind her back. Ivy quickly noted the fae's stiff padded vest extended down to her hips. Ivy needed to temporarily incapacitate the fae. She drove her knee into Alyssum's back between her shoulder blades, shoving the warrior to her knees. From the corner of her eye, Ivy caught a blur of movement on the coliseum floor.

Far below, Alion whirled. He lashed out, elbowing Rime in the face. The Winter Prince's head snapped back. Eight fae guards fought each other while Selleth's and Devain's guards stood aside, next to the royals on the lower stairs. Devain still commanded his attendings to stop. And Orion shouted back a complaint that the orcs hadn't been employed to rein Spring in.

With Rime down, Alion turned his attention to Orion. His morning star nearly slammed Orion in the head, but Orion dodged and followed up with a punch to Alion's jaw.

Ivy felt herself being thrown to the side, and her world seemed to slow. Her thigh collided with the column first, followed by Alyssum's body slamming into Ivy's chest, knocking the wind from her lungs. Ivy's grip loosened. Alyssum's elbow slammed into Ivy's ribs before she reared back. Ivy's lungs screamed for air as she rolled away, just missing another thrashing from the spiked morning star. Ivy grabbed an arrow, but before she could run and nock, Alyssum grabbed Ivy from behind. She squeezed Ivy's neck and trapped one of Ivy's arms and torso. Already out of breath, Ivy's vision blurred, a headache blooming.

Vines shot forward, responding to Alyssum, wrapping from column to column in a frenzy, cocooning them in a warped, living tomb.

Desperate, Ivy gathered her remaining strength and slammed the tip of the arrow just below the fae's hip. Alyssum yelped, and Ivy wriggled free while grabbing her knife. Spinning in a fluid motion, Ivy slammed the hilt into the warrior's temple.

The fae crumpled, and the vines thunked to the ground, unmoving. Ivy had bought herself enough time to get to the double doors.

"Halt, Alion! That's enough." The Summer prince's voice was somewhat muffled by all the vines piled around her.

Ivy crawled back to the lip of the stairs, gulping air and forcibly ignoring the pain in her upper back. Devain was holding up his hand, keeping the orc warriors at bay, though they were now poised near the bottom steps of the coliseum. Devain frowned in Ivy's direction then turned to Selleth. "Your elf will need to pay for her injury to my attending."

"Your attending is in Winter territory," Orion shouted, still redirecting and dodging Alion's attacks. "They struck first, attacking a guest under Winter protection."

"Your attendings will face justice in the Winter Court," Rime added.

Ivy discretely buried her knife in her belt. She lifted her chin and forced air into her jabbing lungs. Overhead, Ash cried out, headed in Orion's direction. Of course, the flying blue rat was coming to the rescue *now*. Then again, later was better—all the little dragon could do was ruin clothing. *Not helpful.*

Alyssum stirred; she'd be conscious soon. Ivy scrambled to the warrior's side, an apology on her tongue, and ripped out the arrow. Without the ability to glamour the tip, she couldn't leave it behind. Ivy grit her teeth and limped for the door. Orion would find her a healer; everything would be fine. She'd probably spend the next couple of days in the infirmary, rather than in the woods, which stung more than her wounds.

The double doors were only steps away. Ivy wanted to believe the worst was over, but she sensed trouble gathering at her back. Her fingers grazed the latch, but before she could pull, she was yanked backward, nearly knocking her off her feet.

This time it wasn't vines grabbing at her; it was another elf.

Emmyth Phiro stared down her nose as if Ivy was dung on the bottom of her shoe.

Ivy's mouth dried, realizing she was well out of Orion's sight. He assumed she was safe. No one was coming to her rescue.

"When you poke a bear, Ivy," Emmyth began, her fingers digging into Ivy's arm, "don't be surprised when claws sink into your back."

"Let me guess, you didn't receive an invitation to the Aequus." Defiance rose inside Ivy. "So, you poisoned the minds of the attendings."

The councilor wrenched both of Ivy's arms behind her. Ivy fought to escape, but Emmyth was skilled and unwearied. Ivy's wrists were quickly bound together with a length of vine.

Emmyth dragged Ivy toward Alyssum who was pushing herself into a seated position. The fae brought a hand to her temple, not seeming to notice Emmyth marching closer. Ivy wished the councilor would draw close enough to the stairs to reveal herself, but Emmyth was no fool.

"No one is going to believe that dazed-Alyssum caught me and tied me up," Ivy argued.

"Creatures believe whatever suits their self-interest."

"This is obscene!" the Summer prince's booming voice echoed beyond the coliseum. "Release the Winter prince."

Ivy startled. Someone had Rime? A guard? Alion? Was Orion safe?

Alive?

A jolt of fear rushed through Ivy's limbs. She struggled against the vines at her wrists despite the ache in her back.

"I could've killed the Spring warrior, like you did to my family," Ivy provoked Emmyth. She hoped to create an opportunity to wriggle away or be discovered by a guard on rotation. Something. Anything. "Wait, no. You couldn't even be bothered to get rid of us yourself. You sent Seekers to murder us."

Emmyth lifted Ivy's wrists, driving Ivy to her knees. The councilor dug around in Ivy's satchel, despite her attempt to twist away. It was no use. Emmyth pulled out the little blue box that Wirenth had given her at the elven Gathering, which was the last thing Ivy had expected.

"Smile for the elves of your House," Emmyth said. "You don't want to make a poor, *last* impression."

Ivy shuddered, then her trepidation turned to indignation as Emmyth triggered the box. Emmyth had systematically annihilated Ivy's family members one by one; playing her sister's image, the remnant of her existence, was beyond a violation. The tender familial memory became twisted by Emmyth's vile game. Ivy wrenched her arms away, furious, but Emmyth held firm.

The blue box projected the pond with lily pads carrying massive blooming flowers and the wild orchard beyond. The scene unfolded. Ivy couldn't look away. Her sister, Iris, appeared, calling to her daughter, Calla. When Tomas, Iris's husband, teased her, his words felt surreal. At the end, Emmyth activated the box for a new memory. She angled the cube to record Ivy's face. She ground her teeth, indignation flaring, the blue box watching her with the weight of a thousand eleven eyes. She could only imagine what elves at the next Gathering would think when they saw her in this unknown, snowy location. Would they see the tears in Ivy's eyes as defeat or fury? Did it matter?

"The Council is corrupt," Ivy mouthed. She realized it was a futile message thanks to the ghost of a sneer on Emmyth's face. No one would see the projection.

Emmyth tucked the blue box into her cloak pocket. At the injustice of everything from her family to the lies told to the Spring, Ivy shot to her feet, ramming into the councilor. Ivy slammed with her head and shoulder into Emmyth's chest, throwing her back. Ivy shifted her balance and kicked, aiming for Emmyth's head. But the elder elf was battle worn, her reflexes immediate. She ducked, then gave two quick jabs to Ivy's stomach. Ivy doubled over, coughing. Emmyth grabbed Ivy's upper arm and dumped her at Alyssum's feet, still beyond the fae and orcs' line of sight.

"Alyssum," Emmyth said, her voice full of false humility, "I caught the traitor."

Alyssum cocked her head, her pupils too constricted for the dim evening.

"I trust you can take it from here, Alyssum." Emmyth pressed her hand into Ivy's back, keeping her in place.

Yes, she looks completely capable. Ivy kept her sarcasm to herself as she subtly worked to loosen the bonds.

"I win." Emmyth's hard words stilled Ivy. The malice in her voice chilled Ivy to her core.

Emmyth's free hand shot to Ivy's belt.

Ivy took a ragged breath. Emmyth retrieved Ialant's knife, and the blade flashed in the councilor's hand. Fear trickled down Ivy's spine. Would the councilor dare kill Ivy here?

Emmyth lifted the blade, then cold metal bit into Ivy's back. The knife dove deep where the morning star had already mangled her flesh. From under her shoulder blade rose a searing, frightening kind of pain. Ivy tried to bite back a startled cry as she felt the wound tearing. Emmyth clapped a hand over Ivy's mouth with the edge of her cloak, muffling the sound.

"Never pretend to be me," Emmyth whispered. She cleaned the knife on Ivy's sleeve and then slipped the knife into Ivy's belt.

Ivy tried to suck in a breath, her body desperate for air. With every inhalation, the stabbing pain renewed with repeated, efficient brutality. Ivy blinked, watery tears brimming.

"Don't dance unless you know the song," Emmyth hissed. "At least you're predictable. Your father had everything, but he stepped on my toes. He was predictable, too."

Ivy wanted to claw out Emmyth's eyes, but all she could do was struggle for shallow breaths. Each inhale seemed to lance her lungs. Her heart fluttered like a careening hummingbird, scrambling to fly with a broken wing. The weight of Ivy's knife promised revenge—so close but unreachable at her own waist.

"Alyssum," Emmyth snapped.

The councilor's stern voice jerked the Spring fae out of her stupor. Alyssum grabbed Ivy's shoulder and yanked her back toward the Summer prince. Emmyth gave Ivy a flat stare, blocking any retreat to the castle as the warrior dragged Ivy down the stairs. With every stabbing breath, Ivy suspected that Emmyth had punctured her lung. Perhaps worse.

On the bottom step, Selleth stood unharmed and apparently unruffled as pixies flew like bees around her. The princess cast an imperious glance as Ivy stumbled, trying to keep her feet under her while the Spring fae shoved her forward. Ivy held her head high, refusing to be cowed by Selleth's cold gaze, though every fiber of her lungs screamed for her to give up and crumple.

Ivy blinked back tears as she shuffled past Orion. His guards stood next to him, their swords sheathed in a show of peace, if not surrender. Summer fae guards and three orcs surrounded Winter, not holding them exactly, but showing that they could. Seeing Ivy, Orion pushed through the Summer guards, trying to reach her, his face drawn.

"Don't even think about it," an orc said. Despite her blurred vision, Ivy recognized the speaker. Magdud. The orc's voice then dropped low with reassuring words meant for Orion. Or perhaps for Ivy. But she couldn't distinguish a single syllable over the blood pounding in her ears.

Alyssum spun Ivy around to face the stunned Summer prince and the rest of the chaos. Two orcs were dragging Alion away to the stairs as he shouted about the thousands of fair folk lost to war. Rime pressed a hand to his nose, blood gushing between his fingers.

Orion ignored Magdud and pushed toward Ivy.

Alyssum lifted her morning star; the smooth handle kissed Ivy's neck, the spikes poised over Ivy's carotid artery. Prince Devain's nostril's flared. The air thickened with tension, and the Winter guard's hands slid to their hilts.

Alyssum wavered on her feet. Ivy hoped the club wouldn't slip.

Orion stepped toward Ivy, and the smooth portion of the wood dug into Ivy's neck. She choked. Orion jumped back, and the club relaxed. Prince Devain's brows knit in confusion or anger. Probably both.

"Whatever you may think about Ialant Balrel, Ivy is not responsible for his mistakes," Orion said. "Release her."

Orion turned his attention back to Selleth. Blood was smeared across and behind his ear. If he expected Selleth to speak for Ivy, he was disappointed.

"Even Ialant's ideas," Alion shouted, ignoring the growling orcs restraining him, "were poison, just like the seeds he grew."

The thought of her father and the Council presenting the fae courts with seeds as a means to destroy the humans disgusted Ivy. Her stomach twisted, bile rising, but she couldn't swallow with the club at her neck. Her father regretted his decisions, but even so, the damage was real.

Slightly lifting her chin, Ivy focused on breathing. Trying not to choke, she forced herself to calm. With her attention higher, she noticed the nearly invisible, tiny dragon-shaped blotch circling in the sky.

"The war continues," Alion shouted. "We refuse to comply."

"Peacekeeping is the elves' *only* responsibility," Alyssum said as her club pressed against Ivy's neck. "Yet, they failed the Mother. Failed us all."

Orion pointedly glared at Devain who cleared his throat and finally interjected. "We will discuss this in the Summer Court. Not here."

Rime muttered a complaint about Devain's incompetence under his breath, still holding his bleeding nose.

"Alysatraee delivered a future councilor into our hands," Alion spoke as if to everyone, but then his attention focused on his sister. "If we end Ivy's life, one life, it will send a message to all the elves—the fae will not abide."

The warrior jerked her morning star harder into Ivy's throat as Orion lunged toward her. Someone ripped Alyssum away from Ivy, but the spikes clipped her neck. She fell forward, unable to even catch herself with her bound hands. Before she slammed into the ground, Orion wrapped his arms around her, keeping her upright as she struggled for each breath.

"You'll be fi—" Orion's face drained of color.

Ivy panicked. Orion couldn't reassure her. He couldn't tell her everything would be fine.

Fae couldn't tell lies.

The situation was bad. Really, really bad. Ivy's eye's welled.

"Get a healer," Rime shouted.

She dimly recognized the Summer attendings being dragged away. Devain stood alone, and Ivy realized he'd commanded his guards to seize Alyssum. The shouts of Rime, and Selleth's demands echoed in her ears. The tumult faded to a din as Ivy focused on Orion. Each breath burned. Orion's hand was pressed to her neck.

"Your attending crossed the altar, first," Selleth droned in a commanding voice. "That offense cannot go unanswered, as is our right in our land."

Orion's collar was smeared red. Her blood. He shouted something to Selleth. Ivy reached out and touched his cheek. Her arms were heavy and her fingers numb. She recalled the feel of his skin, rough and warm with corded muscle. She wanted to hold that memory, to take it with her into the dark crowding the edges of her vision.

If Ivy died in the fae realm, Orion would lose his magic. She knew it didn't make sense, but in that moment, as her life slipped away with every ragged breath and gushing beat of her heart—she shouldn't care more about Orion's fate than her own. But she did. She wanted to apologize; she never should have come with him. But she could barely move her lips, let alone speak.

Ash lit onto Orion's shoulder. With her long nostril, she dug into a pouch on her stomach, like an opossum. Ivy wasn't sure if she was hallucinating. She had never heard of such a thing.

Orion gasped, just as astonished, as Ash pulled a jeweled ring from her scaled pouch.

How long has she been thieving?

A little huff of black escaped Ash's nostrils as she shoved the ring back. Ivy's body trembled. The dragon dug into her pouch again and procured a chain. The dragon tugged and Brecc's vial appeared. It swung in the air, a seed resting at the bottom.

One single, glorious life source.

But Ivy was in the wrong realm.

39

THE DRAGON'S SEED

Orion grabbed the vial from Ash, ignoring the heated negotiations between Selleth and Devain. Whether the Spring warriors were tried in the Summer or Winter Court, Orion didn't care as long as they were punished. He ripped off the vial's lid and slid the seed into his palm. But instead of joy, Ivy's face fell.

His mind raced, sorting through everything he'd learned from Ivy. Ash settled on his shoulder, her talons digging through his tunic in a sharp warning. Then, Orion remembered. "These seeds are only meant to be taken in the human realm?"

Ivy nodded, her breathing rapid and shallow. He scooped her up, one hand still pressed at her neck. The morning star's cut wasn't deep, but had it nicked an artery? Orion calculated the nearest portal. He fisted the seed, prepared for the moment they stepped foot into the human realm. His magic would be damaged after returning her in a terrible state, but he didn't care. Nothing mattered except saving Ivy.

"Where do you think you're going, Orion?" Selleth demanded.

Two orcs side-stepped, blocking Orion. Ash hissed, a tendril of smoke escaping her nostril. Selleth glared a warning, reminding him that he must respect the representative. But her posturing was merely a political game; Orion couldn't wait for dithering over courtly agreements. Let his sister be livid. He still had one option to get Ivy to safety.

Shadow magic.

It no longer mattered if his secret was revealed; he'd lose his ability soon anyway. He closed his eyes, ready to call the shadows.

"Don't be a dimwit, brother," Rime rasped. His hand gripped Orion's shoulder, unraveling his concentration.

Rime had placed himself between Orion and the orcs. Blood still ran from his brother's nose, and a bruise was forming near his temple.

"You're not the only one here who can shadow travel," Rime whispered, too quiet for the surrounding guards to overhear. His gaze flicked to their sister. "You won't get far. Especially not with an injured elf. Selleth's guards can travel, too; only the deadly-best for the princess."

Despite their rift, Orion trusted his brother—well, he *wanted* to. Besides, the deep-seated distrust against the Summer Court superseded their sibling spat.

Prince Devain droned about not knowing who to believe: Orion and Ivy, or his own trustworthy Spring warriors.

"Your warrior attendings gravely injured an elf under the protection of King Eldrin," Orion barked as Ivy shivered in his arms.

"The Elven Houses know Alysatraee's law," Rime added. "They may revolt if your attendings don't suffer swift punishment."

Selleth and Devain's arguing renewed, even more heated. It was the Summer's reign, but the crime was committed in Winter territory. Near the base of the stairs, the restrained

Spring warriors stayed silent while Summer guards held them. Or protected them. It was difficult to say for certain.

Orion pulled Ivy tighter against his chest. Ash jumped down onto Ivy's satchel, wriggling her way inside. Orion assumed she was escaping the cacophony, but then the dragon popped back out with a small, bulging bag in her jaws.

"Look through that pouch for a purple stone," Orion directed his brother. "It heals."

Rime dumped out the stones, then pressed the correct one into Ivy's hand. Though far less potent than a seed, it was better than nothing.

"Leave your attendings in the Winter Court for questioning," Selleth demanded. "Our trial. Our dungeon."

Under Ivy's cloak, her tunic was slick. The scent of copper hung in the air, and Ivy's face had grown pale. Orion shifted his arm around Ivy's back, securing her, and his elbow knocked into something metal. The knife. He froze. He couldn't let the weapon clatter to the ground. He also couldn't allow the guards to find it. The complications were piling up; he had to get Ivy out of this place.

He called the shadows.

But they didn't respond.

Orion frantically scanned the coliseum. Selleth's focus was on negotiations, and the Winter guards' attention was on Summer's movements. But only a step from Orion, Rime stood with hands clenched, sweat on his brow. Orion sensed his brother's intent—to hold the shadows at bay.

"Don't," Rime labored to whisper each word. "Your plan. It won't work."

Magdud rested a heavy hand on Orion's shoulder, whispering a prayer or advice, he wasn't sure. She'd maneuvered herself near Orion, close enough to pounce on him if he attempted to flee.

"Give that stubborn Summer prince your assurance," Orion hissed at Rime. "Tell Devain you'll escort the warriors. You will personally *promise* that his attendings will be treated respectfully. We need this meeting over. Now. Because that humorous little *present* you gave Ivy is going to land her in a prison."

"If Selleth would just allow the Golden-boy-Devain to take his attend—"

"She won't," Orion interrupted. "She would rather watch Ivy die than let our father perceive her negotiation as weak. She's in her right to hold the Spring fae, and she will settle for nothing less."

Ivy tightened her grip on Orion's tunic, her word barely audible. "Emmyth."

"I know. I know," Orion assured her. They would deal with the elves later. "Save your energy."

Rime interrupted Prince Devain, mid-sentence, offering what Orion had demanded: the Winter prince's personal assurance. Magdud's attention vacillated between Devain and Ivy, her brow scrunched. The orc seemed to hold her breath as they waited for Devain's reply.

"I agree," Devain said.

Magdud dropped her hand away from Orion, relaxing a fraction. But Orion only grew more impatient. He stepped back, ready to race Ivy to safety.

"On one condition," Devain added. "Orion must be the escort. Of all the Winter fae, he's the only one with compassion for Summer Court."

"After what your attendings did to Ivy, I wouldn't be so sure," Orion said, irritated at another assumption about his dryad nature.

Magdud shot him a look of warning; she was right. If he wanted to help Ivy, this was the fastest way.

"I will oversee your attendings to the dungeon," Orion

agreed through gritted teeth. "And I will request that the guards treat the prisoners respectfully."

Prince Devain pressed his lips together, as if uncertain.

"They will not be harmed," Orion added as he looked at Selleth, his eyes narrowing with an unspoken threat. She had better approve or he'd make her life a misery.

Rime's lip curled as he regarded their sister. Orion wished his brother hid his disdain better, if only to encourage Selleth to be agreeable for once in her life.

The princess gave a shallow nod. "Your attendings will not be harmed before their trial."

The deal was struck. Rime breathed a sigh of relief, but the tension in Orion's shoulders tightened. The Summer guards moved at a glacial pace, handing over the Spring fae.

Orion pivoted and marched toward the stairs. Selleth deigned to move, but only to intercept him, her face serene, set like porcelain.

"Where are you going?" Her voice was calm, but Orion recognized her simmering fury.

"To the dungeon," he said, "by way of the infirmary."

"I'll deal with this," Selleth said, looking from Ivy to the seeping injury at Orion's hairline. "Escort the attendings, as promised. Then get yourself stitched together. Our father doesn't care for those who spill his blood carelessly. If you're going to be an attending, you should at least try not to humiliate him by acting like a common soldier."

Orion glanced over his shoulder to see Prince Devain watching them closely.

He considered what was best for Ivy, then gave Selleth a sharp nod of agreement. Ignoring decorum, what gossip would come, and his siblings next to him, Orion pulled Ivy close and whispered to her as he strode to one of his guards.

"I'll be as quick as I can," he said. "I promise, I'll find you soon. I'll get you through the portal."

Ivy's weak smile in response pained him more acutely than any twisting knife in his belly.

"I'm sorry I chased you across half of Trinth." Orion's voice trembled.

Ivy half-mouthed, half-whispered, "I'm not."

He gingerly handed Ivy to his guard, slipping away her knife as he barked instructions on her care. Orion checked on the healing stone, still secure in Ivy's hand, and he tucked the seed into her other fist. Ivy squeezed, indicating she was aware of the precious cargo.

"Go, be quick to the infirmary," Orion commanded.

His guard rushed toward the palace, past the restrained Spring warriors. As Ivy was whisked away, Alyssum turned her face away in disgust, and Alion growled. Orion would rather pummel them than protect them, but he'd made a promise.

Orion hissed in Rime's ear, "If you'd asked for the official representative position tonight, you could've done something about this mess or avoided the worst of it."

"I spoke on Ivy's behalf," Rime huffed.

"But you don't have the authority to pick your nose right now. You certainly didn't have the right to stop me from taking Ivy to the portal."

"Of course, you don't appreciate me stopping you from making a massive mistake. Of course." Rime shook his head and moved to Selleth's side, his expression dark.

"I'm returning to Carrus soon." Magdud pulled Orion's attention with her simple statement. Her back was to the fae as she explained her plans, then she proceeded back to Summer's side of the coliseum. She wasn't the last guard to return to her place; she'd always been careful not to reveal the extent of her friendship with Orion.

Orion stood alone, and frustration rose within him as Ivy disappeared beyond the upper stairs. Ignoring the urge to rush to be near her, he reminded himself that the healers would stabilize Ivy's injuries and, ideally, they'd facilitate a complete healing. He'd longed for Ivy to stay with him in the fae realm longer, but it was too dangerous. Even the usually mundane Aequus Ceremony had turned to chaos.

Orion strode over to the Spring warriors and the Winter guards surrounding them. "Let's get this over with."

He had someone far more important to protect.

40

FAIR BETRAYAL

Ivy's lungs burned with every breath. Carried in the arms of a Winter fae, his every reverberating step pounded through her body. As they ascended the coliseum steps, over the guard's shoulder, a single figure drew Ivy's attention.

Orion watched her from below with silent, dark eyes. She could only guess what he was thinking as his practiced mask had returned to hide his thoughts. She hated to be parted from him, but she needed the infirmary.

Ivy suffered the only lethal blow of the night—from her own blade.

For a moment during the representative's negotiations, she thought Orion might shadow travel. With the clouds shrouding the stars and moon, it would've been easy. But, of course, he'd hadn't. He'd kept his power hidden for decades, and concealing abilities was the smarter choice. Still, it stung that Orion chose to keep his secret rather than save her life.

She closed her eyes and took a careful breath. Residing in the fair realm was never an option, so she'd never planned to stay with Orion for long. She'd kept her heart aloof—so why did she feel like her very soul was stretched thin with the physical distance between them?

Somewhere between the earthen forests and the finery of the Winter Palace, she'd fallen for Orion. Ivy couldn't simply snuff her feelings like a candle. When she opened her eyes, she found Orion, again. The muscle in his jaw twitched, his attention on her until she was carried beyond the stairs, and the coliseum swallowed Orion from her sight.

She wasn't sure which was more painful, the thought of her living in the human realm without Orion or the stab wound in her back. She fisted the seed, a last, desperate hope. Ingesting it in the fae realm was a gamble. Would it be akin to eating any ordinary seed, as the lore suggested?

While the guard carried her through the portico, Ivy spotted a lone figure in the distant woods, apart from all others. Emmyth.

Ivy's instincts screamed for her to chase the traitor and reveal her duplicity. But as Ivy's body jerked in response, her lungs caught in a painful reminder, and the guard tightened his grip.

The councilor stood boldly between the budding trees. Emmyth uncrossed her arms, holding Ivy's gaze. She looked oddly serene, apathetic, even. Emmyth didn't care enough about Ivy to feel anything. As if Ivy was simply household refuse the councilor was responsible for burying. Nothing more.

Ivy had played in the councilor's home. Befriended her children. Had even *admired* her. Ivy sickened, unable to rectify the elf she remembered with Emmyth's true, rotted nature.

Inside the Winter Palace, the walls blurred along with Ivy's swirling thoughts; the events of the last few weeks were like a puzzle, scattered across a wobbling table. The pieces nagged at Ivy, begging her to turn them over, but exhaustion threatened.

The empty infirmary bustled with healers as soon as the

guard appeared. He placed Ivy on a bed while explaining what had happened. Flashes of Alion and Alyssum's vitriol spilled into Ivy's mind. They were angry and then Emmyth appeared.

No … the sequence was reversed. Emmyth had appeared to the Spring warriors before the ceremony, and she'd stirred them up. First Emmyth. Then anger.

Ivy stilled as the puzzle pieces began to shift. How did Emmyth know Alyssum and Alion would be the attendings? Devain had mentioned that the twins were last-moment substitutions. A lucky coincidence? Unlikely. Emmyth had manipulated the choice of attendings.

A serious-looking centaur approached, her glasses resting low on her nose. The centaur commanded the room; a human tugged off Ivy's cloak, satchel, bow, and quiver while a gnome scurried to the shelves of tinctures.

As Ivy was rolled to her side, someone sliced the back of her tunic away and cleaned her wounds. Shoving the pain into the recesses of her mind, Ivy's thoughts darted to Nym. Was she safe? Nym must've pushed herself beyond exhaustion to arrive home before the Aequus Ceremony. Still, even if Nym had immediately spoken with Emmyth, the window of time before the Winter hand-off to Summer was impossibly short.

For Emmyth to travel to the Spring Court would've taken at least a week. Between portal locations, dryad permissions, and locating the Spring warriors, Emmyth was truly fortunate. Ivy's heart sped faster, and not just because of the pain.

Even more miraculous, Emmyth knew the Summer and Spring Court intimately enough to know *exactly* which fae would react with such vehemence. And *then* she wrangled those same angered fae into place as attendings.

Each of Emmyth's astounding feats cracked another fissure through Ivy's bones, threatening to break her. Perhaps Emmyth really was guided by the Mother. Had Ivy been wrong from the beginning, merely blinded by grief?

"The elf has bruising and several superficial wounds along her back and neck," the centaur said to her human assistant and the guard, "but what concerns me is the deep puncture wound. It appears that an object slipped under the elf's shoulder blade and penetrated her lung, collapsing it."

The centaur clomped a hoof down and the room jumped, assistants running to fetch the elixirs and herbs as she demanded. For Ivy, hearing her terrifying fears spoken aloud made them all too real. But, at least someone had finally noticed the stab wound. Looking past the obvious, the healer had found the real danger.

"Not to worry, elf," she said stiffly, barely looking at Ivy's face. "Fair folk who live in the human realm believe Winter are callous barbarians."

We're not totally wrong.

"Life is precious to Winter," the centaur healer continued, "they're just sensible about it. When preserving life makes sense, as it does in your case, Winter takes practical steps to intervene with death."

Does it "make sense" because the king and his son have sworn to protect me? Ivy wanted to snap her sarcastic remark, but she saved her breath.

"First things, first," the centaur said as a gnome handed her a vial.

The pressure on Ivy's neck lifted as the guard stepped back. But a burning sensation burrowed into her thoat wound, and Ivy reflectively jerked.

"The discomfort will pass," the gnome said with a soft smile, his sapphire eyes glittering.

Discomfort? Try inferno.

"Unicorn tears and dragon's blood aren't easy ingredients, so hold still," the gnome advised.

Without asking, the Winter guard made sure she didn't move, by pinning her head and shoulders to the bed. Before Ivy could protest, the burning in her neck began again. The purple stone dug into her palms as she fisted it. A whimper escaped her lips, and she promised herself she'd punch this fae guard in the face ... as soon as she could sit up again. As the burning increased, her body tensed in momentary horror, then she half-wriggled, half-convulsed, every instinct blaring for her to flee.

When the burning mercifully began to ease, Ivy's sensibilities returned. Healing from seeds was invigorating, but fair magic was torture. She sourly admitted to herself that perhaps the guard had given her a Winter-like kindness by holding her still.

The centaur gave an approving nod at Ivy's neck, before moving on to assess Ivy's back. While the centaur called for different elixirs, Ivy scrutinized her puzzle.

Orion's very existence indicated that few creatures could easily travel between realms. Yet Emmyth had appeared outside the Winter Palace; logically she'd portaled. Was Prince Devain secretly manipulative and aiding Emmyth? Or did Emmyth inexplicably commanded dryads?

Ivy's stomach twisted as she turned the pieces in her mind. There was one obvious answer to the *lucky* coincidences.

Emmyth had help from a powerful fae.

Which fae was influential enough to orchestrate such an elaborate ruse? A royal who sat on a throne. Acid burned up Ivy's throat, recognizing the most likely culprit—the Summer Queen.

Naturally, the Summer Queen could easily discover which fae would be susceptible to Emmyth's emotional manipulation. The twins were perfect targets given their family's involvement in the war, their combat skills, and their passionate Spring temperaments. Furthermore, as the Spring Court was under Summer's dominion; they wouldn't refuse their queen.

Ivy jerked forward, leaning off the bed as she gagged. The human assistant shoved a bucket into Ivy's face just in time for her to be sick. Ivy broke into a cold sweat. The realization that the Elven Council's lies went further than Ivy's wildest imagination left her empty and shaking.

The Summer Queen couldn't have acted alone. She'd have needed King Eldrin's compliance. Orion had said his father wasn't acting as he'd anticipated, and Eldrin's complicity explained why. The fae courts wanted the war to continue. The elves had presented the idea, but the fae kings and queens not only hid the elven plans—they were helping. Together, they pulled the strings, fooling the fair folk with their duplicity.

Ivy pressed a hand to her sternum, robbed of breath. Between her injuries and revelations, her mind spun.

"Lay back down, elf," the centaur said. "I'm ready to attend to the worst of the damage. This won't be easy."

The gnome lifted a healing vial just as footsteps bound into the infirmary. Rithmat entered and he rushed to speak with the guard, whispering in his ear.

"Take the elf to The Tower." Rithmat low tone was still plenty loud for elven ears.

"What?" the guard balked.

"You heard me," Rithmat hissed before turning to the centaur. "We are moving the elven guest, immediately."

"The elf's lung has collapsed, which may prompt the other to follow," the centaur huffed. "She's not yet properly treated. If you remove her, it may cost her life."

The gnome popped up next to Ivy's hand and in a flash, he wriggled a finger inside Ivy's fist. He muttered an incantation under his breath before Ivy even thought to pull away the seed he seemed to reach for.

"From Zel," the gnome mouthed. "He—"

Ivy cried out as the guard lifted her, her pain blinding her to the rest of the gnome's words. No one commented on the gnome's actions; they hadn't noticed, or they simply didn't care. As Ivy was marched away, the gnome gave her a mournful look, his once glittering eyes now seemingly dull. Were his eyes dimmed with worry or from expending dark magic into the seed she still held? She wished she knew.

The guard carried Ivy and followed Rithmat through the castle, his expression tight. They advanced quickly, and the castle windows soon disappeared, replaced by solid walls of rough stone and burning torches. Ivy wasn't sure what The Tower was, but it clearly wasn't a blissful retreat filled with flowers and honey.

She suspected Rime, Selleth, nor even Prince Devain were privy to their parents' misdeeds. Even the fair creatures of The Tree House were blindly following orders, while only knowing partial truths, relying on the Council's promises of safety.

Ivy's breathing grew more shallow and rapid. The most powerful fair folk intended to ignite the war between the realms. And they were prepared to win at all costs. The only whisper of a chance the realms had at peace now pivoted on an impossible task.

The elves had to overturn the entire Elven Council before the Centennial.

Like Devain said, the fae courts had to listen to a united, unanimous Elven Council. But unless Ivy warned her kind, the Houses wouldn't force a change. There would be no one to stop the Elven Council and the Fae courts. And it seemed that the royals had every intention of burying the truth along with Ivy.

So, Ivy did the only thing she could—a last desperate

attempt to save herself and the knowledge she held. She lifted her hand to her lips, and she swallowed the seed.

Follow Ivy and Orion in *Elven Council in Ashes* as they fight to bring down the Elven Council, figure out where they fit in the realms, and find their happily-ever-afters.

Fast-paced with twists and turns in both realms. Don't miss Ivy and Orion's next adventure, along with orcs, dragons, dryads, elves, fae, devious villains, and loyal friends.

Follow Kristin J. Dawson to receive book announcements >>
Amazon
Bookbub
Subscribe to her newsletter for insider news and giveaways!

ACKNOWLEDGMENTS

I had so much fun writing this story while I was at home with my family during the global shutdown. I'd actually written this story concept with the elves and seeds—and their corrupting effects—almost a decade ago, but it was an urban fantasy set in Colorado! It just goes to show that writers should hold onto story ideas because one never knows when it might be the perfect time to take them "out of the drawer" and into the world.

Thank you to everyone for your patience as I moved to a new city and then polished this story for you! Phew! It was a long time in the making.

Thank you to my beta readers and also to my writer friends who reviewed many iterations of this story, especially Kathleen Gooch who did the initial copy edits and Paul Tallman who helped refine the magic system. Also, thank you to my readers who hopped over to Vella and paid to read the earlier version. I appreciate your feedback and incorporated your ideas based on your votes!

The Deranged Doctor team was incredibly patient as they lent their talent to this gorgeous cover!

And, finally, thank you to my team at Oliver Heber Books, including my editors S. E. Welfonder and Dan Hilton!

About the Author

Kristin loves chocolate (*quality* chocolate, because ... life is short!), research (I know, I know, who loves research ... *raises hand*), English movies (especially with my mom or my sisters), and reading fantasy novels (by Jeff Wheeler, Melissa Caruso, J.K. Rowling, and ... a thousand other great stories with fun characters and lots of tension!).

I was born in L.A., grew up in Utah, spent a short stint in Bristol, England, then ended up in the Pacific Northwest. I've been here ever since!

Note: When Oregonians say, "I live in the country," they're not talking about living near cornfields or cows. They're talking about the woods. The woods! (I know, it's not like the farmer stories I grew up with, either.)

ALSO BY K. J. DAWSON

Epic Fantasy Adventure

The Unchosen Omnibus

-female protagonist with a massive character arc

-cunning female mentor

-kingdom-ending stakes

-magical linguistics

-sweet romance

Unravel the mysteries, secure the smartest alliance, win the crown

Realms of Alysatraee

Elven House of Ivy

Elven Council in Ashes

Romantasy

The Poisoned Prince

-best friends to {sweet} romance

-hidden royal

-bantering elves

-battle for the crown

-stand-alone romance with a happily ever after

A royal huntsman. An illegitimate daughter. And one heart—delivered on a silver platter.

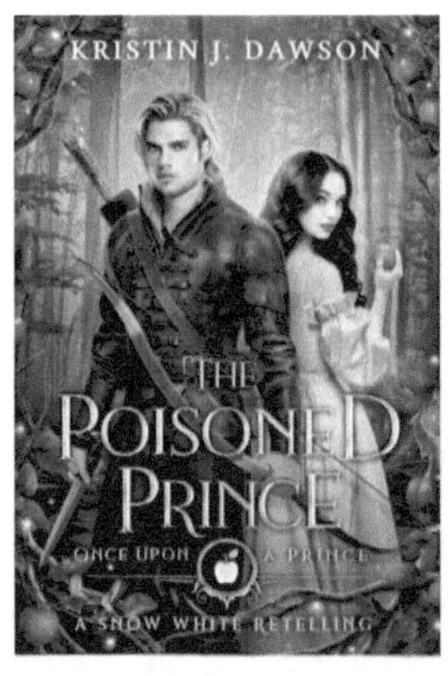

www.ingramcontent.com/pod-product-compliance
Lightning Source LLC
Chambersburg PA
CBHW020522110726
47899CB00004B/1213

* 9 7 8 1 6 4 8 3 9 6 5 9 5 *